THE WARRIOR'S PATH

BOOK ONE OF
TALES OF GORANIA

KARIM SOLIMAN

THE WARRIOR'S PATH

Copyright © 2018 by Karim Soliman

Edited by Felicia Sullivan
Cover art & design by Stefanie Saw

ISBN-13: 978-1-72000-634-3
ISBN-10: 1-72000-634-2

For my beautiful wife May, who believed in me more than I did.

The Northern Sea

Skandivia

Rusakia

Koya

Koyan Sea

The Endless Sea

Bermania

Mankola

Boiling Eyes

Murase

Byzontan Gulf

Byzonta

Cursed Waters

The Great Desert

GORANIA

PROLOGUE

Whispers of prayers replaced laughter and witty remarks. No one was playing brave now. Since those mountains loomed over the horizon, Noah's gallant companions became pious.

"We rest here," the old caravan master announced, his voice strong for his age. Ironically, that wrinkled man was the only source of reassurance for a green caravan guard like Noah. Unlike the muscular men in this company, the old caravan master had been keeping his calm since they departed from the city, as if he was leisurely walking his horse by the lake of some shady oasis, not braving the perils of the bleak desert with a caravan that would definitely be tempting for wandering bandits. With the edge of man's world in sight, mortal robbers of flesh and blood should be the least of anyone's concern right now.

All men dismounted, and so did Noah. An order to rest should be an easy one to comply with, if only there was a tree trunk to tie his horse to.

"Open your eyes and watch, boy." The caravan master must have noticed Noah's perplexity. The old man was still on horseback when he nodded toward the other guards, who took down a few barrels from the cart. The men implanted the barrels in the sand and now they had a few hitch poles for their horses. Holding his horse by its reins, Noah trudged through sand to tie his courser to one of those implanted barrels.

"You have to dust your hands a little bit if you want a barrel, boy," a muscular guard snapped at Noah when he approached a hitch pole.

"Easy on him." The caravan master glared at the muscular fellow. "It's his first ride as a guard."

The guard smirked. "I rode ten times already when I was his age."

"And that's why you trembled when you saw the demons' mountains, right?" Noah taunted.

The muscular guard shoved him, and suddenly, all other guards were mad at Noah, yelling and cursing and wagging firm fingers. Surprised by their exaggerated fury, Noah stepped back, his hand reaching for his sword.

"Enough, you fools!" the caravan master bellowed. "Couldn't you make your fuss a little louder?"

The muscular guard pointed his finger at Noah. "You should teach that boy how to hold his tongue."

"And you should pick an opponent your size," the caravan master rebuked the muscular guard. He beckoned to Noah. "Come."

Noah caught up with the old man, who nudged his horse away from the caravan just enough to be out of earshot. *Time to teach the green guard a lesson*, Noah thought. He wasn't in the mood to hear lessons. However, he should be grateful to the old man who had prevented an upcoming bloody clash. It was needless to say who would have bled if Noah had drawn that sword in front of a dozen furious guards.

"Tell me, boy," said the caravan master, "what did your parents tell you about demons?"

Noah rubbed his head, trying to recall anything he might have heard from his parents. "They never talked about them."

"Exactly." The old man leaned toward Noah. "The men behind us are not much different from your parents; they never say the name of the dwellers of the Great Desert." He nodded toward the distant mountains. "Especially when we are so close to the lands in which they reside."

The notion of being merely a few miles away from some demon unnerved Noah. "You think if we mention them, they may—"

"It doesn't matter what I think, boy." The old man gestured toward the guards. "I just want you to understand that these men are nervous so that you don't get into trouble again. Because if you do, I won't be there to stop them from killing you."

The caravan master wheeled his horse, but before he rode away, Noah said, "You are not afraid because you know those demons do not exist, right?"

The old man pulled the reins of his horse and took in a deep breath. "Two days ago I was on my way back to Kahora when I saw that man coming out from the Great Desert on a black stallion. My men, terrified, thought he was a demon chasing them, but when he came closer, we realized he was nothing but a lost traveler who would kill for a sip of water."

The old man's tale confused Noah a bit. "What are you trying to tell me? That the Great Desert is inhabited by men like you and me?"

The old man turned to him. "I'm trying to tell you that not everything you hear—"

"A *leopard!*"

While Noah was looking around to find the beast, he heard a roar followed by a grunt, and then a few men hooting. A guard had struck the leopard dead with a thrown spear, Noah deduced after he found the beast's corpse at last. The sight of a dead leopard was much more relieving than a live one. Especially if it was moving toward you.

For some reason, the old man didn't appear impressed at all though. He even looked concerned as he gazed at the vacant desert behind them. "We must leave now, men. Mount your horses," he urged his guards who had barely gotten a rest. The order made them disgruntled, but no one dared to disobey the veteran caravan master.

Noah found the courage to approach the old man and ask, "Something wrong?"

"The Ghosts." The caravan master was still gazing at the horizon. "They have sent an eye, and the eye saw us. Now they know we are here."

"Ghosts? But I thought you didn't believe in——"

"The Ghosts are different from the demons, boy. They are *real*. I saw the corpses they left behind." For the first time, the reserved caravan master sounded nervous. "Now put your arse on a saddle."

Noah swallowed. He had never wielded his sword in a real fight. "You know how to defeat them, right?"

"No one fights a Ghost, you naïve. I grew old because I always ran away. Now move or we leave you behind!"

Noah didn't need more persuasion to sprint toward his horse. He hurriedly untied it, but there was that heavy barrel which was still stuck in the sand. He called out to the guards to help him return it to the cart, but no one paid him heed as they were already mounting their horses.

"Forget the damned barrel! You are hindering us, boy!" The caravan master nudged his horse onward, the rest of the guards following him. Noah, jumbled by their rush, struggled with the stirrup before he swung up into the saddle.

And then a shriek echoed in the desert.

"Merciful Lord!" One of the guards looked back, his jaw dropped. Noah didn't need to be a seasoned guard to know what that shriek was. The terrified look on everybody's faces said it all.

It was the shriek of a Ghost.

1. MASOLON

The smells struck Masolon first when he stepped inside. The smell of the sweaty men cramming the tavern, of mutton served to their creaking tables, of burnt incense battling the other two smells. The incense was losing the battle, Masolon had no doubt, yet those sweaty men were still devouring and gulping and jabbering. Amazing thing what those men could do with their mouths at the same time.

"Any help, *stranger*?" The stout tavern keeper glared at him. And Masolon was thinking no one had noticed his arrival. Was it that obvious he didn't belong to this place?

He leaned to the wooden counter she was standing behind. "I am looking for Kuslov."

"What for?"

"I was told he might need my services."

"Is that so?" She arched an eyebrow. "He hasn't shown up tonight yet."

Masolon shrugged. "I can wait."

From the way she looked him up and down, he could see the impression of his ripped tunic. "You're not going to make trouble with that sword on your belt, huh?"

Unless I have to, Masolon thought. "I will be as still as the chair I am sitting on."

"We shall see. And one more thing, darlin', we don't offer drinks for free here."

Goranian coin was something he lacked in his first day in the great city of Kahora. And he wasn't going to trade his shield nor his horse for a tankard of ale. *She might be interested in my tunic, though.* Well, he would drink from the fountain outside if he must.

Masolon found a vacant chair at the corner and threw himself on it, every muscle in his body crying for sleep after his journey in the Great Desert. 'Exhausting' wouldn't do justice to describe his passage through the prohibited lands of demons. 'Deathly' might be the word. He was still not sure if he had died already and this was the afterlife, though. At a certain moment, he had felt as if every small part of his soul—if a soul was made of small parts or even big—had abandoned his body. At *that* certain moment, he had turned into a dead man, or perhaps one of the demons of the Great Desert. Only when his hollow stomach growled did he realize that 'Masolon' still existed. Because demons would never get hungry. Even if they did, they wouldn't have growling stomachs. But who would ever know?

With the back of his hand, Masolon wiped the beads of sweat that popped on his forehead. Midnight was coming soon, and not even a hint of a gentle breeze entered that accursed tavern through the window next to his seat. He should be grateful though. That smelly tavern was paradise compared to the Great Desert. The Goranians called it the Great Desert and his clansmen called it *Si'oli*; 'Hell' in his native tongue.

Masolon had no plans after surviving Hell, or even before. He had just mounted his horse and headed to the end of *his* world. Now he had a plan, and that plan was Kuslov. With Kuslov there would be coin, and with coin there would be mead, bread, and a chamber in a tavern. The more the coin he got, the *warmer* his chamber would be, that veteran caravan master from the Murasen desert had told him. Anyway, a chamber was the least of Masolon's concerns, as it should

6

be for any of the Ogono warriors. *He should have warned me of the bloody odorous mutton though.*

His grandfather's lengthy tongue lessons were paying off so far. Though the Murasens' accents sounded different from what Masolon used to hear in his sessions, he could follow the boisterous debate at the next table about the sweetest voice in the Murasen realm. The only two meaningless words in their blabber were *Abla* and *Mehra,* names of two women, Masolon guessed. Soon his guess became a certainty when the debate turned into a boyish rant about anything in those two women other than their voices. If Masolon's father was here, he would shorten their tongues with his own blade.

People started to leave the tavern and Masolon was still waiting, his eyelids heavy. Was it possible that Kuslov had already come and gone, and that tavern keeper had simply forgotten to inform him? Masolon gazed at her, but she never looked where he sat, not even by chance. Maybe he should go and ask her, but he was too tired to leave his seat.

"Hey you!" the tavern keeper called to him. "It's only a couple of hours before dawn! I must shut the place now."

Masolon realized he had dozed for a while, and now he was the only one in the tavern. "Perhaps I should try my luck another—"

His stallion tied outside the tavern was whinnying. A quiet stallion it was, yet not at this moment. Something, or probably *somebody* must have enraged it. *Not more than three men,* Masolon estimated from the thudding footsteps. What could be the odds that those fellows were just passersby at this late hour, and they just thought of bothering his horse for no specific reason?

Masolon drew his sword and hurried to the door.

"What are you doing?" the stout tavern keeper asked, her eyes wide in alarm. Masolon was already outside in the Fountain Plaza when she finished her question.

The place was abandoned except for three men, two of them armed with falchions, one with a sword. The latter held Masolon's untied horse by its bridle.

7

"Drop the damned sword!" The three thugs pointed their blades at Masolon, their nervousness not lost on him. Yes, they outnumbered him, but his towering stature must have intimidated them. As the case would probably be with most of the people in this land. Three weeks, and not a soul had he reaped. Fighting those bastards should be enough to stimulate his idle muscles. In each ugly face, Masolon could see the cowards who had burned his mother and his sisters alive. Was it strange they always looked ugly, those brigands?

"Leave the damned horse first." Talking to them was useless, yet he wanted to make sure they were eager to die tonight. "*My* horse."

"Not anymore," snarled one of the thugs. "Do you have a problem with that?"

They were leaving Masolon no other option. "You are three." He sighed. "This is not going to be a fair fight."

The same thug smirked. "Life is unfair, you fool."

"To you, I mean." Masolon swung his sword as he lunged at him. The robber tried to block Masolon's strike with his falchion, howling in agony when his hand took the strike instead. With a backhanded swing, Masolon slashed the abdomen of the second robber, stepping sideways to evade the stab of the third thug who left the horse to aid his miserable fellows. Masolon's move, however, wasn't fast enough to prevent the robber's blade from scrapping his skin. Now infuriated more than hurt, Masolon sliced the robber's neck with one clean swing, dark-red blood bubbling out of the gaping wound.

"To me!" Masolon turned to face the remaining robber who had lost his hand. "I will rid you of your pain!" Masolon gnashed his teeth as the thug sprinted away. He hadn't been there when the cowards had burned his mother's shack and fled; a grave mistake that had ruined Masolon's life beyond repair. But today no thug would run away. *Not tomorrow, not any day else.* Masolon had nothing for the likes of those scum but death, be it quick or slow.

"Enough! You're wounded!" the stout woman yelled at Masolon from behind him. After making sure the way was clear she

8

approached him to check his bleeding arm.

"Merciful Lord!" She looked alarmed. *Too religious for a tavern keeper,* he thought idly. "We must find Bumar to stop the bleeding! Come with me!"

Her voice wasn't harsh anymore, making him wish he had been wounded earlier to earn her pity. A glance at the fountain of the plaza made him realize how thirsty he was. Usually, after the blood work, Masolon felt as if he wanted to drink a whole river, but this time a river of water wasn't what he wanted.

"Before I go anywhere," he grinned tiredly, "can I have a drink first?"

2. MASOLON

Only the scent of lavender reigned over the torchlit hall of Bumar's house. Masolon was relieved to realize that not all places in Kahora smelled like its tavern.

A servant ushered Masolon to a wooden seat and disappeared inside the house. Right in front of Masolon was a desk on which piles of books and scrolls were stacked up. If only his grandfather had taught him how to read the Goranian tongue…

Clad in a loose cotton tunic, a beefy, round-faced man dragged forth a wooden table, placing it at Masolon's left. "They say you defeated three men on your own," the beefy man said, his voice deep and calm. His accent was nothing like what Masolon had heard in the boisterous tavern.

"They were maggots, not men," Masolon spat.

"The tools, boy!" the beefy man demanded, giving Masolon a studying look. According to the tavern keeper, that was Bumar, the most skillful healer in the city, if not in the entire kingdom. "The sand and dust that cover your hair and clothes made me think in the beginning that you came from a neighboring Murasen village. Now I'm quite sure you are far away from home."

Masolon stared into Bumar's silver eyes, which were not less soothing than his hypnotic voice. "I have not met many people here, but to me, you seem far away from home too." From his brief experience with Murasen skin, Masolon had seen all shades of yellow and brown, but not red.

"Impressive." Bumar grinned. "You have more than your muscles to reason with."

Masolon shrugged. "It was not hard to notice that."

"Maybe you're right," said Bumar. The servant returned with a rattling metal box and laid it on the table next to Masolon. "I was born in the Kingdom of Bermania, but I spent most of my life here among the Murasens. They consider me as one of them."

The table beside Masolon was now full of bandages, metallic tools he had never seen before, and bottles with pungent odors. "I hope you know what you are doing," he said.

"I have been a healer for three decades, young man." Bumar bent over Masolon's arm to check it. "Your wound is not very deep, so don't worry." Grinning, he nodded toward his shiny tools. "I won't need them."

"These things? I have watched uglier blades cutting into my flesh." *As if something like a 'prettier' blade even exists.*

"I don't need any ugly blades tonight. It's just this to cleanse your wound." Bumar raised a piece of cloth soaked in a potion in front of Masolon's face. "But I have to warn you; it may hurt you much more than you think."

Masolon could feel the sting when the piece of cloth touched his wounded skin. Not the worst pain he had suffered from, but still, it caught him off guard.

"Don't you have a story to tell me?" Bumar asked. "Something about you? About where you come from? What you do here?"

A story to tell? Masolon did have one, but where should he start? From the first horse he had ridden at the age of four? From his night watches around the mountain foot to chase and hunt down those bastards who were used to raiding his village? From his last quarrel with his father, the great chieftain of the most feared clan in Ogono?

11

Masolon could see his square face now. Tall and broad-shouldered, his father stood clad in his brown woolen tunic.

We cannot be like them, Father!

We must be, or they kill us all!

We cannot punish someone for the guilt of someone else. You taught me so.

Do not remind me of what I taught you, Masolon. They killed your mother and your sisters! With or without you, I am taking the men at first light to burn the bastards' village to ashes!

I cannot let you do so.

Stop me if you dare, then.

His father drew his sword, his glowing eyes betraying his determination to slay anyone standing in his way. Anyone. Even his own son.

"Hey."

A gentle slap on Masolon's cheek brought him back to the present moment.

"A bad dream?" Bumar asked.

A bad memory, Masolon thought. "Did I talk in my sleep?"

"You're not only in dire need of sleep, young man." Bumar wrapped a bandage around Masolon's arm. "You need someone with whom you share the load you bear in your chest. Otherwise it will be your mind talking to you."

"My mind?" Masolon sighed. "At least we can understand each other."

"Nothing is as confusing as a voice coming from your head." Bumar tied the bandage tightly. "We are done."

"This is it?" Masolon stared at his wrapped arm. "No red hot blades?"

"The stinging mixture will do. Just cover your wound and it will heal. No water on it."

That went easier than Masolon had expected. "Thank you." He rose up to his feet and headed to the door.

"Where are you going?" Bumar sounded more disapproving than inquiring.

Masolon stopped, looking over his shoulder. "Are we not done with the wound?"

"We are." The calm healer wore a stern face now. "But do you think I work for free?"

Masolon didn't think so. He just hoped. "I cannot repay your services if truth be told. Coin is something I lack."

"Of course you lack the coin." Bumar peered at him. Escaping the healer's silver eyes was impossible. "Because you are not from here. Not from Murase, not from anywhere in Gorania."

Masolon knew he should deny that. He had seen the fear in the eyes of Goranian men upon telling them where he came from. "How do you know?" he couldn't help asking the healer.

"Because I read about you, young man. *The Outsiders*; I know they do exist." Bumar reminded Masolon of his grandfather; a man who seemed to know all the answers, but when he talked, he just raised more questions in your mind than you already had.

"That makes you all Outsiders to me, if you get what I mean. . ."

"Look at you." Bumar scanned Masolon with his eyes, as if he beheld some peculiar creature. "Despite your strange accent, your silky black hair is Mankol, your facial features Byzont, your fair skin Bermanian, your muscular body Skandivian. This is how our ancient ancestors looked."

Bermanian, Byzont, Skandivian; too many new words for one day. Hopefully, they were not synonyms of 'demon' in the Goranian tongue.

"But our tongue," Bumar kept staring at the wondrous creature standing in the hall of his house, "how did you learn it?"

"My grandfather taught me."

"And who taught your grandfather?"

Masolon felt hesitant to go on with that particular part. Even his father used to laugh at it. "He spent some time with the mages of Cawa. Speaking the Goranian tongue was one of many things they taught him."

Bumar gaped at Masolon. "The mages of Cawa?"

"I understand if you do not believe in mages. Not all of my people do."

"What is *Cawa* exactly?"

Masolon was surprised that it was not the mages that took the healer's attention. "An ancient fortress that no one can enter without the mages' permission." Actually, nobody in Ogono was sure of Cawa's existence. "Trust me, I cannot help you go there if that is what you want."

"Not for the time being." Bumar's grin grew wide. "Listen. I'll help you repay my services. I happen to know someone in urgent need of a skillful swordsman like you. You can spend the night here if you want, and tomorrow I will take you to him."

A night under a roof. Bumar's munificent offer aroused Masolon's doubts. A few minutes earlier, he had been denied from leaving without paying for the healer's services. "Now you make my debt heavier," he said cautiously.

"The price I demand is nothing you can't pay. After we meet Kuslov tomorrow, you will tell me everything about your homeland and your faction." Bumar glanced at the piles of scrolls and books. "I had better make sure I have enough ink."

Had Masolon heard that right? "The man we are meeting tomorrow is called Kuslov?"

"Yes." Bumar furrowed his brow. "Do you know him?"

"No." Masolon couldn't help laughing. Like his wise grandfather had told him once, the games of destiny were hard to understand sometimes.

3. MASOLON

A night in Kahora was hot, a morning was hell. Though not like the hell Masolon had survived in the Great Desert, of course. In *Si'oli*, the sun curtained the sky with its blaze so white he couldn't see the sun itself. The sun of Kahora was not that mean, though mean enough to force the good people of this city to abandon its streets for a while.

"Kuslov is a foreigner, like me…and you," said Bumar as they walked through the vacant streets, heading to the smelly tavern. "Born in the frozen kingdom of Rusakia, kidnapped by Mankol bandits when he was seven, and sold as a slave to a merchant from Eahor. When I first met him a few months ago, his wound was much worse than yours."

Masolon chuckled. "Is this how you always make new acquaintances?"

"How am I supposed to make them? I'm a healer, young man. Soldiers and mercenaries hurry to me when they're wounded. That's why someone like Kuslov comes to me when he seeks new recruits."

Recruits? "What is he? A warlord?"

"No, he is something else: The best tracker who has ever lived in Gorania. I swear he sees and hears what we can't. The ground that

15

looks plain to you has many stories buried in it, and only his eyes can read those stories."

Masolon wasn't impressed at all. His clansmen had the eyes of hawks and the ears of owls. "I do not understand," he said. "Why would a tracker seek a recruit?"

"Because of Kuslov's profession, he has connections with many merchants. Most of the time he seeks guards for the caravans of his wealthy friends."

When they reached the vacant plaza, Masolon gazed at the sulky man inspecting the ground in front of the shut tavern, head looking like a fur ball with all that heavy black hair covering it.

"Kuslov!" Bumar called out cheerfully. "What are you up to?"

"You see these two dead bodies?" Kuslov kept his eyes fixed on the thugs' corpses. "A fight happened here. A horse robbery, I presume." He pointed to the ground next to the tavern doorstep. "This is where they untied the horse and dragged him, but..."

"But what, master of all trackers?" Bumar glanced at Masolon, winking.

"It doesn't make any sense." Kuslov rubbed his heavy hair and knelt, scanning the terrain around the two dead bodies. "These two were slain by the same blade." He squinted at the ground for a moment before he went on, "They had a third partner who fled this way." He pointed to the street ahead. "Badly wounded."

"So?" Bumar grinned. "What's the odd thing about that?"

Kuslov rose and looked at Bumar at last. "Their opponent was only one man, Bumar. And he defeated them." He stared at Masolon, pointing a forefinger at him. "What is this?"

Masolon looked Kuslov up and down. He wouldn't even need his blade to tear that arrogant tracker apart. "This is Masolon," Bumar replied on his behalf, holding Masolon's arm. "He's what you've been looking for."

"I've been looking for four warriors, and this is only one." Kuslov gave Masolon a studying look. "He looks fine, though. Six feet three inches is not a bad height for a warrior."

Not a bad height? Come on! You need to stand on your toes to reach my chin! Masolon suppressed a mocking smile.

"Tell me, young man," Kuslov addressed Masolon, "how many men have you killed before?"

"How high can you count?"

"What on Earth is this accent?" Kuslov turned to Bumar. "Is he right in the head?"

"He is fine." Bumar chuckled, glancing at Masolon. "He is just coming from a very faraway rural place."

"A stranger desperate for silver. Well, well," Kuslov mused. "When was the last time you used that thing?" He nodded toward the sheathed sword strapped to Masolon's belt.

"Last night." Masolon slowly drew his sword, raising its stained blade before the tracker's eyes. "To retrieve my horse from three outlaws." He gave Kuslov a lopsided grin. He could swear he spotted a smile that lasted for a heartbeat on the Rusakian's face.

"Is your horse wounded?" asked the tracker.

"No."

"You're in. Tomorrow after sunrise at the northern gates."

"I am in for what?"

Kuslov didn't answer as he glanced at the keeper who arrived to open the tavern for its customers, a different keeper from the stout one Masolon had met last night. *Is the sight of dead bodies on the street a normal thing in this country?* Masolon wondered, finding it strange that the tavern keeper didn't even seem to notice the corpses on his way. *And I thought I was the barbarian here.* Obviously, the Goranians were not the civilized people he thought they were.

"Don't forget the time and place. There'll be some good silver waiting for you," said Kuslov, his voice low. "Now if you'll excuse me, gentlemen, I have to get my morning ale."

The tracker followed the keeper into the tavern, leaving Masolon and Bumar outside. Not sure about the outcome of that encounter, Masolon asked the healer. "What just happened?"

"You have earned a place on one of Kuslov's jobs." Bumar

17

grinned. "No need to thank me."

Kuslov himself didn't look much different from the thugs Masolon had slain last night. What if the job was simply a raid or a murder?

"What do you think you are doing?" Bumar extended his arm, stopping Masolon from following Kuslov inside the tavern. "When Kuslov says 'tomorrow,' then it's *only* tomorrow."

"Do you trust him?"

"I knew him before I knew you, *stranger.*"

"However, you seemed keen to not reveal my origin to him."

"The people here will run from or after you if they know your origin, young man." Bumar took Masolon by the hand, urging him to walk away from the plaza. "Let's go back to my place. I cannot wait to listen to everything you know about your world. As a start, what do you call your homeland?"

"Ogono."

"Ogono," Bumar echoed, his eyes wide with excitement. "What does it mean?"

"Paradise." Masolon knew better than anyone else how ironic that name was. After the Doom had reduced his homeland to scorched, cursed ground, the people of *Paradise* turned into blood-thirsty beasts, and mercy became a sin. "What about Gorania? Does it have a meaning?"

Instead of giving Masolon an answer, Bumar repeated 'Ogono' more than once, as if he was trying to master its pronunciation. And he was faring badly so far. 'Ogono' became 'Ogano' then 'Ogana' and finally 'Gana.'

"So, Gorania has no meaning?" Masolon asked again.

Bumar gave him a strange smile before he held Masolon by the arm. "We have a lot to talk about, young man."

4. SANIA

Sania knew their howdah slowed the caravan. If the decision was up to her, she would mount a horse instead of that stupid camel. But who was she to object to her lord father's order? When her father said the howdah was more honoring to her as a noble lady, then it *must* be honoring. Still, a question irked her; what was the point of teaching a child something she wouldn't be allowed to do when she grew up?

"Are we sure we can make it to Burdi and return before nightfall?" Meryem fidgeted on the seat opposite Sania's.

"You don't miss my brother, do you?" Sania teased Meryem, leaning forward toward her.

Meryem gave her a dismissive wave then she let slip a guilty smile.

"Someone is shy here." Sania held Meryem's knees and shook them playfully.

"Stop being silly!" Meryem pushed her hands away. "I shouldn't have come with you in the first place."

"I'm doing you a favor, foolish girl. Unless you haven't had enough of your prison."

Meryem wanted to say something, but she looked hesitant. She let out a deep sigh, gazing at the desert through the window of the howdah. "At least he is in Arkan these days. Who knows how many days he is going to spend in his castle this time?"

Sania felt a bit guilty for taking the poor girl away from her husband. "I'm sorry for not taking that into consideration, Meryem. I just thought you might be bored of poetry lessons and sewing."

"You don't have to apologize, sweet." Meryem gave her a grateful smile. "I've joined you of my own will because I really feel bored, especially of poetry lessons."

"I don't hate all poetry if truth be told. Some of those love poems are—"

"Nonsense. *All* those love poems are nothing but nonsense, Sania. I didn't marry my champion, and neither would you. It's your lord father who decides who your worthy husband will be. I will be surprised if he hasn't decided already."

Sania's *worthy* husband had to be a lord of a great house like hers. To the likes of her father and Meryem's, marriage was nothing but a move in the power game. Sania and that poor girl were mere pawns.

"You might be luckier than me," said Sania. "You were wed to a good man."

"A good man that I barely know." Meryem gazed through the window, her arms folded. "Do you know who your lucky suitor is?"

"I know nothing. It's too soon."

"Too soon for what?" Meryem asked. "You're seventeen, pretty girl."

"So what? You were nineteen when you were wed to Feras, *old girl!*"

Meryem laughed. "It was your brother who showed up late. Father was waiting for him."

Sania giggled. She loved the company of her sweet sister-in-law, a flower that was slowly withering thanks to some absurd lordly plans. Sometimes Sania envied the commoners who didn't have so many rules to abide by in their lives. While she could not pass the gates of Arkan without informing Dawood, those commoners were not obliged to take anyone's permission before going anywhere. They would ride their horses in the streets whenever they liked to.

They were simply free.

A crazy idea crossed Sania's mind. "Meryem, do you know how to ride a horse?"

"Yes, my father taught me when I was ten."

Of course, to ride it only within the walls of your manor, Sania thought. "Very well." From the window of the howdah, she yelled, "STOP!"

Captain Dawood commanded his memluks to halt. Mounting his horse, he approached the howdah. "Is everything alright, milady?"

"We want to get down, Captain."

"In case you may want to know, we are only two miles away from Burdi, milady."

"Great. That's exactly where we want to get down."

The camel master responded to Sania's request after he got Dawood's approval. With a few incomprehensible words, the master ordered the camel to sit back down. She wondered if camel masters knew the tongue of those beasts for real as the Tales said.

Sania stepped down, Meryem following her. "Dismount! Yes, both of you!" She gestured to two memluks, who in turn exchanged a look with their confused captain.

Dawood turned to Sania. "Milady?"

"I said dismount," Sania snapped at the two men, ignoring Dawood. "We will take your horses."

"Sania, what are you doing?" Meryem asked, her voice low.

"Just follow me," Sania told her before she shouted at the two men, "How dare you ignore an order from your lady? Get down now!"

Reluctantly, the two memluks dismounted. Sania held the reins of one horse with one hand, using the other hand to grab the pommel of the saddle.

"Sania!" Meryem hurried to her. "You are not properly dressed for this!"

"I wear breeches under my skirt. What about you?"

Meryem exhaled. "I do as well, but—"

"Then do as I do."

Carefully, Sania put her left foot in the stirrup. Still holding the reins, she stood on her left foot, swung the right leg over the horse's back, and landed smoothly in the saddle.

"Your turn." Sania tilted her head, Meryem gawking at her.

"I…usually get some help to do that," said Meryem cautiously. "But I'll give it a try."

Meryem struggled for a short while to maintain a steady foot in the stirrup. With a little help from the nearest memluk to her, she mounted her horse.

"Now you look like a real horseman!" Sania hooted. "Ready for a race?"

Meryem looked alarmed. "What race?"

"To Burdi. The town is only two miles away, the captain says."

Meryem gazed at the vacant horizon. "I see nothing ahead."

"That's the best part. Come on! When was the last time you mounted a horse in a boundless area like this?"

"That could be dangerous, milady!" Dawood nudged his horse onward and stopped it next to Sania's. "Please, there is no need for this."

"I'm sure you and your men can catch up with two ladies, Captain." Sania glanced at Meryem to make sure she was steady on her beast. "Ready, old girl?" she teased her sister-in-law.

Meryem gave a nervous chuckle.

Sania nudged her horse into a trot, giving Meryem a chance to keep pace with her. But Sania was impatient to fly in this endless desert. It had been impossible for her to ride a horse at its full speed within the walls of the castle of Arkan.

Meryem didn't look comfortable with her horse. "Slow down, Sania," she said as Sania was cantering already. "Forget the stupid race. I'm out of it."

What race? Sania had almost forgotten Meryem's presence. Her mind was busy recalling all the instructions she had learned in her horse riding lessons. She was told how to gallop, but she had never tried it. If she harmed herself today, she might be locked up in Arkan for good.

Sania leaned forward, slightly raising her body from the saddle, maintaining a firm grip on the reins. When she pressed with her legs, the horse went faster. She kept pressing, and the beast kept increasing its pace.

She was flying now.

Behind her by a decent distance, Meryem squealed, but Sania didn't bother slowing down to understand what the panicky girl was saying. Maybe Sania should return to her…after she was done flying.

The memluks caught up with Sania, galloping on both sides. She pressed more with her legs to outpace them.

"Slow down, Lady Sania! I beg you!" Sania heard Dawood's voice coming from her right, but she kept her eyes fixed on the town appearing on the horizon. There was no fun in rivaling those horsemen. She had better spread her wings and race with those ravens heading to the town. She had never felt alive as she did at this very moment.

"Lady Sania!" Dawood cried. "The horse needs to rest!"

While Sania wished she could fly forever, unfortunately, Dawood was right. Pushing her butt down, she sat up straight, moved her knees away from the saddle flap, and pushed her heels down. Keeping her legs on her horse's sides, she gave a firm tug on the reins, and then loosened them again. The beast was stronger than the mare she rode in Arkan, and for a moment she felt like crying for help, but at last her horse responded and slowed down to a canter. *Yes, yes! You're mine now!*

When she reached the town, she realized that she had left Meryem behind by a whole mile or more, forcing the memluks to split themselves into two groups. And there was still the camel and his master. While waiting for Meryem, Sania entertained herself by walking her horse around Dawood and his men.

"That was enough for today, Lady Sania." Dawood followed her. "I have a family in Kahora."

"For today, Captain." Sania hadn't got enough, but the poor captain might have a heart attack if she went for another run.

Meryem arrived on her trotting horse. "You must have lost your mind, foolish girl!" she blustered.

Sania gestured to her to calm down. They shouldn't quarrel in front of Dawood and his men.

"You scared me to death!" Meryem shrieked.

"That's a shame. Don't tell me you didn't enjoy the ride, old girl." Sania grinned. "Come on, let's find our house."

Dawood led them to the other side of the small town, away from the buzz of the marketplace. Sania gaped at the palm trees towering over the lone one-story house. The only trees she had seen that tall were those of the castle of Arkan; trees that had an army of gardeners in Arkan taking good care of them. What about the trees of an abandoned house?

"The tales about her were true, apparently," Sania muttered as she dismounted outside the house.

With Dawood's help, Meryem joined her on foot. "What tales? And about whom?"

"Princess Nelly." Sania watched Dawood unlock the oaken door. "The sister of my Rusakian grandmother."

"She must be the one behind that fair skin and auburn hair." Meryem grinned, playing with Sania's hair.

"Unfortunately Feras wasn't that lucky." Sania laughed. "He is dedicated to his grandfather's path as you see."

"So, what are those tales?"

The oaken door creaked when Dawood pushed it open.

"She was a sorceress." Sania sighed. "That's why she was kept here."

Meryem's jaw dropped. "That's one of your silly jokes, isn't it?"

Sania wasn't joking, and neither did the abandoned palm trees, the legacy of the mysterious Lady Nelly.

Sania waited for Dawood's men to finish inspecting the house from inside to make sure it was safe for the two noble ladies. "What if we encounter a demon here?" Meryem asked warily. "This house must have become haunted after all those years."

"Don't be stupid. Demons only exist in the Great Desert." Sania hoped that fact was true. She wouldn't deny she was a bit afraid herself, but what are the chances she might get this close to a sorceress's house again? "You know what you should fear for real? Snakes and rats."

The memluks stepped out of the house when they were done with their important task. Sania took a torch from them and entered the dimly lit reception hall, urging the hesitant Meryem to join her.

"Seriously." Meryem kept looking around as she entered. "What are you looking for in this place?"

"Something more interesting than poetry books." Sania scanned the place. For an uninhabited house, the furniture was not in bad condition at all, even less dusty than her own bedchamber. Somebody—hopefully, not some*thing*—must be attending to the house of the late Lady Nelly. A shiver ran down Sania's spine at the thought. "A sorceress's house should be full of peculiar, *interesting* things, right?"

Other than the peculiar cleanness of the house from inside, Sania didn't find anything interesting. Even this cleanness didn't seem to have anything to do with sorcery. The late Nelly might have found a way to perfectly seal the gaps that might let in dust and sand.

Sania was astonished when she found Nelly's jewelry in her bedchamber. All those years and none of her family had thought of collecting those precious items and taking them back to the castle. The unguarded house would make a great prize for burglars. Unless they knew it was *guarded* already.

"You think of what I'm thinking?" Sania asked Meryem.

"You mean the jewels? That's a bad idea, Sania. You can never know what sort of a curse she casted on these things."

"Who said I can never know?" Sania picked up a diamond necklace and hung it around her neck. "How do I look?"

Meryem shook her head. "You look cursed to me."

"Silly old girl." Sania went out of the bedchamber and searched the other rooms. If Lady Nelly had been a sorceress for real, she must have assigned a particular chamber to practice her forbidden hobby.

"Alright. We had enough of this ride today," said Meryem. "Let's start our journey back to Arkan before the night falls."

"After this one." Sania opened the door of the last chamber, and from one quick glance, it looked like the rest of the rooms in the house. A few chairs and a table in the middle, and adjacent to the wall facing the door was that cupboard...

"Are you done now?" Meryem held her by the arm. "Let's get out of here."

"Wait." Sania pushed Meryem's hand away. That wasn't a cupboard for utensils and all those useless belongings she had found; that was Lady Nelly's library. The secrets of the mysterious sorceress must be hidden in those scrolls and books.

"Hold this for me." Sania handed Meryem the torch since she needed both hands to pull one huge book from the shelf, so heavy that she quickly let it land on the table. The book title, *CHEMISTRY,* was written in big, bold Goranian characters on the hard cover. As Sania browsed the book and saw those symbols and figures and arrows, she realized how ridiculous this idea was.

She grabbed another book, a smaller one, written in a tongue she couldn't comprehend. "Ancient Rusakian?" she guessed. She put it on the table and picked up more books. Many of them were written in Ancient Rusakian, only five in Goranian: *Weapons and Poisons, The Science of Body, The Secrets of Boris the Wise,* and of course, *Tales of Gorania.* The last book was dated to the thousandth summer.

She nodded. "Our search wasn't in vain."

Meryem gave the books a quick look. "Still, sewing is more interesting. Who would want to read those Tales again? We had enough when we were children."

"I'm talking about these." Sania nodded toward the Rusakian books. "I'll ask Feras to find us a tongue tutor."

"You want to learn a new tongue to be able to read these books?" Meryem raised her eyebrows. "That's a long way, Sania."

Sania shrugged. She had all the time in the world. "We will need Dawood's help to…" Turning to the door, she eyed the bow lying on a stone shelf next to the door. How hadn't she noticed it when she entered?

"What was she?" Sania muttered as she approached to have a look from a closer range. "A sorceress? A scholar? Or a huntress?"

"Maybe it's not hers," Meryem offered.

Sania had once tested the weight of a bow and how tight a bowstring could be. "It is hers." She held Nelly's light bow with one hand, like the archers she saw in her castle, and pulled the bowstring with the other. "It is crafted for feminine arms. I'm taking it."

"You are not short of cursed items, reckless girl."

Sania hung the bow onto her shoulder. "I'm already cursed behind the walls of Arkan, Meryem." She scanned the room one more time to make sure she hadn't missed any worthy item. "Let's call Dawood to carry these books for us."

5. MASOLON

Right after sunrise, Masolon rode his horse to the agreed upon place to find seven Murasen horsemen waiting there. Kuslov showed up shortly thereafter and waved at them to follow him outside Kahora. Having no idea where they were going or for what purpose, Masolon expected to know more details from the tracker. He spurred his stallion onward, going past his fellows to reach Kuslov at the front of the pack.

"Not now," Kuslov said before Masolon could even pose his question.

Behind them, the walls of Kahora disappeared and now it was only the desert surrounding them. But this desert was not the Great Desert. Nothing was like the Great Desert. Here at least he could glimpse a hill or a palm tree every few miles, a lizard or a snake creeping across the sand, a shadow of an eagle hovering over their heads. But in the Great Desert, nothing alive existed. No whistles of dusty wind that would scrape the skin of your cheeks, not even a rock to blotch the dull yellow painting with any color. If death had a color, it would be yellow. If death had a sound, it would be silence.

Kuslov stopped by a hill ten miles away from the city, wheeling his horse to face his band of men. "Boys, we have been hired to rescue someone's son from the hands of a gang of nomads. If any one of you feels uncomfortable about this mission, he can return to Kahora at once."

"Who hired us?" one of the men asked, his voice a bit high-pitched.

"Someone who will pay us well if we bring his son back." Kuslov glanced at the other horsemen and added, "Alive, of course."

They laughed, but the man with the high-pitched voice didn't. "I hope he does. Them gangs usually ask for ransoms not far from reasonable."

Kuslov gave him a cold stare. "If I say he will pay us well, then he will. Rescuing our hirer's son is all you must worry about." He turned to his small army. "Any more concerns?"

"Where are we heading?" another horseman asked.

"Where I believe I can find those bastards," Kuslov replied impassively. "I have my reasons to believe they are somewhere near the city of Demask."

No one else uttered another word. Kuslov shot his men an inquiring look as if he was making sure they were done asking. "Good. Let's go."

Masolon kept his horse cantering next to Kuslov's, nothing ahead or behind except the sand. It had always been the sand since Masolon started his journey to Gorania. Sand in the Great Desert, sand in Kahora, sand between Kahora and Demask.

"Is it all desert here?" he dared to ask the tracker.

"Sand is the most thing you are going to see in Murase, foreigner," replied the tracker, his eyes scanning the terrain around them.

"What about the other realms?"

This time the tracker furrowed his brow and turned to Masolon. "You should know the answer if you are from one of those other realms. If you haven't been there already, you should see the green Bermanian fields, the snow lands of Durberg, the rainy coasts of Kalensi, and the rocky mountains of Sergrad."

"Snow?" Masolon had never seen it in his life. "How far are these lands?"

"It all depends. If you are traveling with a caravan, you will probably avoid the Mankols' territories, and after eight days you will see the first snowflake. But if you are on your own and reckless enough to head north directly, you will only need three days to cross Mankola, provided that you use the Skandivian map to make sure you don't get lost in the middle of nowhere."

Masolon hadn't used a map to cross Si'oli. And even if he had one, it wouldn't do him any good in the heart of nothingness. He had only survived that crossing because he was destined to. *Everything happens for a reason. Nothing happens by chance*, his grandfather had always told him. Trusting the queer games of destiny was the only option Masolon had.

"I see you rely on no map," Masolon remarked.

"Maps are for green travelers like you." Kuslov gave him a mocking grin. "For the seasoned ones, the sun and the stars are enough."

"You must have traveled a lot until you learned how every grain of sand looks."

"I don't know how every grain of sand looks, but they all know me."

Masolon's ignorance about Gorania was the only reason for him to tolerate Kuslov's arrogance, hoping the veteran tracker might say something useful. Yet his patience was not endless. "Even the sands of the Great Desert?"

Kuslov's eyes widened when he heard the Goranian name of Si'oli. "The Great Desert is where our world ends, young man." He looked over his shoulder then he said to Masolon, "The folks riding behind us don't love talking too much about the residents of those cursed lands."

The right side of Masolon's mouth quirked in a smile of victory. "You say you never passed through those cursed lands?"

"No man has," Kuslov replied a bit defensively. "Those who tried to reach the Other Side never returned."

"My grandfather did return."

Shaking his head in disbelief, Kuslov said, "You can never know if he told you the truth. You were not with him when he returned, were you?"

"I was not." Masolon wasn't even born at that time. "But he brought me something from your lands." He leaned toward the tracker as he added, "Your tongue."

"*Our* tongue?" Kuslov narrowed his eyes. "Where are you exactly from?"

"As Bumar told you, from a very faraway rural place." Masolon enjoyed teasing him. Now the cocky tracker realized he was not any longer the one who knew everything here.

Their conversation ended as Kuslov busied himself with the inspection of the surrounding terrain. In a short while the tracker raised his hand, and the horsemen behind him slowed down until they all stopped. He dismounted and bent over some faint hoof prints. "Same tracks I spotted at the kidnapping site," he announced. "Fourteen, all mounted."

"Fourteen? You knew we were outnumbered from the beginning, didn't you?" One of the horsemen scowled, his voice holding the tone of a rebuke.

"Aye." Kuslov smirked. "I didn't wish to disturb you in your lovely ramble. Now get ready to stain your hands with some blood."

* * *

Being outnumbered wasn't something new to Masolon, yet he missed the bow he had lost in his dreadful passage through the Great Desert. Hopefully, he wouldn't need it today.

According to Kuslov, the Master of Trackers, the kidnappers were hiding in a village called Bahna. The peasants had obviously abandoned the unpaved street to flee from the burning sunlight, seeking shelter in their hovels. Masolon would doubt they might find anything alive in this deserted place if it weren't for some cackling hens and barking dogs.

"Look at the shut doors and windows." Mounting his horse, Kuslov contemplated the hovels all around him. "They knew there would be blood the moment they saw us coming."

It is not the heat then, Masolon thought, gazing at a two-story granary at the end of the street. The window of the second floor would make a perfect spot for an archer to defend that hideout from intruders. "Stop," Masolon said to Kuslov, but the tracker's response was only a cold stare.

Ignoring Kuslov's look, Masolon swung down off his saddle and went past the tracker, heading to the granary. He stood for a moment, letting his honed eyes and ears explore the area surrounding the granary, but they found nothing dubious. As he resumed his solo march, his ears caught the snapping of a bowstring. In less than a heartbeat, he dove behind some rubble, evading an arrow that hit the very spot he had been standing on one second earlier.

Lying behind the rubble, Masolon looked for his companions. Kuslov and the other six men had dismounted, and now they were advancing swiftly toward the granary from two directions to distract the window archers. Masolon rose from his hideout and ran as fast as he could toward the granary front door, ignoring the arrows hissing over his head and the men crying behind him. When he reached the door, he took a deep breath as he waited for his companions to join him one after the other. To both his surprise and relief, he realized that, despite all the cries he had heard during his mindless sprint, his party had only lost one man. Well, so far. If Kuslov was right in his estimate of the kidnappers' numbers, then most likely, the man he had lost wouldn't be the last.

Masolon pushed the door open without stepping inside, arrows coming to receive the unwelcome visitors. "Stay here," he said to his fellows. Moving adjacent to the wall of the granary, he turned around it until he spotted another window. The wooden granary wouldn't be harder to climb than the slippery rocky hills of his homeland.

Masolon vaulted atop the wooden windowsill. He warily watched the two archers, making sure they were still aiming at the door in anticipation of any attempt to storm the granary. *I can only take one of them by surprise.* Gripping the hilt of his sword with one hand, holding the handle of his shield with the other, he rushed through the window, stabbed the nearest archer in the back, and blocked the expected arrow from the other archer. With the very shield that caught the arrow, he hit the archer in the face, then sliced his belly with his blade. When the archer fell, Masolon realized he had just locked himself up with ten swordsmen in this cursed granary.

"To me, fellows!" Masolon yelled, ten blades shining by the sunlight streaming through the open windows, hasty footsteps cracking on the wooden stairs. His fellows would be here to aid him in a few moments, but he had to survive those few moments first.

Masolon stepped back to evade a deadly blade. Lunging forward, he stabbed his nearest opponent. With his shield in the other hand, he blocked a strike by a second attacker then swung his sword, slashing his opponent's chest. The remaining eight nomads turned their sights away for a moment to face Kuslov and his men, and a moment was all Masolon needed to plunge his sword into the back of a third nomad. He swung his blade at a fourth one, the nomad managing to save his chest from the blow, but not his arm. Masolon didn't let the wounded bastard be tortured by his pain and sliced his neck with another strike.

Kuslov, who was now engaging the nomads with his fellows, displayed his good skills in swordplay. No doubt he was unmatched as a tracker, but as a warrior, he was just fine. He bellowed with his men, whose fighting skills weren't much better than their ability to growl, whether in fury or in agony. Either way, the mess they had created was enough to get the job done, but not without casualties. For the six nomads they killed, they lost two men.

"Here is our bounty." Masolon pointed to a young, good-looking man tied up to a beam at the corner. "I hope they did not hurt him." He watched one of his fellows untie the kidnapped man.

"Good fight." Kuslov nodded his chin toward Masolon. "You did the right thing when you came to join me."

Masolon nodded in acknowledgment. Now the tracker addressed him without that usual tone of arrogance. Masolon could even feel a sense of recognition in Kuslov's voice.

One of Kuslov's companions was counting the corpses. "You said fourteen, Kuslov. We only killed twelve."

"Are you sure we killed twelve?" Kuslov made a tour in the bloody granary, kicking the bodies as he passed by them until a nomad woke up from his sleep, grunting. Without hesitation, Kuslov drove his sword into his chest, silencing him for good. "They are twelve now."

The same companion stared at Kuslov, his jaw dropped for a moment. "What about the other two?"

"May they burn in hell. Who cares if they have gone to fetch food or to piss in the desert?" Kuslov glanced at the rescued young man. "We got what we came for. If you want to wait for them, then suit yourself."

The Murasen fellow didn't argue.

Kuslov turned to Masolon. "Take us out of here."

Masolon led the way outside the granary, looking around for any hiding nomads. After making sure the way was clear, he motioned the rest to follow him with the rescued hostage. As they got away from the granary, the rescued man approached Masolon. "Meeting you is such an honor, good sir. I'm Galardi, and I believe we shall meet again when we go back to Kahora."

An honor. Instead of mocking the word, Masolon nodded as he went to his horse. Had it not been for silver, that Galardi might have rotted in that bloody mill until the end of the days.

6. MASOLON

It was Masolon's third night in Bumar's house, the only place in Kahora for him to return to. Yes, the mission was done, but he was still broke. Silver was yet to come in one day or two, Kuslov had promised.

Before the start of their second 'history' session, Bumar's servant handed Masolon a cup of a warm drink, the scent of which unfamiliar but not unpleasant. "It's anise," Bumar clarified when he noticed Masolon's hesitation. "After a tiring day like today, you need something to help your muscles relax, and hopefully, help you sleep well." Bumar took another full cup from his servant and carefully sipped. "In Bermania, we prefer chamomile despite its bitter taste because of its potency. What about you? Do the people of Ogono drink or smoke anything to calm their nerves down?"

You should not have asked. Masolon laughed. "Cow blood."

Grimacing, Bumar almost spat his drink.

"I am certain your chamomile is less bitter," Masolon scoffed, finishing his cup in one gulp.

The healer called the servant to collect the empty cups after they were done with their warm drinks. "From what I heard from you yesterday, the similarities between our worlds are more than their

35

differences." Bumar browsed the scrolls he had been filling with his writing for a whole day. "You are divided into clans, we into kingdoms. You fight for land and resources, and so do we. We both believe that the Great Desert, or *Si'oli,* is a cursed place. You worship one god, like most of the Goranian factions—though we use different names to call Him. You have the Doom, we have the Last Day. Except that your Doom has happened already."

Wondering if one cup of that anise would be enough to help him sleep, Masolon rested his buttocks on his bed, which was a mere cotton carpet in the hall. "If you believe the Last Day is like our Doom, then you must warn your people and start looking for a new homeland."

"We are already warned, Masolon." Bumar gave him a hollow smile. "The Tales of Gorania have told us about the demons' coming to our world. It is only a matter of time before they break free from their curse and flee from the Great Desert."

Now Masolon understood why Goranians would never welcome him if they knew where he came from. In the beginning, he thought they doubted his tale about crossing the Great Desert. Now he realized that they were afraid he might be telling the truth.

* * *

The cotton carpet was a more comfortable bed than the burning sand of the Great Desert, but it never stopped the nightmares. This night his father was paying him another visit, red-eyed, blood covering his tunic and his huge sword. Masolon tried to call to him, but his voice didn't come out.

"Coward," his father spat, pointing his greatsword at a familiar shack set on flames. "You did nothing to avenge them."

"Kill the coward," another voiced urged, but Masolon saw nobody.

"Kill the traitor!" More voices joined in. "Kill the kinslayer!"

Masolon found himself fallen on the ground, his father standing at his head, the blade of Erloss shimmering in the sunlight. "Kill the kinslayer!" His father lifted his fearsome greatsword with both hands.

"Masolon."

Bumar's voice woke him just at the right moment. His father was about to crush his skull.

"Someone called Galardi has sent for you," the healer said. "He's waiting for you at the tavern."

"He is? You mean right now?" It had never crossed Masolon's mind that Galardi was serious about meeting him again.

"You're not in trouble, are you, young man?"

Masolon rose to his feet. "It is the man I rescued from the nomads."

"You must have left quite an impression."

Usually, I do. Not always a good one, though. Masolon strode to the door. "Do not sleep and leave me outside. I will not be late," he promised as he opened the door and stepped outside.

The Kahorians who hid from the blazing sun during the day thronged the streets at night, making it easier to go to the tavern on foot than on horseback. Passing by the market, Masolon listened to the clamorous chorus of yelling merchants, bargaining buyers, whinnying horses, and banging blacksmiths' hammers. He found the Fountain Plaza less noisy when he reached it, but the smell. . . Would he ever get used to that mutton?

The stout tavern keeper greeted Masolon with a genuine smile when he stepped inside. "Darlin,' Kuslov is there." She nodded toward the table at the farthest corner of the tavern, where both Kuslov and Galardi were sitting.

"Bring me my ale there. Kuslov is paying tonight," Masolon told the stout woman, then left her to join the two awaiting men.

Kuslov produced a clinking purse when Masolon sat. "Your cut, young man," said the tracker, and it felt a bit too awkward. Masolon taking his reward in the presence of no one other than the very man he had rescued? *The man who was honored to meet me?*

"No shame, Masolon. We all knew it was a matter of business.

37

Please take your silver." The handsome fellow grinned as if he could sense Masolon's concerns. The concerns that vanished the moment the full pouch landed in Masolon's hand.

A serving girl brought Masolon's drink to the table, Kuslov following her with his eyes until she disappeared in the crammed tavern. "What I hate about this city, besides its weather, is the brothels."

Galardi narrowed his eyes. "There are no brothels in Kahora, Kuslov."

"That's why I hate it." Kuslov took a big gulp of his drink.

"You may travel to Demask if the matter is urgent," Galardi suggested.

"Oh, please!" Kuslov snorted. "The whores in that brothel were uglier than me."

Masolon drank his ale while the two men recalled their memories in the Demask brothel. Despite his grim face, Kuslov had the ability to make you smile. In fact, it was his grim face that did the trick so well that you could not stand the sight of a grin on it. On the other hand, Galardi was nothing like Kuslov. His smile was pleasant, his voice honeyed, his black hair combed, his cloak elegant and neat. The only thing he had in common with his Rusakian friend was his short stature.

"What is your story, Masolon?" Galardi asked. "You came from some faraway place, I was told."

"Yes." Kuslov took another gulp and mocked Masolon's accent when he said, "*A faraway rural place.*"

"Don't mind my Rusakian friend. He was never renowned for his mannerly behavior," said Galardi to Masolon. "I'm just curious to know why you left your home and made your long journey here."

Masolon had no doubt that Galardi or anyone else would loathe him if they knew his *story*. The first Goranians who had found Masolon stranded in the Murasen desert almost killed him because they believed he was a demon. "What difference would that make?" he asked. "Would you take your silver back?"

"No." Galardi tittered. "I want to know because I'm a merchant. You see, everyone has a gift. You wield swords, I make deals. Trading is what I'm gifted in, Masolon, and a trade is what I want to make with you. My father is a reputable merchant in Kalensi, and I have been working for him for a decade. Currently, I'm about to start my own business, and to do that, I need my own men. I have Kuslov to guide me through the lands of Gorania, and I want to have you to lead my army."

"Your army?"

"The roads are ruled by bandits, Masolon. Caravans need guards for protection, and guards need a true warrior to lead them, not some mercenary who would undertake that role as a profession." Galardi took a sip from his tankard, giving Masolon a studying look. "So what do you think?"

A cure for my restless soul, Masolon thought. His sin would never be undone. But he might earn his salvation, his peace, if he saved innocent souls and reaped accursed ones.

"I will lead your army," Masolon announced. "But I will never be your assassin."

"Understood." Galardi grinned. "I'm traveling back to Kalensi today. Once my caravan is ready, I will summon you. Meanwhile, you have two months to recruit your men."

"Two *months?*" Masolon echoed in disapproval.

"Do you need more time?"

"I need less." *Before I starve.* Masolon didn't know if the silver in his purse would suffice him that long.

Galardi shot him an inquiring look.

"Alright." Masolon tapped his fingers on the table, smiling nervously. "What am I supposed to do in those two months?"

"I told you. Recruit."

"Curse you, Galardi! That's not what he's asking about." Kuslov slammed his tankard on the table. "He's asking about the silver."

"Ah, I see." Galardi's smile was back. "You have enough silver already as long as you stay away from whores and gambling."

"Gambling. The Contests." Kuslov stared at Masolon. "That is exactly what you need, young man."

"Drunk again, Kuslov?" Galardi taunted.

"That is where you will find your recruits." Ignoring the young merchant, Kuslov wagged a finger at Masolon. "Some of the fighters there are well trained, even better than the lords' regular soldiers. Besides, you may earn some silver if you do well in the fights."

"Too much silver even." Galardi nodded. "If he comes from a faraway place as he says, then he is unknown."

"High odds." Kuslov's eyes were still fixed on Masolon.

"Alright then." Masolon gestured to them with both hands. "Would any of you care to tell me what you both are talking about?"

7. MASOLON

According to Galardi and Kuslov, the Contest was a Goranian tradition where contenders fought for the title of the City Champion. Every few months, a Contest was held in a different city, and the next one was going to be held in Inabol, the capital of the Byzonts. To Masolon, the whole thing was nothing but absolute absurdity. Fighting in Ogono was always a serious issue, a matter of life and death, not some stupid sport for a hollow title.

The only part that mattered about those Contests was the fighters. He might encounter a few fine ones to recruit for his army. *And the silver*, Masolon thought, glancing at the purse of coins he had received from Galardi. He had no way of knowing whether this purse would carry him through the coming two months or not.

Bumar advised him to follow a caravan heading to Inabol unless he wanted to travel in circles around the mountains of Sergrad. The best place to find a caravan was the Dusty Plaza, where all caravans gathered to drop or collect their goods.

Masolon didn't find the Dusty Plaza much dustier than the rest of the city. Perchance it had earned its name from the travelers who got dusty on the road to this city in the heart of the desert. *Dusty, sweaty, and thirsty*. Masolon still remembered his miserable condition the day

41

he had arrived in Kahora.

After asking a few men, merchants most likely, Masolon found the caravan he was looking for. One cart was already loaded with carpets and cloth of various colors, the other still half-packed with barrels. A black-haired man clad in a gray tunic and black breeches was overseeing the lads carrying the barrels to the second cart. *This must be the man in charge.*

The black-haired man glanced warily at Masolon when he saw him coming ahorse. "Need help, young man?" he asked.

"I was told you were heading to Inabol." Masolon stopped his black stallion in front of the caravan master. "I hope you do not mind showing me the way."

The caravan master looked him up and down. "I wonder what a Mankol is doing in Murase, and why he would be heading to Byzonta."

To be mistaken for a Mankol was safer than being identified as an Outsider. "We are all taking care of our business, are we not?"

Chewing on his lip, the caravan master nodded. "How much are you going to pay?"

"Pay?" Masolon didn't see that coming. "For what?"

"For protecting you on the road."

Masolon chuckled mockingly. "With what? Those barrels?"

Apparently, the caravan master didn't have a sense of humor. "I have an army to take care of my business, Mankol man. If you don't want the Ghosts to rip your heart out, you will need my protection."

Ghosts and demons; the people of Gorania believed so much in them. Masolon should think twice before mocking that man again.

"Let me worry about myself," Masolon said in a serious tone this time. "I will keep my distance, neither too close to burden you with the task of protecting me nor too far to lose your track on the road."

"Make no mistake then. I will ignore your screams for help."

The agreement sounded fair to Masolon. After the lads were done loading the second cart, the black-haired master sent one of them to summon his warriors. Shortly after, ten horsemen made their way through the plaza and joined the caravan. While Masolon was waiting for the rest of the mighty force to assemble, the caravan master mounted his horse and ordered his men to move. *For real? His army is ten horsemen?*

The caravan headed west, Masolon keeping himself one mile or less behind it. Whenever they moved, he spurred his horse onward. Whenever they halted, he took his rest. When darkness fell, they camped, leaving Masolon no other option except doing the same. Worried that those men would leave him behind once they woke up, Masolon found himself waking up every hour to make sure they were still in his sight. Unable to sleep at all after dawn, he waited until every man in the caravan woke up and mounted his horse. They were ready to move now.

When Masolon resumed his journey, the sandy terrain disappeared from the horizon, the sun's heat much milder. The caravan turned around the mountains of Sergrad in order to reach Inabol on the third day. The mountainous area surrounding the city reminded him of the mountains of Ogono, his homeland.

When he reached the walls of Inabol, he could estimate thirty Byzont archers atop the bulwark. The spearmen at the gate stopped all carts to inspect every barrel and every box. Since Masolon had nothing but his horse, they let him in without delay. While the caravan was still being searched, he couldn't conceal his gloating smile as he went past the black-haired caravan master.

"Where can I find the arena?" Masolon asked one of the spearmen standing at the gate.

The spearman gave him a studying look that made Masolon regret the question. "We call it the amphitheater, foreigner," the spearmen said gruffly, then nodded his chin pointedly toward the crowd behind him. "Just follow them."

Masolon followed the crowd swarming toward the same direction like bees returning to their hive, which was too large to miss. The 'hive' was a huge, round, stone structure with no roof, and from inside came out a massive buzz of *bees* that had arrived already. An

43

audience he had never had in Ogono for his raids.

Masolon dismounted and tied his horse to a hitching post outside the amphitheater. He strode to the thronged entrance, which was guarded by three tall, beefy men, even larger than those spearmen guarding the city gate. One of them stopped Masolon with his massive arm. "The pass first."

"Pass?"

"Hmm. Another foreigner." The doorman nodded toward the people showing a piece of paper to the other doormen. "You see that thing? Only those who have it are allowed to watch the Contest."

"I am here to be watched, not to watch."

"Is that so?" The doorman looked at him quizzically then called over his shoulder to a short, slender lad standing behind him. "Risto! Take this last-minute champion to Admastos. If there is no room for him, make sure you bring him back to me."

The lad hurried to Masolon and ushered him inside through a narrow corridor that reeked with sweat and...*Do I smell piss?* Masolon curled his nose, but that would never help. The stench had filled his airway already. *I will be thankful next time I smell mutton.*

The stinky corridor led to a wider hall thronged with a boisterous crowd of disgruntled men who were apparently waiting for their turn to enter one particular chamber. Taking Masolon by the arm, the slender lad made his way through the masses. "It's Risto!" he bellowed, banging on the door with his fist. When the door was slightly opened, the crowd grew mad. "No one enters, or we take no more bets today!" he hollered at them, and to Masolon's surprise, the angry mob calmed. No one dared to follow him as the lad took him inside the chamber.

The chamber itself was crowded and noisy. More than twenty men surrounded the mustached fellow sitting behind a desk, piles of papers on its top. "Master Admastos!" cried the lad. "Can you enlist this fighter?"

Admastos was too busy to even look at him. With one hand he was writing, with the other he was taking coins from those men surrounding him. Risto repeated his question two more times before Admastos replied without turning to him, "Put him on Antram's team. He can take one more fighter as far as I remember."

Team? Since Kuslov and Galardi hadn't told Masolon anything about teams, he had assumed he would be fighting on his own. The Contest was more complicated than he thought.

Masolon followed Risto outside the chamber, back to the hall, then through the narrow corridor. As they descended the stairs to an underground floor, Masolon said, "I thought only one fighter could win the Contest, not a bunch of them."

"The point of fighting in groups in the first tier is to eliminate as many contenders as we can before we start the following ones." Risto glanced at him. "Survive this round, and then you are on your own."

"*Survive?*" Masolon echoed in disapproval. "Do I have to kill to entertain the crowd?"

"Sweet Baizent!" Laughing, the lad turned to Masolon. "Haven't you even watched one single fight before? Because you sound like a novice though you look like a Contest beast."

Risto ushered Masolon to a dusty, sweaty room where his three fellow fighters were waiting for him, wooden poles lying over the floor. "Choose your weapon, Champion," Risto urged Masolon, the mockery obvious in his voice. "Your fourth fighter, *Duke*," the lad addressed a bald, dark-skinned, mustached fighter before he hurried away.

Assuming that the poles were the 'weapons' from which he should choose one, Masolon picked up the thickest pole to test its weight.

"Your first time?" When the mustached *Duke* approached, Masolon realized that he was as tall as him.

"Without a real blade? Yes."

"You can still hurt a man with this wooden thing if you make the best of the muscle in your arm. Whatever happens, don't turn your back on an opponent unless he surrenders or passes out."

Masolon felt much better after he made sure he wouldn't need to kill anybody today. "We shall see." Masolon smiled as he watched the other two fellow fighters swing their wooden toys. He doubted if they had held a real blade in their lives, unlike the bald fellow, who looked like a true warrior with his sleeveless tunic that revealed his muscular arms.

"My name is Antram," said the bald fellow. "I participated in a few Contests, and I can tell you it's too unlucky to face Artony at such an early stage."

"Who is Artony?" Masolon asked.

"Who is he?" Antram's raised eyebrows betrayed his astonishment. "He is a veteran champion of the Contest, but not this time." He wagged a finger in front of Masolon. "This time, I am going to beat him." He pointed the same finger at Masolon and the other two as if he was the man in charge of this small band. "You three will keep the others off me. Today it should be me and Artony alone."

"We shall see," Masolon repeated.

The veteran fighter was expecting some cooperation, it seemed. "Listen, I will not let you ruin this fight with any sort of recklessness. This fight *is* the Contest, novice. Let's win it first, and then you can do whatever you want. Until then, you will listen to what I say. Do you have a problem with that?"

"With commanding fingers?" Masolon stared at Antram's damned finger then back at his grim face. "For certain."

Antram lowered his finger at last. "I need the silver, novice. I assume you need it too."

Who in this stinky room does not? Masolon almost said, were it not for the horn blowing outside.

"You hear that?" Antram asked. "One calling for us to enter the arena, another one to start the fight. Don't ever stop fighting until the herald announces a winner."

8. VIOLA

To Viola, it was just another day in one of those regular Contests. All she had to do was give Admastos the gold she wanted to bet on Artony before she joined Ramel in the amphitheater to watch the fights.

That slender lad Risto hurried to her when he saw her enter the amphitheater. "Lady Viola." His wide grin revealed his missing tooth. "Please." He ushered her through the stinky corridor she knew very well. Despite his slender frame, he always managed to make his way swiftly through the throng. She felt the sweaty men following her with their hungry eyes, but she ignored them. She hadn't brought enough daggers for all those bastards.

When Risto took her by the hand into Admastos's chamber, she pushed a coin of copper into his pocket. The lad thanked her with another grin, so ugly she almost changed her mind about the coin. A frown would suit him more.

As usual before the start of the fights, Admastos's chamber was nothing but a barn. The bettors besieged Admastos's desk, all of them talking at the same time. Those couldn't be men; those were cattle. Even cattle wouldn't produce such noise.

"Busy, Admastos?" she asked, raising her voice to make herself heard over the din.

"Viola herself is here!" Admastos rose up from his seat, his arms open, ignoring the mob around him. "Risto, show those gentlemen their way out. I have more pressing matters now!"

The furious men protested and cursed when Risto shooed them away. One of them shoved the slender lad into the wall.

"What on Earth are you doing?" Admastos bellowed at the reckless man who lost his temper. "Get out of here, or I swear I'm not accepting any more bets today!"

The bettors directed their fury at the reckless man and sent him outside the room, a few of them even apologizing to Admastos and his lad. In seconds, the chamber was amazingly peaceful.

"You too, Risto." Nodding toward the door, Admastos motioned his lad outside. Risto groaned as he left the room, his hand on his back.

When they were alone in his chamber, Admastos grinned at Viola. "Aren't you pretty this morning?"

She was used to his flirtation. The Byzont wasn't bad looking with his short black hair and mustache, but she preferred the company of someone else.

"Your gold." She handed him a pouch of golden coins, knowing she would collect ten other pouches instead of that one. "You'd better prepare our gold because we're in a hurry today. We leave the moment the last fight is over."

"One day someone will beat Artony, and Ramel will lose his gold." His hand slid over her arm. He had never dared to touch her before.

"Touch me one more time," she twisted his wrist with a firm two-handed grip, "and I'll break your hand."

"Alright, alright! I understand!" he wailed. After she let him go, he rubbed his wrist. "By Baizent's head! What is your problem?"

"If you can't run away with something, don't snatch it," she hissed.

"Your master has an awkward taste in women."

Viola glared at him. "I have no master." And she walked away.

"Really? Then what is Ramel to you? A lover mayhap?"

The bastard had gone too far. She drew a dagger hidden in her clothes and threw it, barely missing his neck on purpose. The Byzont stared in terror at the dagger stuck in the wall right behind him.

"You're lucky Ramel still needs you." Viola stabbed her finger at him. "Otherwise, you're a dead man."

Stunned, Admastos didn't dare to answer back. Obviously, he had learned the lesson.

"Make sure our gold is ready, dear." She tilted her head, her voice softened. Feeling excited, she stepped outside the master's room. *I should have done that long time ago!* It was nice to break the routine of those Contests from time to time. Making bets, watching Artony win, collecting her booty and, sometimes, returning with Ramel. Ramel didn't attend all Contests, but that part of her routine, returning with him, was her favorite part.

"He is available for you, boys." She casually stepped past the bettors waiting for their turn outside Admastos's room. After passing through the masses of people who thronged the corridor and the tiered seats in the open-air area, she found Ramel in his usual place, among the crowd. Spotting him wasn't hard with the dark gray coat he wore over his black tunic.

"I wonder when you will decide to watch the fights from a balcony, as all elites do." She contemplated his well-groomed black beard when she sat next to him, breathing in his scent of lavender.

"You cannot feel the thrill of the Contest with the company of those hypocrites." He nodded toward the balcony to their right. "Look at the crowd here." He spread his arms, like a lord standing before his underlings. "They will shake the arena with their roar. They will chant the name of their champion. Isn't it beautiful to share those moments with your subjects?"

Sometimes she was irked by Ramel's delusions of ruling the crowd. To him, the matter was much bigger than just winning some gold from his bets on warriors he had trained himself. He never forgot he could have been a commander one day if it hadn't been for those bastards who had released him from service. Bastards, who happened to be a bunch of lords.

"It would be more beautiful," her fingers slid over his coat, "if we shared those moments with—"

"Here he comes," he interrupted her, pointing to Artony, the brawny blond who stepped confidently into the arena, followed by his fellow fighters. "The Champion." He remained seated while everyone else rose, cheering for their favored fighter.

"The Champion." Viola nodded, turning her hollow eyes toward the field.

The other two groups entered the arena. Now the three groups formed an imaginary triangle on the field while they waited for the horns to be blown. In anticipation of the start of the first round of the Contest, the whole amphitheater was silent.

The clamor started when that dull *DAAAAAA* came out.

A storm of dust arose when two groups charged at each other. Artony's group was one of them. "*Duke* Antram has become wiser now," said Ramel, a hint of mockery in his voice.

"Who's Duke Antram?"

"The bald man with the mustache." Ramel pointed him out of the third group who held their ground, leaving the other two groups to crush each other. "Duke or not, he is a good fighter, though not good enough to stand a chance against Artony. Artony crushed him three times before."

"What about the others?" She gazed at the three fighters listening to Antram's instructions.

Ramel shrugged. "They are nobodies." Amid the mixed yells of fighters, Antram bellowed at his men, "*As one unit!*" They rushed together toward a fighter from the second group, a lone fighter who foolishly decided to charge at the *nobodies* on his own. Maybe he wanted to flee from being thumped by Artony's group.

A muscular *nobody* outran his fellows in this short sprint and reached the reckless fighter before them. With both hands grasping his pole, the nobody swung his wooden weapon, smashing his foe's nose. The unfortunate fool swayed for an instant before Antram knocked him down with another blow.

"*Stay together, champions!*" Antram cried. Accompanied by two fellow fighters, Artony was hurrying with his wooden pole and shield toward the nobodies.

When the muscular nobody charged at Artony, the veteran champion swiftly evaded his hit and struck him hard on his back. The nobody fell to the ground, and now Artony had only Antram to deal with as his mates had knocked the other nobodies already. This fight was almost over.

But wait, the muscular nobody rose. Roaring, he drove his pole into the belly of one of Artony's mates, whose back was sharply bent by the massive blow. Without waiting for his opponent to recoil, the raging nobody pulled him by his hair, whacking his head against the wooden pole to which he was still pinned by the abdomen. The nobody turned to the second mate, who was the first to strike, and hit the nobody in his shoulder. Howling like a wolf, the nobody toppled the pole from his foe's hands by a mighty strike and followed it with a final blow to the face.

"What is this man made of?" Ramel's mocking smile was gone. Was he worried about his gold?

"He's just a novice," she muttered. "Artony will easily beat him."

Artony was nearly done with Antram, who looked exhausted by Artony's consecutive blows. The Champion gave the *Duke* one final strike in the jaw before he turned to face that stubborn novice.

The two remaining fighters advanced toward each other. With an overhead strike, the novice tried to hit Artony's head. The Champion countered with his shield, its wooden rim splitting the novice's pole into two. Surprisingly, the unarmed novice lunged toward Artony, giving him a ferocious headbutt. The former champion flew in the air, landing hard on his back.

The astounded crowd gave an *Oooh*, and then silence reigned over the arena. Viola herself was shocked when she saw Artony rise, the lower part of his face flooded in red. Was it a broken jaw or nose? She couldn't tell.

"Interesting." Intrigued, Ramel leaned forward. Viola did not know what was interesting about losing his bet.

The fates smiled upon Ramel when one of Artony's fellow fighters rose and picked up a weapon. The novice was now unarmed *and* outnumbered.

Artony's returning mate charged at the novice. The novice rolled his body on the ground, evading a horizontal swing. In a heartbeat, the novice pivoted on his left foot and lunged at his opponent, falling with him on the dusty arena, showering him with rapid punches until his foe collapsed.

The novice grabbed his fallen foe's weapon and turned to face Artony, but the Champion didn't give him a chance, stunning him with a mighty blow with his wooden shield. The novice lost his balance as well as the weapon he had just plundered.

With hurt pride, the Champion didn't wait for his opponent to rise, and swung his wooden pole to smash the novice's face. The novice rolled away, and Artony's pole hit the ground. Roaring with fury, Artony charged with his shield and pole, slapping the novice's face and hitting his elbow. The novice tottered, trying hard to keep his feet on the ground until Artony gave him a decisive blow on his head. At last, the novice lost his consciousness.

"We have a winner!" the Contest herald announced.

The spectators hailed their champion, their *bleeding* champion, who looked so furious that he left the arena without greeting his crowd. It was his hardest win ever, and Viola doubted if any of the coming rounds would be that tough. As expected, Artony would eventually win this Contest, and she would return with Ramel with *their* gold.

"Behold the Champion of the coming Contests," Ramel muttered, staring at the muscular novice who restored his consciousness and dragged his feet until he exited the dusty arena.

"You can't be serious, Ramel," she said in disapproval.

"Agile like a jaguar, hard like a rock," said Ramel, as if he didn't hear her.

"His moves are too naive."

"And ferocious." Ramel looked at her. "He fights like a bloodthirsty savage."

"Such a savage can do nothing more than exhausting your well-trained fighters. Eventually, he will lose to them."

"You are right." Ramel rubbed his chin. "If he is trained, he will be invincible."

Viola studied Ramel's face. He was thinking of something, and she knew what it was. "You are not bringing him to the Pit, are you?"

He grinned. "I am."

9. MASOLON

With a swollen face and an aching elbow, Masolon was exiting the amphitheater alongside his comrade in battle Antram. For a first-timer in the Contest, it could have gone worse; a bunch of fellow fighters had told Masolon, but he utterly disagreed. If any of those weaklings had been paying attention to his fight against Artony, they would have definitely seen how Masolon had been close to victory. *If not for that bastard who unexpectedly decided to rise and distract me...*

Antram ambled next to him, his face gloomy. "It is alright, Antram," Masolon said. "We fought well."

"Quite an opportunity to miss," Antram grumbled. "I've never been that close to defeating him."

Nonsense. He did not even touch Artony. Masolon kept his thoughts to himself since he didn't want to argue with Antram, who was serious about the Contest and particularly his supposed rivalry with Artony. "Forget about it for now. When is the next Contest?"

"The herald told me there would be another one in five weeks in the Jewel."

Masolon wondered if his accent had not aroused Antram's attention yet. "The Jewel, you said?"

"The Jewel, yes." Antram sensed Masolon's ignorance at last.

"*Paril*, mate. What is the matter with you?"

"Nothing. Just a man from a very faraway rural place." Masolon borrowed Bumar's expression. Before Antram might feel curious about his origin, he asked, "So, Paril is a big city like this one?"

"Paril is like no other city. The greatest and most beautiful place in the world. Wherever you look, you see either its green fields or its blue sea. The air there is pleasant, not flaming like the hell of Murase, not freezing like that of Rusakia, not as dry as in Mankola."

They reached the hitching post, and surprisingly, Masolon's horse was still there. Maybe the thieves in Byzonta were not that interested in horses.

Masolon began untying his horse. "That lad calling you *Duke*; what was that for?"

Antram peered at him. "You don't know for real? Or you just want to mock me like the others?"

"Mock you?" Masolon jerked his head backward. "Why?"

"Because everybody thinks I just name myself after House Antram. Nobody believes I am really the third of my name in the house that used to rule Lapond."

Masolon couldn't help chuckling, his horse nickering as if it shared his opinion of this farce.

"I'm used to that." Even Antram himself didn't appear bothered.

"Forgive me, *milord*," Masolon jeered at him. "May I just ask: What on Earth you are doing in this amphitheater, away from your castle?"

"I have no castle to go to," Antram said casually. Obviously, he had narrated this story a hundred times before. "Not after that tyrant Charlwood sentenced all my family to death."

The hits Antram had received in today's fight must have harmed him deep in the head, yet his tale seemed to be an amusing one. "Why?" Masolon asked. "What happened?"

"My father, Lord Aurel, disputed with that bastard on lands that had belonged to our house for decades. I still remember the clopping hooves of the horses coming from the horizon. The knights were everywhere, killing and burning anything alive. I was a boy when I fled the massacre. I ran like a fool in the forest until bandits found me and raised me as one of them."

"One of *them?*" Masolon had thought of asking Antram to join Galardi's caravan with him. After Antram's little tale, Masolon cautioned himself to slow down.

"Don't give me that look," said Antram. "They taught me how to defend myself and survive. I may have committed some bad deeds, but I had no choice. After ten years of living with outlaws, I abandoned them and started wandering the realms of Gorania.

"The only thing I was able to do was wield a sword. Fooled by my skin color, the commander of the castle of Kurdisan thought I was a Murasen and hired me as a guard. After spending two years there, I heard of a Mankol lord in desperate need of mercenaries. And mark my words, my friend; mercenaries are very well rewarded in these bloody lands.

"I fled Kurdisan with dreams of endless pouches of Mankol gold, but unfortunately, my new master was vanquished in the first battle. I was lucky enough to survive though, and from then on, I thought I had enough trouble in my life. The Contests seemed to be a good alternative. No, the pay is not that good, but the risks of that path are nothing compared to what I've been through."

A confusing fellow, Masolon thought. Despite Antram's questionable past, Masolon detected some good in him. "Alright then." Masolon swung up into his saddle. "How can I find you again if I want to?"

Antram grinned. "Just follow the Contests."

* * *

Believing that he could remember the way to Kahora on his own, Masolon rode to the gate of Inabol without looking for a caravan to guide him on the road. The spearmen on duty paid him no heed, busy inspecting all carts going outside. Unlike the Murasens, those Byzonts were suspicious of everything entering or exiting their city.

One coin of copper was all he got from his journey to Inabol. Compared to what he had earned from Kuslov's job, that was a pittance. *If only that bastard stayed on the ground a bit longer...*

Masolon was nearing the mountains outside the city of Inabol when he felt he was being followed. Looking over his shoulder, he spied two horsemen on his tail. One of them was a girl actually. A tall, slender, black-haired girl.

The horseman waved at Masolon. "We mean no harm."

"I mean to harm if I want to," Masolon said menacingly as he wheeled his horse to face his two followers. Only a fool would stop for two strangers on the road. But the man, his beard neatly shaved, clad in a dark gray coat, didn't look like a brigand.

"No need for any surprising moves," said the neatly-shaved man. "My name is Ramel and this is Viola, my assistant. I was interested in meeting you after I saw your performance in the arena against Artony."

"What performance?" With an innate instinct, Masolon's hand reached for the hilt of his sword. "I was vanquished in the end."

"I understand your doubts. However, you have to know that I'm here for the good of both of us."

"How do you know what is good for me?"

"Don't you want to be a Contest Champion?" Ramel asked wryly. Curious to know the end of this gibberish, Masolon let him continue, "I hardly remember anyone who can bear the heavy blows you endured. It's as if you are made of iron, not flesh. Your muscles are toned, your movements swift, yet you don't have the skill for the Contests. But this is something I can fix. I can make a legend out of you."

Ramel paused, as if waiting for Masolon's response, but all he got was silence.

"I'm not a charlatan, if that's what you think." Ramel grinned. "I used to train elite military troops."

"You used to train elite military troops and you want to train me?"

"It's a long story. I shall tell it to you on our journey to my pit."

Their journey? To his *pit?* What was going on?

"It looks awkward for a big boy like you to be scared." Viola was pretty until she gave him that crooked smile.

"It is not me who should be scared, young lady," Masolon said coldly.

"That's the spirit, Champion!" Ramel hooted. "Come on! Let's ride away from here!"

"And go where?"

"You don't believe I can train you, right?"

"My doubts about *why* are much bigger than about *how*."

Looking at Viola, Ramel pointed to Masolon. "Straight and to the point. I like this fellow!" He turned again to Masolon. "So, you know everything has a price."

For certain. "I am listening." Masolon kept his hand near the hilt of his sword.

"I take a cut from your prize, in addition to the bets," Ramel explained. "Since you are a new fighter here, odds will be high against you. Higher odds mean more gold. Names like Artony and Vaknus are not currently bringing in as much gold as they used to."

Masolon stared at Ramel, astonished upon hearing Artony's name.

"Yes, yes." Ramel nodded. "What were you thinking of? Artony and all other names you might have heard in people's chants in the previous years were crafted by me. Renowned warriors you now see have come from Ramel's Pit. They usually step in strong, brave, and tough, yet naive when it comes to skills and technique. After a few months, they emerge as legends."

Masolon recalled how Artony fought. The notion of finding more skillful fighters in Ramel's Pit to recruit was tempting, yet there was something about Ramel that made Masolon skeptical. "It is a nice story you tell. I believe there is only one way to be sure of it."

Ramel seemed to understand what Masolon meant. "I will be glad if you do so." Ramel dismounted, handing Viola the reins. Masolon had to admit he was surprised how Ramel simply accepted the challenge.

Keeping an eye on Ramel, Masolon swung down off his saddle, tied his horse to a tree and unsheathed his sword. Ramel looked amused when he did the same, his sword matching the length of Masolon's. Thanks to Masolon's height, he would easily outreach Ramel. Not much challenge expected in this duel.

Masolon charged, Ramel simply blocking the strike with his sword. In a blink of an eye, Masolon found his foe turning around before he felt Ramel's blade scratching his right leg. Had the duel even started?

"I could have cut your knee," Ramel pointed his sword at Masolon, "but I need you with both legs."

"This is nothing but a scratch."

"It's a scratch because I *wanted* it to be so. Do you want to go on?"

For the first time, Masolon found someone who could wield a sword faster than he. In answer, he returned his weapon to his sheath.

"Good." Grinning, Ramel sheathed his sword as well and returned to his horse. "Now you know *why* and *how*. Follow me."

10. MASOLON

Apparently, destiny had a plan for his redemption. He had met Bumar, who in turn had led him to Kuslov, and eventually to Galardi. And only when Masolon thought he had found a starting footstep for his path, he found himself heading somewhere else in the company of Ramel and his dubious assistant Viola. Either Masolon's journey to the Inabol Contest had changed the course of his destiny, or that had been the plan from the beginning.

"So, Masolon," Ramel called out, "where did you learn how to fight?"

"My homeland," Masolon said simply, recalling Bumar's warning about revealing his origin. He didn't want to talk about it anyway. All the memories of his early days of sword wielding brought to mind his father's face. "What about you?"

"I learned everywhere. I wandered the six realms of Gorania to acquire the ways of each faction. Now I can tell where a warrior comes from by the methods with which he fights." Ramel glanced at him, smiling mockingly. "Unless he fights without a method."

"Maybe he comes from a realm you have never been to."

"You're not a Koyan, are you?"

"You can say I am far away from home. What about you?"

Ramel exchanged a quick look with Viola. "You can say I am far away from home too."

Bumar, Kuslov, Galardi, and now Ramel. They were all different, yet they were all the same. They were all far away from home. Was that part of being a Goranian?

Masolon spent the rest of the journey asking about anything crossing his mind related to the six realms Ramel had wandered. He kept asking, and Ramel kept answering. The veteran trainer didn't show any sort of boredom, unlike Viola, who shot Masolon a few uncomfortable looks.

Only one mile remained to reach Ramel's Pit, which was located near a Bermanian village called Shunri. There, Ramel trained two types of warriors: one for warlords for their endless battles, and the other type was for entertainment.

"Unlike what you may be thinking, I always keep my best warriors for the Contests," said Ramel. "Soldiers die quickly in real battles. It's a pity to waste time and sweat on them." He looked at Masolon, wagging his finger. "Don't tell anybody why you are here. Understood, young man?"

When they arrived, Masolon understood why Ramel's headquarters was called the 'Pit.' The whole place was built on a vast land depression. An amphitheater was erected, resembling the arena Masolon had seen in Inabol. And not far from that amphitheater came horses' whinnies. Was there a stable nearby?

"Impressed?" Ramel must have noticed the stunned look on Masolon's face.

"'Pit' is an understatement, I must say."

"A clever builder helped me construct my Pit," said Ramel. "He knew I needed tough conditions for my training field. Here, air is dry and wind is scarce. This makes you tolerate exhaustion better than anybody else."

Masolon spotted a dozen fighters in the Pit busy with different activities. Some of them were dueling in pairs, others practicing archery. For a moment, all eyes were on the newcomer, some with curiosity, others with carelessness, before everybody resumed what they were doing.

"Welcome to Ramel's Pit, Champion." Ramel clapped Masolon on the shoulder. "Ready to begin?"

"Do we not need to have some rest first?"

"*We?*" Ramel repeated cynically. "Who's we? I didn't say I needed rest."

"Maybe the big boy is tired and wants to lay his back for a while." Viola sneered.

Masolon shot her a hard look. "I did not ask you to speak on my behalf."

"Knock it off," Ramel snapped at both of them. "Viola, go make sure we have a bed ready for Masolon." He turned to Masolon. "Get your sword and follow me."

Viola lingered for a while until she received a glare from Ramel. Masolon watched her drag her feet away from them.

"Don't stand still like a stupid rock," Ramel urged Masolon, his voice rough. "When I say 'follow me,' you follow me. If you really want to be a champion, then do what Ramel says."

Masolon took a deep breath. Obeying orders as a subordinate was not something he was good at. It was another thing he might need to learn.

"I thought we were going to this amphitheater," said Masolon as he followed Ramel, who went past the arena and moved forward.

"Not now. I have a better start for you."

They were approaching sparring fighters on a dusty field ahead, men's roars blending with the clanging of steel. "Those men are almost ready to shed their blood on the battlefield." Ramel contemplated his students. *His victims.* No doubt, Masolon didn't like how lightly his mentor regarded their lives. According to Ramel, they would die anyway, and the lords' wars always needed blood to water their battlefields with.

"Don't underestimate these dogs," Ramel said, still not looking at Masolon. "Speaking of skills, they're not the best, but they'll tear you apart unless I stop them."

Masolon would argue later about who would tear whom apart. "Improving my skills is the reason for bringing me to your Pit, right?"

Ramel finally looked at Masolon and held his shoulder. "I'll ask you something. Forget the previous chattering we had and focus on your training. Can you bear this?"

When Masolon nodded, Ramel looked excited. "That's much better!" The owner of the Pit yelled at two sparring fighters to stop, and beckoned them over.

"You must stop them from killing you without you killing them," Ramel said to Masolon in a low voice. "This novice is yours, warriors!" He pushed Masolon forward. "Finish him off!"

"Most probably I will kill you after I am done with them," Masolon promised.

"Let me see what you got, boy," Ramel scoffed. "Unleash your wrath!"

* * *

It was nearing midnight when Masolon dragged his feet to the chamber Ramel had shown him. Beating those two opponents hadn't been a big task, but the whole day was quite a long one. He hadn't rested his body since the early morning as Ramel was testing his stamina from the very beginning.

A long day with an awkward turn of events. Instead of returning to Bumar's house with a sack full of silver, he would spend a night in Ramel's Pit. And who knew how many more nights he would spend here? He had better deal with Ramel and his nonsense until he recruited the men he needed for his own company.

Lingering at the back of his mind was, what if Ramel's proposal was the best he got? What made him so sure that Galardi would wait for him until he was done recruiting an army? What if Galardi assigned someone else to the job? What if after two months, the merchant simply forgot about him?

Shaking his head, Masolon roused himself from his doubts. How did he consider, even for a second, pursuing Ramel's path? What had happened to his oath to punish every marauder his sword could reach? Apparently, the spark of vengeance was fading. The clink of silver had its magic.

Admit it, Masolon! It is all about silver!

He could hear the voice of his mind. Yet what was the shame about that? Was he supposed to let himself starve in the lands of Gorania?

"Hey you, big boy." Viola's mocking voice interrupted his self-conversation. "This is not the time or place for daydreaming. You may resume your dreams on your mattress inside."

Masolon realized he was standing by the door of his chamber, staring at the dusty ground. "Mind your business."

"You think of quitting. I can see it in your eyes."

"Oh really?" Masolon chuckled mockingly. "I did not know you were a soothsayer."

"I'm not a soothsayer. I'm someone who doesn't need funny accents to sense who doesn't belong to us." Despite her pretty brown eyes, she looked like a snake when she hissed, "Like you."

"And who are *us*?" Masolon asked. "You and Ramel?"

"We're bigger than you think." She raised her chin. "We're the league that rules all Contests of Gorania. But a foreigner like you will never understand what Contests mean to Goranians. Many peasants may have never heard about their lords, but they can tell you tales about our champions and their heroic victories. They fill their bellies with barrels of ale while chanting our warriors' names in every tavern in these lands. We're the true rulers of Gorania, big boy."

She knew he was not a Goranian, but obviously that didn't scare her. It would be fun to know what might scare this wicked viper.

"What is a girl like you doing here with a bunch of warriors?"

"Is this your way of flirting?" she countered.

"Flirting? With *you*? Not in a hundred years!" Masolon hadn't laughed that loud in a long time. Maybe she was the only girl he had chattered with so far in these lands, but wooing her? The thought had never flashed through his mind. Not that she was bad looking, because she was certainly not. It was something about the way Masolon felt every time he crossed paths with her. An uncomfortable feeling that always kept him on his toes whenever she was in sight. Most probably, the feeling was mutual.

His mocking tone had enraged her; he could tell from the glare on her face and the clench of her fists. While it hadn't happened intentionally, that didn't prevent him from enjoying the moment.

"One day you will regret this," she said menacingly.

Masolon waited until she walked away before he pushed his chamber door open. Normally, he wouldn't let that scum of a woman get away with her menace, but at this very moment, he had a bigger concern. A much bigger one of the highest priorities. *Getting some sleep after quite a full day.*

11. MASOLON

Masolon wondered why he didn't smell anything cooking.

His stomach growled when he woke in the morning. There must be some kitchen here. Or did he have to hunt his breakfast? Maybe it was part of Ramel's absurd training.

He wandered the silent Pit, looking for anybody to ask him how he was supposed to get his food. The amphitheater was abandoned, and so was the dusty ring. The only sound he heard was the snorting of horses coming from the stable. Masolon went there, but he found no one, except the horses of course. He must have woken up too early.

His ears caught a humming sound. Behind the stable was a thatched building that Masolon assumed was a barn. However, he discovered this barn happened to be the Pit's dining hall. Already ten brothers-of-the-Pit were there, sitting at the long table in the middle of the hall, devouring their white breakfast.

"What is this?" Masolon asked the nearest brother, nodding toward his bowl.

The brother didn't look at him when he answered, "Milk with wheat grains and black dates."

"What sort of food is this?" Masolon asked in disapproval.

"Your breakfast." Holding a similar bowl, Viola came in from the door connecting the dining hall with what appeared to be the kitchen.

"I thought you were Ramel's assistant, not his cook." Masolon smirked.

"I'm here because our cook doesn't feel well today." She pushed his bowl over the table toward him. "Finish this. You will need strength for your training."

"Will it kill me?"

"Not unless a date seed gets stuck in your throat."

Masolon allowed a wry chuckle. "Why should I believe you?"

"Only because Ramel still wants you alive."

He does for the time being, but what about you? Still suspicious, Masolon turned to the same brother he had asked about the contents of the bowl a minute earlier. "Do you mind?" Without waiting for his permission, Masolon switched his bowl with his neighbor's.

"You!" snapped the brother. "What do you think you are doing?"

"I am giving you a full bowl." Masolon kept his eyes on Viola, waiting for her to interfere before the wrong man got poisoned, but the viper's face was as cold as ice. "You should thank me."

"Are you serious?"

"I always am." Masolon was addressing the dubious brother while looking Viola in the eye. "Now eat the bloody thing before I change my mind."

Out of the corner of his eye, Masolon saw the brother eat from the damned bowl at last. "Afraid I might kill you?" Viola laughed. "Don't worry, when it comes to that, I would go for knives." The crooked smile on her face slowly faded into a hard look. "You still have the chance to leave if you want. Leave now before you are in too deep, and I promise no one will harm you."

You harm me? Men twice as big as she could only try. "I never killed a woman in my life, but there is a first time for everything."

Viola arched an eyebrow. "Are you threatening me?"

"Just reciprocating."

"I was offering, not threatening." She curled lip. "And my offer

67

stands until you step into the arena."

Silence fell over the dining hall after she exited it, and only now did Masolon notice that the other brothers were watching. When he looked at them, they pretended they were busy with their almost empty bowls. Maybe he should have his breakfast now lest he show up late at the arena. To his surprise, the breakfast didn't taste bad at all thanks to the sugary black dates. Recalling Viola's hint, he chewed carefully so as not to swallow a seed. *Hopefully, we get a real meal at the end of the day. Not...this.*

The moment Masolon stepped out of the thatched hall, he saw Ramel coming to him. "You're late." Ramel motioned him to hurry.

Masolon caught up with him and both men headed to the amphitheater.

"Did you sleep well after yesterday's fight?" Ramel asked.

"*That* fight; what was the point of it?" Masolon asked.

"You can't just do as I say without asking questions, right?"

"Forgive me for my rudeness." Masolon smiled crookedly. "I am sure you have a point and I want to know it."

"You mean you believe it was pointless. Because you *believe* you fought perfectly, don't you?"

"You asked me to beat those two without killing them and I did."

Except for two sparring fighters, the amphitheater was empty when they entered. Not much space was allocated for spectators in this arena, but the field itself was as vast as the one Masolon had seen in Inabol.

"That fight revealed the flaws in your swordplay," said Ramel. "You took too much time to end that encounter."

"I thought this would be more entertaining to the crowd."

Ramel arched an eyebrow, staring at him for a while. "You may have a point, I must say, but you miss what the whole thing is all about."

The sparring trainees stopped when they saw their master standing at the edge of the ring. Ramel gestured to them to resume what they were doing.

"The Pit, the arena, those fighters and you; is it all about entertainment? Of course not. It's all about gold and silver," Ramel went on. "And you only earn gold and silver by winning Contests, not by entertaining the crowd. That is your profession from now on, Masolon. You win those Contests, and both of us will enjoy their lives. All I ask is to keep your attention in this Pit to what I tell you, and later you will get drunk with whores whenever you please."

"When will I be done here in the Pit?" Masolon asked.

"When I say you're ready." Ramel picked up a wooden pole from a long wooden counter at the corner of the arena. "New students usually need six weeks."

"What about almost ready students?"

Ramel regarded Masolon with amusement, standing between him and the weapons counter. "You still don't want to understand."

Roaring, Ramel lunged forward with his pole. Masolon dove to evade his charge, rolling his body on the ground toward the wooden counter, and snatched a pole. Still lying on his back, Masolon used the length of his pole to block a smashing strike from Ramel, and in a heartbeat he kicked Ramel in the legs.

"Not bad." Ramel curled his lip in disdain. "Still not ready though."

Masolon pushed to his feet. "You cannot be serious."

"I am serious about my business, Masolon." Ramel looked him in the eye. "I always earn a lot from the Contests and I always will. Do you know why? Because I know what it takes to run this business. The way you fight might have worked before, but not in my Pit, not in *my* Contests. I don't care about the thousand ways you have learned to slay a man with a steel sword. I only care about one way to knock out an opponent with a wooden pole. *My* way."

That bastard thinks so much of himself. "What is this speech for? I was about to defeat you a few moments ago, if only you did not stop the fight all of a sudden."

Ramel patted Masolon's leg with his pole. "Your hit here won't cause as much harm as here." He slid the pole up to Masolon's knee.

"Not if I hit you harder."

"Power is not everything. It is the spot of your strike that makes the difference between a decisive victory and a clear defeat. You will find yourself surrounded by four or even more opponents who have beaten all your fellow fighters. For each foe, you will only have one chance to knock him out. If one of your strikes fails, you are out. That's what makes winning a fight with wood harder than with steel." Ramel threw his pole and held Masolon's arm. "Your blow doesn't start from here." He jerked the arm away and pointed to Masolon's eyes. "It starts from here. Your eyes should drive your arms, Masolon. Keep them open, and don't let anything distract them."

"Eyes drive arms," Masolon muttered, gazing at the viper approaching them.

"A message from your lordly friend." Viola handed Ramel a sealed envelope, glancing at Masolon. "I see you are still here."

Masolon grimaced. "Why would I not be?"

"What is it, Viola?" Ramel asked.

"Nothing." She shrugged. "Just wondering how long this big boy will remain obediant."

"He will." Ramel snickered. "After he earns a Champion's night with a Rusakian wench, he will!"

Heedless of Ramel's nonsense, the viper stared at Masolon. "A bird hates its cage, even if it is made of gold."

"Come on, Viola. I cannot understand your thoughtful poetry." Ramel patted her shoulder gently and returned the envelope to her. "Listen. Keep this with you until I'm done with our new champion. We have a long day today."

"I will be waiting for you," Viola said to Ramel, surely not happy with the way he dismissed her in Masolon's presence. Now avoiding Masolon's eyes, she turned her back on them and left.

"Not a bad skirt, huh?" Ramel smiled wickedly when he caught Masolon following Viola with his eyes. "But she's better than nothing."

Masolon harrumphed. "I am sure she is a capable assistant."

"Capable? Yes, she is. She *assists* me very well!" Ramel guffawed, and so did Masolon. Although he never felt comfortable with Ramel either, he had to admit that his company was not too dull, to say the least.

"Why do you not participate in those Contests yourself?" Masolon asked.

"Why should I?" Ramel shrugged. "To earn gold and keep my bed warm? I am enjoying all these pleasures already without a drop of sweat. That's why I train men like you, Vaknus, Artony, Edson, Tharmen, and others." He grabbed the thrown pole and spun it fluidly. "Time to teach you some combinations. Defend yourself, boy!"

* * *

Masolon's first week in the Pit didn't go as planned.

Unlike how easy the idea appeared, recruiting brothers-of-the-Pit to his army was futile, and after a few attempts he learned why. It was the gold. Since warlords would always pay higher than merchants, only a moron—like Masolon—would join him.

Though Masolon didn't care about Ramel's Contests, he still expected his mentor to teach him some of his fluid moves, including the one he had beaten Masolon with in their first encounter. That never happened. All Ramel had been doing for seven days was watching Masolon spar barehanded with two opponents, and saying 'again' every time Masolon beat them. If there was something Masolon had mastered in his first week, it was how to pronounce the word 'again' in a perfect Bermanian accent.

"Let's make things more interesting." That was Ramel starting a new week. And indeed he made things more interesting by surrounding the sparring field with a ring of fire, sparing a couple of feet as an exit. "If you push your opponents into the fire, you will follow them," Ramel warned him, but his opponents didn't receive the same warning. Much more interesting now.

71

Day after day, the ring was getting narrower, and yet Ramel didn't seem to have had enough fun. By the end of the sixth day of the second week, Ramel let in one more opponent. Still, Masolon was winning, but after receiving a few more punches in the face. Every day one more opponent joined the ring of fire, adding more bruises, but the result never changed, and 'again' never stopped. Near the end of the third week, Masolon found himself facing eight opponents, the fire already consuming the thin air of the Pit. It took an eternity to persuade those eight opponents to lie on the ground and stop fighting. *I would have been more persuasive with my sword, though.*

"Again."

He felt like crushing Ramel's neck when the word rang in the Pit.

"NO!" Masolon blustered.

Standing outside the ring, Ramel glared at Masolon. "I said 'again.'" Ramel's voice was menacing.

"This is insane." Masolon stepped outside the ring through the two-foot exit.

"Masolon!" Ramel shouted. "You cannot leave the ring before I tell you!"

But Masolon had enough of this farce. "This absurd ring of fire has nothing to do with what I saw in the Contest!"

"Are you questioning my methods?" Ramel snarled.

"Yes!" Masolon didn't flinch, an awkward silence following his curt reply. Apparently, Ramel hadn't seen that coming.

"Come," Ramel said as he strode away from the fire ring. For a moment, Masolon had thought of leaving that Pit for good, but he found himself following Ramel to a chamber he hadn't entered before.

"This is where we should have started." Masolon gazed at the five rows of racks full of all sorts of weapons, all crafted in wood.

"It is not that simple," said Ramel, his face still grim. "You cannot master all these weapons without heavy sparring. And you cannot endure heavy sparring without improving your stamina."

So all the madness about the blasted fire rings revolved around stamina. "Why do I need to master *all* those weapons?" Masolon asked.

Ramel smiled in amusement. "What is your favorite weapon? A sword or a spear?"

Ramel was back to his games. Masolon mused for a moment then he said, "If I say 'sword,' you will give me a spear, right?"

"No, I will give you this." Ramel grabbed a war ax. "Do you have any idea how to block an ax strike? The best way to know is to learn how to use the ax itself."

"I did not know we could use axes in Contests."

"Wooden axes, wooden swords, and in some Bermanian Contests they give you a horse and a lance. Horsemanship is something highly regarded in Bermania."

Not more than it was in his homeland. There, a man who couldn't mount a horse was not a real man. And they never used saddles, bridles, or reins to steer their horses, only hands and thighs. Masolon couldn't wait to test how any of those Bermanians would fare against him on horseback.

"Alright then," said Masolon. "I am ready to start."

"Do you know what this means?" Ramel asked.

"For certain." Masolon knew it meant more weeks of mounting horses and endless sparring with axes, swords, and poles. "No more fire rings."

12. SANIA

Sania sat by her mother's bed, watching the healer's potion work at last. The old lady had stopped coughing, and now she was falling asleep. After one long sleepless night, Sania's sick mother needed a truce.

The sun must have risen already. Sania had seen the effect of the potion a dozen times before, and she knew that the coming few hours could be her only chance in the whole day to get some sleep. When she returned to her bedchamber, which was next to her mother's, she took Nelly's bow instead of going to bed. Now could be the best time to try her new bow. Only half an hour, and then she would hurry to her bed. Half an hour wouldn't harm anybody, right?

She strapped the quiver she had borrowed to her back. Pushing the door of her chamber open, she found her maidservant Fadeela at the corridor.

"Milady." Fadeela scurried to Sania. "Let me carry this for you."

"Quiet," Sania whispered. "I can handle myself. You stay here in case Mother...I mean Lady Ramia wakes up. I will be in the backyard in case you want to find me."

Sania left Fadeela behind, skipping down the faintly lit stone stairs to the vestibule of the castle. Guards at the main door stared at her as she approached them. *Yes, bastards. Who said that only men can wield a bow and arrow?* She glared at them, forcing them to avert their eyes and give her a courtly nod. As she traversed the courtyard, she felt that every guard was following her with his eyes and wanted to yell at them to mind their own damned business.

The palm trees crammed the backyard of the castle. Here she had plenty of targets to shoot at. Recalling how she saw the archers do this, she drew an arrow from her quiver and nocked it onto the bowstring. Before she made a full pull back, the bowstring slipped from her hand. Startled, she screamed, realizing that she dropped the arrow from her hand before letting loose the bowstring. Flying an arrow came out to be harder than it seemed.

Sania didn't look around to know if the guards were watching this; she was quite sure they were. They must be laughing at her foolishness, and that made her more determined to make this happen, to shoot an arrow at one of those palm trees.

She picked up the arrow from the ground and nocked it one more time. Straining her wrist, she pulled the bowstring and loosed the arrow, which struck the ground twenty feet away from her. A longer journey this time, but not higher. What was she doing wrong? Perhaps she should raise the bow when she shot.

Sania drew another arrow from the quiver. Raising her bow arm, she shot the arrow and watched it soar in the air. To her amazement, the arrow missed all those trunks and hit the stone wall behind them.

"Nice shot!"

Her brother's voice came from behind her. If he had seen her first shot, then he wasn't mocking her.

"Lord Feras." She sketched a bow to her brother, the Lord of Arkan. The creamy doublet he wore contoured his broad shoulders and slender waist, his black beard cleanly trimmed as usual.

He came closer. "I assume from your presence here that Mother is alright."

"She is asleep. I'm afraid that once she is awake she will choke again." Sania sighed. "I'm really worried, Feras. Three weeks, and her condition is only getting worse."

"Nineteen days," Feras corrected, his eyes on her diamond necklace. "Since you returned from Burdi."

"That's nothing but a coincidence."

"There is no coincidence, Sania," Feras said firmly. "When your grandfather sent Nelly to Burdi, it was no coincidence."

"I thought she went there by her own choice."

"Well, he sent her, and she agreed."

Feras always knew more than she did about anything, but why would that surprise her? The heir of Lord Ahmet must be well readied for that day when he assumed his father's seat.

"You saw her?" she asked him.

"I never did. I was a babe when she left. We were all forbidden from visiting her in Burdi."

"Because she was a sorceress?"

"More than a sorceress, Sania," Feras said with a shiver. "She was…evil."

Sania waited, but he said nothing more, as if she was supposed to understand what he was hinting at.

"What kind of *evil*?"

"A kind any man would have exterminated." Feras tilted his head. "If it hadn't been for love."

"Grandma?" Sania chuckled mockingly. "I never thought there were real love stories, especially in our glorious house."

Feras gave her a studying look. "I know what you are hinting at, sly girl. One day you may understand that love does exist in your glorious house. You will find it, but not in the sweet words you read and hear in your poetry lessons. You will find it deep in the simplest deeds you might not appreciate."

Good heavens! Sania had lived long enough to witness a moment to remember; when her elder brother, the valorous Lord Feras Ahmet, gave her a lesson about love.

"Simplest deeds, huh?" Sania snorted. "Tell that to the sick lady upstairs. I'm sure she appreciates Father's *simplest deeds*."

Feras curled his nose. "Don't you feel you are harsh about Father?"

"I hope he proves me wrong when he receives the news of his wife's sickness."

"You really disappoint me, Sania. I thought you became a woman with reason, but you still think like a child. What do you expect him to do? Father is battling the Mankols to defend the northern borders of our kingdom, to make people like you safe in their homes."

"Ah, I understand now. Mother should be grateful then. I will tell her when she wakes up."

"I don't ask you to thank him, but don't blame him for doing his duty for his faction."

"What about his wife? Isn't she part of his bloody faction?"

"She is," Feras said. "But he knows she is in safe hands. Don't you agree?"

"Who are you fooling? He never cared about her. Her mission was done after she gave him his children."

"What is this folly?" Feras snapped.

"The truth, brother." She glared at him. "I'm not a child as you think. I understand the game I'm part of. It is only a matter of time until I become a pawn like Mother and Meryem."

Feras shook his head. "I hope you only lost your mind. Worse things could have happened to you in that cursed house."

"Rest assured, Feras," she said, "I'm not haunted by a demon, and I didn't lose my mind."

"You had better be sure of that." Feras exhaled again. "Mother needs care, and you will be on your own in the coming days."

"I am always on my own. Even on the few days you honor us with your presence in the castle, you are not here, *brother*."

Feras didn't look offended. "I'm talking about Meryem. I'm sending her to her parents in Demask to be taken care of." He allowed himself a faint smile. "After a few months, you will be an aunt."

Sweet Meryem! Losing her only companion in this prison was really bad news. "So, you will feel relieved only because you know she is in safe hands. Is that it?"

"Meanwhile, I will be riding with my men to the western borders, where I will be joining forces with your uncle."

"Are you going to a war?"

He shushed her, looking right and left. "We don't want to start panic here. We're not sure yet of the Byzonts' intentions, but we've received some news about their movements near our western frontiers. If they dare to come too close, we will simply vanquish those bastards and send them back to their territories."

For the first time she felt worried about her brother. Maybe she really cared about him after all. "When will you come back?"

"Hopefully, soon." He sighed. "Until then, I'm asking you to keep your eyes on Mother." He glanced at her necklace. "Get rid of anything that might harm her. I will tell Dawood to return everything you took from Burdi. "

She was about to protest, but his eyes betrayed his determination. Whatever she was going to say, he wouldn't allow her to keep everything she took from Nelly's house. But what about one thing?

"I yield the necklace and the books," she said.

"*And* the bow."

"The bow stays here."

"It could be cursed, Sania."

"And it could be not. I'm sure it's the only bow I can wield."

Her brother's silence gave her hope.

"On one condition," Feras wagged a firm finger, "the bow stays *here*, in this very yard."

13. MASOLON

Finally, the moment Masolon had been waiting for had come. After weeks of quarreling with Ramel and sparring with his apprentices, the Master of the Pit had announced him ready for the Contests. Tonight was Masolon's last night in the Pit, and for this occasion he was having a warm rabbit soup with Ramel in his room.

"You know nothing about the Tales of Gorania, do you?" Sitting on a stool, Ramel stirred his bowl. "They used to tell us that thousands of years ago a great Bermanian king called Goran had conquered all other kingdoms and united all the realms under his banner to become the first emperor of Gorania. He reigned for forty golden years, during which the great cities of Gorania were built. The Tales say that in the era of Goran, mills had no room to store the grain, and the surplus was fed to the birds."

"How true are those Tales?" Masolon asked.

"They are as true as virgin whores." Ramel sniggered. "Those Tales were written centuries ago by some drunken clerics. Don't let their appearances and hollow speeches fool you. Those blasted clerics are no different from farmers, carpenters, and blacksmiths. They do what they do because it's their profession. At the end of the day, they're men, young man. Men who need to drink and whore to be ready for another laborious day of their miserable lives."

Masolon hadn't encountered a Goranian cleric so far. He assumed they were like the holy monks of his homeland, except that they neither drank nor whored. Becoming one of those monks was a great honor that only a few in Ogono were worthy enough to earn. Here in Gorania, Ramel himself would fare well as a cleric.

"You do not believe those Tales?" Masolon took a sip of the rabbit soup.

"Please. Feeding excess grain to the birds? What sort of merchants did they have in those days?"

"And King Goran?"

Ramel put down his empty bowl. "If the Tales were right about his army, then why not? Imagine an army of Bermanian cavalry, Skandivian infantry, and Byzont archers. What force can stop that? Give me such an army, and I would conquer the six realms."

"You would make a horrible king. I have seen enough in the Kingdom of Ramel's Pit," Masolon teased him.

"I might be a horrible king, but I'm quite sure I'd be a great emperor." Ramel grinned. "Some haste, young man! Finish your soup and mount your horse. You shall depart for Durberg tonight."

"Durberg? What for?"

"You thought you would leave my Pit and go back home? You have a Contest to win, and the next one will be held in Durberg in seven days. I want you to catch a caravan that's going to travel tomorrow from Lapond to Maksow. I will catch up with you after I finish some matters."

"Of course, you will." Masolon gave him a hard look. "To take your cut."

"I will take my cut whether I come or not." A confident smile lifted the right corner of Ramel's mouth. "It is the moment when the people of Durberg start chanting your name that I don't want to miss." He pushed to his feet and grabbed a rolled map from his desk. "I already told them to ready your horse. Do you know the way?"

Knowing the map of Gorania by heart was one of the skills Ramel had stressed. "I will go north."

Ramel seemed to be waiting for more. "That's it? North? That's really promising." He handed Masolon the rolled map. "Don't lose this, or you'll be lost."

Masolon drank what remained in his bowl and took the map from Ramel, spread it out, and tried to locate Durberg on it. "I knew it. I told you I would go north." He still couldn't read all Goranian words, but he only needed to recognize the drawing of the name of each big city.

"Northeast," Ramel corrected. "Going north means heading to the Northern Gulf. And trust me, you don't want to face coastal raiders before your Contest. It will be a deadly practice session. You shall follow the snow to the northeast until you reach Maksow, then north to Durberg."

Despite Masolon's absolute failure in recruiting the army Galardi had requested, he couldn't resist the temptation to pass by the merchant in Kalensi and see if there was any news about his caravan. No doubt that would make his journey to Durberg longer; something Ramel wouldn't be happy about.

"No need to worry," Masolon reassured Ramel, and rose to his feet.

"I only worry about my gold, Masolon. The little rumor that has reached my ears makes me worried indeed." Ramel looked at him quizzically. "You were recruiting caravan guards in the Pit, weren't you?"

Well, not recently, Masolon wanted to tell him. After his early attempts in his first week in the Pit, he had given up the idea. "A plan for the future will not harm." He tried a careless smile. "I had no idea where my training was going to take me."

"Now you do have an idea, right?"

"I told you, no need to worry."

"It is you who will need to worry if you think of messing with my gold." Ramel glared at him. "Becoming a caravan guard is *not* one of the reasons for which I wasted the previous six weeks of my life."

"Should I say it for the third time?" Masolon had no doubt Ramel would be upset when he left him, but why start the quarrel now? Two weeks still remained for his appointed time with Galardi.

"Don't forget your companions. The road is not always safe." Ramel motioned him toward the corner of his chamber where his new 'companions' lay. On the floor next to his sword rested a steel shield, a bow, and a full quiver.

"A Rusakian shield can stand a strike by a Skandivian ax," Ramel explained. "And this Mankol bow combines the balance of power and range."

Masolon glided his fingers over the tight bowstring. *And a steel shield?* he thought, testing the solid smooth surface with his fist. Surprisingly, it wasn't much heavier than his wooden one, but it felt different in his hand. Though this might sound strange to a peasant who would wish for nothing but peace for the rest of his life, an Ogonian like Masolon would hardly wait until he found an excuse to try his new gear. "Your gifts are gladly accepted."

"They cost me a few golden coins, but you're worth it, Champion."

"You will not regret it." Masolon left the chamber with his new companions. "I will see you in Durberg."

Masolon's horse was ready as Ramel had promised. To take it out of the Pit, he pulled it by the bridle until he reached the leveled fields of Lapond. The city was only a few hours from the Pit, but who said he needed to catch that caravan departing for Maksow?

14. GERVINY

The ironwood skeleton of the coach creaked as the horses trudged on the heavy snow. The wooden thing was the same age as his father, if not older, but no one could convince the stubborn old man to get rid of this relic. The Lord Marshal of Rusakia deserved a more elegant ride.

"No foolish acts today." The blue eyes of his father were fixed on him.

The old man would never change. *I am twenty-one, and he still treats me as if I am his little boy.* "Why should I act foolishly?"

"You ask me?" His father curled his lip with distaste. "Why don't you ask yourself?"

Gerviny wondered what his father's harsh tone was about. He knew the old man would never love him like he did his late brother Elov, but usually the Lord Marshal had a justified reason to get angry at his only son.

"You know what I'm talking about."

Old Larovic was in a bad mood today, like he was every day. Although Gerviny had been a child at his brother's funeral, he still remembered the smile on his father's face in his conversations with Elov.

"I will be grateful if Lord Larovic clarifies what he is talking about," Gerviny said.

"The girl. She is not your bride yet." His father wagged a finger. "Don't *ever* forget that."

His father was hinting at Gerviny's little…adventure with his former squire's sister. Three years had passed, and still his father rebuked him. Maybe the Lord Marshal was still weeping over the gold he had paid to buy the squire's silence. The whore's curves were worth every coin though.

"Is that what you are here for?" Gerviny couldn't suppress his mocking smile when he recalled that night in her chamber. "To prevent me from ruining this *honorable* marriage? I never thought you bore any affection toward Sanislav." Truth be told, Gerviny never thought his father bore any affection toward anybody at all.

"You are even naiver than Sanislav's daughter." His father shook his head, giving him the look that Gerviny always hated. The look that betrayed his disappointment in his sole heir.

"I'm not naive," Gerviny snapped. "It's you who never shares his plans with me."

"Do you really need me to tell you that this marriage is about Sanislav's castle, not him or his worthless daughter? With Durberg and Sabirev in our hands, our house will be the most powerful house in the North." His father *tsked,* looking his son up and down. "After my death, you will be the most powerful lord in Rusakia."

"I will." The moment Gerviny realized how that might sound, he hurriedly said, "May the Lord of Sky and Earth bless you with good health."

His father gazed through the window at the white terrain. "I talked with Sanislav already about my desire to bind our houses through this marriage, so everything is arranged. However, you will do the talking with him as if nothing has happened between me and him. You will ask for his daughter's hand in marriage, as if it is your own decision, your own desire. I will be watching and say nothing."

Not a big task to worry about, Gerviny believed. "You can count on me, Father. I know how to handle this."

"You do?" his father scoffed. "You only know how to bed lowborn whores."

"You underestimate your son, milord. You have never seen how I treat delicate highborn ladies to judge me."

"Perhaps I am going to see very soon. The girl might show up today and spend a few moments with us. Show me your best."

"Not a problem." Gerviny tried to look confident. "I've made prettier girls fall for me."

A hint of a smirk barely lifted the right corner of his father's mouth for a second. "I doubt you've met a prettier girl."

Gerviny wished he could mock his father's standards of beauty, but he would never dare. The last time he saw Halin had been five years ago in a feast in Maksow, but he remembered well that she had never grabbed his attention. The girl was skinnier than a stick, like a skeleton dressed in silk. He had to admit, however, her blonde hair wasn't bad at all.

Gerviny didn't exchange another word with his father until the coach passed the iron gates of the ancient castle of Sabirev, Rusakia's Last Shield. Gerviny had often heard the tale of the Mankols' invasion that had been broken at the frozen walls of this fort ten centuries ago. When winter came, the Rusakians sallied out of Durberg and Sabirev and ran the barbarians out of their motherland for good. *A stupid, frosty piece of stone.* His demented father was the naive one here to be that desperate to seize control of such a remote castle. Instead of strengthening his status in the North, the Lord Marshal should rather secure a seat for his house in the King's Council in Maksow, in the capital, in the royal palace, away from this dull monument. *Why am I surprised in the first place?* To someone who was fond of anything old like his father, this historical castle was a holy place.

Gerviny and his father put on their fur coats when the coach stopped. Gerviny opened the door and stepped down first, offering his father a hand to help him out. "I'm not that old. Get out of my way." Larovic's answer to his decency was frustrating as usual. Gerviny hoped the guards in their reception from the castle were not paying attention at this moment.

The captain of the Castle Guard saluted the Lord Marshal and his son before he escorted them inside. As the captain strode through the vestibule ahead of them, Gerviny leaned toward his father. "Where is Sanislav?" he whispered. As a display of respect, the lord of this cursed castle should be in the Lord Marshal's reception the moment he stepped out of the coach.

His father didn't look bothered, though. Usually, he looked bothered for no particular reason, but this time, he didn't even heed Gerviny's concern. When Gerviny dared to repeat his question, his father only gave him a glare, as if saying, 'What did I tell you in the coach?'

All Gerviny's protests about Sanislav's lack of respect vanished when he entered the great hall and his eyes fell on the blue-eyed girl standing next to her towering, broad-shouldered father. The two gaunt grooves that used to be in Halin's face had become two rounded rosy cheeks, completely changing the way she looked now. Even her long blonde hair looked prettier on her new face. He allowed his eyes to scan her lithe frame, which had acquired a bit of flesh, giving her bosom and hips the perfect size.

"It's an honor meeting you, Lord Marshal." Halin gave his father a courtly bow. A statue of stone would melt to this epitome of beauty, but his father would not. The proud Lord Marshal barely smiled at her.

"Lord Gerviny, welcome to our humble castle." She beamed at him, hesitantly offering him her hand. Smitten, he was clueless for a moment before he laid a kiss on the back of her hand. The hardest part was letting her hand go.

"We all know what we are here for." Sanislav grinned, glancing at Gerviny. "Let the old men discuss their boring matters while Hal shows you the castle."

What could be interesting in such a castle? *Show me something else,*

Halin, Gerviny thought. All he could do for the time being was let his imagination go wild. A few months of patience and this perfectly sculptured body would be his.

Delighted, Halin led the way on their tour. He shouldn't ever forget that he could charm any girl, and Halin was no exception.

"I love your fragrance," he remarked. "That's purple rose, right?"

"Oh, thanks. Yes, it is." She blushed. "Are you interested in books, Lord Gerviny?"

"Just Gerviny, Halin. And yes, but a certain type of books."

"History?"

"Romance," he lied, but he could wager that was her favorite kind.

"Really?" She sounded more glad than surprised. "I thought men were only concerned about war."

"I'm like no other man, Hal." He winked at her, and she giggled. *Where are you, old Larovic, to watch your son and learn?* "How did you form your opinion about men, though?"

She playfully gave him a dismissive gesture. "It's not what you might think."

"Are you telling me that you never had victims before?"

"Victims?" She laughed. "Maybe. Nobody told me though."

A flower locked in this prison. Gerviny must be so lucky that the games of destiny led him to her. "You must be bored here in this castle."

"My father doesn't let me stay here for long. Since Mother's death, I have become his companion in his travels."

"Traveling is fun indeed." Now Gerviny was quite sure he was lucky that nobody had ever proposed to her. *Fools.* "Have you ever been to a Contest before?"

"Father never took me there. What could be interesting about watching men clubbing each other?"

"Don't judge before you try. Besides, there is a ball after the fights end."

"A ball? That sounds interesting."

"Very well. You are attending the upcoming Contest with me. It is going to be held in my city, in Durberg." And she would be in his palace to attend the ball. *Accidents* might happen when wine played with minds. "Your father won't mind if you go with your betrothed on your own, right?"

15. MASOLON

The trees lined the cobblestone road to Kalensi, the rain showering Masolon and his horse for an entire hour. The rain stopped for another hour, allowing the warm sunlight to dry his clothing before the clouds agglomerated to start a new shower. The sun and the clouds kept playing hide and seek until nightfall, the moon taking the sun's place in the game.

The rain was much less on the next day. Thanks to the map, Masolon was able to identify the right way at the crossroads, managing to reach the marketplace of Kalensi before dusk. It was so close to the sea he could smell the brine in the cold breeze.

Ramel considered the Skandivians the finest footmen in Gorania, and Masolon didn't disagree when he saw them. The Sons of Giants, they called themselves. They weren't ten feet tall as they claimed their ancestors had been, but still, they were taller than the people he had seen in Murase and Byzonta. They were as tall as *him*, as his clansmen in Ogono, which made it hard to understand how a short fellow like Galardi belonged to the Sons of Giants. Ramel might be right, after all, about the drunken clerics who wrote the Tales of Gorania.

After he had asked about them, Masolon realized that the merchants knew Galardi and his father so well. It was the son he was looking for though, and the son wasn't there.

"Most probably he is one day away from Themus as we speak," a merchant told Masolon. "He will spend some time in Byzonta, so he will not be back sooner than two months later."

Themus? Two months later! Masolon spread the map to find the city, which lay there in the far southwest of Gorania. *Blast!* All those days he had spent in Ramel's cursed Pit were for nothing. Masolon's fret about finding new recruits, his arguments with Ramel, his wrangles with Viola; all were for *nothing*.

Calm down and come to reason. It is not over. Those two months could yet be gifts from destiny to grant him more time to find the men he was looking for.

Wake up, Masolon. The merchant must have traveled to Themus with his own army. He does not need you now.

Now he had to deal with the current situation. Galardi was gone, and only Ramel remained. He should catch up with that Rusakian Contest to give any meaning to his ridiculous training in the Pit.

Without having any rest, Masolon left Kalensi and followed the road to Durberg. A bunch of travelers told him he had no other alternative than going by the coast if he wanted to take part in that Contest. But he must be cautious in order not to attract the coastal raiders' attention. "There are two ways to pass through the deadly coast of the Northern Gulf," said one of the travelers. "You go there with an army that no one dares to follow. Or you go there on your own and pray the bastards don't notice you."

Days went by too fast. As Masolon approached a village called Horstad near the Skandivian coast, he was sure he wouldn't reach his destination on time. Only two days remained.

The thick smell of brine saturated his nose, making him feel nervous as he was passing through the coast of the Northern Gulf, yet his dire need of sleep was stronger. Half an hour later, he gave in when he reached the coast. Behind the trees, he dismounted, tied his horse, and lay on the damp grass to rest his heavy eyelids.

It hadn't been too long before his eyes suddenly opened. He heard something; he was sure of it. When he pushed himself to his feet to hurry to his horse, a thrown ax intercepted his way, missing his nose by a hair. He dodged two more thrown axes, accompanied by roars of attackers coming from the woods. Raising his head, Masolon saw two raiders sprinting toward his hideout. They were getting so close he only managed to shoot one of them dead with his bow before he slew the second with his sword. He looked behind the trees to make sure it was over, but it was not. Four more men were charging at him.

"A deadly practice session indeed, Ramel," Masolon muttered.

He charged ferociously, swinging both his sword and shield, felling two of his opponents; one dead and the other with a broken jaw. With his blade, he blocked the ax of the third raider while hitting the fourth attacker in his nose with the rim of his shield. He returned to the third raider, hammering his head with the same shield and finishing him with his sword. Masolon then faced the raider with the broken jaw and slashed his neck. Only the one with the broken nose remained.

"Come on, scum!" Masolon growled. The last opponent bellowed in return and lunged forward. With his shield, Masolon fluidly parried him before he struck him dead in the heart.

"Does anyone else wish to die tonight?" Masolon roared at the vast valley ahead of him. Only now did he realize that his arm was slightly wounded.

"Crush him!" a cry came from behind. Masolon found a dozen men sprinting toward him, blocking his way back to his tied horse. If they ringed him, he would definitely be doomed. In two heartbeats, he shot two men dead, and before he nocked the third arrow onto the bowstring, he heard the whinnies of horses coming from behind the raiders.

Nine armored horsemen, Masolon counted when they appeared from the woods. Galloping, they charged, and luckily, not at him. The raiders' chances of surviving the cavalry attack were nil, but they did stand their ground, letting the knights' steel blades reap their wicked souls. Nine strikes, not a single one wasted. Those horsemen must have done that thousands of times before.

Masolon's rescuers were not Skandivians. From what he had learned in the Pit about Goranian kingdoms, he could tell from the lion sigil on their breastplates that they were Bermanian knights. One of them approached Masolon and took off his helm, revealing his short brown hair and deep-set brown eyes.

"It's unwise to make noise in a deadly place like this one, but in your case, this helped us hear you," said the knight. "What do they call you?"

"They call me Masolon." *And sometimes the Foreigner.* "I am grateful for your coming."

"We are the coast watchmen, and I'm Frankil." The knight turned his eyes toward the corpses of the raiders Masolon had slain. "You defeated eight men on your own." Frankil looked impressed. "We may need someone like you."

"Someone like me to do what?"

"To protect the helpless people of these lands and punish the likes of those bastards who attacked you," said Frankil.

"That is the job of the lord of these lands, not mine."

Frankil grinned and exchanged a quick look with the nearest knight to him. "The lord of these lands is a bit occupied these days. In fact, he has been so for a year, leaving his subjects barehanded against outlaws. That's why we decided to stand for those helpless people."

Masolon glanced at the lion sigil on Frankil's Bermanian armor. "You and your men are far from home. May I know what brought you here?"

Frankil exchanged another look with the same knight. "You can say I have debts that I need to settle."

"Debts?"

"Sins, Masolon. Don't you have any *debts* you wish to release your soul from?"

For certain he did. *The worst of all debts.* Why would he not join that wandering knight who sought redemption? Oh, yes, he remembered now. "I will be indebted to someone if I do not leave at once." Masolon mounted his horse and turned to Frankil and his knights. "Why do you not do those peasants a favor and teach them how to defend themselves? You nine are seasoned warriors after all."

Frankil rubbed his head for a moment. "Sounds like a good idea. It would sound better if you helped us in this."

Ramel and his viper would love that. "I may think about it, but not before I am done with the pressing matter I have for the time being." Masolon held the reins of his horse, kicking its flanks to start cantering.

"The village of Horstad is not far away from here." Frankil's voice came from behind Masolon. "We will meet there again, I presume."

I know we will. We must.

Masolon's horse galloped, the trees around him becoming shorter and more scattered as he was getting away from the bloody coast. To avoid falling into ambush one more time, his eyes kept scanning the field ahead, his mind still there with Frankil and his knights. Their path was similar to what he was seeking. It *was* what he was seeking.

If only he had met them earlier...

16. MASOLON

Masolon shivered as he reached Durberg, the City of Ice that lay in the north of the Rusakian Kingdom. His shoulders were freezing as if the snow was falling on his bare skin, not on the woolen coat Ramel had given him. He had never seen snow in his village, unlike the Rusakians who seemed to be very familiar with snow much more than sunlight.

There was no need to ask where the amphitheater was. Like the Byzont bees, the Rusakians were heading toward the same destination. But those Rusakian bees were hindering him in the narrow streets of Durberg, and he was running out of time.

"Out of the way!" Masolon demanded, yet not a single person bothered to make way for him. When he spurred his black horse into a canter, they realized he wasn't messing with them. Ignoring their insults and protests, he kept moving until he saw the magnificent amphitheater ahead. His ride was almost over.

A spearman suddenly appeared in his way. "You! Halt!" The Rusakian guard advanced, holding his spear toward the cantering stallion, leaving Masolon no option but to pull the reins. Neighing in protest, the horse raised its forelimbs as it stopped just in front of the reckless guard.

"Are you insane? You could have killed somebody!" the guard exclaimed.

"Forgive my foolishness, sir. I am a stranger who needs to catch the Contest." Masolon kept his tone as quiet as he could, not seeking trouble at the moment.

"If you are telling the truth, then you are late." The guard pointed the spearhead at Masolon's chest. "You will hardly find a spot to watch from. People are filling the arena already."

"I am here to participate, not to watch."

"I should arrest you for your foolishness." The guard lowered his spear, looking around. "Listen, I'll let you go, but you must do me a favor." He produced three silver coins from his pocket. "I am not allowed to enter the arena on duty. Take this silver and put a bet for me on Vaknus. If you don't find me at the gates, ask where Androvsky is."

Masolon was hesitant to take this fool's silver. "Is the reward worth the risk of giving your silver to someone you just met?"

"It is worth killing you if you think of fooling me." The guard pushed the silver coins into Masolon's hand. "Make no mistake; the guards at the gates will never let you leave the city until they know that Androvsky's debt is paid."

"I travelled hundreds of miles to win this." Masolon winked as he slapped his horse to move, the guard making way for him. "I guess you will kill me anyway."

The remaining distance was short, but the street leading to the amphitheater was getting more crowded as Masolon approached his destination. *Blast! Ramel could be there already.* What should he tell him if Ramel saw him just arriving?

Masolon dismounted when he spotted a tavern opposite the amphitheater. He tied his horse to the wooden fence and sprinted toward the arena. Inside the arena was a mess. The corridors were too narrow to accommodate all those *bees*, everyone yelling and cursing and pushing. Two men started a quarrel that escalated into a brawl with fists and kicks. The flock stopped moving forward as

95

more men hurried to separate the two angry men. After a few minutes, the throng resumed their slow march until Masolon found himself in the open seats area. Now he had to move in the opposite direction of this crowd to find the damned master of this Contest. *"Where do you think you are going, you fool?"* Masolon ignored harsher statements as he pushed his way back through the endless masses. A slender hand grabbed him by the arm.

"The first corridor to the right, second chamber downstairs." The young woman leaned toward him, and it took him a moment to realize it was Viola.

"I did not enlist my—"

"I did. Go now."

Masolon didn't like the glare she gave him, but he had no time to waste with her. Following her directions, he went downstairs and found his seven fellow fighters in the second chamber. A team of eight men would be battling another team of the same size. That was going to be a real mess.

A lad called them to move out to the ring. Masolon and his fellow fighters went through a dimly lit tunnel that took them upward to the center of the show. The herald approached them, followed by two lads pulling an unsaddled horse by its reins.

"Line up," the herald demanded, then he counted them. "You," he gestured to Masolon, "on horseback."

An unsaddled horse, as in the old days of Ogono, was presented; Masolon wouldn't ask for more.

The lads handed Masolon a lance after he mounted the horse. "Don't start before the horns!" the herald warned as he scurried to the opposite side of the ring where their adversary team lined up. Another horse was brought to them.

"No need to remind you, fellows." Masolon's eyes were fixed on the herald, who was still giving the other team his instructions. "Their horseman is mine."

The herald and his lads left the ring, and after one minute, the horns were blown.

"Charge!" Masolon shouted, spurring his horse onward toward his counterpart. As Ramel had taught him, Masolon hauled the lance and waited for the right moment to drive the wooden thing into his opponent's chest. Howling with pain, the horseman fell to the ground.

Masolon wheeled his horse and helped his fellows finish their opponents. "Out of my way!" he yelled at his men so as not to hit them with his horse or his hefty weapon. He knocked down four more men, his fellow fighters defeating the remaining three. A crushing victory for Masolon's team.

The crowd hailed the winners of this round as they were leaving the field. "They love you, foreigner." A fellow fighter nudged Masolon, nodding toward the clamoring spectators who waved at him. Some of them even rose to their feet, yelling incomprehensible words.

"What do they say?" Masolon asked.

"*Prava, neznakomits.*" His fellow fighter grinned. "They still stick to their ancient tongue in some parts of Rusakia."

Whatever '*prava nenzakomits*' meant, those maggots were taking these stupid fights more seriously than they should. Masolon had slain hundreds of men in *real* fights in his homeland, but no one had cheered for him. In Ogono, fighting was a bloody duty, not a silly game.

Round after round, whether on foot or on horseback, Masolon knocked down whoever stood in his way, earning the crowd's applause at the end of each fight. When dusk came, the herald announced the end of today's fights. All those people should come the next morning if they wanted to know who would become the Champion of Durberg. *More chants for you tomorrow, Masolon.* He had to admit to himself that he was starting to like those chants.

While exiting the amphitheater, he found Viola waiting for him outside. "That was a good performance," she said. "Survive the coming fight and reach the final round."

"Survive?" Masolon smirked. "What were you watching exactly?"

"Ah! I didn't tell you?" Viola smiled wickedly. "Your next encounter is against Artony and Vaknus. Together."

* * *

The sky was clear that evening when Masolon went to the tavern for a drink. There, he found a familiar bald head.

"Antram!" Masolon called. "I was wondering when I would see you."

"I told you before, just follow the Contests." Antram gestured to Masolon to join him at his table.

"How did things go with you in this one?" Masolon asked after taking a seat.

"I lost to a lucky bastard last round. My lance was so greasy it slipped from my hand." That bald fellow would never admit that someone else had outdone him. "He is your fellow fighter in the next round against Vaknus and Artony." Antram took a swig of ale. "I heard that you crushed every opponent you faced."

"My lucky day, perhaps." Masolon chuckled, leaning back to his seat.

Antram looked around cautiously before he said, "I have news from Bermania. They say Lord Di Galio is recruiting volunteers for his army. What do you think?"

"I am not sure, Antram." Masolon recalled his conversations with Frankil and Ramel about lords and soldiers. "I hope he is a worthy lord as you have been seeking."

"A lord who pays in gold is a worthy one to join. Gold is good."

"Is he worth *dying* for?"

"I don't care how noble the cause he fights for is. A mercenary follows his lord as long as he pays." Antram drank half of his drink in a gulp. "What is your problem, Masolon? I didn't know you were a cleric."

"I am no cleric, Antram. I am just a man who wants to earn his gold without staining his blade with forbidden blood. Those knights who followed their lord's orders and burnt your family alive did not care how *noble* the cause they were fighting for was." He looked at Antram beseechingly. "Because their lord was a *worthy* one to follow."

Antram bent his head down at that part. After moments of silence, he looked at Masolon. "You may have a point, but what do you suggest? Run for a Contest after the other? Is that it?"

"Listen, my friend, this land is plagued with outlaws everywhere. Those bastards are who we should raise our blades against," said Masolon, recalling Frankil's invitation. "We can do this together, Antram. We will find someone who will reward our services for that."

"Forget this blabber for now." Antram drained the remaining half of his cup with another gulp. "You have a Contest to win tomorrow. I heard that King Bechov will be there and he might honor the winner himself."

"And my fellow fighter? The lucky bastard who defeated you, what is his name?"

"Blanich. I heard somebody in the arena referring to him as the Rusakian noble."

"Why do they refer to him as the Rusakian noble, *Duke* Antram?" Masolon sneered.

"Because he is." Antram leaned back in his seat. "He *was*."

* * *

The rumors about the arrival of King Bechov proved to be true. The four fighters of the semi-final were ready in the arena, but the Contest master himself had warned them not to swing a pole before His Majesty found his seat and gave them his royal permission to start.

The snowfall had stopped that morning, but the air was still cold, making Masolon feel a slight numbness in his fingers and toes. He flexed them, swinging his leg forward and backward a few times. The draw put him on foot in this round next to his mounted fellow fighter, a handsome horseman with blue eyes and dark hair.

"Are you really a noble as they say?" asked Masolon.

"I'm not here to prattle," Blanich replied curtly. "Let's beat these two, and then it is between me and you in the final."

That Rusakian was obviously less talkative than Antram. "You are not one of Ramel's fighters, are you?"

Blanich curled his lip in disdain. "Ramel who?"

The Rusakian's question was the answer Masolon was looking for. *That handsome youth may cost Ramel a lot of gold today.*

Drums and trumpets declared the king's arrival. The royal party entered with a cheering from the crowd. A forced cheering, Masolon believed. After waving at his subjects, the king gave the fighters the permission they had been waiting for.

Both mounted, Blanich and Artony hauled their poles and spurred their horses to a gallop. Without any previous agreement, Masolon and Vaknus stood still in anticipation for the outcome of the coming clash. Each horseman thrust his pole toward his opponent, but only one fell off his horse, and that one was the good-looking Rusakian *noble*.

Masolon ran toward his fellow fighter to aid him, but Vaknus intercepted. The wooden poles collided a dozen times, both fighters seeking a vulnerable spot to hit until Masolon struck Vaknus's leg, and the veteran fighter fell on his back.

Scurrying toward Blanich to help him, Masolon saw Artony run over the young Rusakian with his galloping horse. The crowd thundered, plainly shocked by the brutal attack. "It's your turn now!" Artony howled, wheeling his horse to face Masolon.

"You coward!" Masolon blustered, sprinting toward the galloping horse. At the last moment, he stepped left before jumping to Artony's right, striking him with fury in his chest. The surprising charge made the champion of Inabol Contest fall on his shoulder, bones cracking loudly the instant the body hit the ground hard.

It wasn't over yet. Vaknus rose and lunged at him, hitting his torso with a heavy strike. Masolon fell on the ground, his pole still in his grasp. He rolled to evade a blow from Vaknus, and swept his foe's legs with his pole. Pushing to his feet, Masolon kicked Vaknus's weapon from his hand and laid the tip of his pole on Vaknus's forehead. The crowd roared, urging Masolon to give his fallen opponent the finishing strike.

Masolon wanted to smash that head, but that was Vaknus under his feet; not Artony. *You cannot punish someone for the guilt of someone else.* Those had been his own words to his father. He couldn't break them now to quench the fire of his fury or to please those people.

Masolon let his pole fall beside Vaknus, and the whole arena hushed. Even Vaknus didn't try to rise to his feet, staring at Masolon in anticipation. The veteran warrior seemed to be waiting for Masolon's next move, but Masolon was done for this round.

A clap coming from the royal balcony echoed in the silent arena. King Bechov himself. Then a storm of applause shook the whole place. Those sheep needed their shepherd's approval before hailing the winner of this round.

The Contest master was checking on Blanich when Masolon strode to him. "He's alive," announced the Contest master. "But I doubt if he's ready to fight you in the final."

"What does this mean?" Masolon asked.

"Don't you get it?" the Contest master grinned. "You're the new Champion of Durberg."

* * *

A long time had passed since he heard the music of clinking silver.

Masolon came out of the Contest master's room after he had received his prize. Waiting for him down the corridor was a man clad in a fine gray coat.

"I was wondering when you would appear," said Masolon, opening his clinking pouch.

"I was never to miss your chant." Ramel grinned, taking his cut from Masolon's prize. "Why were you late?"

"I made it to the fights, and that is all that matters to you," replied Masolon.

"Masolon, don't ever dare to risk my gold and silver," Ramel warned, holding Masolon's shoulder with a firm hand. "You heard that?"

Masolon pushed Ramel's hand. Both men glowered at each other until a bald man approached them, clad in a white coat decorated with the white bear sigil of the Rusakian Kingdom.

"Congratulations, Champion," the bald man addressed Masolon. "You are requested to attend the feast held tonight at the palace of Durberg."

Ramel didn't look surprised, unlike Masolon. "*Requested*? By whom?" Masolon asked.

"King Bechov. Find a clean outfit, and don't be late."

King? Masolon's jaw dropped as he watched the bald man leave the chamber. *He said 'king,' right? The king will have the honor to meet me!*

"Lucky bastard! You owe me for that," said Ramel. For a moment, Masolon had forgotten that his mentor was still here.

"I might owe you for training me, but that does not make me your slave."

"Slave? You're going too far, Masolon, and the whole matter is quite simple. All I request is that you make sure you participate in every Contest."

"For how long?"

"Are you still recruiting for your caravan? Or do you have other plans that I don't know of?" Ramel peered at him. "What are you thinking of, Masolon? You want to be a mercenary and join an infantry squad of some lord, and live every day as if it is your last? I am offering you a life you wouldn't even dare to dream of. A life of wealth and fame. How can you refuse that?"

Antram arrived at that moment.

"Something wrong, brother?" asked Antram, eyeing Ramel

suspiciously.

"Everything is fine," said Ramel. "I will be waiting in Kahora for you in seven weeks, Champion. Don't disappoint me."

Antram followed Ramel with his eyes until he left. "Who is this man and what does he want from you?" he asked.

"It is a long story I may tell you later. Right now I want you to do something for me." Masolon handed Antram a purse of a few golden coins. "A guard at the gate is expecting his prize. I would give it to him myself if it were not for tonight's feast."

"Someone has bet on you?" Antram scoffed.

"He did not." Masolon winked. "But I did."

17. MASOLON

For a man coming from the harsh lands of Ogono, setting foot in Durberg Palace was like entering a totally new world.

The first thing that struck Masolon when he stepped into the vestibule was the huge golden chandelier that hung from the high ceiling with a chain that seemed a bit too small to hold the weight of this massive breath-taking thing. *How did they do that?* he wondered, but the question that really niggled at the back of his mind was: *Why the risk, to begin with?*

The paintings on both sides of the wall didn't impress Masolon that much, though. Since he was totally ignorant about the history of Rusakia, he had no clue what events those paintings depicted, but he could guess the general idea anyway. *Glorious victories of the great Rusakian kingdom,* he thought, glancing at the clashing armies on the snowy battlefields. Back in Ogono, Masolon's people loved to boast about their glorious victories too, yet there was one small difference.

The blood in Ogonian 'paintings' was always real.

A page approached Masolon, urging him politely to head to the big hall at once, and Masolon didn't linger. The instant the guards posted at the big doorway let him in, he realized he had seen nothing yet.

Instead of one golden chandelier, Masolon found three here, each one of them thrice as big as the one in the vestibule. And in addition to the hundred candles on each chandelier, there were also a hundred crystals that reflected the light like a hundred stars shining in the space above this boisterous place. Music played by a band to entertain the guests blended with people's loud chatter and laughter. Judging by their embroidered elegant attires, Masolon was the only common guest here.

Atop the dais at the end of the hall sat King Bechov with his retinue, his golden crown glimmering above his gray head. His face was grim, and so were the faces of the men chattering with him. Away from the dais, the hall was more delightful; men and ladies drinking, laughing, and dancing. Masolon couldn't help staring at three pretty girls standing on his left, and much to his shock, one of them smiled as she noticed him peeking. When she left her friends and came toward him, he swallowed.

"You must be the city champion," said the young lady. "I'm Halin, daughter of Lord Sanislav."

"My name is Masolon, milady." Masolon's eyes were fixed on her gorgeous fair-skinned face, her oval blue eyes. "It is such a pleasure."

She looked him up and down. "You are not a demon as they say."

"No, milady." He smiled. "I do not know why they say so."

"Mayhap it's the losers who say so to justify their defeat against you." Halin nodded her chin toward him. "No doubt your strength and skill are unmatched, but what you did to your opponent was really noble. That sort of chivalry has become rare these days." She sighed. "Even demons can be chivalrous."

"Thank you, milady."

"Enjoy the feast."

His heart drummed hard when Halin smiled at him before she returned to her friends. Masolon wasn't sure of what he exactly felt, but he surely felt good. Halin was the prettiest girl he had ever talked to.

"Welcome, Champion." The same bald man from the

amphitheater interrupted a stream of dreamy thoughts in Masolon's mind. "Are you having a good time?"

Masolon nodded.

"Good." The bald man gave him a brief smile. "In a few minutes you will be standing before His Majesty King Bechov. You will not say a word. Just smile and bow to His Majesty when he honors you. After you are done, step back while still facing him. We do not turn our backs on His Majesty. Understood?"

Masolon nodded, having no problems with those rituals of respect. Still, they were a bit exaggerated to him. Everybody in Ogono always honored their chiefs, but that never prohibited anyone from speaking up before them.

"Good." The bald man kept his artificial smile. "Come with me."

Masolon followed the bald man to the dais. The hall grew hushed when King Bechov stood.

"The last Contest I attended was forty years ago." The old man's voice was surprisingly strong. "I know I am renowned for my low opinion of those games. I have always believed that the Rusakian soldier who sacrifices his life for his motherland is the real champion of this nation."

Masolon wouldn't disagree with that, but he felt that old Bechov had chosen the wrong time to share his low opinion of the Contests. This man was supposed to honor him, right?

"However," Bechov added, "I saw today a true warrior. A man who had not only the strength and mettle of a Rusakian warrior, but also his nobility and honor. Although he doesn't belong to any of the noble houses we know of, he has earned his presence among us tonight. He may advance now to be recognized."

"Move on, Champion," the bald man urged in a low voice. Recalling the bald man's instructions, Masolon stepped forward toward King Bechov and tried to give him a bow like the one he saw the others do.

"Lord Marshal, please." Bechov gestured to the lord standing beside him. The Lord Marshal handed Masolon a full clinking pouch.

"From now on, you will be addressed as Masolon, the Champion of Durberg." The guests clapped when Bechov hung a medallion over Masolon's neck. Masolon gave the king another bow and stepped away without turning his back. Music was played again and the guests were back to their babble.

Nothing changed after the King's recognition. All these fine people, including Lady Halin, had forgotten about Masolon's existence in this hall. *Although he doesn't belong to any of the noble houses...*The king had said it so bluntly. This was no place for a commoner.

Masolon felt like leaving, but it was hard not to follow the gorgeous Halin with his eyes. She was his age or a bit younger, he presumed. Surely she belonged to some lucky lord, who in turn did belong to *any of the noble houses.* A lucky lord of blond hair and blue eyes like hers, like that young fellow standing on his right.

"I see you've got a good taste, *Champion,*" the young lord said, the scorn obvious in his voice. He nodded toward Halin. "I wonder who might resist those pretty eyes, or that artfully sculptured body." He turned to Masolon, a wry smile twisting his lips. "But there are a few things the likes of you must know before stepping into such a place. Being here among the finest people in Rusakia doesn't necessarily mean you are one of them. Take a look. You see those pages, servants, and musicians? They are also here, like you, for a certain purpose, not because they belong here. If *Lady* Halin calls a serving boy to bring her a drink, it doesn't mean he may have a chance with her."

A mocking smile came over Masolon's face when he saw Halin giggling with another lord. "What about your chances among the likes of you?"

The wry smile on the lordly scum faded as he grabbed Masolon by his coat. "How dare—"

Masolon's hand was faster than his mind when it gripped the lord's wrist and pushed it away. The lord's grab had started a fire in Masolon's nerves, and for a moment, he wasn't aware where he was when he balled his hands into fists.

No, Masolon. Not here. Not now. His mind stopped him before he might smash the bastard's pretty face.

"You heap of filth!" cried Gerviny.

And that was when the clamorous hall grew hushed. The jolly guests had ceased their blabber, the band their music, making Masolon come to his senses. *This is not Ogono,* he reminded himself, feeling the weights of the stares of everyone in this cursed hall. Everyone, including King Bechov himself. The best thing Masolon should do now was leave this feast at once.

"Halt! Halt if you are man enough!" Gerviny yelled when Masolon left him behind. Ignoring the blustering lord, he continued on his way to the hall door to leave. Before he reached the doorstep, Gerviny grabbed him by the shoulder and punched him in the face. The hit was more surprising than painful, but it infuriated Masolon nonetheless. *Not here,* he told himself, feeling his hands balling into fists. But instead of returning the blow, he lifted one hand to his nose to make sure it was not bleeding. He badly wanted to ruin the lordling's handsome face, but one more time, he told himself, *Not now.*

"This is not the place for scum like you!" Gerviny spat.

Masolon could have taught the spoiled lord a lesson if he had stood against him toe-to-toe in a different venue. "One day you will not be hiding behind your title." Masolon smirked and left the hall, the heat inside him overcoming the cold air of the white gardens outside. Enraged for not answering Gerviny's hit, he wanted to punch the nearest tree with his bare hands. But when Halin's charming smile crossed his mind, his tension faded. The feast wasn't totally bad, was it?

Quick thudding footsteps; someone was stalking him. Chasing him. *Gerviny.* Alarmed by the mental picture of the Rusakian lordling attacking him from behind, Masolon gripped the hilt of his sword as he turned, and the first thing he saw was a hand reaching for a sword in a curved sheath. Without too much thinking, Masolon drew his blade, and so did his deadly stalker at the same time. As it had done a thousand times before, his trained sword arm made a swift swing, slashing at the abdomen of Masolon's foe. The latter made a quick step back, his curved blade clanging against Masolon's.

"Hey! Hey! Stop! I'm no enemy!" the stalker cried, his voice attracting the guards' attention. As they reached for their swords, he waved at them, urging them to stand down. "Nothing to worry about, brothers. It's all right."

Masolon contemplated the stranger clad in a brown woolen coat matching the color of his skin, eyebrows thick, nose prominent, chin pointy, dark stubble on his cheeks. He was a bit shorter than Masolon, yet his shoulders were well framed. Or did they look so because of the layers of wool he was wearing?

"What is the matter with you?" asked the stranger, his look and accent not Rusakian at all. "Is this how you greet someone?"

"You drew your sword on me."

"Because you drew yours first!"

Maybe the stranger was right about this particular part. But maybe Masolon was right about attacking him as well, who knew? "Who sent you after me?"

"Nobody sent me, brother. Calm down." The stranger gestured with one hand as he sheathed his curved sword with the other. "I'm Ziyad. Don't you remember me?"

"I know no Ziyad."

"You don't know my name, but you must have seen me inside." Ziyad pointed his thumb backward toward the palace door. "I came here for the feast with the band."

"You are too agile for a musician." Recalling Ziyad's quick sword block, it was hard not to doubt his motives. Gerviny might have sent him to avenge his pride.

"And you are too dignified for a Contest fighter."

"I will take that as a compliment."

"I saw all that happened inside the hall. I was playing with the band of course, but I saw what was going on. You must admit you've earned Lord Gerviny's rage, especially after King Bechov scolded him in front of everyone. Shame you missed that part."

"Good for him," Masolon gloated. "He was the one who started it."

Ziyad winked. "*She* was the one who did."

"She?"

"His betrothed. Come on, brother, it was obvious. You grabbed too much attention at that feast. You should have seen how she followed you with her charming blue eyes. If I were Gerviny, I would kill you."

She did? "It is me who will kill you if you fool me," Masolon warned.

"Is it too hard to believe? Because she is a princess and you are...nobody?"

"Enough." Masolon held Ziyad's arm, looking around to make sure no one was listening to this. "This is not the right place for such a conversation."

"Exactly! This conversation needs a drink!" Ziyad grabbed Masolon by the arm. "Come on. I know where you can find the best wine in this city."

Masolon found himself walking with Ziyad to the horses. "Are you used to sitting with people you do not know?"

"Now you sound like my late mother, may the Lord of Sky and Earth have mercy upon her soul." Ziyad nodded to the stable boy when they found their horses. "You tell me about the Contests, I tell you how you charm a girl."

"You?" Masolon couldn't hide his mocking smile.

"Don't underestimate my skills, brother." Ziyad held the reins of his horse. "You're handsome and strong, and that might work. But if you want to occupy any girl's mind and heart, you should have a sweet tongue. Do you know how to tell a story? Girls love stories. They love listening to them, and they love telling them too. You see? You should do both; telling and listening. Telling comes first. If they love what you tell, they will tell you their own stories, and you *must* listen."

Masolon patted his horse. "I am good at listening, I guess."

"There will be nothing for you to listen to if you don't make her talk. And she won't talk if she feels you're boring and gloomy. Got the idea?"

Wooing a girl was a way simpler task in his village. "What do you suggest I should start talking about?"

Ziyad looked amused that Masolon was seeking his advice. "Most of them will ask you 'where do you come from?' You're more likely than anybody else to hear that question because both your look and accent are so confusing. Girls love to hear about places they haven't been to. You should see their faces when I start telling them about the majestic Murasen desert and its legendary immortal Ghosts, the bandits I faced in my journeys, the feasts I attended in the different corners of Gorania."

"You faced bandits, you say?"

"From the nomads of Murase to the axmen of Skandivia."

"I believe destiny has sent you to me for some good reason." Masolon grinned as he mounted his horse. "Now tell me about the majestic Murasen desert and its legendary immortal Ghosts."

18. MASOLON

The tavern was noisy and crowded when Masolon entered with Ziyad. Even among this throng, Antram's bald head was unmistakable.

Masolon introduced them to each other. "Ziyad, a wandering musician and bard from Murase. Antram, a veteran Contest fighter from Bermania."

"A veteran Contest fighter?" Ziyad grinned. "The beauties of Durberg will love that!"

The Murasen's awkward first acquaintance with Antram earned him a hard look. "My friend has a different taste in women." Masolon squeezed Antram's shoulder, trying to lighten the atmosphere a little bit.

"No way!" Ziyad teased. "Who can resist Rusakian blondes?"

"I'm sure they can resist *you*," Antram said.

This introduction is becoming worse than useless. About time Masolon got to the main subject. "Interested in earning some gold, Antram?"

Antram was interested, no doubt; Masolon could see that in his anticipating eyes. "Gold, you said?"

"Yes."

"Where?"

"Kahora."

Antram glanced at Ziyad then asked Masolon, "What did he tell you?"

Masolon nodded his chin toward the Murasen bard. "He knows someone who needs capable warriors to protect his caravans."

"The Master of the Merchants' Guild," Ziyad added. "I didn't say I knew him in person. But I know how to reach him."

Antram looked skeptical, chewing his lip in thought. "Gold is worth the risk," he said after a moment. "I'm in."

"I do not think this can be worse than following the Contests," Masolon teased the bald fellow.

Antram grinned. "When will we travel?"

"As soon as we finish our business in Horstad," said Masolon. "Someone there might be interested in joining us."

"Horstad? Are you bringing Skandivians in?" Ziyad asked curiously. "They could be the finest footmen in Gorania, but they won't be useful in the Murasen desert. We need horsemen, brother."

"Exactly. That is why they are *not* Skandivians, brother." Masolon winked. "At first light, you depart for Kahora. By the time we join you there, you will have arranged with that Guild Master."

"First light?" Ziyad tapped his fingers on the table. "About time I had some sleep then."

"We should all get some rest," Masolon agreed. "Let us go."

The three fellows headed upstairs to their chambers. Masolon stopped in the corridor when he found two men helping a severely injured man enter his room, bandages wrapped around his shoulders, arms, left leg, and most of his face.

"What is it?" Ziyad asked.

"I think I know this fellow." Masolon followed the two men with his eyes through the open chamber door, watching them lay the injured man on his bed. After they had left the room, Masolon entered to confirm his doubts.

"Blanich?" Masolon asked in a low voice. "Can you hear me?"

"Who is it?" The injured fellow turned his covered face toward

113

him. After a moment of silence, he said tiredly, "You are the one from the Contest. Masolon, is it?"

Masolon managed a smile. "We did not have our duel after all."

"That's a shame," Blanich said bitterly. "We will never know who would have won that duel."

Out of the question, Masolon almost said, but he would play along for now. "Maybe in another tournament."

"This is not what the healer told me. My limbs will never again be the same as before."

Other than his name, Masolon knew nothing about Blanich, and yet he pitied the broken young man. Sometimes death was a mercy, and in Blanich's case, surviving a horrendous accident in this way—if anyone would call this surviving—was a fate Masolon would only wish for his bitterest enemies.

"I know a veteran healer in Kahora," Masolon offered. "He must have a look at you."

Although most of Blanich's face was hidden, despair was obvious in his eyes. "I appreciate your concern, Masolon," he sighed, "but I'm afraid it's of no use now."

"You have nothing to lose if you go." Masolon glanced at Ziyad and Antram, who stood by the doorstep. "I will send you with my friend Ziyad. He is leaving to Kahora tomorrow."

Blanich paused for a moment before his eyes betrayed his submission. "I don't know what I could do to return the favor."

"You may worry about that after you recover." Actually, Masolon wasn't sure if Bumar could handle a desperate case like Blanich, but again, what was there to lose? "I shall see you in Kahora."

Masolon padded to the door and closed it as he exited, his two fellows outside staring at him. "Our plans didn't include your broken friend." Ziyad started, not a hint of rebuke in his voice though.

"Now it does," Masolon stated. "Will you be able to find Bumar the healer?"

Ziyad grinned. "Kahora is my mother, Masolon. Now I must run away before you give me another task." And just like that, the

Murasen bard walked away as he headed to his chamber. "See you in Kahora, brothers." His voice rang in the quiet corridor before he slammed the door of his room shut.

"I don't know why you brought this fellow with you," said Antram, staring at Ziyad's closed chamber door.

"Do not let his blabber deceive you. He is not just a man who knows how to wield a sword; he has a mind that is even sharper than his blade."

Antram shook his head, a nervous smile plastered on his dark face. "You always have a point, Masolon. But sometimes I feel I'm not quite sure I understand your plans."

Neither do I. "There are no plans. We just do what we are destined to do." That was what his wise grandfather had taught him.

"Destined? Don't we have a choice in what we do?"

"Of course, we have a choice."

"No, we *don't.*" Antram frowned. "Can I choose to become a wealthy merchant like your friend Galardi?"

"No, you cannot." Masolon patted the pommel of his sheathed sword. "Men like you and I know no way to make a living except with a blade. But we *choose* not to be outlaws, and we are comfortable with that." He studied his friend's face. "Unless you still miss your old friends who raised you up."

"You're not serious." Antram wrinkled his forehead. "Now, what are you going to do with that fighters' master Ramel?"

Ramel wouldn't be happy about the whole notion, Masolon knew. Not after those weeks in the Pit. "I will tell him. But not before we make sure we have—"

"*Are you done blabbering, you two?*" an angry voice came out of one of the rooms. A resident opened his door and yelled, "We're trying to get some sleep here, you—"

The angry man froze the moment he saw Masolon and Antram. Two towering men blocking the corridor, sheathed swords hanging from their belts. "Never mind," he croaked before he retreated to his chamber and slammed the door shut behind him.

"Speaking of choice," Masolon chuckled, nodding toward the door of the angry man's room, "that fellow has just chosen to do the right thing." He clapped Antram on the shoulder. "We shall move at dawn to Horstad. Sleep well."

* * *

Except for a few dogs barking every now and then, no one was around when Masolon and Antram arrived in Horstad. All doors and windows were shut. The whole village appeared to be asleep until four armored men appeared from four directions to surround the two unexpected guests.

"Stand down, fellows." Masolon gestured with open hands. "I am Masolon, and this is my friend Antram. We are looking for Frankil."

"You came back, Masolon." Clad in his plated armor, Frankil approached from behind him. "And you brought someone else with you to join us."

Masolon gave Frankil a wide grin. "Actually, it is *you* and your friends who will join us."

Frankil arched an eyebrow. "I'm curious now. Come with me."

Masolon and Antram followed Frankil until they reached another group of four knights sitting by a campfire.

"I remember this fellow." A black-haired knight pointed his finger at Masolon, but Masolon didn't remember him. The only one he had talked to was Frankil.

"I told you he would come back, Bergum." Frankil motioned Masolon and Antram to join the ring. "I'm listening," he told Masolon, who sat next to him.

"Alright then," Masolon began. "You and your friends have chosen to desert your home for a noble cause. Would it matter if you fulfilled your mission somewhere else? Away from Horstad?"

Frankil seemed to be weighing Masolon's words. "Horstad needs us."

"How many people live in this village? A hundred? I know

thousands of people who need your help. *Our* help."

"Thousands? Counting you and your friend, we are barely a dozen."

"The strength of our enemy is not in the numbers; it is in the reputation. No one dares to raise a blade against them, but we will."

"*Our* enemy? *We* will?" Bergum chuckled mockingly. "Are we one band already?"

"Bergum, not now please," Frankil rebuked his friend.

"Listen, brother. I'm not ready for another journey to fight for some people I don't know," Bergum announced. "The people of Horstad know us, and they are kind enough to give us the food they can spare."

"The people we will go to pay in gold," Masolon addressed Bergum, glancing at Frankil. Gold had persuaded Ziyad and Antram. Gold would persuade anybody.

The right side of Bergum's mouth quirked upward. "I might change my mind in this case."

"We are not mercenaries." Frankil glared at Bergum then turned to Masolon. "I will never let anyone dictate to me who I should kill because he pays me, Masolon. I told you I would never spill an innocent's blood with my blade."

"You can refuse the gold if you want," said Masolon. "But do you have a problem with slaying some Ghosts?"

Frankil shot Masolon an inquiring look.

"You don't mean the Ghosts of the Murasen deserts, do you?" a red-haired knight next to Bergum asked.

"Don't be a fool, Danis," Bergum teased. "Ghosts only exist in your nightmares."

"Obviously, someone in Kahora disagrees with you," Antram spoke at last, addressing Bergum. "And he's ready to pay in gold for those who would kill the Ghosts that *don't* exist."

"I heard you can't see them when they attack because they attack in the dark," said Danis. "And the beasts they ride don't leave tracks on the ground because they don't gallop. They *fly*, for real."

Masolon's eyes were on Frankil, who was plainly unhappy with what he was hearing. "Those Ghosts could be demonic or men of flesh and blood like us," said Masolon. "But the fact we are certain of is that they *do* exist. And no one has even dared to face them. We can. And we will defeat them."

"Don't they have competent fighters in Murase?" Frankil asked doubtfully.

"Don't they have competent fighters in Skandivia to protect this village?" Masolon countered.

"The lords might have abandoned their subjects, but I won't."

"I am not asking you to abandon anybody."

"You're asking me to leave Horstad."

"They are Skandivians!" Masolon chuckled. "Peasants or not, fighting runs in their blood. I am sure we can teach them how to defend themselves."

Frankil gazed at the fire for a moment then said, "You seemed reluctant when I asked you to join us. Now you're determined to travel to the end of Gorania to do exactly what I asked you to do here. Does gold matter that much to you?"

"I have seen what hunger does to good men, Frankil." The first spark of war in Masolon's homeland was seizing a granary. "If that gold prevents me from turning into an outlaw, then yes, it matters that much to me."

Frankil exchanged a look with his fellow knights. "We've sworn to stay as one party. So either we all stay here in Horstad or we all ride to Kahora. What do you say, brothers?"

19. FERAS

On horseback, Feras glanced at the thousands of Murasen troops following him and his lord uncle to the mountains of Sergrad at the eastern borders of the Byzont Kingdom. "I believe we should stop here, Lord Munzir," Feras suggested.

"Why should we?" Munzir asked. "According to our scouts, those scared Byzonts are trembling behind the walls of the castle of Sergrad."

Deep inside, Feras cursed the day King Rasheed had sent him with his uncle to deter the advancing Byzont troops. He hadn't felt good about the news of the enemy marching toward Kahora. "Still hard for me to believe that Byzonts would dare to venture into our lands," he said, his full armor rattling with his horse's trot. "They haven't raised enough cavalry since their glorious defeat against the Bermanians. They know their swordsmen will be crushed under the hooves of our memluks' horses."

"We are marching by the King's orders," Munzir snarled.

Feras exhaled, trying not to react to his uncle's aggressive tone. "The King gave his orders based on Lord Memot's information." He knew how Memot's name could boil the blood in his uncle's veins; the fruit of three decades of rivalry between the two veteran lords.

"Besides," Feras pulled the reins of his warhorse, gazing at the mountains ahead, "our orders were to stop the advancing enemy troops, not to invade their lands. We have reached the mountains of Sergrad, and yet no sight of a Byzont helm."

Thousands of hooves and boots halted. Feras could see the fury in his uncle's eyes.

"I didn't give you the permission to stop, Feras!" Munzir growled.

"If I were the Byzonts' leader, I would ambush the memluks in the bumpy valley at the foot of these mountains. It will be the best battlefield to slaughter our cavalry."

Munzir wheeled his horse, facing Feras's. "This is *my* army. I am the one who says march, I am the one who says halt!"

Feras gritted his teeth. "As you say, milord."

Munzir steered his horse toward the mountains once more, the horde resuming their march following their leader. Feras spurred his stallion onward as well, keeping his eyes on the mountaintops. *What was King Rasheed thinking when he decided that this clueless man could spearhead an army?* If there was one thing Feras's uncle was good at, it was his incomparable gift of deluding His Majesty. A seat in the throne hall with King Rasheed would suit Munzir more than a saddle on the back of a warhorse in a battlefield, and yet, according to what Feras had heard, it was his uncle who had insisted on leading the troops headed west to deter the advancing Byzont army. *Is this all about proving himself more valuable to the realm than Father? That politics was not his only area of...*

Feras was sure he caught glimpse of one head on the last mountaintop. *A helm.* "Take cover!" Feras hollered when the helms became too many, and they were not hiding any more. One moment later, hundreds of hissing arrows were falling upon his troops.

"*Raise your shields!*" one of the captains behind Feras barked. "*Shields up!*" another one yelled, but none of these loud orders stopped the screams of their shot soldiers. The Byzont archers positioned up the last mountain were hunting Feras's men like sitting ducks.

And this was just the beginning.

From around the rocky corners ahead of Feras emerged a battalion of the infamous Byzont heavy infantry. Well-trained soldiers clad in steel armor wielding long halberds and glaives, all of them roaring as they charged at the vanguard of the Murasen army. The memluks behind Feras roared in return as they advanced to meet the incoming Byzonts, but they were almost crippled on the uneven grounds of this valley. Launching an effective cavalry charge to crush and outflank the Byzont infantry here was nearly impossible, and the shrewd Byzonts knew it.

But the Murasens, under the wise command of Lord Munzir, did not.

A mix of fury and fear washed over Feras as he watched a Murasen captain drag the horse of his stuttering uncle away from the battlefield. *Blaming him is of no use now, Feras. Think. Think. Think!* he told himself as he watched the Byzonts infantry lay waste to the unorganized memluks, listening to the horrendous song of hissing arrows and shrieks of agony. *We are doomed here to the last man if we don't stop these deadly showers.*

"You!" he bellowed at the spearmen's captain, who was fortunately still alive. "Rally your men and—" An arrow struck the captain's chest before Feras might finish the damned order. "Blast!" he blustered, the grunting captain falling to the ground. *I will have to do this myself!* "SPEARMEN! TO ME!"

The scattered spearmen gathered behind Feras, whizzing arrows still hunting them. "Advance and form a spear wall behind the memluks! Now!"

Standing here was not less deadly than behind the slaughtered memluks, so the spearmen advanced anyway. "Faster! Faster, you slow bastards! Form the damned spear wall!"

The entire spearmen battalion was now ahead of him. Standing shoulder to shoulder, they held their weapons and shields toward the Byzont infantry. "No gaps! Steady! No one shall pass!" Feras bellowed as the Byzonts charged, their swords clanging against

Murasen shields. "Stab!" As one unit, the aligned Murasens thrust their spears through the attackers' trunks and limbs. Swiftly they restored their wall formation, their shields blocking the Byzont blades from breaking the Murasen line. The Byzonts didn't give up and charged more than once, but the spearmen didn't falter. Shield then stab; that was what they were trained to do. "Yes, yes! Keep it like that! Hold your ground like leopards!"

Hoping his spearmen would hold the Byzont infantry at bay for a while, Feras turned to the remaining swordsmen behind him. "Follow me!" He pointed to the mountaintop. "Let's slaughter those dogs!" He beckoned the archers at the rearguard over. "You too! To me!" Thanks to his father the veteran Lord Ahmet—who was a real military commander, not like that pretender Munzir—Feras knew about the narrow passage between two particular mountains in the middle of the Sergrad range. A passage that would take them to the other side of the mountains, where the Byzonts usually lurk to ambush their enemies. *High time we gave the Byzont scum a taste of their own medicine.*

The armor of the Murasen soldiers rattled behind Feras as they defiled through the narrow passage. Since it was practically impossible to shoot anybody here, the screams of agony halted for a while. But that only lasted until they reached the end of the passage. Once they started scaling the mountain from the other side, the arrow volleys were back.

Feras had to dismount to ascend the mountainside with his soldiers. "Shields up!" he demanded, two hissing arrows rattling against his wooden shield, soldiers of his own shrieking behind him, but there was no looking back now. He would lose a lot of men in this ascent, and he knew it. But he also knew that he would save a lot more. All arrows falling upon him and his men were arrows not falling upon the valorous Murasens holding their ground on the other side. *They are holding their ground, aren't they?* Well, the only way to know was to go up, vanquish those Byzont archers, and take their position on the mountaintop to watch.

More arrows hit Feras's shield as the deadly showers got even heavier. *They won't be throwing everything they have if we are not doing the right thing.* "More haste, men! More haste! We are almost there!" he announced, his archers at the rearguard now close enough to send arrow volleys in return. "That's it, you leopards! We have them now!" His archers' interference wasn't the most effective—given their position on the mountainside—but it relieved his swordsmen from the Byzont showers a little bit, giving Feras and his infantry a slight boost in their momentum. "We have them now!"

Feras was among the first Murasens who made it to the mountaintop. Enraged at the Byzonts' death trap, enraged at his uncle's foolishness, he roared as he led the charge. Swinging his saber, he chopped off the arm of one archer without even bothering to finish him off. He lunged at another Byzont, the curved blade of his sword cleaving across the archer's belly. A third Byzont almost took him by surprise, but Feras's shield caught the Byzont blade at the last second, his saber plunged through the attacker's guts.

With a quick look, Feras scanned the battlefield. His men had already thronged the mountaintop, hacking through every archer standing in their way. The Byzonts were putting up a good fight, Feras would give them that, but their defeat was only a matter of time. "Archers! Hold!" he barked, raising one arm in the air. With another quick look, he found a clear path to the cliff overseeing the battle ensuing at the foot of the mountain. While his soldiers were still putting the Byzont archers to the sword, he sprinted to the edge until he reached a spot where he could watch the clash in the valley. His spearmen still persisted, but the Byzont heavy infantry was slowly gaining ground. *We need to hurry back to them before they falter.*

When the last of the Byzont archers surrendered, Feras called out to the captain of his own archers. "I want you and your men to assume shooting positions at the cliffs." He pointed to the Byzont heavy infantry that outnumbered his spearmen in the valley. "Shoot at their rearguard, you hear me? Shoot until we drive them back."

Feras summoned all the swordsmen around him and led them

down the mountainside, then through the narrow passage, until he rejoined his worn-out spearmen. "Leopards of Murase!" he hollered, making sure the swordsmen behind him as well as the spearmen ahead heard him well. "Charge!"

The recently coming swordsmen gave the struggling spearmen some momentum, and now the Murasens were on the offensive for the first time in this valley. Feras's archers had already been thinning the Byzonts' ranks for a while with a storm of arrows descending upon them from the very mountains of Sergrad. Panting, he scanned the battlefield to assess the current odds, but for several minutes, the Byzonts seemed to be holding their ground after their brief retreat. Though he was aware he had deployed all his forces into the battle, he glanced at the abandoned valley behind him, hoping he might figure out a way to break this stalemate.

And that was when he heard one of his men cry, *"They are retreating! Run them out!"*

Feras pushed his way onward, bellowing, "Hold!" He yelled again and again as he sprinted to catch up with the men chasing the Byzonts at the frontline. "Hold, I say! Hold!"

With the aid of his captains, Feras managed to rally his scattered troops before they might pursue the Byzonts too deep into their own territories. Another trap might be waiting for Feras's men there. Looking back, he contemplated the battlefield crammed with hundreds of corpses from both sides. It was hard to say who had won today. The shattered Byzonts did not seem likely to launch a counterattack any soon, and his broken army wouldn't be able to advance beyond this point.

"Bury the dead and take the wounded out of here," he ordered his men. "We are returning to Kahora."

"Wait!" It had been a long while since Feras heard the voice of his helpless uncle. Mounting his horse, the 'fearless' Lord Munzir advanced toward his nephew, the soldiers making way for him. "You cannot give such an order without my permission, Lord Feras!"

"We are done here," Feras said curtly.

"We are done only when we achieve victory."

Feras took off his helm and tossed it on the ground at the hooves of his uncle's horse. "Then go and achieve this victory yourself." He stalked past his stunned uncle and demanded a horse.

"Feras! I didn't give you my permission to leave the battlefield!"

You mean the battlefield you were absent from? Feras ignored him as he headed to the horse brought to him and swung up into the saddle.

"You can't ignore an order from a senior lord, Feras! There will be consequences for that!"

Consequences? Like what? Telling King Rasheed? So be it. Let him tell His Majesty that his nephew had ignored him in front of his men. In return, Feras would tell the King about his uncle's *leadership* on the battlefield that had almost led them to a massacre. Maybe Feras had gone a bit far in showing disrespect to his lord uncle, but nothing would make him regret it. From now on, he would never obey a fool on a battlefield. Especially if it was Lord Munzir.

20. MASOLON

Since they were travelling along the eastern Bermanian borders, Masolon let Frankil lead the eleven horsemen headed to Kahora. *No one would know Bermanian lands better than a Bermanian.*

On the first day of their journey, they encountered a small caravan that surrendered to them, mistaking them for a band of brigands. Even when Frankil assured the travelers that they were free to go with their goods, they seemed wary of him and his band. *They think he is toying with them,* Masolon reflected. After the caravan vanished in the forest, he asked Frankil, "Do they not trust the armor you don?"

"A few respect the honor of the armor they don these days." Frankil glanced at his brothers-in-arms. "The likes of us are fools in the eyes of some."

On horseback, Antram approached Masolon when Frankil went ahead of the group to resume their ride. "Maybe we should have been paid for safe passage."

Masolon glared at his bald friend. *Does he miss the ways of those who raised him up?*

"Just a thought. Don't mind me." Antram nudged his horse onward.

At noon on the third day, a colossal structure of stone loomed ahead, towers reaching for the grey clouds. "We shall turn around the fortress of Karun, passing by the Lionsmouth Lake." Frankil was not suggesting; it was just an announcement. When Masolon checked his map, he felt that Frankil's route might not be the shortest one to Kahora. *No one would know Bermanian lands better than a Bermanian,* he reminded himself.

They spent the day taking a wide turn around the western side of the fortress. They camped by the lake Frankil had referred to, and the next morning they resumed their journey south toward the Lapondian woods.

"A Rusakian scout." The red-haired Danis jerked his chin toward a distant frame of a horseman on their left. Bergum dared him to bet on that, and shortly the two of them rode after the distant horseman, who disappeared behind the horizon the moment his chasers made their move. To Masolon's surprise, Frankil and the rest of his knights didn't pay heed to the two gone bettors.

"Should we not ride after them in case they need our help?" Masolon asked Frankil.

"They will be back soon," Frankil casually replied. "Nobody catches a Rusakian scout."

"What if he is *not* a scout?"

"He is," Frankil insisted. "The Rusakians always scout this area whenever Karun is not under their dominion."

Masolon chuckled. "Do they lose it so often?"

The Bermanian captain heaved a sigh. "It is really absurd as it sounds. Both Bermanians and Rusakians have been claiming that ancient fortress for ages, and what is the end result? An endless toll of dead men and youths at the walls of that worthless piece of stone."

Perhaps Masolon should tell Frankil what his late father would do to defend a worthless piece of stone on his own ground. "You cannot blame both sides for the bloodshed. You cannot blame the rightful claimant for defending what belongs to them."

"How can you tell who the rightful claimant is? It was the Bermanians who built the fortress in a region that was given to them after the Imperial Split. On the other hand, the Rusakians insist that the very piece of land on which the fortress was constructed belonged to the Rusakians' territories *before* the reign of Goran the Great." Frankil gave Masolon a studying a look. "Can you sort this out?"

The fort belonged to the Bermanians, the lands to the Rusakians; quite a dilemma indeed.

"Raze the fortress to the ground. Return the land to the Rusakians. Pay the Bermanians so that they can build another fortress elsewhere," Masolon suggested after giving it a thought.

"Not bad for a new king," Frankil scoffed lightly. "I wish handling those matters could be that simple. On the borders between every two neighboring kingdoms, you will find a *Karun*, like that one.

"You know what? Though I never highly regard him or his *glorious* deeds, I believe in Goran's approach to settling all those border issues."

"What was Goran's approach?"

"Conquer all realms and eliminate the damned borders."

Shortly, Danis and Bergum returned like Frankil predicted. From the frown on Bergum's face, it was easy to tell who won the bet.

On the sixth day, they were crossing the Lapondi forest. "Back home," muttered Antram, who must be contemplating his childhood playground. Masolon wondered what kind of games a child raised by bandits would play, but he decided to keep the question to himself. It wouldn't be wise to feed Antram's yearning to his wild past.

Two days later, the terrain grew dusty, the green fields a rarity now. They were nearing the Murasen realm.

"You take it from here," Frankil told Masolon while they were camping at their eighth night on the road. "None of us have ever been to Murase."

"Then prepare for a sun you have never seen before." Masolon nipped from the almost empty wineskin, saving one sip for Frankil.

"Say farewell to this darling. Murasen ale is not as sweet as her."

"No need, Masolon." Frankil nodded in appreciation. "Thanks."

"Trust me." Masolon offered Frankil the wineskin. "This could be the last drop of fine wine you may drink for good."

Frankil pressed his lips together, a strange smile on his face. "I don't drink at all, Masolon. I killed my brother the last time I did."

Masolon needed a few seconds to figure out that Frankil was not jesting, for a change even. "A brother-in-arms?"

"*My* brother, Masolon. The one my mother gave birth to."

That is a sin worth abandoning home for. Masolon knew it would be rude if he laughed at the coincidence of meeting a fellow-kinslayer. "Did Bergum and Danis and the rest kill your brother too?"

"What is this nonsense? No!" Frankil let slip a laugh. "We were a cavalry squad in Ramos, and I was their captain. The night I did what I did to my brother, I decided to leave Ramos and Bermania for good. Bergum and Danis found me on the road and tried to persuade me to come back, but it ended up the other way. By the end of the month, seven more brothers-in-arms joined us in Skandivia."

Masolon could easily understand what Frankil had been going through, but his brothers-in-arms? They were too good to be true. "You sure they have nothing back home to return to?"

"Have you ever fought alongside the same group of men for a year or even a month?" Frankil gazed at Danis, who was contemplating his prize, which used to be Bergum's dagger. "When you do, you will understand how firm the bond between us has become." He looked at Masolon out of the corner of his eye. "If there is someone I should worry about, it will be you. I don't know if you have anything back home to return to."

The former captain had no idea. Even if Masolon felt homesick for any reason, he would never brave the Great Desert one more time. He had survived it once, but he could not be that lucky twice.

On the ninth day, Masolon's new band was entering the sandy realm of Murase from its northwestern corner. The proud Bermanian knights didn't protest at the beginning of their first visit to the

Murasen kingdom, but Masolon would bet Danis they would whimper tomorrow.

Next day they made it to Kahora at last. "The sun is blazing like hell," Bergum complained as Masolon led his company to Bumar's house through the streets of Kahora.

"You have not seen hell yet." Masolon chuckled. According to his experience with Murasen weather, it was just another normal day. Summer was yet to come.

Antram spurred his horse onward to be next to Masolon's. "We will be in big trouble if your Murasen friend doesn't find that cursed Guild Master."

"You may have no reason to trust him, but you have no reason to doubt him either," Masolon said.

"I just have a bad feeling about him." Antram shrugged. "I hope I'm wrong though."

"I hope you are wrong too." Masolon dismounted when they reached the house that looked deserted. He knocked on the door ten times, but not a sound came from inside.

Antram exhaled impatiently. "That's not promising."

"We do not need Bumar to find Ziyad. I know where we can find him." Masolon swung up into his saddle and kicked the flanks of his horse. "Follow me."

Thanks to the blazing sun of Murase, the streets of Kahora were almost abandoned. Soon Masolon and his small army made it to the Fountain Plaza, where the sweaty tavern lay. Masolon hoped they were not serving mutton today.

His Murasen fellow was chattering with the stout tavern keeper when he arrived. "Masolon! You're back!" Ziyad received him with open arms.

"I did my part," said Masolon as his company entered the tavern. "What about you?"

"Wow!" Ziyad exclaimed. "You've brought a whole army of brothers!"

"An army? Are you waging war here, darlin'?" the tavern keeper asked.

Masolon nodded toward a vacant long table, and the men headed for it.

"There's no war, so don't worry," Ziyad said to the tavern keeper. "We'll resume our talk later, beautiful."

Now twelve men were sitting at the long table, Masolon at its head, Antram on his right, Frankil on his left. Determined not to give Ziyad a chance to brag about his inglorious conquests in bedchambers, Masolon made sure his introduction to Captain Frankil and his knights was a brief one.

"Now tell us," Masolon said, "how was your meeting with the Guild Master?"

"You mean Master Sayeb? It wasn't hard to find him. I told you," Ziyad winked, "Kahora is my mother."

"Be specific," Antram said gruffly. "Did you persuade him to hire us to fight the Ghosts?"

"Hire us, yes," replied Ziyad. "But not for the Ghosts."

"Why not?" Masolon asked, frustration creeping into him.

"I told you," Antram slammed his massive hand on the table, "I had a bad feeling about him."

"Brothers, brothers, listen." Ziyad waved at them. "He likes our notion of attacking the brigands in their dens instead of waiting for them to defend the caravans. But he says he is not ready to send a bunch of brave men to their doom."

"So?" Masolon prompted.

"Four of his caravans were raided at the Northern Road by a group of nomads in the previous two months. Nobody knows the exact location of their den or their exact number. But according to a few survivors from those raids, they are between twenty and twenty-five."

"All mounted, of course," said Antram.

Ziyad nodded. "Exactly."

"Blast!" Antram turned to Masolon. "We must find more men to join us."

"If we're going to do that, we must do it soon," Ziyad said. "Sayeb has been waiting for long already."

"Captain," Masolon said to Frankil, "do we need more men to face those nomads?"

"Assuming those nomads are lightly armored, then no, we don't."

Bergum smiled crookedly. "Bermanians are the best horsemen in Gorania, my friend."

Ziyad grinned. "We can never know until they face Murasen memluks."

"And I hope we never know," Masolon concluded. "Ziyad, go to that man called Sayeb and tell him we are ready for his mission. Make sure you come back here once you finish with him. We have some arrangements to make."

"As you wish, *Commander.*" Ziyad saluted him and rose to his feet. "I will see you soon, brothers." Only Danis greeted him back, Antram shaking his head.

"We will get some rest for today," Frankil announced when Ziyad was gone. "At first light we scout the Northern Road to find those nomads."

Masolon leaned back in his seat, his hands clasped behind his head. "What if we make them find us?"

21. MASOLON

The plan was simple. A caravan of four carts on the Northern Road loaded with empty boxes and barrels, each cart ridden by two men who appeared to be unarmed thanks to the cloaks they wore over their heavy armor. Four of Frankil's knights surrounded the caravan, pretending to be its guards.

"What if they don't come today?" Frankil was next to Masolon on the first cart, sweat pouring down his face. He, as well as everyone else, must be melting under their cloaks. The sun this morning was even harsher than yesterday.

"They will, Captain," Masolon replied.

Frankil gazed at the horizon for a while then asked, "Isn't it strange that I still don't know anything about you, Masolon?"

"What do you want to know?"

Frankil chuckled. "I'm not sure where to start. You defeated eight Skandivians on your own. *Eight.* I wonder where you learned how to fight. I'd say Skandivia, but you were lost in the Northern Gulf when we first met. And of course, your accent is anything but Bermanian. Actually, your accent is nothing I've heard before."

"Have I not told you yet? I am from what you call the *Other Side.*"

"The other what?"

"*East! We are being followed!*" Danis called out urgently.

The moment they had been waiting for had arrived. A cloud of dust approached, hoots and screams echoing in the endless desert.

"What are those fools doing?" Frankil curled his lip. "Warning us before they attack?"

No, striking fear into our hearts before they attack us with steel. The nomads evoked memories of Masolon's past by doing what his clansmen did in their raids.

"The horses! Now!" Both Masolon and Frankil threw their cloaks away and cut all straps tying their horses to the cart.

Ziyad ripped off his cloak and spurred his horse to a gallop. "Death to you, scum!"

"Ziyad, wait!" Frankil yelled. "We must attack in formation!"

But it was unlikely that Ziyad would wait. The Murasen bard was already closer to the nomads than to Masolon's company. "The bastard is going to get himself killed." Masolon kicked the flanks of his stallion and galloped, trying to catch up with his reckless fellow.

"No, Masolon!" Frankil's cry came from behind him. "Antram, wait! Blast! This is a mess! Danis! Bergum! Wedge!"

It was indeed a mess, like it had been in the old days. Masolon and his clansmen had never attacked in formation. They simply attacked, their swords swinging, reaping their enemies' souls.

Ziyad had already slain a nomad with his saber before Masolon slashed the chest of another. On his right, Antram struck a third nomad dead. But that wasn't the end of it. The bloody event was just starting.

"Ziyad! Antram! Together this time!" Masolon wheeled his horse, and so did his fellows, facing the nomads' rearguard. The Bermanian knights charged from the other side, Frankil at the head of the wedge, roaring. Steel clashed with steel, tearing through flesh, smashing the bone beneath. The Bermanian wedge shattered the nomads' band.

"Chaaaarge!" Masolon ordered, Ziyad and Antram galloping with him. Half of the remaining nomads engaged Frankil's knights, the other half starting to flee. Today wasn't another plundering day. Today the predator was the prey.

"Regroup! Regroup!" Masolon commanded. He didn't want his band to be scattered in this vast desert without knowing what might be waiting for them. He had the victory he had wanted, and that was what mattered.

"Those bastards don't deserve to live, Masolon!" Ziyad protested.

"Let them spread fear among the rest of them," said Masolon. "Let them know that the Northern Road is not theirs anymore."

"We should talk before we make another raid together, fellows." Frankil didn't seem glad despite the victory. "This chaos mustn't happen again."

Masolon nodded, not wishing to argue with the Bermanian captain. This *chaos* had brought them a crushing victory.

"What are we going to do with those two?" Antram nodded toward Frankil's knights. At the hooves of their horses, two nomads were down on their knees.

"Tie them to your horses," said Masolon. "We need something to sweep the Northern Road with."

* * *

Their entrance to the Fountain Plaza had brought an audience this time. People dared to abandon the shade inside their houses and gather around Masolon and his fellows as they tied the two nomads to two erected poles. Even the attendants of the smelly tavern abandoned their mutton and ale to watch. None interfered, only watched, murmuring among themselves.

"This is an unnecessary fuss, Masolon," Antram muttered, looking around. "We could just take our gold and leave."

For Masolon, it wasn't all about gold. Every nomad reminded him of those savages who had set every house in his village on fire, with his mother and sisters inside one of them. Every nomad reminded him of what his father had wanted him to be, of why he had driven a blade into his father's abdomen.

Pretending he was tightening a knot around the nomad's foot, Antram said, "On your left, four footmen wearing the leopard, the sigil of the Murasen Kingdom. Those are memluks, Masolon. We are in trouble."

"Everything is going to be alright, brother." Masolon patted his friend on the shoulder, not even looking at the soldiers. He and his fellows were heroes today. Why should they be worried?

The sight of Bermanian knights piqued some curiosity, teasing the imagination of the throng. Masolon heard them talking about an alliance between the two great kingdoms of Murase and Bermania. Others mumbled about the incapability of their King's memluks, who were supposed to protect them instead of waiting for the help of a bunch of *foreigners*. Fury crept into the crowd's murmuring, and an angry mob wasn't something Masolon desired.

"Good people of Kahora!" Masolon waved at them, glancing at the four footmen standing silently among the throng. "Behold your vengeance!"

Not many reacted to his display.

"What is the matter with all of you? Can you not recognize the filthy faces of those who have given themselves the right to steal your coin?"

Nods, voices of approval, and curses.

"Can you not recognize the filthy faces of those who have given themselves the right to kill your loved ones?" With every word Masolon said, the clamor grew louder. "Here they stand before you! What would you like to tell them?" He extended his arm toward the two nomads. The Fountain Plaza rang with curses, the sound of it lovelier than the Contest chants to Masolon's ears.

"Today every bandit has learned a lesson!" Masolon hollered. "There will be a price for their crimes. And that price will be their heads! Today we wage war on those scum!"

"*War! War! War!*" the crowd roared with him, a shiver running down Masolon's spine as he opened his arms.

"You! Stop this farce!" the memluks cried as they approached Masolon, a moment he had been anticipating.

"The King's memluks have arrived!" Masolon addressed his crowd. To the footmen he said, "Those bastards are ready to be served the King's justice!"

The crowd cheered for the memluks as Masolon had wanted, knowing it would be hard for the footmen to ignore that.

"The King's justice doesn't include dragging men on the ground for a hundred miles and humiliating them in the plaza of the King's city without even the King's permission," one of the footmen spoke gruffly.

"It was only thirty miles, soldier." Masolon gave him a lopsided smile, the plaza ringing with laughter.

"You and your gang are not entitled to implement the King's law." Surrounded, the memluk did his best to keep his composure.

"Gang?" Frankil frowned.

"Yes, my friend," Masolon said, "we are a gang." He turned to the memluks. "An honorable gang of warriors."

"Leave the brave men alone!" someone from the crowd demanded. "You'd better help them, you worthless memluks!"

The memluk pressed his lips together. He must have realized who was in charge here.

"I told you, they are yours. Do whatever the King's justice dictates." Masolon nodded toward the nomads and turned to his fellows. "Let us go, brothers." Leaving the Fountain Plaza as hailed champions was much better than being dragged from it as prisoners.

"I told you it was unnecessary," Antram rebuked Masolon after they got away from the plaza. "What were you thinking?"

"It went well, brother," Ziyad said. "Calm down."

"It went well thanks to the crowd," Antram corrected. "Next time we will be arrested."

"There will be no next time," Masolon announced. "What do you think, Captain?" he asked Frankil, whose face had been stern since their return from the Northern Road.

Frankil shook his head, a smile creeping over his face. "You are reckless."

"You should have known better," Masolon teased him. "What did you expect from someone who passed through the Northern Gulf on his own?"

Frankil chuckled, and Masolon couldn't ask for more. A laugh wouldn't suit the Bermanian captain.

"We should find a meeting place other than the tavern," Antram suggested. "We don't want to attract any attention for a couple of weeks at least."

Masolon couldn't disagree. The smell of the tavern wasn't something he would miss anyway. The rest voiced their approval, and Ziyad mentioned an abandoned hill only one mile away from the western walls of Kahora. While the Murasen fellow was suggesting going now to the hill to have a look at it, Masolon was busy with the slim frame of a woman standing in his way.

"Missing me, big boy?" She tilted her head, a crooked smile on her face. He knew she would be looking for him, and he would be seeing her.

"Oh, *big boy*!" Ziyad hooted. "We should leave you now!"

"You should indeed." Masolon sighed. "I will catch up with you soon."

Viola waited until his fellows went past her, a slight smile on her face. A smile of a viper who had found her prey. "You have new friends now," she stated, her eyes fixed on him.

"What do you want?"

"That's a good question. What do I want? What do I want?" She tapped her chin as if she was thinking of an answer. "What about slitting your throat?"

He smirked. "You can try."

"You were wondering what I was doing in the Pit. Well, arranging bets and enlisting the contenders are part of my duties, but that wasn't what Ramel hired me for in the first place. Did anybody tell what it was?"

"Was it anything other than warming his bed?"

Surprisingly, she kept her composure, her chest rising and falling as she heaved a deep breath of air. "My first task was to kill one of his fighters," she said. "One who decided on his own to break his agreement with Ramel. The fool thought he could simply flee, and he did...for three days."

"Are you threatening me again?" Masolon leaned forward. "I can crush your neck with my bare hands."

"You would be dead already if it were not for Ramel," she hissed. "The only reason you are still breathing is that he believes he can still earn gold from you. I can't wait to see his face when he knows about the Contest you missed."

Did I? Masolon had been busy training peasants in Horstad, recruiting warriors for his *gang*, and slaying nomads in the desert. Too busy to understand what Viola was talking about. "What Contest?"

"The Contest of this very city." Her smile returned. "Unfortunately you arrived one day late. I'm sure he will understand you were too preoccupied to remember."

22. FERAS

The king's page ushered Feras to the small hall of the royal palace. The letter he had received in Arkan didn't say who was going to attend this meeting with King Rasheed, but from the chosen venue, he could tell there wouldn't be much of an audience today.

Only his lord uncle was waiting in the hall when he entered. They hadn't seen each other since their *victory* at the mountains of Sergrad. "Lord Munzir," Feras curtly greeted his lord uncle who silently nodded.

The king's page closed the door of the small hall, leaving the two relatives alone. Feras picked his seat on the same side of the table to find something else to look at other than his uncle's face. The place was so quiet their heavy breaths sounded too loud. As time passed, Feras found himself growing uneasy, his eyes on the closed door, impatiently waiting for anyone else to join this gathering. Lord Munzir was nervous too; Feras could tell from the way he rocked his legs.

"His Majesty, King Rasheed," announced the king's page from the door. Munzir and Feras rose to their feet when the king stepped inside. About five or six years younger than Feras's father, the king looked as young as Feras with his thick black hair and flat belly.

The door of the hall was shut, and that meant no one else would attend this meeting. Now Feras had a clue what this meeting was all about. He couldn't wait for his uncle to start talking about the glorious battle of Sergrad.

King Rasheed gestured to them to be seated. "Honorable lords." His Majesty's voice was cold and firm. "We have a traitor among us."

Even Lord Munzir looked surprised at how the king started the meeting.

"Feras, you have proven your worth as a commander in battle," Rasheed said, his voice still cold despite the praise. "Tell me, if you were the Murasen king who had lost half of his western army, what would be your next move?"

First, there was that announcement of the traitor among them, and now the king referred to the battle of Sergrad. A connection between the two topics was hard to find. To answer the king's question, Feras should weigh his words carefully. Nothing could be more dangerous than an enraged king who might make a harsh decision because of an ill-chosen word.

"I wouldn't leave my western borders vulnerable to the Byzonts, sire." Feras tried to look confident. "The day the battle ended, I would send for reinforcements from the central region of Demask."

His Majesty gave Feras a long, studying look. "That is exactly what I did *not* wish to hear."

Feras's heart pounded vigorously.

"Byzonts rarely fight outside their lands," Rasheed said, his eyes fixed on Feras. "You should refer to the history of your enemy to understand him. For centuries, they have been at war with the Bermanians. They know very well if they blink while guarding their northern borders, they will wake up to find Bermanian knights besieging Themus."

Rasheed glanced at Munzir. "The Byzonts' attack was a decoy. As we speak, Dehawy is taking an army of Murasens and Mankol mercenaries to our northern regions. If I did what Feras said, the northern front would be thin against those assaults."

"Dehawy?" asked Munzir. "But why?"

Feras didn't find anything surprising in that. Dehawy was not the first of the king's cousins to betray him. What Feras was worried about was his father, Lord Ahmet.

"Who can possibly be helping him?" asked Feras.

"I don't want to accuse anyone by name right now, but you are the only lords I can trust in this realm," Rasheed replied.

Feras noticed the concerned look on Munzir's face. Speaking of a traitor from inside brought to his mind a familiar name he had discussed with his uncle before.

"We need to keep our eyes and ears open these days," said Rasheed. "We have Mankols in the north, Byzonts in the west, Dehawy in the east, and the Lord knows who else is involved in this plot. While Lord Ahmet is already leading our northern army in Bigad, Lord Munzir will command our reinforcements in the central region of Demask."

The scowl on Lord Munzir's face was unmistakable. He had always been the King's spearhead. Removing the veteran lord from the western region of the capital meant he was no longer the man of the hour.

"I don't recommend moving our troops between regions right now," said Rasheed. "Feras, your mission is to replenish our western army as fast as you can. The safety and security of Kahora citizens are now your responsibility."

Kahora! The king's trust was thrilling. Munzir must be mad with rage at the moment.

"You may leave now, honorable lords." Rasheed gestured to his vassals.

Feras saw the glow in his uncle's eyes. Without saying a word, he let Munzir stride in front of him toward the door of the hall.

"And Feras," Rasheed called out, "I have received some obscure news about a *warriors' gang.*"

Feras nodded. "It's nothing but a band of mercenaries, sire. Sayeb the Merchants' Guild Master hired them one month ago."

"It is not a band of mercenaries anymore. Our youths join this band with every battle they win." The king rubbed his chin. "In such a critical situation, and as a guardian of Kahora, you must be fully aware of every single event that happens in your city. A wicked conspiracy is threatening our realm, and as you see, we are not sure yet how many other realms are involved in it. Amidst all of this, a band of mercenaries appears from nowhere at this particular time. Coincidence must be your last assumption to interpret what goes on, Feras."

"You are absolutely right, sire."

Rasheed looked Feras in the eye. "I know you will do what is right for your people. Now go."

Feras didn't find his uncle when he left the hall. He must have gone past the gates of Kahora already. Surely, Lord Munzir didn't like the consequences of his nephew's actions that had exposed the veteran lord's incompetence as a military commander. And regions like Kahora in the west and Bigad in the north needed *real* commanders like his father and him, of course. His lord uncle should admit the king had put him in the right place, in Demask, away from all the trouble of the frontiers.

Feras shook off his thoughts. Munzir shouldn't be occupying his mind now. He had an assignment to finish in order to prove he was worth the King's trust. The Warriors' Gang would be the start.

23. MASOLON

Neither the columns of marble inside Sayeb's house nor the two silver chandeliers impressed Masolon, but the platter of mutton did. Flavored with garlic, olive oil, thyme, and pepper, it tasted nothing like the mutton of the smelly tavern. He considered if perhaps Sayeb's cook wasn't that good, it was the tavern cook who was too bad.

"Are you done?" asked the round-faced Guild Master.

"Almost." Masolon licked his greasy fingers. Nothing remained of the mutton, though there were the bowls of red potatoes and yellow grapes.

"The Ghosts struck last night," Sayeb announced calmly as if he was saying 'good morning.'

"Are we sure it was them?"

"They slaughtered a whole caravan on the Northern Road, sparing only one man after chopping off his hands." Sayeb's face was as still as a mountain. "He couldn't see them in the darkness, but he heard their horrifying voices."

One survivor. "And they sent a message, did they not?"

"A straightforward message to us: the desert is their kingdom. If we attack their kingdom again, they will attack ours."

"You Murasens have been exaggerating those Ghosts," Masolon said. "They are just another band of nomads."

"Nomads or demons, I have never seen one in my life, thank the Lord of Sky and Earth. But I know they have been ruling the Murasen desert since the beginning of time. And obviously, they have earned their name for some reason." Sayeb leaned forward. "The question is, what are we going to do? Their message has had quite an impact this morning. Every merchant and traveler is scared of stepping outside the walls of Kahora. If the news flies away from here into nearby and distant cities, our trade will be ruined for good. Especially with those rumors of a coming war with the Byzonts."

"I guess you know what I am going to do." *He wants me to tell him I am going to fight those Ghosts. Why does he not just ask directly?*

"Masolon, if anything happens to you and your good friends, I won't be able to live with that."

"We vanquished the nomads in their nests before. We can do it again."

"With a band of thirty fighters?"

"They are true warriors."

"Even the new recruits?"

"I train the new recruits myself." Masolon exhaled. "They are ready."

"Very well." Sayeb nodded. "I hope they fare well without you."

What is this nonsense? "Humor was never one of your qualities, Master Sayeb."

"I'm a humorous man indeed, Masolon, but not when it comes to my gold." He spread his hands open. "How do you think I've become the Merchants' Guild Master?"

"What is it then?"

"You are summoned by Lord Feras," Sayeb said at last. "He invites you to come to the castle of Arkan."

"*Invites?*" Masolon echoed in astonishment.

"You are his guest," Sayeb confirmed. "Don't let this fact fool you. You *must* arrive at the castle before tomorrow's sunrise."

"What would a lord want from me?"

"I don't know. His messenger said nothing more than I told you."

The notion of Lord Feras's *invitation* was hard to digest. Little chance any good might come from it.

"This is farce," Masolon mumbled. "He must wait until we are done with the Ghost—"

"He must nothing," Sayeb cut in. "He's a lord, young man. When he says you come, you do so without a question. Any other action will bring nothing but trouble. And trust me, no one can help you if you fall in trouble with the likes of him. You'd better save your recklessness for the outlaws you butcher. Now tell me: who's going to lead the band until your return?"

"I do not know. I never thought of that."

"You should make up your mind fast if you don't want to arrive late at Arkan."

Masolon had better decide before someone else made the decision. If the leader in his absence wasn't Antram, Ziyad, or Frankil, who else could be?

"It will be Frankil." The Bermanian captain seemed to be a better option than the other two. He wasn't only the most seasoned warrior in the gang, he was also more self-possessed than the quick-tempered Antram and the raving Ziyad.

With a preoccupied mind, Masolon left Sayeb's house. He should mount his stallion and hurry to his fellows to inform them of the news. But someone was mounting his tied horse. Masolon's hand reached for the hilt of his sword…although he knew he was no robber.

"Come on, Masolon." Ramel swung down off the saddle. "Is this how you greet a friend?"

"What do you want?"

"It has been a while." Ramel shrugged. "I thought I should I pay you a visit."

"I am grateful." Masolon smirked. "Anything else?"

"Is this your way to welcome me?" Ramel asked. "I always

wonder what I sowed to reap this hatred. You are now what you are because of me. Despite being a commoner, you had the chance to stand one foot away from the Rusakian king himself and charm a lovely princess because of me. Travelers to Kahora tell tales about the mysterious Masolon and his gang of warriors because of me. Because of what I taught you."

A grin must have slipped over his face when the brief memory of Halin's smile overwhelmed his thoughts.

"You taught me to fill your coffers," said Masolon after restoring his composure.

"I'm not saying I'm a cleric, Masolon. But I'm sure I didn't do anything wrong to you." Ramel shrugged. "Training is my profession, and I see no shame in naming a price for it. You already name a price for your profession, just like me. What makes you different?"

"Maybe we should not be different at all. I should choose my own path while you pursue your own."

"We had an agreement, Masolon." Ramel clenched his jaw. "I was clear about it when we first met, and *you* concurred."

"You cannot tie me for eternity." Masolon glowered at him. "Let us name a price for your services, once and for all."

"It will be a huge price." Ramel rubbed his chin. "Considering my loss because of the Contest you missed in Kahora, considering what you are earning now and what you are going to earn in the future thanks to my drills, it won't be less than ten thousand golden coins."

That greedy bastard. "We cannot reach an agreement like this. You know I cannot afford that sum."

"I am not deceiving you, Masolon. I really want to end this," said Ramel. "I am tired of arguing with you before every Contest, of worrying about my gold and silver. Gold and silver are all I seek, and I will find them. I will make new champions—I am an expert in this. Yet I am not going to release you from your pledge before you pay for it."

When someone like Ramel assures you that he is not deceiving you, you must be quite certain that he is. That was why Masolon mulled over the devil's proposal, trying to figure out an alternative one. *He is not likely to accept haggling over the price he demands, is he?*

"I have a way out for you," Ramel offered. "One last Contest. Only one Contest to win, and you shall never see me again."

"That is it?" Masolon said doubtfully. "What happened to the fair price?"

"That Contest will do," said Ramel. "It's the Contest of Paril, boy. You are completely unknown to that city, even to the whole kingdom of Bermania. Your odds will be extremely low, and as I have told you before, lower odds mean more gold."

Afraid Ramel was omitting something important, Masolon kept his eyes fixed on his trainer's face, trying to detect any hidden intentions.

"All right I'll tell you." Ramel looked irked. "Betting is a sort of entertainment for any city, but in Paril it's an enormous business. I knew men who grew wealthy after winning extremely risky bets. However, losses are disastrous, young man. Anyone from Paril should think twice before putting his gold on you. Anyone but me of course. I can get my fair price if I arrange a number of big bets with the help of my friends in Paril. It will be one bet with a colossal return."

"Is that it all?"

"Yes." Ramel nodded. "But beware. This can only be done once. Losing this Contest will ruin me and you as well. The Blue-Blooded will be involved in this, and you surely don't want to mess with their gold. Even if you survive them, you will be mine forever."

"The Blue-Blooded?" Masolon echoed.

"The highborn, Masolon. The lords and nobles of Bermania." Ramel paused until two passersby were out of earshot. "Each one of them commands an army. Despite their wealth, they still care about the gold they earn from those Contests. I promise you, they will hunt you for life if you make them lose a coin of silver."

24. MASOLON

The sweat poured out of every inch of Masolon's body, though the sun was a bit gentler today. A storm of thoughts overwhelmed his mind as he followed the tar-paved road between Kahora and Arkan. A poorly paved road, but without it, everything looked the same in this desert. Every now and then he came upon a bunch of palm trees, and again it was only the damned yellow.

Worry and curiosity consumed his mind. Well, it was all worry in the beginning, but later, curiosity was gradually getting the better of him as he started to believe that Feras's 'invitation' was a real one. It should be. *It must be*. Otherwise, the lord of Arkan would have sent a squad of memluks to take Masolon with them, not just a messenger with a scroll.

The notion that concerned Masolon was the gang. His meeting with his brothers had been a brief one when he told them the news, but Antram's grim face was worrying. He hoped his ill-tempered fellow wouldn't be a source of trouble for the new leader.

There was also Ziyad. A tough warrior, but a troublesome fellow with his unleashed tongue. Masolon's presence had prevented many small conflicts from snowballing into big clashes, which made him wonder what might happen in his absence.

"...charmed a lovely princess..."

Masolon tried to pretend he hadn't heard Ramel's words, but he couldn't. He didn't want to. And yet they imposed themselves on the rest of his thoughts. The faces of Frankil, Antram, and Ramel faded away, and only Halin's face with that pretty smile was the one his mind *loved* to remember. A daydream that Masolon wished would never end. Part of his mind had its reasons to believe it. *The rumor reached Ramel. You can see the fire from the ashes that has remained.* But the other part insisted that it was nothing but a delusion. She was a lady and he was…well, he was Masolon, and that meant everything to him. But he must be frank with himself, none of the Blue-Blooded would care.

The Murasen sun was magnificent only when it fell down. When it became just hot instead of *too* hot. It was falling in the west where the castle of Arkan appeared, its towers looming over the horizon. As Masolon approached, he spotted the archers atop the bulwark ready with their bows. Slowing his stallion to a trot, he identified himself to them. Shortly, the portcullis was raised, four spearmen and a page at his reception.

"Welcome to the castle of Arkan, Masolon." The page grinned. "Lord Feras wanted to meet you tonight. Unfortunately, he is still busy with the engineers at the towers. He will meet you tomorrow early in the morning. Until then he asks you to make yourself at home."

That was a good start, better than his expectations. "Send him my greetings." Masolon managed a smile. "I will have a walk in the courtyard to enjoy the night breeze."

Masolon dismounted, letting the spearmen take his horse. It was true he hadn't entered a castle before in Gorania, yet he felt the guards and archers were more than there should be. The rumors of war seemed to be right.

Torches were scattered in the castle yard, making it look as if the sun had risen over Arkan at night. In the backyard, Masolon could see the redness of the palm dates despite the darkness. Looking down the palm trunk he beheld a big round wooden plate fixed on the trunk itself. He thought he saw circles drawn on that plate and one arrow hanging to it. Out of curiosity, he walked toward the palm tree until he was one foot away from it to inspect that wooden plate.

His ears caught that whizzing sound. Instinctively, he bent his head back to evade the arrow that hit the wooden plate and would have missed him anyway. Alarmed, since he hadn't expected a hostile action in this place, his eyes sought the shooter.

And what a pretty shooter she was, he had to say.

Although she didn't wear a tiara or a diadem over her loose auburn hair, he could tell from her embroidered white dress and the maid standing beside her that she was highborn. But definitely, she wasn't a Murasen. The girl's fair skin wasn't burned by the blazing sun of these lands.

"I am so sorry! I didn't mean to scare you!" Looking alarmed, she dropped her bow and hurried to him. Then her alarmed face turned into an infuriated one and she snapped, "What are you doing here in the first place?"

Masolon couldn't help chuckling at the abrupt change of her tone.

"I noticed you are blind for not recognizing my practice range, but I didn't think you were deaf as well," the girl continued, her childish manner masking her offending words. Masolon liked her spirit.

"I thought I was sighted, but I have just realized how blind I have been," he said.

"What is this?" The girl arched one fine eyebrow. "A sort of poetry? You don't look like a poet."

"I am not a poet for sure." He chuckled again. "I am Masolon. Lord Feras sent for me to meet him."

"I'm Sania, his sister."

Masolon didn't know whether it was good or bad news. From now on, he had to carefully pick his words.

"Are you surprised all the time?" asked Sania.

Masolon laughed at the way she teased him. "Forgive my candidness, Lady Sania, but you do not look like the Murasens I see every day."

Sania blushed. "There is a reason for that. My grandmother was a Rusakian." She pointed to the bow strapped to his back. "Do you mind if I see this?"

Masolon handed her the bow, and she looked impressed as she held it with both hands. "That's quite a heavy bow." She gave the bowstring her best attempt to pull it, but failed. "Curse that!" She burst into laughter, her sweet voice causing a brief twitch in his chest. "Where did you get your bow? From the Mankols?"

"It is a Mankol bow indeed. You must be an expert in archery."

"Of course, I am." She chuckled, then her hazel eyes widened. "Wait. You are not a Mankol, are you?"

"I am afraid I am not."

"Not a Byzont, I presume?"

Masolon hoped that Ziyad wasn't raving when he told him that girls liked to hear about places they didn't know. "I am not from anywhere in Gorania."

"Better for you." Sania chuckled cheerfully. "Now seriously, where do you come from?"

"Ogono. It is behind what you call the Great Desert."

Sania's large eyes betrayed her astonishment, or most probably her fear. "What *we* call? Alright, you scare me for real now."

"I am not trying to scare you. I am just telling you the truth."

Sania shook her head. "No one lives outside Gorania. I mean no *human*."

"I am not surprised to hear so, milady. Yet I can assure you there is a whole world behind the Great Desert."

"A whole world of..." Sania didn't dare to say it. Like Kuslov had told him before, Murasens didn't like to talk about the residents of the *Other Side*.

"A whole world of men and women of flesh and blood, like here," said Masolon. "Except that the men there have forgotten their humanity and live like beasts, the strong feasting on the flesh of the weak."

"Interesting. I thought that Outsiders only existed in legends. Everyone in Gorania believes so." She kept studying his face as if she was making sure he was a real man. "But here I am, talking to one of them right now."

"I do not bite."

"So far." A smile lit up her pretty face. "Alright, you deserted your...people because of their brutality. Have you found it any different here?"

"Not really, milady. If truth be told, Gorania is no less brutal than my homeland."

"You must be regretting coming here."

"Not yet." He grinned. "I have met many good people so far."

"Are they as lousy poets as you are?"

He didn't remember the last time he had enjoyed chattering with someone as he did at the moment. "I do good poetry with this." He pointed to the shiny blade of his sword, and she giggled. And how lovely she looked and sounded when she giggled.

"So you have a new home now," she said. "Do you feel any sort of belongingness?"

"I am starting to. Faster than I thought."

"I can't tell whether it's good or bad not to belong to one particular faction for your whole life." Sania glanced at the Mankol bow she was still holding. "A free wanderer like you has the luxury of picking what fits him best, not fitting himself to what he finds. My brother doesn't have the blessing you have. He must choose from Murasen swords, Murasen armor, Murasen horses, and of course a Murasen princess."

"Your brother loves his homeland, milady. Nothing bad in this."

"Don't get me wrong. I love my homeland as well. What I mean is that wielding a Mankol bow, for instance, shouldn't deny my pride of being a Murasen, right?"

"Absolutely, milady." He glanced at Sania's maid, who approached her mistress and whispered to her. Sania dismissed her with a hand gesture.

"You are an interesting person to meet, foreigner." Sania returned his bow to him. "I believe there is more to hear from you. Unfortunately, I must go now. We may continue our conversation another time."

Another time? He could only wish…

Sania hurried after her maid, Masolon following her with his eyes until she was out of sight. He should thank her lord brother for choosing such a perfect timing to ramble with those engineers.

"Evading that arrow wasn't easy at all, I have to say."

Masolon turned when he heard that familiar, soothing voice. What on Earth was the beefy healer doing here? And most importantly, how long had he been standing and watching?

"That was just a reflex." Masolon shrugged.

"Your reflex wasn't fast enough."

"What are you talking about? It did not hit me."

"Really?" Bumar shot him a mocking smile. "You're badly hit, good friend."

Masolon tried to ignore the joke, but his smile exposed him badly. "What are you doing here? I sent you a friend of mine to take care of."

"You mean the pile of broken bones your friend Ziyad brought with him? His case was a desperate one, but not to me. I restored his bones to their normal positions, and when he left my house on his feet, he walked with a limp. In a few months, he will walk normally.

"After that Lord Feras sent for me to take care of Lady Ramia's health." Bumar made sure they were out of earshot before he spoke again in a lower voice. "Your great news has reached the lord of this castle. Somehow he knows I know you. Yesterday he asked me a few questions about the man called Masolon."

"What did you tell him?"

Bumar tilted his head. "Not everything I know about you."

That should be reassuring. "So I am not in trouble."

Bumar glanced at the wooden target Sania was shooting. "Not yet."

THE WARRIOR'S PATH

* * *

It was morning when the page ushered Masolon to a small room on the ground floor. Though there were two seats opposite that neat desk at the end of the chamber, Masolon chose to stay standing for no specific reason. A few minutes later Feras showed up, the faintest of smiles on his long face. He was younger than Masolon had thought, but he could be as young as he pleased; he was still the lord of this great fortress.

Feras stared at Masolon for a while, and to Masolon's surprise, he didn't go to the seat behind the desk. "You don't seem to be at ease." He picked one of the two seats facing each other, motioning for Masolon to sit. "Was my hospitality not enough for you?"

"Pardon me, milord." Masolon sat opposite Feras. "I just cannot help wondering why I have earned the honor of your hospitality."

"If I had any suspicions about you, you would be standing before me in your chains." Feras leaned toward him. "Besides, I assume you did nothing wrong to be worried about."

"I am sure about myself, but not about *you*, milord."

That did catch the lord off guard, it was plain. "While I admire your frankness, I advise you to be careful." The lord smiled nervously. "There is a fine thread between honesty and rudeness."

There was a reason why Masolon would go for a duel with swords rather than an exchange of words. Words could be twisted, manipulated, misunderstood. But swords? Nothing was as true as a clean swing of a blade.

It could never be 'misinterpreted.'

"I did not mean to offend you, milord."

"I'm quite certain you didn't ride through the desert to do that," Feras said dryly.

"I rode through the desert only because you summoned me, milord."

Feras raised his eyebrows, as if he had just realized that Masolon was right. "Indeed, Masolon. I summoned you because I wanted to listen to you."

Why so vague? "Something specific you want me to talk about?"

"Your aspirations, Masolon. A man like you seems to have a vision."

Finally, something less vague. "My vision is a simple one, milord. A peaceful land for the weak."

"That's the lords' duty, Masolon," Feras argued. "Do you want to be a lord some day?"

Do I not? Masolon couldn't help imagining how different his first conversation with Halin could have been if people had to use the word 'lord' to address him. For certain his brief encounter with Gerviny would have been different too. *Far more different.* "If I understand lordship right, it is earned by birth, not chosen by whim."

"How about becoming a governor?"

Masolon might not be seasoned in politics, but he was not a fool who might miss the trap in Feras's question. "I prefer leading warriors on battlefields."

"For what? Glory? Or gold?"

"For the helpless."

"But you're paid for that, aren't you?"

Another trap. "I need some gold for food and shelter, yes."

"If you ask me, you earn too much for a hero."

"I never claimed to be a hero."

"But the people say so."

"Is there something wrong with that?"

"No. But you don't have the authority to recruit troops and wage war in my lands."

"Is your authority more important than your subjects' security?"

Feras arched an eyebrow. "If I let everyone recruit mercenaries to have his own army, our country will end up torn by a civil war between a bunch of struggling parties under the claim of protecting the peasants' rights." He paused for a moment. "Especially, when one of those armies is led by a foreigner who recruits warriors from different kingdoms."

Had the lord of Arkan brought Masolon here only to warn him? Because if he did believe that Masolon's gang was a serious threat, he would have arrested Masolon and disbanded his gang already. "I trust your judgment, milord." He looked Feras in the eye as he leaned forward toward him. "I am sure you will do what is best for your subjects."

Feras held his gaze for a moment, both men judging each other. The only difference between them was that only one of them had the power to obliterate the other.

"You may leave now, Masolon," said Feras evenly. "But you have to bear in mind that my duty obliges me to keep my eyes on you. If I know that you or your gang are threatening our kingdom, *my subjects*, I won't hesitate to execute you all."

* * *

Well, there were much worse ways to end a meeting with a lord, right?

Masolon had already packed for his journey to Paril. As he stepped outside into the courtyard, the sunlight hit his eyes, forcing him to shield his face as he walked toward his horse. From the whizzing sound coming from the backyard, he could tell there was some activity in the practice range this morning. Without too much thinking, he found his feet taking him to the same palm tree of the previous night, his horse neighing as if he was calling him to come back.

And there she was with her light bow. His heart pounded when she smiled upon seeing him coming. *Blast!* She looked even prettier than last night.

"Here you are again, foreigner," Sania teased him.

Totally stunned, Masolon smiled without saying a word.

"Are you alright?" she asked. "It seems you didn't sleep well."

157

Masolon realized he had been absent-minded for a few seconds. "I never felt better, milady. In fact, I am thankful for the sunlight that reveals to us the beauty of...things."

"Beauty of things?" Confused, she looked around. "Perhaps you mean those palm trees scattered in the yard?"

"No, not the palm trees. I mean you...your face."

Sania blushed when she laughed. "For a poet, you're not so smooth in flirting."

"I did not mean to." Masolon swallowed. "I just say what I think."

"You mean I was ugly last night?" she asked playfully.

"Of course not! Last night you looked...good. But today, you are...I mean sunlight makes us see...better."

Sania giggled, and he couldn't blame her for that. Surely, he looked and sounded like a fool.

He harrumphed as he tried to recollect himself. "I came because I heard the arrows hissing." *Seriously, you can do much better than that.* "I just wonder how you can practice in this bright sunlight. It must be confusing to your vision."

"I am a Murasen, foreigner. Murasens are accustomed to this sun." She smiled again when she asked, "How did your meeting with Lord Feras go?"

Even Masolon himself was not sure. "He said I was free to go, so I believe the meeting was not that bad."

"You are not leaving so soon, are you?"

Alright, Masolon shouldn't fool himself. She was not actually concerned, and he had to be certain of that. She was just asking out of...courtesy. *Yes, courtesy. Nothing more.* "I have some matters to take care of in Paril before I go back to Kahora."

"Paril? That's a long way to the northwest of Gorania. I thought your gang wanders only around Kahora."

Masolon's eyebrows rose. *She knows about the gang. She knows who I am.*

"My maid told me you are the leader of the Warriors' Gang the people have been gossiping about," Sania went on, arching one fine eyebrow. "You made quite a display in Kahora, I was told."

Masolon must be smiling from ear to ear, like any sane man would in this situation. Who would get enough of listening to this lovely girl while she was talking about him like that?

"What else did you hear about me?"

"That my brother would arrest you."

Not the answer he expected, but it wouldn't harm, would it? "Do you think I deserve to be arrested?"

"Of course not. Dedicating yourself to the helpless is a noble mission."

Keeping this conversation going on was Masolon's noble mission right now. "What if one day I have to disband this gang by your brother's order, milady?"

She furrowed her fair brow. "Why would he give such an order?"

"To protect his subjects from a possible threat."

"This doesn't make any sense. You are the one who protects his subjects from the threats on the road." She paused for a moment before she added, "It's the name of your band that might be a threat though."

"That name cannot be changed," he jested, but she didn't seem to be listening to him. His heartbeats rushed madly when Sania stared at him.

"You don't look like a threat to me." She smiled sweetly.

"Uhh…thanks, milady." Masolon had no idea what he was thanking her for. The heat in his head was fogging his thoughts.

"I think I'm done practicing today." She glanced at a patrol guard approaching them. "Good journeys to you, Masolon."

'*Masolon*' sounded sweeter than '*foreigner.*' Even all the barrels of ale in the tavern of Kahora wouldn't make him drunker than he felt right now.

25. ZIYAD

Those Bermanians would never stop grumbling about the weather. Ziyad should tell them what summer was like last year. They could have cooked their potatoes without using fire in the heat of the noonday sun.

The new leader had gathered the whole gang in their new nest, a hill near the western walls of Kahora. Forty warriors were listening to Frankil's instructions about their formation in their next fight. *Forty!* Still, without Masolon, a big stone of the fort was missing. Yes, Frankil was a good man, who could also be ruthless when necessary; Ziyad had been there when the Bermanian captain slaughtered those nomads with no mercy at all. A commander who was always serious about the task at hand, but still, he was not Masolon. He didn't have that aura you would feel when you look at and listen to that towering, broad-shouldered foreigner. But to give Frankil some credit, Ziyad had encountered a few nobles who lacked that commanding aura too. Anyhow, it didn't bother him who might lead the gang as long as that leader ensured that the pouch in Ziyad's pocket was always full.

But obviously, the leadership matter bothered someone else.

Ziyad didn't like the scowl Antram had been wearing since Masolon announced Frankil their leader. *What is your problem, bald fellow? Did someone tell you that you were Masolon's second-in-command just because you used to be a duke?* Honestly, Ziyad didn't care if Antram's story about his noble bloodline was true or not. The ill-tempered fellow was a fierce fighter, Ziyad would give him that, but a leader? He was not born for that.

"The Ghosts will be our next target," Frankil announced, the news looming large in the minds of the Murasen members of the gang, Ziyad himself included. The Ghosts were more than the fear of his childhood and manhood. They were the slayers of his loved ones, the very reason why he had begged his uncle to teach him how to wield a sword when he was a boy of six. *Blast! That was a long time ago, Ziyad,* he told himself, staring at the other Murasen brothers who were certainly like him; men who had never had the chance to raise their blades against a single Ghost. Those who had that chance never lived long enough to narrate their heroic stand against the soul reapers of the Murasen desert.

"Who is that fellow?" Ziyad nudged Antram, pointing to the sulky man ascending the hill on horseback, hair black and heavy. Ziyad had already guessed who the newcomer was, but he wanted to break Antram's silence.

The bald fellow exhaled. "That must be Kuslov who Masolon told us about. A Rusakian tracker who has the eyes of a hawk and the nose of a hound."

The tracker looked a bit surprised when he joined them. "I thought they were exaggerating when they said that Masolon had an army."

"Was it hard to find us?" Ziyad teased him.

"That's what I do for a living, young man." The tracker looked from Ziyad to Frankil. "You must be Captain Frankil, the leader. I'm Kuslov. Masolon left me a brief note about your quest. Are your men ready?"

"When do you want us to start?" Frankil asked.

"We had better finish this before sunset, so I say we start now. We will be easy prey for those Ghosts when the darkness falls." Kuslov paused, giving the band members a moment to digest his urgent instructions. "And let me tell you something, young men; I'm not ready to die today."

"You heard him, warriors," Frankil addressed his men. "To your horses." The captain fluidly mounted his horse and asked Kuslov, "Where will we start?"

"Where they were last seen," Kuslov replied. "The Northern Road."

* * *

The Warriors of the Gang were too quiet today. Quieter than the silent desert, which wouldn't remain dormant for long. Autumn was coming soon. And autumn in Murase didn't mean fallen dry leaves— trees barely existed in these lands—it meant sandstorms. A foe that could prove as deadly as the Ghosts themselves.

The small army stopped where the massacre had happened yesterday. When Kuslov dismounted and crouched, Ziyad trotted forward to watch the Rusakian work from a close range. The terrain was so plain he didn't understand what Kuslov might find in these sands.

"They didn't leave any tracks as usual," Ziyad commented, prompting the tracker to speak.

Kuslov turned his head, obviously not happy to be interrupted. "Young man," he said, "do you trust your eyes?"

Ziyad wasn't sure what this question was for. "Maybe not as you trust yours."

"At least, we have something to agree about."

"You tell me, Kuslov, what did you find?" Frankil asked, focusing on the task at hand as usual.

"A real Ghost doesn't leave tracks behind him nor try hard to hide them, Captain," Kuslov remarked.

"Those we are tracking are not the Ghosts then," Frankil concluded.

"Or the Ghosts are just men of flesh and blood." Ziyad recalled what he had heard about those poor travelers. What sort of men could slaughter women and children so mercilessly?

"They are headed northwest." Kuslov mounted his horse and nudged it to a trot, eyeing the ground with caution, making Ziyad wonder how long it would take to find those bastards at this pace. But no one should ask the Rusakian to rush. If he lost their trail, Ziyad and his fellows would wander the desert for eternity...if they could survive that long. In reality, the Bermanians wouldn't survive a few more hours without water here.

For hours, Ziyad rode next to Kuslov, trotting when he trotted, stopping when he stopped. He waited for a word from the Rusakian, but the tracker said nothing until it was nearing dusk.

"We should return to Kahora while we still have time to reach it before nightfall," Kuslov said after a lengthy ride.

"We will not return until we finish this mission," Frankil insisted.

"We can come back tomorrow and resume your mission."

"We keep following their tracks until the sun falls to Earth, and tomorrow we resume from where we stop."

The tracker didn't protest as he spurred his horse to a trot yet again. Ziyad kept following him, hoping he could spot a horse hoof or a footprint, but he saw nothing on the endless sand, and that was when he started to doubt that the Rusakian was fooling them. Because even if there were any tracks, how could he see them in the dim light of dusk?

The army stopped when night fell.

"Should we make fire for our camp?" Bergum asked.

"No," Antram snapped. "That will expose our location."

Frankil looked from Bergum to Antram then asked Ziyad, "I presume you know better than any of us. What do you suggest?"

"Those Ghosts can see in the dark anyway," Ziyad said. "I say we make a fire to see them as well."

Antram shook his head in disapproval. "If what you say is true, then we are just making their mission easier."

"So be it," Frankil decided. "Instead of making a fire in the center of our camp, we surround our camp with it so that they don't surprise us."

The Bermanian captain split the band into five groups of eight, each group guarding a position in an imaginary wide circle, but not too wide so that they could warn each other if one group spotted any threat.

Ziyad was the first in his group to take his turn on the night watch. The stars glittered in the clear sky like bright diamonds floating on a quiet, dark-blue ocean. A sight he couldn't enjoy in Rusakia where the sky was always grayed by a curtain of heavy clouds.

Yet something was wrong tonight. Usually the wind blew gentle breezes at night, shaking the fronds of those scattered palm trees, which was not the case *this* night. Right now no sound was coming from the desert but utter silence. *The sound of death,* Ziyad thought.

"*Over here!*" Danis cried.

Ziyad drew his sword as he scurried to the red-haired Bermanian. The whole gang held their weapons and hurried to where the cry came from.

"Where are they?" Antram asked nervously.

"The thudding footsteps came from that way." Danis pointed his finger at a dark spot in the desert. Ziyad grabbed a flaming branch from the campfire and cautiously ventured into the darkness.

"What are you doing, Ziyad? Come back here!" Antram yelled.

Ziyad would be glad to do as Antram asked *after* he found the intruder. He was sure he heard something approaching. Slow thudding feet. *This is not wise, Ziyad,* he told himself, knowing for certain that he had better stay behind the campfire with his brothers.

And then came the roar. All he remembered was his fall on his back, Antram's growl, and his fellows' cries.

"*Ziyad! Ziyad!*"

"*Talk to me, brother!*"

"*Are you hurt?*"

He could hear them, but for a few seconds, he had forgotten how to talk.

"Cursed demons!" Ziyad raised his head, his heart beating again at last. "What was that?"

"He is alright!" Danis announced, holding Ziyad's shoulders. "He is alright, folks!"

"Gracious Lord," Frankil muttered. "Antram was fast enough."

Ziyad had heard Antram's voice amid the clamor. On his left, the corpse of a desert leopard lay in a dark-red pond of blood. Standing in the same pond was Antram, the dark red splattering his face and his tabard.

"You saved me." Ziyad gave him a tired smile. "I thought you hated me, brother."

"Now I do." Blood dripped from Antram's sword. The gash in the leopard's neck was so deep it had almost severed its head.

"Your watch for tonight has ended," Frankil told Ziyad. "I hope I find you alive when the sun rises."

Ziyad hoped so as well. He hadn't lived all these years to become some leopard's supper. He knew they were here when he lay on his side, his eyes open. The silent desert felt it. That silent desert had sent that leopard to warn them, the same fashion it had warned his father before. It was really unfortunate that his father hadn't listened, and a whole caravan had been slaughtered on a quiet night like this one.

Frankil's voice woke him at first light. "Let's move, brothers. We have a long day ahead."

Obviously, the Ghosts hadn't paid them a night visit. Not yet. Perhaps they would tonight.

Ziyad rode next to Antram, both following Frankil and Kuslov. "I feel sorry for ruining your outfit," Ziyad said.

"You will feel sorry indeed if you don't buy me a new one," said Antram.

They were moving faster today. Kuslov, who was leading the group with Frankil, didn't stop to check the tracks as he had done yesterday. Only once they had to rest for the sake of the exhausted

Bermanian brothers of the gang.

"Curse these lands," Bergum muttered. "I'll kill that Guild Master if he doesn't pay us fairly this time."

The sun was heading west when Kuslov stopped them and dismounted to scrutinize the ground. "Quicksand," he announced.

The Murasens called it the Sand Sea, though it was not that kind of a sea you might swim in or sail through. That curse of a sea was designed to do one thing and one thing only: swallow whatever fell into it. As Ziyad's uncle had once told him before, *The only way to survive a fall into the sand sea is not to fall into the sand sea.*

"They are there." Kuslov nodded toward a hill at the horizon, in the heart of the sand sea. "The perfect location for a hideout."

"How can they reach it while we can't?" Frankil asked.

"There must be a passage." Holding his horse by the bridle, Kuslov walked, staring at the ground. "It's here." He turned to them. "But we can only cross this one man at a time. The passage is too narrow."

Ziyad looked around at his fellows, making sure he was not the only one confused here. The Rusakian tracker was talking about a passage that did not exist. The terrain was nothing but plain sand all around them except for that hill.

"What are you waiting for?" Kuslov gestured to them to move. The tracker's honed eyes must have spotted something they couldn't.

"You heard him, fellows." Ziyad dismounted, urging the rest to do the same. The warriors held their horses by their bridles and walked their beasts as Kuslov did.

"Stick to the line, everybody. Keep your eyes on the brother in front of you as long as he is still on his feet. One misstep and the quicksand will swallow you," Kuslov instructed as he led the group. "And one more thing; if you see a brother trapped in the sand, don't try to save him for any damned reason. The sand will swallow you both."

"Do as he says, brothers!" Ziyad waved at the horsemen behind him. "Stay close to each other!"

166

Normal sand and the sand sea looked exactly the same, but somehow Kuslov could spot the difference. They didn't exaggerate when they said the tracker had the eyes of a hawk.

"*Help!*" a cry came from behind Ziyad, a cry he hoped he wouldn't hear because he knew the consequences. As he expected, the Murasen fellows at the rearguard had already reached out for the brother whose knees had sank below the sand.

"Leave him!" Kuslov shouted, but he was too late. Two more brothers had stepped into the cursed sands already.

"Somebody pull them out!" Frankil yelled.

"No! More men will fall!" Kuslov insisted.

"We can't watch them die!"

"There's nothing we can do for them! Move forward!"

The brothers near the three trapped fellows took off their tunics, tying them together to make a chain. But the sand was faster. Before they made a single chain, one head was buried already, the sand swallowing the rest of its meal.

"*Keep your feet steady!*"

"*Don't let me die here!*"

"*Hold on tight!*"

"*We'll get you out!*"

"*There's nothing you can do! Leave them, you fools!*"

Everyone had lost his mind. Everyone was screaming. Only two screams in particular faded away as the sand filled the throats of two drowning fellows.

And then, silence. The warriors of the gang were mute, staring at the evil sand that had swallowed their fellows.

"Wake up, wake up!" Kuslov clapped. "They're gone! Make sure you follow me right this time."

Ziyad and Frankil exchanged a look. "I'm afraid he's right," said Frankil. "There's no good of staying here. Move and they will follow you."

The screams of the drowning fellows still echoed in Ziyad's head as he carefully moved onward, focusing on Frankil's boots in front of him to make sure he was stepping on the same spot. It would be a shame if he failed now while he was getting so close to those Ghosts.

"Shields up!" Antram called. "Archers at the hilltop!"

"Those cunts!" Ziyad unstrapped his shield and raised it in time to catch arrows knocking on the wood. "Kuslov! Have we crossed the quicksand yet?"

Men cried, horses whinnied.

"Kuslov!" Ziyad urged. "Answer me!" It was raining arrows, and deathly sand was on both sides. *Not the best time or place to become deaf, you Rusakian bastard!*

"From this point, spread out!" Kuslov instructed. "Don't spread sooner!"

Ziyad waited until Frankil made it to Kuslov's spot. The moment Ziyad joined them, he sprinted forward, leaving his horse behind him. His charger would hinder him if he ascended the hill with it. *Another fight, my friend*, he would tell his horse. *I have to fight this one on foot.*

The arrows hammered his shield as he went uphill. Glancing over his shoulder, he realized he was leading the attack, Frankil and Antram right behind him. The instant he reached the hilltop, Ziyad drew his saber and slashed an archer's abdomen. "Bleed, you scum!" Ziyad roared, watching blood pouring out of the dead archer's belly. *So, the Ghosts do bleed like men, huh?*

"What are you looking at?" Antram bellowed as he stabbed another archer. "Fight, you fool!" he chided Ziyad.

Ziyad estimated more than thirty Ghosts atop the sandy hill. Now it was a fair fight. Raising his shield at the right time, he blocked a soaring javelin as he charged at the spearman, and before the spearman could throw another, Ziyad chopped his hand off. The spearman howled in agony until Ziyad drove the curved blade into his chest, cutting off his screams. He wrenched the javelin from his shield and thrust it into another Ghost's torso. "DIEEEE!" he roared.

The fearless brothers vanquished the mortal Ghosts. Ziyad

wondered if those bastards still earned their name after they crammed the hilltop with their corpses.

"Wait!" he yelled at Bergum, who was about to stab a Ghost fallen on his back. "Not yet! Not yet!" Ziyad hurried to the Bermanian before he might kill the last surviving Ghost.

"Want to finish him yourself?" Bergum panted. "Be my guest." He took a step back.

"You! Are there others?" Ziyad laid his blade over the Ghost's throat. For the first time, he had a chance to contemplate the face of one of them. No horns or long ears. No dagger-like canines in his jaw. Even his facial features weren't as ugly as in the tales.

He was just a nomad.

"Speak, you filthy dog!" Ziyad jabbed his neck with his blade. "Where are the rest?"

The Ghost spat, uttering curses in the Old Murasen Tongue. "I'm not playing, son of a whore!" Ziyad spoke in the same old tongue, then stuck his curved blade in the nomad's hand, the nomad shrieking in agony. "Speak, or I will make your death slower than you can ever imagine!"

The fallen nomad was still screaming.

"Not the answer I'm expecting," snarled Ziyad, plunging his sword into the other wrist.

"Stop…stop!" the nomad wailed, hardly able to breathe between gasps.

"Ziyad!" Frankil yelled. "That's unnecessary!"

"You should have seen my father's corpse," Ziyad snapped at the captain, and then he turned back to the howling nomad. "Say something useful, or the next thing I cut will be your member!"

"They are coming." The nomad grimaced. "All of them."

"Coming where?" Ziyad jabbed his chest, but the nomad didn't talk, his eyes closed. "Don't pass out now!" Ziyad slapped him. "Wake up, you cunt!"

"That's enough, Ziyad." Frankil glared at him. "Finish him off."

"Not before we know what he knows!"

"He won't be able to tell you anything." Bergum flipped the nomad's body, showing Ziyad the gash in his back. With all this lost blood, the rascal was probably dying now.

"Come on, brother," Antram urged him. "It's over."

"Haven't you heard him?" Ziyad argued. "He said they were coming."

"Let them come." Antram stood tall. "We shall give them another day like this one."

Like this one? No, not enough. Ziyad would never be satisfied until he made sure that the Ghosts didn't exist in this world any longer.

26. SANIA

Sania let her brother hold her hand as they descended the stairs together. The Bermanian healer was waiting in the vestibule by the order of the Lord of Arkan who wanted to thank him in person for his efforts, and so did she. What the healer had done for her mother was a real miracle. A few weeks earlier the old lady was dying. Today she could even walk on her own.

"You're a source of pride to all Bermanians, Bumar," said Feras. "I hope my humble reward is up to your expectations."

Bumar gave a courtly bow. "Serving you is an honor, milord."

"Five memluks will escort you back to Kahora," said her lord brother. "They are waiting for you outside."

"I don't have enough words to express my gratitude, milord."

"You are returning to your gang, aren't you?" asked Sania, the impact of her question on Feras's face not lost on her.

"I'm not sure what you mean, milady," Bumar replied. "I'm not a member of the Warrior's Gang. They're all valiant heroes, and I'm just a healer."

"I thought you were a friend of Masolon's." *A friend who can tell me more about him.*

"I can't even tell." Bumar shrugged. "But I daresay there's a sort of chemistry between us."

"Chemistry?" Sania echoed.

"Yes, milady. When there's chemistry between souls, they get along with each other swiftly. Some need a longer time to do so. Others never get along at all."

"What sort of *chemistry* did you feel, Bumar?" she asked. "You are a man of knowledge and wisdom, and he, I presume, is a ruthless, heartless barbarian."

"Appearances can be deceiving, milady. A pure pearl is always hidden in a rough shell."

"Well said." Sania tilted her head, impressed by Bumar's eloquence, which nearly matched his unparalleled healing skills. "Where did you read that?"

"Not anywhere, milady." Bumar gave her a toothy grin. "Just a mere fruit of decades of experience."

"We don't want to hold Bumar, Lady Sania. The noon sun will be harsh today." Feras harrumphed. From his grim face, Sania could tell there was something in the conversation he didn't like. The healer noticed too. With another courtly bow, he took his leave and went to the door, Sania resisting the urge to call out to him. She wanted to hear more, but honestly, she didn't dare to ask. Not in front of her stern brother.

Now on their own, Feras leered at her. "Is there something you didn't tell me about?"

"Something like what, brother?" she asked innocently.

Feras took a deep breath. She knew her brother was suspicious of something, but of what? She recalled every word she had just said and found nothing wrong about it. Maybe because she had mentioned Masolon? What could be the problem with that? Nobody had told her she was forbidden to speak his name.

"Nothing," said Feras. "I just feel. . ." He stopped when the page hurried to him.

"My apologies, milord." The page handed him a sealed scroll. "We

172

have an urgent message from Bigad."

Bigad, the region her father ruled. What sort of urgent news might come from there? To Sania's surprise, she found herself a bit worried.

Feras dismissed his page and broke the seal of the scroll. The way his eyes twitched while reading the scroll piqued her curiosity.

"Is Father alright?" she asked worriedly.

Feras looked right and left, then took her by the hand and headed to the hall. "Out," he ordered the guards standing by the door.

"You're scaring me, Feras," she told her brother after the guards closed the door behind them. "What happened to Father?"

Feras seated her opposite him. "He's alive, if that's what you're asking, yet he's in grave danger. We all are, in fact. Dehawy is leading a rebellion in the eastern region, while his new allies, the Mankols, have already captured the castle of Kurdisan in the north."

Kurdisan was the Murasens' northern shield—her brother always said that to justify their father's absence. Its fall meant that the whole region of Bigad was in danger.

"What about Father? Where is he now?"

Feras let out a deep breath of air. "He has retreated to the southern bank of the Blue Crescent to defend the city. All he can amass right now is four or five thousand men against an enemy twice as strong as him."

Sania's military experience was as good as Feras's skill in sewing. "Can't you send him a few thousand of your soldiers to aid him?"

"Only my uncle can." He ground his jaw. The fact that he didn't like the idea of seeking their uncle's help was no surprise at all. "I need reinforcements to face the Byzonts coming from the northwest."

Byzonts, Mankols, and a rebellion. May the Lord have mercy. "Coming where?" she asked.

"Here, to the castle of Arkan. That's why you and Mother must go to Kahora before it's too late. It's not safe here."

"That is not going to happen," she snapped. "Mother can't stand the sand and the dusty air outside."

"Can you just use your reason for once instead of blustering like a child?" He glared at her. "This very castle will be besieged in three or four days. A siege is something we can never know when it will end, especially in a situation like this one, where our troops are busy engaging the enemy on different fronts. Currently, Kahora is the safest place in the whole kingdom, and the safest place in Kahora is the royal palace. I'm quite sure Mother will be taken care of better than here."

Sania had been to the royal palace once and she had never liked it. Yes, the chambers, the food, and the clothes were much better than here. But the formalities were unbearable. Lots of bows and the 'Your Highness' and 'Your Majesty' thing. She had to be dressed in her finest outfits wherever she went as she might run into some lord or even worse, the king himself. Even in her own chamber she should look well to the royal maidservants. Still, she couldn't deny the royal palace would be more comfortable for her mother Lady Ramia. The only problem—which could be a big problem, mind you—was the journey from Arkan to Kahora. It might not be that long, but not for her sick mother.

"I need a howdah," she told her brother.

"Of course," Feras agreed. "Now pack as fast as possible. I want you to leave before dusk."

27. MASOLON

There were two big differences between Ramos and Kahora; the looks of their people and their weather. To someone who had spent a few months in Murase, summer in Ramos was like a paradise.

The sight of ripe red apples in the marketplace piqued his attention. "I hope you can pay for this," said the merchant dryly when Masolon snatched one apple from the box. With the other hand, Masolon took a silver coin out of his pocket and made it visible to the merchant's eyes, still not looking at him. He didn't want anything to distract him from enjoying the sweet juicy fruit.

"Murasen silver!" exclaimed the merchant. "You don't look like a Murasen, stranger."

"I am not from Gorania, if that makes you feel better." Masolon picked up another apple.

"That's another silver coin," said the merchant.

Masolon glared at the merchant. "Hey, I said I am a stranger, not a fool."

"I'm sure of that. Is it your first Contest?"

"No."

"I mean in Paril."

"Yes." Masolon was bored of the curious merchant. If it weren't for his irresistible apples…

"Then I wish you a good fight." The merchant paused for a moment then said, "Nobody told you what really goes on there, huh?"

"Is there something I should know besides knocking my opponents out?" Masolon bit into the third apple.

"The bets."

"There are bets in every Contest."

"The bets in Paril are something else," the merchant said in a low voice. "Lords and elites are involved in this Contest, which means an unbelievable amount of gold at stake. Those men don't let anything happen by chance. Do you understand what I mean? Someone may simply *ask* you to let your opponent win. Trust me, son, you'd better do what he says. If you want to return to your family, you must not earn the enmity of those people."

"Excellent." Masolon tossed the apple core onto the street. "Because I do not have a family to return to."

"Then make one. Buy a house, meet a girl and get married, have children. Even soldiers do that."

Masolon laughed. That merchant must be feeling so lonely that he wanted to talk to anybody about anything.

"What makes you laugh?" the merchant asked, confused.

Masolon ignored him as he approached the nearby blacksmith, gaping at the greatsword the craftsman was sharpening with a grinding rock. The etched hilt was long enough to be gripped two-handedly, the broad blade shining like a diamond. The artfully crafted weapon reminded Masolon of his father's huge sword, which he had always been eager to wield. Because it could swiftly take a man's life, it was called Erloss; 'Mercy' in Masolon's native tongue.

"How much is this one?" Masolon asked the occupied blacksmith.

"This one is sold already." The craftsman didn't look at Masolon.

How disappointing. "But surely, you can make another one."

"You will have to wait, then. I have a full week ahead."

Masolon couldn't stay away from his gang that long. "Did the buyer pay you yet?"

The blacksmith sighed as he finally turned to Masolon. "We work by norms, young man. I gave him my word."

Masolon wondered how those Bermanian norms would fare against Murasen gold. "How much did he promise you?"

The blacksmith peered at him. "You that desperate to get it?"

You have no idea. "Just name your price." Masolon gnashed his teeth.

The blacksmith looked Masolon in the eye. "Seven golden coins."

Masolon produced ten golden coins from his pouch. "And three for your trouble with your buyer."

The craftsman couldn't conceal his smile. "That's too generous of you, young master. Just give me a day, *only* a day, until I'm done sharpening and polishing the sword."

Masolon returned the coins to the pouch. "Your payment stays with me until I get hold of *my* sword. I will be back to you tomorrow."

Masolon left the marketplace. Before nightfall, he found a vacant chamber in a tavern to spend the night in. This time he wasn't in a hurry. He still had one day before the beginning of the next and *last* Contest. The only window in his room was so small he could hardly get his head out to breathe some cool fresh air from outside. In Murase, the windows were huge, yet there was no breeze to let in.

Just before dawn, Masolon woke. He left the sleeping city on his horse, trotting in the green fields outside its walls. Since he set foot on the Bermanian soil, he didn't remember he had seen that yellow color except in the lemon farms. Even the hills were curtained in green. According to the map Ramel had given him, Masolon was now passing by the Green Hills. He wondered if there were other hills with different colors in the Bermanian realm.

The Green Hills were ten miles outside Paril. The notion of spending the night at the hilltop was tempting, but he was afraid his horse might get injured while ascending that steep hillside. The wind at the hill foot was just right. Cooler than in Murase, yet warmer than in Rusakia. Murase and Rusakia. Halin and Sania. Two highborn ladies from two different kingdoms. He remembered how hard his heart beat when he saw Halin, but his heart pounded harder when he met Sania. There was something he liked about her company. The way she teased him without much reservation, the way she was being herself, not acting according to what her title dictated. What might be his chances with...? *No!* He wouldn't allow his mind to even entertain the possibility.

In less than a couple of hours, he reached Paril, the Jewel of Gorania. What caught his attention were the building colors that seemed to be following a certain pattern. The first quarter he passed by was all blue, the next green, the third red. The streets were wider than those of any city he had ever visited. The towers of the royal palace of King Wilander touched the sky of Paril so high they could be seen from anywhere in the city.

Follow the noise. That piece of advice worked here too. Finding the majestic amphitheater of Paril wasn't hard at all. And what an amphitheater it was. Quite fitting for the biggest Contest in all Gorania.

Masolon wasn't a bit surprised to find his name listed in the contenders' roster. Viola was here no doubt, yet he couldn't spot her in that thronged venue. Having no time to check his fellow fighters' names, he hurried to the fighters' chambers to gear himself up. One of the arena boys was still there.

"You are too late, sir," said the boy. "All contenders of the first round are out to the stage and they will be starting at any moment."

"Forgive me." Masolon grabbed a wooden pole and a shield. "I am not so clever when it comes to roads." Noticing that his wooden gear was heavier than any of those of the previous Contests, Masolon swung his pole to feel its weight with both arms. "Something is wrong with my pole."

The boy took the wooden weapon from him. "Looks fine to me."

"It is heavier than usual."

"Because it's a Lignum Vitae," the boy explained. "The heaviest wood in Gorania."

Masolon contemplated his wooden weapon. With a well-driven blow, that pole could do some damage. *Real, bloody damage.*

"Wait," the boy demanded, Masolon leaving the chambers. "You will need this." He tossed a wooden helm to Masolon.

Masolon wasn't used to wearing anything on his face, especially when he fought. While putting it on, he could feel his breath blowing in his face. He wondered how Frankil and his knights fought with their iron helms.

"Hurry up, sir," the boy urged.

Masolon dashed through the corridor which led at its end to the field. Once he stepped into the arena, his ribs were shaken by the crowd's roar. Why was he nervous this time? Was it because of the stage packed with excited spectators? He was the Champion of Durberg. The Contest of Paril would be his second and last accomplishment to release himself from Ramel's pledge. The Contest of Paril would cover the damned 'fair price' of his training.

"You! Hurry up! You are about to be eliminated!" a fighter with a familiar voice cried.

Masolon strode toward his fellow fighter to confirm his suspicions about the face hiding behind the helm.

"You still don't recognize me, do you?" the fighter asked mockingly.

"What are you doing here, Artony?" Masolon asked dryly.

"Doing what you are supposed to do. Now get your arse here on my right."

The notion of fighting alongside Artony was hard to digest. What was harder was Artony's presence in this Contest in the first place. Would he let Masolon beat him when they met in the final round? That made sense as an explanation. As usual, Ramel didn't leave anything to chance.

The horns were blown, announcing the start of the first fight in the Contest of Paril. Masolon wasn't sure if he was allowed to hit his own fellow fighters, but he did hope he was. The temptation to smash Artony's face was hard to resist.

"Even if Ramel wants you to win, I won't make it easy," Artony said, determined to provoke him. "It will be the most painful victory you will ever earn."

"Curse you both," Masolon muttered, looking at their two opponents who charged at them. He gripped his heavy pole from the middle with both hands and rushed toward the attackers, roaring in fury. Before their swung poles reached him, he struck the two opponents in their bellies with two consecutive hits from both edges of his pole. Without delaying his finishing blow, he raised his pole from its end and hit his opponents with the full length of his wooden weapon, knocking them out. The battle ended as soon as it started, the crowd roaring in utter excitement.

"A good start, Champion," Artony said sarcastically, clapping. "I thought you might need to warm up."

"I cannot wait for the final round to crush you." Masolon smirked. "May the Contest draw bring you to me in the next round."

"Hey, you! Move over! We have a fight to start!" growled a fighter from the next contending team.

Vaknus? Masolon recognized his voice. Apparently, Ramel had taken every measure to ensure he would come back to him with his gold. The two fighters Masolon had just beaten could be Ramel's men as well. Would it be surprising if all the fighters of this Contest had come from, or even passed by the Pit?

Unlike what Masolon had expected, the draw of the following round resulted in an encounter between Vaknus and Artony. It would make sense if they met in the last round before the final, but this soon? Maybe Ramel was not in control of everything as Masolon had suspected.

The two veteran fighters showed much rivalry in their duel, making it hard to predict who was going to win. As Masolon had no real harsh feelings toward Vaknus, he wished good luck to Artony. *This Contest will be your last as well, you bastard.* The two former champions parried each other with their poles crossed. When

Vaknus's weapon flew away, Artony flipped his pole, sweeping his opponent's leg, and then he raised his weapon with both hands to give Vaknus, who was on his back, an overhead strike. *That is right, bastard. Win this to face me.*

But the finishing blow never came. Artony lowered his weapon, and Vaknus raised his hand declaring his surrender. The bastard was copying what Masolon had done in the Contest of Durberg, and it worked. The throng burst into cheering and clapping to the 'chivalrous' winner, who stood, raising both arms toward his crowd to greet them back. Nothing but a stupid show, yet the bastard was enjoying it.

The next rounds barely brought any challenge for Masolon. In every fight, Masolon finished his opponents with a few strikes, and every time he left the field he met Artony entering his next fight. The bastard was still winning, which was exactly what Masolon wanted. *Bring me the final fight already.*

After beating his opponent in the semi-final round, Masolon lay on a wooden seat in the corner of the arena, waiting for Artony to win his fight to face him in the final.

"You're fighting well today." Looking over his shoulder, he saw Viola holding the bars that separated the crowd from the fighting arena.

"I have not started yet."

"That's what I thought." Viola nodded. "You know pretty well how bad I want you to win." She was threatening him, Masolon knew.

"I have an agreement with your employer." *Your lover, you whore.* "Once I win, we will part ways." Leering at Viola, he leaned forward toward her. "I swear if I see you again in my way, even by coincidence, I will deal with you as I deal with those bandits I slaughter. You are not any different from them."

The crowd behind her roared. It must be Artony beating his opponent.

"His name was Theronghar," said Viola, a slight smile on her face, as if not bothered by Masolon's menace. "A huge Skandivian, taller and bigger than you. Ramel's plans for him were even bigger. After winning five Contests, the Skandivian decided to settle in his homeland as a fisherman." She chuckled mockingly. "Skandivians love the sea, you know, and Theronghar was no exception. He wished he could spend the rest of his life beside his *love*, and I made sure his wish was fulfilled."

The throng shook the amphitheater with their roar again. They cheered for the winner, who was...*not* Artony. What had happened while Masolon wasn't watching?

"Best of luck, big boy," said Viola. "I will be waiting for you."

Masolon ignored her, trying to understand what was going on. The point of Artony's participation was to make sure that Masolon fought one of Ramel's men in the final. Obviously, the plan didn't work after Artony's loss to some unknown contender. *Why did you lose, you bastard?* Anyway, that didn't change the fact that Masolon would have to vanquish his opponent in the final to pay his debt to Ramel. Such a shame he wouldn't be able to break Artony's bones in the arena as he wanted.

Putting on his helm, Masolon's foe waved at the herald that he was ready for the fight. Masolon himself was impatient to start. Gripping his pole from the middle with one hand, his helm in the other, Masolon pushed to his feet and stepped into the arena.

"You fought well with the helms," said the opponent. "Although you haven't tried them before in the Pit."

Masolon's jaw dropped. That voice sounded like...no, it didn't sound *like* him. It *was* him.

His mentor wasn't among the crowd today.

28. MASOLON

"This is not possible!" Masolon exclaimed when Ramel took off his helm, revealing his well-shaved face. What on Earth was the bastard doing in the ring? His place was among the crowd, not *here*. "Why?"

"This is the duel you were looking for, isn't it?"

"What brought you here, Ramel?"

"You, Masolon. You brought us all here."

Masolon's mind was in a whirl. "What happened to your fair price? Did you decide to give up your gold?"

Ramel gave him a crooked smile.

"There was no bet in the first place, was there?"

"That's not true," said Ramel. "The big bet is there, and I will get my gold. But no one said that the bet would be on *you*."

Masolon felt that numbness creeping all over his head. *The bet was on Ramel?*

"The idea of bringing you to this Contest was based on your low odds," said Ramel. "You are still less renowned than Artony and Vaknus, and this makes betting on you more risky, hence more profitable. After a second thought, I asked myself the same question you asked me before: Why don't I participate in the Contest? What if

183

I make one huge bet on the most unlikely winner of two unlikely finalists? You have no idea how much I'm going to earn today."

"What about Artony and Vaknus? Why did they join this Contest?"

"Some distraction won't harm. As usual, you made it late to Paril. I knew that your busy mind wouldn't notice my name in the contenders' list. I was pretty sure that I would be invisible as long as Artony and Vaknus were here." Ramel waved with his helm to Masolon. "That piece of wood helped a lot not ruin the surprise I was preparing for you. You don't know how I am going to enjoy this fight!"

Four lads from the arena entered the field, two of them pulling two horses, the other two carrying a lance for each contender.

"Put on your helm, Masolon." Ramel put on his own helm and mounted his horse. "You have no idea how badly you are going to need it today."

Masolon understood the words, understood that he should wear that helm in his hands instead of staring at it. Why was he frozen like a statue?

"Come on!" Ramel cried. "Or I shall pierce your head with my lance!"

Knowing that a bastard like Ramel wouldn't mind doing that, Masolon had no option but to pull himself together. He covered his head with the helm, mounted his horse, and gazed at Ramel who waited at the other end of the arena for the horns to be blown.

The final round of the Contest started. Ramel was the first to spur his horse onward, while Masolon, still muddled by Ramel's appearance, needed two more seconds to get himself into the fight. *Nothing has changed, you fool,* he reminded himself. *It's still just another fight you have to win.*

Both riders held their lances as the two horses galloped toward each other, Masolon's eyes fixed on Ramel's trunk. Tightening his grip on the heavy wooden weapon, he waited for the right moment to drive his lance into Ramel's torso to finish that matter once and for all. But just before that *right* moment, his horse whinnied out of pain when Ramel's lance hit it. The stallion swayed and was about to lose balance and fall, but managed to keep its four hooves on the ground, making its way to the end of the arena field.

Masolon wheeled his horse to face Ramel, who reached the other side of the field. His trainer knew exactly what he was doing. First, it was Masolon's horse; next time it would be Masolon himself.

From the way Masolon's horse limped, it was obvious it was seriously hurt by Ramel's hit. "Come on," Masolon patted his horse's neck as if he was encouraging it to summon all the power it could. Most probably this would be the last charge of the brave horse. *You must finish the duel in this very charge,* he told himself. *Focus, you bastard!* In a few seconds, a clash of wooden lances was going to happen.

A trot, a canter, then a gallop. Masolon, who had been raised by the fiercest Ogonian warriors, was certain he could transition his horse's gait faster than Ramel, but the latter did surprise him with his smooth horseback riding. *Focus, Masolon. This is your turn.* As he kept reminding himself who he really was, what he was capable of, the Ogonian warrior held the lance firmly, eyes on nothing but the spot he aimed to hit. Ramel closed on him with his galloping horse, and the anticipated clash happened. A painful one this time… for Masolon himself.

Hit in his left shoulder, Masolon fell off his horse, the earth and the sky twirling as he rolled several times on the dusty arena. Frustrated by his second failed attempt, shamed by the dust that covered him, he rose to his feet, watching Ramel parade with his horse in front of the crowd. Was that the dance of victory?

"What is this, Masolon?" Ramel trotted toward him. "This crowd deserves a better show than this pathetic one. After all, I wasn't that bad as a trainer. I am sure I have taught you something that makes you fight better than an old lady."

At a loss for words, Masolon was allowing Ramel to enjoy the moment. No words could help a dismounted man against a mounted foe. What he needed now was a crushing blow to deliver to this bastard.

"Very well." To Masolon's amazement, Ramel swung down his horse, threw his lance, and grabbed the wooden pole strapped to his back. "Come on!" he shouted. "Show me your best moves!"

Masolon grabbed his pole as well and made a combination of a few swings, an attack he had learned from Ramel.

An attack Ramel easily deflected.

"So predictable," said Ramel, parrying Masolon's pole. Now on the offensive, Ramel roared as he charged, his swings fast and relentless. Masolon blocked them all, gasping as if he was climbing a mountain. On the other hand, Ramel, who could be the fastest foe he had ever encountered, looked tireless. "That's what I call a fight!"

"Eyes drive arms," Masolon muttered, catching his breath.

Ramel charged again, his pole tearing the air in different directions, making Masolon feel as if he was facing five opponents at the same time. So far his pole was always in the right place at the right moment.

Until Ramel's pole struck his abdomen.

Masolon grunted, bending his back. Ramel followed the first hit with another massive strike on his already hurt shoulder. Masolon growled, yet still standing his ground.

"Why have you done this to yourself, Masolon?" Ramel swung his weapon thrice at him. Masolon only blocked one blow, but he failed to do the same with the other two. Again he growled.

"You could have become the greatest Contest fighter of all times of Gorania," Ramel snarled. "But you always insisted on following your sick mind!"

Masolon found it hard to cope with Ramel's unbelievably fast pace. He received three more strikes, followed by a fourth one on his head. The helm saved him from losing his consciousness, but the shock of the heavy blow worsened his confusion. He felt as if a whirlpool had swallowed him.

"How can you be so ungrateful?" Ramel hit him once more in the torso. Masolon stepped back, still refusing to fall down. "I offered you a life that every Goranian dreams of. Wealth, fame, pleasure; what else do you want? Is death what you seek? You can die when your hair is grayed. But if you are so eager to die young, I can fulfill this wish for you!"

With the uttermost rage he had displayed thus far, Ramel struck Masolon with his pole in an unmatched speed. Masolon blocked a few hits before his own weapon flew away from his hands.

"Isn't that painful?" Ramel smirked as Masolon shielded himself with his bare arms. "Maybe for a normal person, but not for the great Masolon!"

Masolon crossed his arms to prevent Ramel's pole from reaching his body or head, and his trainer seemed to be enjoying that, torturing his reluctant apprentice.

"*Masolon the Brave!*" a cry came out of the crowd. Cheers hailing his name grew louder.

"You like it?" Ramel asked nervously. "The crowd is hailing to you. Is that what you want? I can bring you more if you wish."

Ramel wasn't enjoying the show anymore, Masolon could tell. The crowd's reaction had ruined his amusement. With the edge of his pole, Ramel struck Masolon in his left knee, but Masolon didn't fall. "Ah! I forgot! You are the man with iron flesh, aren't you?" Hitting Masolon in the other knee, Ramel's tone sounded more nervous than cynical. Masolon dropped to his knees, his hands on the ground.

With the tip of his pole, Ramel removed Masolon's helm from his head, the wooden weapon scraping his forehead. "Do you still want to release yourself from your commitment? I shall grant you what you want." Ramel looked exhausted when he took his breath. "You won't see any Contest again in your life. I will lock you in the Pit and make an example of you until the worms eat your bones." He put the edge of his pole beneath Masolon's chin to raise his head. "Don't ever think it's easy for me to destroy something I crafted."

"I am not your craft," Masolon said weakly.

"You can still talk. That is really impressive."

"Eyes drive arms." Masolon threw himself on Ramel's legs and fell with him on the ground. Ramel, who lay on his back, kicked Masolon in the face and rolled his body fluidly away from him.

"Nice try." Ramel was again on his feet, Masolon lying on the ground. Masolon desperately dove again, but his trainer was out of his reach when he jumped.

"Give up, you fool," Ramel snarled. "I will hurt you more if you don't stop."

Ramel dragged Masolon by his tunic and kicked him at the back of his head. Masolon fell on his face, his senses in disarray. He could barely hear Ramel's faint voice saying, "You foolish bastard! Look at yourself! Are you happy now?"

With his crumpled body, Masolon felt like sleeping when his eyes closed. Ramel's voice was gone, and the last thing he recalled was the faint voice of the Contest herald announcing, *"We have a new champion for the Jewel."*

29. VIOLA

Viola had never been interested in those stupid fights like the crowd she was sitting among. But today's fight was an exception. For her first time ever, she was watching the whole encounter without missing a move, having no doubt that Ramel would teach that arrogant scum a lesson. Masolon had thought he was invincible, but today he discovered the truth the hard way thanks to Ramel, who wasn't going easy on him at all. Her favorite part was when Ramel dismounted to face Masolon on foot; an utter humiliation for the supposedly invincible fighter.

While she wanted to keep watching Ramel lay waste to Masolon, she couldn't wait for the fight to end, for the moment she could look Masolon in the eye after his disgraceful defeat and let him know that she had been watching and enjoying every second of it. She would tell him this every day until he rotted in the Pit. She knew Masolon would either try to kill himself or escape, and she wished he could escape. She would even help him do that just to get an excuse to hunt him down with her daggers. *He wouldn't be a harder target than Theronghar.*

"Artony!" She waved at Ramel's fighter who was looking for her among the throng.

"Your big boy is not doing well," said Artony as he found a spot for himself beside her.

"My big boy?" Viola pursed her lips. "I don't think he deserves the honor."

"Look, Viola. I don't like that fellow either, but I don't understand the reason behind your deep hatred toward him."

"He doesn't belong to us."

Artony snickered. "Did he turn you down?"

"What are you talking about? Are you out of your mind?"

"No, I am not. But I see you hate him without any obvious reason...to us."

"From the moment I saw him, I knew he didn't belong to us." She turned her face away from Artony to watch the duel. "I warned Ramel more than once about Masolon. I was sure he would not succumb easily."

"Ramel doesn't listen to anybody. What made you think he would listen to *you?*" Artony chuckled scornfully.

"What do you mean, Artony?"

"What I mean is that you are thinking so much of yourself. You are deluded, Viola. Do you really believe you are anything special to Ramel? He has known as many as a hundred women."

She frowned. "This is not true."

"Wake up, Viola." He snapped his fingers. "Everyone in the Pit has a role to play. I understand my role, and I am satisfied with it. I guess you understand your role too."

"I take care of all of his arrangements. Without me, he wouldn't be able to collect his gold."

"Taking care of his gold is *one* of your roles." Again, Artony smiled wickedly. The he glanced at her reminded her of Masolon's disdainful looks. Actually, he looked like Masolon right now.

"You want to know why I hate Masolon?" She glowered at him. "It is that look in his eyes," Viola hissed, one hand snatching a dagger from inside her coat before stabbing Artony in the abdomen, the other hand on his mouth to suppress his cry. The mocking smile disappeared from his face. Forever.

Viola looked around, making sure nobody noticed what had happened thanks to the heat of the encounter between Masolon and Ramel. She rose up from her seat, leaving Artony dead in a pond of blood. The panic started when she heard the thud of his body falling to the ground, dead.

"Murderer! Stop that wench!" cried one of the spectators, pointing at her.

She had to move quickly. The way to the main door was too crowded to consider as an escape, so she dashed up the amphitheater to reach the fence at the top. When a chaser blocked her way, she bellowed, "Get out of my way!" Without hesitation, she threw a dagger at her chaser's throat. She climbed the fence and looked at the other side of it. The height was deadly, she realized.

"What is she doing?" one man from the crowd cried. "She will fall to her death if she jumps!"

Viola clutched the fence, looking at both sides. Chasers were approaching her, and it was time to decide whether she would let herself be caught, or try her luck from that height. She wished she had enough daggers to slay all her pursuers, and after that, she would go to Masolon and even Ramel and slaughter them both.

Gazing again at the outer side, she let herself go.

30. MASOLON

"Not yet."

Awakened by the herald's voice, Masolon propped himself up on his palms. His vision was not quite clear, yet he could see Ramel standing in front of him at some distance. Looking over his shoulder, Masolon spotted the weapon he had lost early in this damnable fight.

His lance.

"Now what, Masolon? What are you trying to do?" Ramel's tired voice came from behind as Masolon crawled toward the weapon, doing what his warrior's instinct told him.

"Do you have any idea what you are doing now?" Ramel spat. "Even an amateur knows that you can't use that thing on foot, you fool!" His trainer was absolutely right. A lance would be too long and too heavy to maneuver. "Put your hand on that lance, and I'll smash your head with it!" Despite Ramel's menacing tone, he sounded weary.

Masolon reached the lance and grasped it with both hands. He started to get himself up on his feet again, looking at his exhausted opponent. A moment of eerie silence reigned over the arena. Everyone was stunned, including Ramel himself.

"You really think you can hit me with that thing?" Ramel snorted.

"Not even in your best form."

Masolon could barely hear Ramel's faint voice, his vision blurred thanks to the hits he had received on his head. Every inch of his body ached. His mind didn't recall anything he had learned at the Pit. Anything, except one word.

"*Again.*"

Masolon's eyes were only fixed on his opponent. His hammered arms could feel nothing but the weight of the lance. Stretching his heavily bruised knees, he uttered a roar. A last one perhaps.

Masolon charged, driving his heavy Lignum Vitae lance into Ramel's stomach. The strike bent Ramel's back and almost knocked him over. Masolon threw the heavy weapon and punched Ramel with his right fist squarely in the nose. Revived by the sight of blood on Ramel's face, Masolon gave his stunned trainer another punch in the same spot on his nose. Ramel blocked Masolon's third punch, but he couldn't dodge Masolon's headbutt that smashed his nose for the third time. Without giving Ramel a chance to spit the blood out of his mouth, Masolon swung a punch that broke his foe's jaw. While Ramel was swaying backward from Masolon's successive blows, Masolon threw himself on his opponent, falling with him to the ground. Sitting on Ramel's chest, Masolon hammered his trainer's face with both fists. He hammered and hammered nonstop, until he lost the count of his punches.

Ramel wasn't responding anymore, blood covering his face as well as Masolon's hands. But Masolon didn't stop. Were it not for the arena boys who hurried to pull Masolon away, he would hammer Ramel's head until eternity.

Without resisting them, Masolon let the arena lads drag him away. He kept his eyes on Ramel who didn't move a muscle, making sure he would never ever move any. "*A healer!*" cried the herald as he scurried to the fallen contender and felt his wrist. "*There's no pulse!*"

Many people yelled, but Masolon couldn't decipher what they said. He didn't bother, though. What mattered now was that his nightmare was over. No more debts. No more Contests. It was time to bid farewell to every arena in Gorania.

Six armored swordsmen stood in Masolon's way as he headed to the exit of the arena. "Halt, Champion," one of them commanded.

"I waive my prize." Masolon stopped. "Just let me through."

"One more step, and you will be the first champion to die in the arena."

"Am I arrested?"

"That is not my decision to make, Champion. But we shall know soon."

"Whose decision is it, then?"

"Mine." A man clad in a blue embroidered doublet and sky-blue mantle came from behind the guards, the black mask he wore only showing his brown eyes. The swordsmen made way for him, slightly lowering their heads in respect.

"Who on Earth are you?"

"I wear this for a bloody reason, naïve one." He pointed to his black mask. "It's me who demands answers here. Now tell me, who pays you?"

Masolon could barely hold his head upright. "Pays me for what?"

The masked man sighed, rubbing his hands together. "Let me tell you a few things about me. When someone lies to me, I know. When I know, I get angry. And when I get angry, believe me, you will regret the day you were born. Is there anything I said you didn't understand?"

That man was one of the blue-blooded highborn, Masolon realized. He must have lost a fortune today.

Masolon nodded. "Everything is clear."

"Good. I need a name, and I promise I will not hurt you."

"What name?"

"The name of the mastermind behind today's mess. The man who destroyed Ramel's empire for good."

"Destroying Ramel's empire was none of my concern. Winning this Contest was all I was thinking of. Ramel's death wasn't anybody's plan."

"Ramel's death wasn't anybody's plan?" the masked man echoed. "What about the murder of his finest fighter? Or do you want me to believe that, by some coincidence, his assistant decided to kill him at the same time?"

The murder of his finest fighter? Did the masked man mean Artony? The good news kept coming. "I cannot talk about others' deeds and intentions," Masolon replied.

The masked man glared at Masolon, his eyes betraying his dissatisfaction.

"Get out of my sight." He motioned Masolon outside with a chin nod. Without delay, Masolon strode past the masked man and his six guards before the masked man might change his mind.

"I wouldn't participate in any more Contests if I were you," the blue-blooded man called from behind him.

Masolon looked over his shoulder. "No one would."

31. SANIA

Two weeks still remained for summer, yet Sania had already seen the harbingers of the dreadful autumn dust storm in her journey to Kahora. Poison Wind was coming early this year. Although the windows of the royal palace were shut, the dust found a way to invade the air inside her mother's chamber.

"You!" Sania cried at two maidservants. "Find me something to stick to the trims! I want to seal all the gaps between them and the wall!" Her mother was coughing and sometimes gasping for every breath of air she took. "The door as well! Seal all those stupid gaps!"

Sania hurried outside to make sure all the windows of the corridor were locked. "Where is this air coming from?" The air in the corridor was laden with dust, which was entering her mother's chamber from inside and outside the damnable palace. "Where is everybody?"

A few moments later, the one who had introduced herself as the First Maid of the women's wing hurried to her. "What's the matter, milady?"

"What was your name again?"

"Fadwa, milady. I'm the—"

"First Maid," Sania cut in. "Yes, yes, I remember. It's just the name that I forgot. The air is too dusty in this wing, and I want you to see to this issue urgently."

The First Maid managed a fake smile. "It's Poison Wind, milady. Even with all doors and windows shut, some dust will enter."

"Then take your girls and seal all the windows," Sania demanded. "Use cloth, cut the curtains—I don't care. But you must do as I say. Now!"

Fadwa pressed her lips together. "I'll see what I can do, milady."

Sania wagged a firm finger at the maid. "If you can't do it, I'll do it myself. This is my mother, do you understand? I'll do whatever it takes to save her."

"I understand your worries, milady. Please, calm down. We'll do our best to help Lady Ramia."

Sania doubted she might see any good from the thick First Maid. She must talk to the king himself. Poison Wind generally blew for a whole week. Her mother wouldn't stand the storm until its end.

Bumar, Sania thought when the First Maid was leaving her. "Wait, you…you told me your name already, I know. Fadwa, yes. Fadwa, I need someone to find Bumar the healer. He's the only one who can take care of her."

"Where can we find him?" the thickheaded woman asked. "He's not a Murasen, is he?"

"No, he's not." Sania ground her teeth. "He lives here in Kahora, though. Ask any of the guards, and they will know what to do."

"I'll see to that, milady. Rest assured." She nodded with her fake smile and left.

I shouldn't have listened to him. Obeying her brother's orders had put her in that delicate situation with those slow servants. She knew that journey wouldn't go well.

Lady Ramia's gasp reached Sania in the corridor.

"Merciful Lord!" She scurried back to the chamber and rushed to her mother's bedside. "Mother, a healer is coming soon." She held her mother's hand with both hands, her mother giving her the faintest smile she had ever seen. Her sick mother could hear her, but she must fight to talk with her locked lungs.

"Ahmet." Her mother coughed a few times just to utter his name. "See him."

"You want to see Father?"

"Am leaving." Her mother coughed again and again. "See him."

"No, Mother. You're going to stay!" Sania couldn't hold her tears from falling. After all this time, her mother still thought of him.

"See him. Leaving…"

"You!" Sania shouted at one of the two maidservants she had ordered to seal the windows. "Find me Fadwa and tell her to come at once. No, wait. Keep working on those windows. I'll go find her myself."

Sania hurried back to the corridor. "FADWA!" she called out more than once. Everybody in the palace must have heard her yells. In a few minutes, Thickhead returned.

"I'm really sorry, milady." Fadwa looked down. "I told them Lady Ramia needed your healer's urgent help, but they said they had a healer in the palace already."

"What is this nonsense?" Sania blustered. "How dare they refuse my request?"

The maidservant looked a bit hesitant then asked, "Shall I let that healer come?"

"No." Sania gave it another thought. "Yes, bring him. Until I talk to His Majesty." She left Thickhead behind her and strode across the corridor until she reached the stairs. Downstairs she asked the guards to take her to King Rasheed. The guards looked nervous when they told her he was occupied at the moment.

"What is it, Lady Sania?" asked Qasem, Captain of His Majesty's Royal Memluks.

"I need to talk to His Majesty." Sania stomped her foot, infuriated. "Now."

"I'm afraid that's not possible now, milady." Qasem gave her a slight bow. "As for the healer, we've sent one for Lady Ramia already."

"I must see him now!" Sania bellowed.

"Milady," Qasem pleaded. "I hope you understand the situation we are facing."

"Your situation?" She glared at him. "What about mine?"

"You didn't hear the bells, milady?"

"What bells?"

"The alarm bells." Qasem leaned forward. "The walls of Kahora are under attack."

32. ZIYAD

Ziyad had never heard the bells in Kahora before, but he knew what they meant. From the faces of his Murasen brothers of the gang, he could tell they knew too.

Half of the gang had gone to sleep early this night. Since their battle with the Ghosts, everything had been quiet. No bandits, no raided caravans. But Ziyad didn't forget the dying Ghost's promise. *They're all coming.* They must have come already.

"Wake up, brothers!" Ziyad cried. "Kahora is under attack!"

Frankil was the first one to rise. "What is happening?"

"The bells, Captain!" Ziyad pointed to the dark horizon, where the city of Kahora lay. "The Ghosts must have come!"

Antram rubbed his face, his voice even harsher than it really was when he said, "We can't be sure of that."

"We can only be sure if we go there! Come on! Hurry up!" Ziyad urged.

"Slow down, brother. That is the memluks' job." Yawning, Antram stretched his arms. "No one hired us to guard the city walls. We haven't even received our gold from the last fight yet."

"Have we turned into mercenaries now?" Frankil asked.

"Since we came here? Yes." Antram shrugged. "Aren't you paid for what you do?"

"I'm paid for doing the right thing," Frankil said. "And I'll always do it whether I'm paid or not."

"Come on, brothers." Antram looked from Ziyad to Frankil. "This is not our fight. We don't even know if there's a fight in the first place."

"So be it. I'm going," Ziyad decided, knowing that arguing was a waste of time. "Anyone else coming with me?"

"We're all coming," Frankil announced, glancing at Antram.

"You're supposed to lead us only on paid missions." Antram shook his head in disapproval. "You're not going to lead me on this ride."

"Your choice. I haven't forced anyone to do what I do, and I never will," said Frankil, rushing off with Ziyad to their horses.

"This is nonsense," Antram mumbled. Despite his protests, he would follow them in the end, Ziyad knew.

"Torches," Frankil demanded of his knights. "Put on your helms. This is going to be a dusty ride."

The Bermanians had fared well with the Murasen summer. Now they had another test with the Poison Wind. Even the sons of Murase couldn't stand the evilest sandstorm of autumn. Summer was leaving a bit early this year.

"Blast!" Bergum, riding behind Ziyad, grumbled. "How do your people live with this?"

"They stay inside their houses if they want to hide," replied Ziyad, recalling those days of childhood when his mother wouldn't allow him to go outside the house in such weather. "Or they put this on if they want to ride." He held the edge of the turban covering his mouth.

"That should be part of a song." Danis sneered.

Antram caught up with them. "A death song."

"You have no idea. The storm hasn't even started." Ziyad wasn't exaggerating. "Three more days, and you will see no more than two feet ahead."

201

The smell of smoke was unmistakable as they approached the eastern gate of the city, the clang of bells getting louder. Ziyad nudged his horse into a gallop.

"Ziyad!" Frankil called out. "I won't say this every time!"

Ziyad knew what the captain was going to tell him; they had to stay together and attack in the formation. *Curse the formation, Frankil,* Ziyad wanted to tell him. This was not a battalion in the disciplined Bermanian army, this was the Warriors' Gang.

Now Ziyad could see the smoke. At first glance, he had thought it could be a building set on fire inside, but it was the gate itself. "Those dogs!" He kicked the flanks of his horse, which was galloping already, until he reached the field in front of the gate, corpses of Murasen soldiers and nomads sprawling on the ground. Ziyad's horse had to step on the dead bodies to reach the charcoaled gate, the dusty air around him laden with the coppery scent of blood.

The warriors slowed down as they entered the city. "Looks like there was quite an unfair battle." Antram let out a deep breath of air. The endless footprints didn't require a tracker to tell the huge difference in numbers between the attackers and the defenders.

"What we encountered in the desert was just a small part of the horde," Frankil said impassively, obviously shocked by the sight as his horse stumbled over a few corpses. "Find survivors."

"You won't find any."

Atop the archers' bridge stood a good-looking Rusakian fellow. The last time Ziyad saw him, he had been a pile of broken bones.

"Blanich?" exclaimed Antram. "Why are you still here? You should be home now."

Blanich fluidly descended the bridge, making it hard to believe he was the same badly injured Rusakian Contest fighter. Seriously, Bumar was a sorcerer.

"Whatever you've come for, you should abandon it now," said Blanich. "I hope one of you is willing to share a horse with me."

Ignoring his request, Ziyad asked, "What is happening here?"

"As you see," Blanich swept a long arm at the burned gate, "blood and fire."

"What did *you* see?" Frankil asked.

Blanich sighed. "I was sleeping in that Mercy Temple when I heard the bells. I thought it was prayer time, then when I realized it was still dark outside, I hurried to see where the clamor was coming from. Hundreds of nomads were raiding the city, butchering everyone they saw, women and children no exception. They were burning everything. Even the temple I hid atop was struck with a catapult. A catapult, fellows! Those bastards almost killed me!"

"Since when have the nomads been using siege weapons?" Ziyad asked in astonishment.

"I think they have some help," Blanich said. "I'm not a Murasen, but I can tell that among the horde escorting the catapult, there are a dozen men whose embroidered outfits don't belong to those people who live in the heart of the desert."

"Where are they now?" Frankil queried.

"Everywhere. They're not disciplined troops. They attack and destroy whenever and wherever they like." Blanich looked over his shoulder. "They can be returning now."

Ziyad didn't believe that was entirely true. Those nomads who had brought a catapult to storm the city hadn't come without a plan. Whether that plan was theirs or belonged to someone else, they were here for something.

"The royal palace," Ziyad deduced. "They will attack the royal palace with their catapult. We must stop them."

"Were you even listening?" Blanich asked. "I said *hundreds* of nomads, and you're not even forty. How many nomads are you going to kill? A hundred? Still, they win, and all you will do is add more corpses to the pile behind you."

Frankil and Antram were both silent, weighing their decision. Ziyad had to admit that the Rusakian had a point.

"We don't have to kill all the nomads," Ziyad suggested. "It's their catapult that we want. Without it, the royal guards might have a chance to hold the palace until reinforcements arrive." He exchanged a look with Frankil and Antram. "What do you think?"

"We will die before we touch that catapult. It must be heavily guarded," Antram suggested.

"Siege weapons usually fall behind at the rearguard." Frankil was clearly considering the idea. "We will hit and run." He gazed at the street ahead. "Even if they engage us, their numbers will mean nothing on this narrow street as long as we stand like a steel wall."

"You heard him, brothers." Ziyad didn't want to give them a chance for hesitation. "Let's do as the captain says."

"We must stay in the formation this time," Frankil insisted, looking directly at Ziyad. "Otherwise, you may get us all killed."

Ziyad nudged his horse. "You stay here if you want. I see you don't have a horse," he said to Blanich as he went past him. Reluctantly, the Rusakian rode with one of the Murasen brothers at the end of the line.

Frankil led the gang through the street, five horses in each row. The closer they came to the Fountain Plaza at the heart of the city, the more dead bodies they came across. Houses and shops were still on fire. Even the fountain of the Plaza was broken, water flooding the ground. So much devastation for no reason.

Frankil raised his hand when he spotted a band of nomads ahead. Not more than fifty, Ziyad estimated. A dozen pushed the catapult, seven on horseback, the rest holding javelins and swords. Not the hardest battle for the gang.

"Charge!" Frankil spurred his horse into a gallop.

Ziyad roared, digging his heels into the flanks of his horse. Obviously, the stunned nomads were not expecting any resistance after defeating the city guards. While the nomads were still turning to face them, Ziyad and the brothers shocked them with their charge. Ziyad went for a nomad's neck with a mighty swing that left the dead man's head dangling. While the horse was still galloping, Ziyad sliced the throat of a nomad on foot with another perfectly-timed strike. Two more nomads growled, but before they might swing their swords, Ziyad's horse rammed into them, knocking them out. "You!"

Ziyad pulled the reins of his horse to halt it right in front of a horrified man clad in an embroidered outfit. *The strangers Blanich was referring to.* "Make the slightest move, and you die!" Ziyad pointed his sword at the stranger, backing him into a corner.

"I'm not with them," the stranger whimpered. "Please, don't kill me!"

Ziyad stole a glance at the narrow battlefield behind him. His brothers were already done with the mounted nomads, and now they were slaying the ones on foot. "The strangers!" Ziyad cried. "We need them alive!" *For now.*

Ziyad's folks needed two more minutes to kill the last of the nomads. Herding another surviving stranger, Bergum approached Ziyad on horseback, Danis and Antram following him. "Do you want to interrogate them this time?" Bergum gave Ziyad a sly smile.

"Mercy! We didn't kill anybody!" cried the new prisoner.

"It's not hard to recognize the eastern accent in your tongue." Ziyad glared at the two prisoners. "I wonder why the men of Shezar would fight alongside the nomads."

"Forget him," Antram urged, pointing to the approaching dark mass of men and beasts at the end of the narrow street. "More nomads are coming ahead."

"Listen!" Frankil demanded, hundreds of hooves clopping *behind* them. "They're trying to surround us!"

Trying? They already did. "Destroy that thing!" Ziyad pointed at the catapult. "We won't die in vain!"

"LISTEN, ALL OF YOU!" Frankil bellowed. "This cursed battle is not over yet! Half of us join Bergum to protect our rearguard! The rest stay with me to face those bastards at the front! No one dies tonight!"

Death is not the end, it's a journey, Ziyad's uncle had told him once. His uncle had better be right.

33. MASOLON

Two weeks and a couple of days had passed since Masolon left Kahora. Since he last saw Sania. He missed her, he had to admit. Yes, a battle raged in his head.

I do not miss her for real. I must wake up.

All right, I will use more proper words; you would like to see her.

That is right.

You want to see her.

That is also right.

Then you miss her.

You got me cornered. Maybe you are right.

Yes, I am. I am always right! Let us ride to the castle of Arkan.

But how can I explain my unexpected visit to her? To her brother?

"Hey you!"

A yell snapped him back to reality, where he was on his way back to Kahora, a caravan on his left by some distance.

"Something wrong?" Masolon called loudly.

A horseman left the caravan and approached Masolon. "Are you heading to Kahora?" the man asked nervously.

"Who are you, and why do you want to know?"

"Kahora is in total chaos. A thousand nomads have stormed the city, burning it to ashes!"

Masolon knew he must be gaping at him like a fool. *Nomads? Inside Kahora? How did that happen?*

"Unless you have a family to worry about, there is no need to go to the city now," the man from the caravan said. "Even if you have one, there is nothing you can do."

"Where is the army of this kingdom?"

"We are not sure. But escapees from Kahora confirm that the remaining troops have retreated to protect the royal palace, leaving the whole city in turmoil. Even King Rasheed is trapped there, unable to do anything for himself or for the princesses who have just arrived from Arkan."

Masolon's eyes widened when he heard the name of that castle. What could be the odds that Sania was *not* among those princesses?

The man's fellows from the caravan called out to him, urging him to return. "We must leave now before the Oasis gets crowded with other caravans," said the man.

"The Oasis?"

"That's where we replenish our supplies. Not far from here. You should come with us."

Masolon paused for a moment. "You say we may meet many caravans there?"

"Perhaps." The man was growing impatient.

"Alright, I am coming with you." Masolon wheeled his horse and joined the caravan. Along their brief journey, Masolon barely spoke while the other horsemen were blathering on about the nomads' raid on Kahora. Some believed they were the Ghosts, who had come to avenge their dead. A few argued that the Ghosts were immortal, so even the Murasen army wouldn't be able to stop them. One suggested fleeing to Bermania, another doubted the idea would work. After they were done with Murase, the Ghosts would unleash their wrath upon the other kingdoms until all Gorania was doomed. It was the Warrior's Gang to blame, the caravan master concluded. Masolon didn't bother convincing him otherwise.

The Oasis didn't exist on Ramel's map because it wasn't a real oasis. The haven of caravans in their long journeys was a two-story building with a huge store in its backyard. The whole place looked like a garrison with the palisade walls surrounding it and the eight caravans waiting for their turns to get their supplies.

The man who was yelling and cursing at the merchants seemed to be the master of the Oasis. Masolon wasn't sure if he could reason with that ill-tempered man, but at the same time, he couldn't wait until the master calmed down.

"We arrived here first. It should be our turn!"

"We come from Shezar! We still have a long way ahead before we reach Kalensi! These mediocre quantities are not enough."

"You are asking too much for this meat! It's too dry!"

The merchants never stopped complaining and bargaining, the guards of their caravans chattering and ranting in the backyard. Silencing this crowd wouldn't be an easy task, but Masolon had no other choice. He found a barrel at the corner and dragged it near the hustle.

"Listen to me, people!" Standing over the barrel, Masolon waved both hands. From the way they looked at him, he knew he had piqued their attention. "Kahora is falling to the nomads, and the only hope to save the city is us! If we *all* do not move right now together, Kahora will be doomed for good!"

Most of the audience hummed in disapproval. "We do not have to involve ourselves in this. Let us wait for the Murasen army to come and settle this issue," suggested one of the merchants.

"I can assure you that if we wait for that army, there will be no Kahora anymore," said Masolon. "Those nomads are besieging the royal palace, and we don't know for how long it will stand."

"Why should we listen to this man?" the master of the Oasis yelled, pointing at Masolon. "Who's him anyway?"

"I am Masolon," he replied. "The leader of the Warrior's Gang."

He saw the impact of his announcement on the horsemen of the caravan he had come with.

"I don't care about you or your gang," the master spat. "Listen, son, this is no place for speeches. I have a business to run here, and you are interrupting it."

"When Kahora is razed to the ground, you will have no business to run, clever man," said a voice from behind Masolon. A merchant had just arrived followed by forty guards. A turban hid his face to protect it from the sandy wind, but Masolon could tell he wasn't a Murasen. Actually, he sounded familiar.

"This man is trying to save your coin," the merchant said to the owner. "No Kahora means that caravans will take other routes very far away from your lovely *Oasis*."

The owner frowned, realizing the mysterious merchant was right.

"Why do you all hire these guards?" the merchant continued. "Are you paying them to travel with you and that's it? Those brigands are our nightmares, remember? Now it is our chance to join forces and lay waste to those bastards once and for all."

No one protested this time. The mysterious man's speech was working. Better than Masolon's speech, to say the least.

"Know this, fellow merchants. If we don't crush those devils today, they will hunt our caravans tomorrow, one by one," the merchant went on. "I can see here around two hundred and fifty men. Led by a gallant warrior, our army can end that nightmare for good."

All eyes turned to Masolon when the mysterious man pointed to him. "This man is the most dauntless and ferocious warrior I have ever met. He is the only one who can lead us in this battle."

The other merchants hummed, looking from Masolon to the mysterious man.

"Am I right, Masolon?" the merchant asked, approaching him.

"You have just come in time." A smile slipped over Masolon's face when he recognized whose voice it was. "Good to see you again, Galardi."

34. SANIA

Dawn was coming, yet the clamoring nomads outside the palace gave Sania's mind more reasons to be restless.

Sitting by her mother's bed, she watched the healer check her mother's pulse. An hour ago he had given the sick old lady a potion to help her sleep. It had stopped the coughing, yet her mother's chest kept wheezing.

The healer's furrowed brow worried Sania even more. "What is wrong?" she asked, but she got no answer.

The healer exhaled. "Emm…I…but…"

Why was everybody in this damned palace slow and thick-headed? That healer needed remedy himself. "But what?" She would yell at him if it were not for her sleeping mother.

"I don't like to be a bad news bearer until I…emm…make sure…"

"What bad news?" Sania asked, alarmed. "Speak up."

"Don't get me wrong, milady. It's the pulse. I believe it's…emm…a bit slow."

"A bit slow?" she echoed, not knowing whether she should fret because it was slow, or feel relieved it was *a bit*.

"Slower than it was one hour ago."

"So?" She waited for him to elaborate. "Sleep slows pulse, right?"

He lowered his eyes. "She's not sleeping."

"What? But the medicine you gave her—"

"Alleviates the cough…emm…but doesn't induce sleep."

"Then do something!" She glared at him. "You can still do something for her pulse!" *Oh Lord, help me! Where is Bumar now?*

"I will try more potions." The healer rose to his feet and checked the metallic box he had put on the table. He took out a flacon containing a red liquid and a flask with a brown one. "It can't be worse," he muttered.

Fadwa pushed the door open. Before Sania might rebuke her for entering without a permission as if she was stepping into a barn, Fadwa started, "I'm so sorry, milady. But the King has given his orders to sneak all the women out of the palace."

"What happened? Did the nomads break into the palace?"

"Not yet." Fadwa shook her head. "But everyone believes it's only a matter of time. They say the royal guards here are not enough to hold those wild masses off. I also heard them mention something about a catapult."

"I don't think it's safe to leave the palace at this time."

"Those savages will slaughter everyone in this palace."

It would be better if those nomads *just* killed them. Worse things could happen to Sania if she fell into their filthy hands.

"How can we even leave the palace if we want to?" Sania asked. "Those dogs are right at our gates."

"Through a secret passage that takes us outside the city five miles away from the western wall, milady. Her Majesty has left already."

Sania glanced at her sick mother. "Lady Ramia can't go anywhere, as you see."

"I will look for two guards to put Lady Ramia on a sedan chair." Surprisingly, Fadwa was resourceful now. Danger must have awakened her thick mind. Still, Sania wasn't sure about the idea. Running away in the desert didn't sound less dangerous than staying in the besieged palace.

"You must decide now, milady." Fadwa was nervous, and who could blame her? "Soon we might not find an available guard in this palace. His Majesty has already mustered most of his soldiers at the front gate."

Last time it was her brother's decision, and he was wrong. This time, she had to make the right decision. "Get those guards." Sania motioned her maid to go. Part of her heart didn't feel well, though.

Turning to the healer, she found him petrified. "What were you doing?" she asked. "Watching me? You should have given her the medicine already."

"Forgive me, milady. The news has just…emm…overwhelmed my mind." The healer put one drop from the red potion into an empty pot, and then he poured a little from the brown potion. "Lady Ramia will need me to…ahem…take care of her health in her escape, right?"

He was looking for a place among the women to save himself. "What about taking care of her health now?" Sania snapped.

The healer gave her a faint smile and resumed his work. The bowl almost slipped from his hands when they heard the *BOOM* coming from outside.

"Merciful Lord! What could that be?" Sania gasped.

"I'm afraid that's the catapult she was talking about." His eyes grew large in terror. "Nothing can prevent those barbarians from smashing the gate of the palace."

Now Sania knew what she wanted to do: get out of here. "Keep working!" she commanded.

The healer looked nervous as he stirred the mixture he had just prepared. Using a narrow glass tube he sucked the liquid up, but before it reached his lips, he placed his finger over the tube mouth. He carefully placed the tube in her sleeping mother's nose and blew through the tube to push the liquid through.

Sania grimaced. "What was that?"

"An attempt to refresh her lungs and heart," the healer said, then repeated the same process with the other nostril.

Fadwa arrived at last, two guards following her with a stretcher. *It's not a sedan chair, but hopefully, it will do.* The two men gently laid her mother on the canvas surface. Lifting the stretcher from both sides, the two guards went outside the chamber.

"They know the way," Fadwa reassured her. "Let's go."

Sania nodded to the healer to join them, a smile of relief slipping over his face. The guards swiftly went upstairs as if they were carrying an empty stretcher. "Be careful! Watch your pace!" Sania cried behind them, and then asked Fadwa, "Have you readied a howdah for us?"

"It will be difficult to do so in the current circumstances, milady," replied the maid.

"The howdah is not a good idea," the healer pointed out. "Camels are too slow. We'll be easily spotted."

"We're not just going to put her on a horse, are we?" Sania asked disapprovingly.

"I'm afraid we have no other option…"

The hallway, as well as all the chambers they passed upstairs, was abandoned. Except for those two carrying her mother, Sania hadn't caught a glimpse of a guard's shadow since she left her chamber. Fadwa wasn't exaggerating the situation at the gate then. It could even be worse than she described.

"Who is that genius who constructed an escape passage upstairs?" Sania asked impatiently.

Fadwa kept her eyes on the guards ahead. "It is built as such to be close to the royal wing."

Sania was too hurried to entertain her eyes with the sight of the crystal chandeliers and the chiseled columns of the hall they passed through. Only now did she realize she was in the royal wing. It was clear that the residents of this wing had fled already.

Fadwa grabbed a torch from the wall as they entered a dark, windowless bedchamber, the air inside packed with dust.

"Mother won't stand that," Sania mumbled, her eyes on the frames of those hasty guards. "Watch your step!" She was worried they might stumble over something in this darkness. No one seemed to be paying heed to her complaints as they moved toward a huge fake fireplace, which acted like a slightly open door for a dark passage behind it.

The downward incline of the passage helped them move faster with less effort. Having Fadwa's torch as the only source of light in this darkness, Sania didn't stop asking the guards to watch their steps. But after many sharp turns to the right and to the left, she didn't bother reminding them as she felt dizzy, the dusty air filling her chest.

They took a while until they reached the straight part of the passage. No inclination, no turns. "We didn't shut the passage entrance," Sania suddenly remembered. "Those savages might follow us if they find that dusty room."

"There are others who still need to flee, milady," said Fadwa. "The King himself is still behind us in the palace."

Sania was surprised. "I thought he had escaped already with his…"

She thought she had heard a faint womanly scream, and obviously she wasn't the only one who did. Fadwa, the healer, the two guards; all stopped without saying a word, even holding their breaths to make sure of what they heard. A few moments later, another faint feminine scream broke the silence.

"Merciful Lord! Where are these screams coming from?" Sania wondered. In her best wishes those shrieks were coming from inside the palace through the thin passage walls. Although none of her companions answered, she got an answer anyway. And that answer was a horrifying cry echoing in the narrow passage.

A cry of a nomad.

35. ZIYAD

Revenge would never bring the gone loved ones back, his uncle had told him once. The old man was probably just worried the idea was consuming his restless nephew.

The first gift his uncle had given him was a saber, so heavy that little Ziyad couldn't lift it from the ground with his child's arms. The child had become a violent, reckless lad, and the uncle regretted what he had sown. That was why the second and the last gift was a harp. It was true, the harp hadn't avenged his father, but it had introduced the reckless lad to an overwhelming new world. A world of music, laughter, and festive nights. The harp had let him set foot in fancy palaces and boisterous taverns, chatter with noble ladies and wenches.

But nights were not festive any longer with the shortness of coin. Playing the harp was not paying off well, and that was when he thought of the other thing he was skillful at: Wielding a sword. He had heard he could earn some silver just for wielding a wooden sword. Becoming a Contest fighter was his next move, but that man from nowhere called Masolon had brought him back to what he was destined to do; avenge his dead father.

"They say your memories flash in your mind before you die," Ziyad muttered, smiling at Frankil, but it appeared the grim-faced Bermanian captain wasn't ready to die now.

"Brothers of the gang! Chaaaargggeee!"

The sonorous voice came from behind them. The man from nowhere was here, in Kahora, in this very street. And the best part was: he was not alone. Looking over his shoulder, Ziyad saw Masolon leading a horde of more than two hundred horsemen through the main street of Kahora.

"You heard him!" Frankil raised his sword, addressing his band of men. "Charge!"

More than a thousand hooves thundered in the street as the two big hordes of horses were ready to clash. With an iron grip, Ziyad held the reins the moment his horse raised its forelimbs. The nomad's horse galloping in the opposite direction did the same before they collided. Ziyad's sword reached the nomad's horse first, the rider falling. The second strike chopped off the nomad's neck. The third slashed another nomad's abdomen. The fourth and fifth struck two more horses. The neighs of dead and wounded horses were higher than men's roars and shrieks. In such a narrow battlefield, it was easier to hit those poor horses either deliberately or by accident than their riders. It was so narrow that Frankil and his knights wouldn't be able to attack in their wedge formation. Today there were no formations; only a mass of horsemen pushing their way through another mass.

Ziyad recognized the roars of Frankil, Antram, Danis, and Bergum, the vanguard of this army. Nothing had been heard from Masolon since his entrance. Whether he was still stuck at their rearguard in that narrow battlefield, or it was Ziyad who had pushed his way too far forward; there was no way to look back to make sure where Masolon had gone. All Ziyad could see now was the next nomad he was going to slay or the swung blade that was going to kill him.

"Chaaarge!"

Masolon was back. But he wasn't behind Ziyad this time; his voice rang from behind the nomads' lines.

"The sly bastard!" Excited, Ziyad listened to the sweetest thunder ever. The thunder of Masolon's horsemen charging at the Ghosts from their arses. If the Ghosts had arses.

Gaps appeared in the faltering nomads' lines. "Punch them hard, brothers!" Ziyad urged his horse forward through the gaps. Masolon howled from the other side, his voice louder and closer. Ziyad couldn't wait to shake hands with him.

"Yield!" Masolon bellowed at the last dozen nomads, pointing his greatsword at them. As they found themselves between a rock and a hard place, the desert dogs dropped their weapons and raised their hands.

"I don't think I could be happier to see you, brother!" Ziyad nodded toward Masolon.

"I hope I am not too late," said Masolon.

Frankil nodded as well. "Just in time, brave warrior."

Masolon gazed at the street, the columns of his army cramming it. "I heard there were more nomads than that."

"Those we have defeated are barely one-third of their men," Blanich said, coming forward.

Masolon looked surprised when he saw the Rusakian, a smile slipping over his face. "The nobleman himself is here. I never thought I would cross paths with you again."

"This time could be the last if we don't leave this city now," said Blanich.

"Not with those nomads still here," Ziyad insisted.

"Remember, brothers," said Antram. "We only want their catapult, and we have it now."

"That was before Masolon's arrival with reinforcements," said Frankil.

"Still, we are outnumbered three to one," Blanich reminded them.

"Sounds like a fair ratio to me." Masolon shrugged. "Especially, if we can work that thing." He nodded toward the catapult standing at the end of the street.

"Danis can," said Frankil, looking a bit confused. "But what do you want to do with a catapult? Do you think we might need to storm the palace if it falls to them?"

"That thing throws stones from a long range, right?" said Masolon. "While we hold them at the front, Danis shall throw stones on their middle ranks and their rearguard."

"Flaming stones, brother," Ziyad added, liking the idea. "We can persuade our new *friends* from Shezar to help Danis."

"Moving that catapult is going to take some time," Frankil said. And if the nomads broke into the palace, the catapult would be useless.

"Then we hold those bastards until you arrive," Masolon told Danis. "How many men do you need?"

Danis thought for a moment then said, "Twenty."

"So be it. To the palace, brothers!" Masolon waved at all warriors of the gang as well as the horsemen he had brought with him. Their small army was surely outnumbered, but Ziyad believed in their chances to save this city. With Masolon's return to lead them, they were fearless no matter how low the odds were. Today they were the real ghosts.

36. SANIA

Sania tried to forget her heavy legs as she hurriedly ascended the inclined passage on her way back to the palace. Fadwa and the healer were right ahead of her, the guards carrying her mother behind her by some distance.

The cries of their chasers never stopped. *They are terrorizing us,* Sania thought. *Those bastards know we are here.*

They were closing in on them, their shouts getting louder. "Are we there yet, Fadwa?" Sania asked breathlessly. "Where is the damned door?"

Fadwa didn't answer, probably saving her breath for something more worthy. Sania had better do the same.

"Here they are!" the healer yelled, looking over his shoulder.

"Keep moving! Don't look back!" Sania was scared her feet would fail her if she saw those nomads from a close range.

Fadwa and the healer made it to the door, Sania joining them a few moments later. The First Maid held the torch to illuminate the way for the two guards. At the end of the flickering light of Fadwa's torch, Sania spied those shadows right behind the guards.

"Faster! Faster!" she cried, making way for the guards to pass through. The moment they stepped into the room with the stretcher, she urged the healer and Fadwa, "Push! Push! Push!" The three of them gave the heavy door—the fake fireplace—their best. Before they could close the door completely, the intruders pushed from the other side. "Help here!" Sania cried. The two guards put the stretcher on the ground and hurried to help them. Ten arms were pushing the door now, but the arms on the other side seemed to be more and stronger. The nomads were gradually forcing the door open.

"Take the sick lady out of here!" one of the guards urged Sania. "We will slow them!"

She wasn't sure what she should say to the brave guard. All she did was nod silently to him then she turned to Fadwa and the healer. "Quickly, follow me."

The healer picked the stretcher up from the front side, Sania and Fadwa lifting from the back. "Move, move, move!" she urged the healer, who was taking the lead as they exited the dusty bedchamber. "To the stairs! To the stairs!"

Not far away from the damned room they had just left, she heard the cries of the two valiant guards. Nothing would hinder those savages now from catching them. Neither she, Fadwa, nor the healer could outrun those beasts. Their doom was inevitable.

"Hold this." Sania grabbed her maid's arm and made her grasp the handle Sania was holding. "I will distract them. You two, hide in any of these chambers and barricade it well."

The terrified maid stared at her.

"Go! Now!" Sania hissed.

The healer and her maidservant hurried with the stretcher toward the nearest chamber to them. After making sure that the nomads hadn't seen them hiding, Sania sprinted across the hall, hitting the floor hard with her feet to make those dogs hear her. She could tell her reckless move was working when she heard their footsteps following her.

She reached the stairs and hurried to the first floor, taking rights and lefts without knowing where they would take her to. The only thing on her mind was running as fast as she could. Being caught by such barbarians would be a horrible fate for her. Out of exhaustion and fear, her heart pounded vigorously, the echo of her chasers' footsteps getting closer. Her legs started to fail her, and she knew she wouldn't be able to keep the same pace for long.

Dashing downstairs, she pushed a door that led to the front courtyard. With her whirling mind, she couldn't decide which direction she should take in that vast area. The menacing voices of her pursuers were getting clearer and she had to act quickly. Having not enough time to consider any better options, she went up the nearest stone stairs adjacent to the palace wall.

It was too late when she realized how difficult it was to run on such broken stone steps. Turning back was not an option as her pursuers were right downstairs. She stumbled a couple of times, and the gap that separated her from her tireless chasers was closing. One of the two nomads dove and caught her foot, falling with her on the stone steps. Lying on her back, Sania screamed in horror and shove the attacker with both legs. The unbalanced nomad tried desperately to cling to the steps, but he fell to the ground, landing on his head.

"You wench!" the other nomad growled.

Terrified, she pushed to her feet and continued her way up until she reached the top. "No!" she screamed. The stairs led her to the top of a keep tower. It was a dead end.

The last nomad reached the top as well. He drew his sword, scanning her with his eyes like a predator that had cornered his prey. With parapets behind her, the only way out was going past that pig.

"I don't need this." He threw his sword aside and carefully approached her. "There is no pleasure in a dead body."

37. MASOLON

As Blanich had told them, too many nomads were still there in the city, making long columns of their men in the narrow street leading to the palace. Yet Masolon was relieved when he saw they were still *outside* the palace. Sania was safe so far, and that was the only thing that mattered.

The archers atop the walls of the palace kept the nomads away by some distance, only a plaza separating them from the main gate. If Masolon pushed the nomads to the plaza, they would be in the archers' range.

Masolon raised his hand to stop his men. "We're giving them a chance to regroup," Ziyad snapped. A fearless warrior, but sometimes a bit rushed.

"Look at their numbers," said Masolon. "In this street, we can only stun a bunch of them before they rally the rest of their men."

"So what are we going to do?" Antram asked. "Wait for them to attack us?"

"We are in no hurry for the time being." *As long as Sania is safe inside the palace.* "And Danis has not arrived yet." Masolon looked back again, but not a sign of the catapult yet.

A nomad advanced ahead of his horde, gazing at Masolon's army.

That was probably their leader, assessing the opposing troops. The nomad must be wondering what Masolon's army was waiting for too.

"You brought that from Paril?" Frankil glanced at the new greatsword strapped to Masolon's back.

"I like its weight and length." That explanation would do for now. No need to bother his brothers with his childhood aspirations.

"Most of the Bermanian infantry use it two-handed in their encounters. It will be much more difficult for you to make swift maneuvers with such a hefty blade."

"Do not worry, my friend." Masolon gave Frankil a lopsided smile. "Just mind your distance when I swing that thing. I do not want to hurt you or your horse with its long blade."

The nomad leader roared, hundreds of his men howling, raising their swords behind him.

"It is happening, brothers!" Masolon bellowed. "Give them nothing but the taste of your steel!" He unstrapped his greatsword, hauling it with one hand, his army answering the nomads with a louder noise. The clash was starting with a battle of roars, both sides showing their guts, but no one wanted to be the first to strike. Masolon had his reasons, but he wondered about those nomads. Did they hope that Masolon's army would fall back upon seeing the nomads' numbers? Those fools had no idea.

"Come on, Masolon," Ziyad urged. "We can win this, even without that catapult."

"I have no doubt," Masolon said. "But if we have a chance to lay more waste to our enemy, why not do it?"

The nomads moved at last.

"Blood and steel!" Masolon spurred his horse onward. "Chaaarge!"

He held the greatsword horizontally the way he would hold a lance, kicking his stallion's flanks repeatedly, urging it to gallop before he collided with his first opponent. With this speed, his sword would tear a horse apart with a single strike.

The nomads' leader rushed toward him. Masolon drove his

greatsword right into his chest without touching his horse. With a backhanded swing, he slashed a horse and chopped off a nomad's leg. Yes, the weapon was heavy, but with its long reach, Masolon's opponents had no chance to clash swords with him. His greatsword reached them first while they were still extending their arms to make a swing.

"*Catapult!*" Cries from behind him announced Danis's arrival. The creaks of the wooden arm reached Masolon's ears when the catapult started hurling flaming stones in the middle of the long column of nomads. In this narrow street, there was no escape for those dogs. The flying fireballs always found at least one nomad to land on. Masolon wondered what those screeches were for. A nomad shouldn't find time to screech before the fireball crushed him. Perhaps it was those who survived the horrible fate.

"Hold your ground!" Masolon commanded as he slashed a neck with the tip of his blade.

"We need to push them to the archers at the walls!" Frankil yelled.

"Not yet!" Masolon wanted to keep his men away from the zone toward which the flying fireballs plummeted with ominous *cracks*. The nomads were trapped. If they advanced, the swords of Masolon's horsemen would be waiting for them. If they retreated, they would be in the archers' range. If they remained where they were, the fireballs would crush their bones. The nomads' only way out was to push Masolon and his fellows toward the catapult.

The gang was like a wall of steel. With their blades stabbing and swinging nonstop, Masolon and the brothers at the vanguard were breaking the nomads' lines one after the other. "Not yet!" Masolon bellowed every time he spotted his troops pushing forward too much toward the fireballs' range.

Even for his muscular arm, the greatsword was still heavy. His swings were now a bit slower as the hefty blade started to exhaust his arm. No horseman from either side dared to come close to him as long as he kept swinging that magnificent steel craft.

"*We're out of stones!*"

Masolon heard the announcement repeated from the lines behind him until it reached him. Now was the time to punch those nomads.

"Atttaaack!" Masolon bellowed. From the sweet whizzing of arrows that came shortly after, he could tell that the nomads had fallen back until their rearguard became in the archers' range.

Frankil and his knights spurred their horses onward and went past Masolon. Moving onward together, the Bermanians formed an iron fist that pushed the nomads backward at a faster pace. "If you don't mind, you're hindering us with your huge sword." Ziyad nudged his horse toward the frontline to join the Bermanians. Maybe his Murasen fellow was right. His greatsword wasn't the right blade for such a narrow battlefield. But it had done some damage, hadn't it?

Masolon's army was getting closer to the palace walls when the gates were open. The archers halted their deadly volleys as heavily armored knights came out. They were not numerous, yet they shattered the nomads when they charged at their rearguard. Those desert men wearing light outfits were meant to fight in an open battlefield, to hit their slower opponents and run. A city with narrow streets could be a trap for them; they should have seen that coming.

The Ghosts were fearless warriors, Masolon would give them that. Refusing to surrender, they kept fighting to the last man, trying to fend off the army tearing apart their front and the armored knights shredding their rearguard. It did not take long before the street became a river of fresh, warm corpses. The crows cawed in the sky above the city, waiting impatiently for the battle to end so they could feast on the flesh of the dead.

Masolon's men, Bermanians and Murasens alike, roared, celebrating their victory. The Murasen knights of the royal palace, as well as the archers, raised their hands in the air as they joined the celebration. Hauling his greatsword, Masolon saluted the caravan guards, who had followed him from the Oasis. They raised their swords, hailing him. Truth be told, his brothers were the ones who had done most of the fighting. Still, acknowledging those mercenaries wouldn't hurt.

Making his way through the clamoring crowd, Galardi approached Masolon on horseback. "I see you have your own army at last." The merchant grinned. "Still interested in joining me?"

Masolon wanted to tell him all he had been through to get the job done. His consuming training in the Pit. His vain journey to Kalensi to meet him. His encounter with Skandivian raiders. His rides in the snow and through the rainy woods. Different paths that eventually took Masolon to what he had been looking for.

"I know we shall make a trade one day," Masolon said.

Galardi acknowledged with a nod. "You know where you can find me." He wheeled his horse and returned to the crowd, motioning his men to move on with him.

"Who leads this horde?" a royal knight cried.

Masolon passed through the celebrating warriors until he reached the plaza in front of the gates. "That is me, Masolon." The brown color of the Murasen knight's armor matched that of his eyes, a leopard decorating his breastplate. "And those are the Warriors' Gang." He extended his arm toward his brothers.

"You and your gang fought well today," said the Murasen knight. "I'm Qasem, Captain of the Royal Guard of His Majesty." He nodded his chin pointedly toward a man in a golden cloak standing atop the bulwark, his hands on his waist. The only person who still kept his calm in this bustle, and now he was nodding. He was nodding to Masolon.

"Well, greeting His Majesty for sending his royal knights would be a nice gesture." Masolon feigned a smile. *A nice gesture indeed. Sending his valiant knights after victory became a possibility.*

Masolon nudged his horse to a trot, going past Qasem. Greeting that king was none of his concern. All he wanted was to make sure that Sania was here and safe. She was the only reason to fight for this city.

Sinking in his thoughts, he barely noticed he had already crossed the open palace gates, and now he was ascending the stone steps to salute Rasheed, King of Murase.

The black-haired king looked younger than Masolon had imagined. "We are grateful to you, brave warrior." Rasheed smiled. "Or shall I call you Masolon?"

"It is an honor for me, sire." Masolon nodded. "It was your wisdom that concluded the battle by sending your brave knights," he lied.

"You show too much nobility for a foreigner who comes from nowhere," Rasheed said, "as far as I know."

Masolon wouldn't deny he felt flattered. "I come from nowhere indeed. But from where I come, we always honor our chief."

"You speak like a lord, yet you fight like a barbarian. I wish all my commanders were like you." Rasheed glanced at an armored man standing next to him, the Murasen leopard sigil decorating his breastplate. The man, who seemed to be one of the king's commanders, looked down. "You and your gang of warriors should be rewarded for your bravery."

"This is too generous of you, sire." Masolon grinned, recalling his last meeting with Lord Feras who had doubts about the gang. Now, the same gang was recognized by the King himself. Could things be any better?

"Nomads!"

A cry from the king's commander brought Masolon back to reality. All of a sudden, nomads were up the bulwark, slaughtering the Murasen archers who were obviously not competent hand-to-hand fighters as their fierce opponents. One after another, they fell like young trees blown away by heavy, sandy desert wind. The warning urged the Murasen knights standing outside the palace to return, but it was too late. The nomads had locked and barricaded the gate already.

"Those dogs!" the commander growled. "We are trapped here!" He drew his sword and hurried to aid the archers at the left flank. Where was the fool going? Wasn't he going to protect his king? Masolon found himself alone, standing against six nomads. All archers at his flank were slain.

"I am not afraid of you, bastards!" cried Rasheed, unsheathing his golden-hilted saber from its jeweled scabbard. "Come on, you filthy pigs!"

The king impressed Masolon with his swordplay. In return, Masolon drew his sword with his right hand and held his steel shield with his left. The nomads must have thought they had cornered him. "He who wants to die first advances!" With his steel shield, Masolon received a strike from a nomad before lunging forward, stabbing his opponent in the stomach. He swiftly swung his hard shield, breaking the jaw of another attacker, following it with a deadly blow with his sword. Two nomads fell in two seconds. As for Rasheed, it turned out he wasn't easy prey at all. The agile king blocked an attacking blade with his golden-hilted sword before turning it fluidly, opening a way for his dagger to dive into the nomad's throat.

There was not much space for maneuvers on that narrow bulwark. Masolon slew a nomad, whose blade was locked with Rasheed's, and at the same time used his shield to block two deadly nomadic swords. Roaring, Masolon charged, holding his shield, edging one of his two foes off the bulwark. The remaining opponent didn't live long enough to hear his fellow's bones crushed by the fall. With an overhead strike, Masolon smashed his skull. The nomads' attack at Masolon's flank was thwarted at last.

On the other flank, the case was different.

Upon seeing the king's commander struggle against two opponents, Masolon sprinted to aid him. The commander managed to slay one of his adversaries, but unfortunately, a deadly strike from the other nomad ended his story.

"I am ending your filthy bloodline now!" Masolon threw his heavy shield and gripped the greatsword with both hands.

"This is not your fight, foreigner. This is between us and them." The last nomad approached with caution, probably weighing the range of Masolon's blade. "You shouldn't be fighting alongside those bastards."

Masolon kept his eyes on his opponent, watching out for any

sudden moves, his ears attentive to all sounds around him to warn him of any attacks from the back. "The only bastard I see right now is you."

"I'm not surprised," the nomad said. "You are nobody but a mercenary who kills for gold, no matter the side he fights for."

Masolon curled his lip in disdain. "I kill thieves like you for nothing."

"Thieves?" The nomad scowled. "What do you know, foreigner, to say so? What do you know? Those spoiled lords whom you are serving are the real thieves. We are the rightful lords of the Murasen lands."

"Your lordship ends today."

Both of them could hear the Murasen memluks ramming the barricaded palace gate. Rasheed was on his way down the wall to open the gates from inside and let his forces in.

"Can you hear that, desert scum?" Masolon nodded toward the gate. "You are alone here. After I am done with you, I will hunt every remaining nomad in this desert!"

"The desert you're talking about belongs to us!" The nomad lunged forward with his blade toward Masolon, trying to take him by surprise, but Masolon swiftly blocked the strike with his sword. The nomad growled, swinging his blade over his head, but again, the two swords locked together for two seconds. Kicking the nomad below his belly, Masolon forced him to step back.

"Where were you when our ancestors were slaughtered while defending their water wells?" cried the frenzied nomad. "Every town and village is built on the corpses of our great grandfathers! How much glory do you find in that?"

"Nonsense!" Masolon glared at the nomad, waiting for him to attack. "What was the sin of the innocent people you killed?"

"What was the sin of our ancestors?" the nomad countered.

"Being born as a son to a murderer does not make you a murderer yourself. You cannot punish someone for the guilt of someone else." *I killed the last one I told him that.*

"Yes, I can! That someone lives in *my* house, which was built on *my* land! Those trade caravans that you are guarding do not offer the fair price for that!"

"You want a fair price? Here it is!" Masolon charged, the nomad managing to block his strikes. With Masolon's heavy sword, it wasn't easy to outpace the agile nomad. After a few clashes of the two blades, the nomad was the one on the offensive now, displaying more skill than Masolon had expected.

Masolon bent down to evade the nomad's blade before he chopped off the nomad's right leg with one massive swing. Howling in agony, the nomad squirmed on the ground. Masolon stood at the head of his fallen foe, watching him die slowly. If the pain didn't kill him, the copious bleeding would. Maybe he deserved a more merciful death, and maybe not. He could be no different from the savages who had reduced Masolon's village to ashes.

We cannot be like them.

Masolon had promised he wouldn't be his father. "You do not deserve mercy, scum." He gave the tortured nomad one last look. Holding his greatsword—his own Erloss—upside down, he thrust it right into the nomad's heart to end his screaming and suffering forever.

Rasheed was still struggling to unbar the barricaded gate on his own. Masolon strapped his greatsword to his back, picked up his steel shield, and headed to the stone steps to give the king a hand. Before he took one step downstairs, he heard that feminine shriek.

"Sania!" Masolon recognized her terrified voice. He turned, scanning the whole area with his eyes until he found her trapped at the top of a distant keep tower. His blood boiled when he saw a nomad approach her. Without thinking twice, Masolon nocked an arrow and aimed, pulling the bowstring. He had never shot from such a distance, but by any means, that pig must not lay a finger on her. Tightening his grip on his bow to keep it steady, he loosed the arrow and followed it with another. The first arrow got the job done, the second hitting the bastard's shoulder.

Masolon hurried downstairs and sprinted toward the tower.

"Masolon?" Rasheed called out to him.

Heedless, Masolon left the king behind him and dashed across the abandoned yard.

Sania was still up there when he reached the stone steps leading up to the tower. He hurried up the stairs and found her sitting on her haunches staring at the dead pig sprawled on the ground at her feet.

"Sania!" A few seconds later, he realized he hadn't addressed her with her title, dispensing with the absurd courtesy. "It is alright, Sania." He carefully approached her, his voice low. "It is only me…Masolon…the foreigner." He took her cold hand to help her up. His first time to touch her, and she wasn't even looking at him.

Sania's legs trembled as she tried to stand with Masolon's help. "Is he dead?" Her voice was tremulous, her eyes fixed on the nomad's corpse.

"He is. It is over now, Sania." Masolon had his arm around her waist, trying to help her walk, but the shocked girl couldn't take one step forward, not with those shaky legs. "Let me take you out of here." He scooped her up into his arms and carefully descended the stone steps. He wasn't dreaming; she was so close to him her warm breath kissed his neck. An awkward feeling overwhelmed his heart. Awkward yet thrilling. Masolon almost forgot the clashing blades, the neighing horses, the fireballs, the blood; everything. With only him and her, he was just starting a new day now.

Not knowing where he should go, he stepped down into the yard, Sania still in his arms.

"Mother!" Her hazel eyes flew open and she pulled herself up. "I must find her!"

Masolon let her down, making sure she could stand on her own. The moment her feet touched the ground, she scurried toward the palace. "Wait!" He hurried after her and caught her by the hand. "You cannot go anywhere on your own until we make sure the palace is safe."

Sania pulled her hand away. "Leave me be! I must find my

mother!" The stubborn girl ignored his warning and dashed away.

"Not without me." Masolon drew his sword and followed her to the palace. He kept his eyes and ears open as the reckless girl raced up the stairs and strode through corridors and hallways without taking into consideration that armed nomads might be still lurking here. When she stopped at one particular chamber, she banged on the door with her fist. "It's me! Open the door!"

A gray-haired man opened the door, casting down his eyes.

"What is it?" She nervously gripped his arms.

"I am so sorry, milady," the gray-haired man said quietly. "There was nothing I could do for her."

38. FERAS

Silence reigned over the cemetery when the two coffins arrived.

The body of Her Majesty was the first to reside in its final destination below the sand, her husband Rasheed standing stoically. The moment the men took Lady Ramia out of her coffin, Sania rushed toward her, wailing. The men carrying the body urged Feras to take his sister away when she insisted on holding her mother's hands and kissing her face, but Feras wouldn't dare go near Sania, especially today. She must be blaming him for their mother's death, and perhaps she was right. If it hadn't been for him, their mother could have been in Arkan instead of her grave. But no, that was blasphemy. No one could change his fate. His mother was destined to die in that place at that time, may the Lord of Sky and Earth rest her soul. But would that convince his sister to forgive him? She had never forgiven her father, and she never would. Especially after he had missed his wife's burial.

The shovels rained sand over their mother, the clerics intoning prayers for mercy to the dead. Even after the men were done with the grave, Sania kept staring at the ground where their mother lay beneath. Perchance he could approach her now.

"Stay away from me!" she snapped the moment he laid his hand on her shoulder. "I don't want to see any of you, ever!"

Without saying a word, he turned and stayed away as she wanted. Now wasn't the right time to talk.

With careful steps, King Rasheed approached, his retinue trailing him. "I understand your grief, Feras, but we need to make some decisions today. Come to the palace as soon you feel ready."

Feras wondered what the king's notion of grief would look like. Rasheed's eyes betrayed nothing but fury. "I am ready whenever you will, sire," said Feras.

"You should see to your sister first," said Rasheed.

People were leaving the cemetery, and still Sania stood in the same spot. *It is over now,* Feras wanted to tell her. His sister was gazing at nothing but sand. When would she realize there was no good staying here? This was how she always had been; emotional and a bit childish. *Too* childish to understand her father's dedication to his country. She blamed him for doing his duty to his homeland instead of appreciating his sacrifice. Did she even think for an instant how her father felt about being away from his family? He would learn about his wife's death from a messenger, and he wouldn't be able to see her off before she went to her grave.

Everybody had left except for the memluks guarding him and his sister. "Let's go now," he said softly to her, but she didn't look at him. "Sania, please."

Her eyes were still wet. "Go where?"

"Wherever you want. We may rest for a while in the royal palace before we return to Arkan."

"I hate that cursed palace. I'm not going there ever."

"I just want you to rest before you travel. You're exhausted."

"I'm not going to Arkan either. I won't be able to stand the sight of Mother's vacant chamber." Sania gave him a dismissive gesture. "Just leave me be."

"Leave you *here*?"

"I can take care of myself." She went past him, leaving him in his astonishment. "And don't send your soldiers to follow me."

"What is this folly? Tell me where you are going."

Sania didn't reply.

"You are not going to the old house in Burdi, are you?" he asked.

She stopped, letting out a deep breath of air. "I am." She resumed her walk away from him.

Maybe it was better for her to be on her own for a while. "My guards will escort you."

From the thousand soldiers he had brought from Arkan, Feras ordered two hundred to escort his sister to the town of Burdi. Too many for such a short journey, he knew, but there could be remnants of nomads seeking revenge for their crushing defeat. Feras hadn't witnessed the battle, but from the ruined city he found, he couldn't tell who might have won. Yes, hundreds of Ghosts died on that day, but the cost was huge. The cost was the city itself. In a morning that would be ever remembered in the Tales of Gorania, everyone in Kahora was either carrying or following a coffin.

* * *

It was hard to believe that the nomads had set foot in the royal palace and a fight had actually happened on the very courtyard Feras stepped on, though. Compared to the ruined city, the palace looked untouched, as if it was thousands of miles away from the havoc.

The King joined him in the small hall, face grim. "You came earlier than I thought."

"It didn't take that long," Feras said curtly, waiting for His Majesty to tell him what he wanted.

Leaning his elbows on the table, Rasheed sighed. "You know, Feras, I thought I was a man of composure until yesterday's disaster."

Feras didn't say a word, waiting for Rasheed to go on.

"What I saw had never crossed my mind in my worst nightmares." Rasheed clenched his jaw. "Part of me still can't digest the sight. Can you imagine? A thousand nomads burning and killing in your great city, and chanting outside your palace before breaking into it. A whole kingdom almost fell to the filthiest dogs of the desert."

In the beginning, Feras had thought Rasheed was wistful because of his wife's death. Good thing Feras remained silent before expressing his condolences.

"She died because I gave that order." Rasheed's eyes were fixed on the empty table. "I should have let her stay *here*, where I was keeping the most of my royal guards."

"You tried to save her, sire, and you were right. They broke into the palace in the end, I was told."

"No one fools destiny." Rasheed grimaced. "Bring me that map."

Feras grabbed a map from a desk behind him and spread it over the table.

"I must say I underestimated the game Dehawy was playing," Rasheed muttered, his eyes hollow. "I never expected him or anyone else to use the Ghosts."

Who would expect that anyway? The desert clansmen had always had their own code; no agreements or deals with anyone from 'outside.'

"Sire, do you think Dehawy really arranged that attack with them, or he just made the best of their raid?"

"It doesn't make much difference; the result is the same." Rasheed stared at the map. "While we were busy with the Mankols at Kurdisan and the Byzonts at Arkan, we cleared the way for the Ghosts to sack Kahora. Afterward, he would march with his troops from the east to save the broken kingdom. A well-woven plot by my dear cousin."

"The Byzonts never came close to Arkan, sire." Feras felt the bitterness of regret. His mother's tragedy had started from the news he had received about the Byzonts' march.

"The Byzonts' role in Dehawy's game was to distract us, I told you. They will never send an army outside their lands because of the Bermanians crouching at their northern borders."

"But the Mankols are not *just* for distraction."

"The Mankols' threat is real. Dehawy must have sold Kurdisan to

237

them. That's why I sent your uncle Lord Munzir to aid your father." Rasheed moved his finger on the map from Demask to Bigad. "While Dehawy might consider marching to Bigad to surround Ahmet and Munzir, you will take his battle to his own ground, to Shezar."

Stunning Dehawy would be better than waiting for his next strike. Still, something was missing. "What about the nomads?" Feras asked.

"Unleash that Masolon on them." Rasheed had thought that through, it seemed. "He knows how to lead men on a battlefield better than our green commanders."

"He is a mercenary," Feras said, not sure about the idea.

"Not anymore. Bring me my seal, and I shall raise him to the rank of Commander. He will be reporting to you."

39. MASOLON

"All hail, Commander Masolon!"

Ziyad will never change, Masolon thought. He should have considered the consequences of accepting the King's generous offer. But who was he fooling? No question, it was an order, not an offer.

Burning the tavern during the Ghosts' raid didn't stop the gang from celebrating the new commander and his new captains. Masolon had no idea where they had obtained it, but a barrel of ale was in the gang's den.

"This is a day when you should drink, pious brother!" Ziyad teased Frankil. The way Frankil curled his lips with distaste made Masolon and Antram laugh.

"Do not push on him, Ziyad," said Masolon.

"What did you call me, Commander?" Ziyad held his ear. "Until yesterday, I was just Ziyad. But starting from today, I will allow nobody to address me by anything other than *Captain* Ziyad."

"You know what?" Antram said. "I prefer just Ziyad the Serious to Captain Ziyad the Ridiculous." Everyone guffawed.

"Where will we be patrolling tomorrow, Masolon?" asked Frankil.

According to Lord Feras, protecting the whole western region of the kingdom had become Masolon's responsibility, and he now led a battalion of five hundred men, most of them memluks camping in Arkan and Kahora. And still, he could accept volunteers from the Murasen youths who were eager to join the *gang,* a name Feras loathed, but there were a few things even a lord could not change.

"Arkan. The location of this fort makes it our most important area in the region." *Yes, the most important in the world.*

"I thought our mission was to drive the nomads out of this region," said Ziyad. "Not to watch over Arkan from the Byzonts."

"Exactly, brother. We cannot undertake our mission without making sure that our back is well protected."

"Masolon has a point," Antram seconded.

Ziyad wrinkled his forehead in confusion." The Byzonts have retreated already."

While Ziyad and Antram were busy in their argument, Frankil leaned closer so only Masolon could hear him. "We are still on our path, Masolon, aren't we?"

"What are you worried about, Frankil?"

"When you came to me in Horstad four months ago, I joined you to help the helpless, not to serve lords."

"We are still helping the helpless with our new assignment."

"But now we're Feras's soldiers. We have to obey his orders whatever they are."

"Feras is a man of honor. He will never involve us in dishonorable acts."

"Power turns men mad. You can't trust a man with power for long."

"Nobody on Earth can impose his will upon us. We will use this new authority to serve our mission, and we will never comply blindly with orders we receive."

"I really hope so, Masolon." Frankil looked doubtful, though.

"Hope? You must be sure, Frankil. We are neither soldiers nor mercenaries. Whatever the banner we fight under, we will remain the Warriors' Gang."

"That is reassuring." Frankil smiled at last. "I hope I won't need to remind you of this conversation one day."

Had Frankil forgotten? It was Masolon who had started that path in the first place.

The path, the path, the path. The path is in a safe place, Commander. You have to worry about your girl.

"Are you alright, Masolon?" Frankil inquired, noticing his friend's absent-mindedness.

"I am fine. Just a stupid headache." Masolon smiled faintly. "Have you ever felt that someone in your head is talking to you?"

Masolon left his brothers to their chattering and ranting and found a quiet spot on the hill to get some sleep. But it seemed a Rusakian fellow had claimed it first.

"I see you have become one of us now," he said to Blanich.

"They never told you, huh?" Blanich chuckled. "I was leaving the city, but your friends made me change my mind. And yes, I think I'm going to stay for a while. I will never return to Rusakia with empty pockets."

Many were here for coin, and who could blame them for that? It was just another profession.

"I wonder what may have happened to the highborn Rusakian," Masolon commented.

Blanich rolled his eyes. "Life has been a bit harsh to me since my father's death."

"You certain it is just a *bit*?" Masolon chuckled mockingly.

"It's a matter of perspective." Blanich grinned. "You know, I was called a bastard, kicked out of my father's house, attacked by a bear once in the woods, stomped by a horse that broke my bones, and just a few days ago, I was nearly buried under a crumbling temple. You might regard my life as a series of unfortunate events, but you know how I see the whole thing? I'm lucky enough to survive all of that."

An interesting fellow, Blanich was. *More interesting than I thought.* "The gang will make use of your luck." Masolon lay on the ground. "Tomorrow you shall ride next to me."

* * *

After sunrise, Masolon took his new captains to the royal palace to get their new armor. No surprise, Ziyad was excited. Antram wouldn't bother as long as he would get paid. Frankil was too reluctant to take off his Bermanian armor, but at last he came to reason and understood that he couldn't lead Murasen soldiers while the Bermanian lion decorated his breastplate.

The King's page told Masolon that Feras wanted to have a word with him. Clad in his new brown armor, Masolon followed the page to a chamber where Feras was waiting for him.

"Now you look like a Murasen commander." Feras gave him the faintest of smiles. "Be seated."

Masolon sat opposite Feras, listening to his instructions about making outposts at the eastern side of the region to alert the city keep to any surprising nomads' raids. The lord also stressed the importance of securing the Northern Road for all travelers, especially trade caravans.

"I will be leaving in two days after I'm done assembling the army marching to the east," said Feras. "Until my return, you have my permission to cleanse our deserts of those nomads. Uproot them before they grow again."

"That will be my pleasure."

"Do you know where Burdi is, Commander?" Feras asked.

"Yes, a small town a few miles away from Kahora, milord."

"Good." Feras looked satisfied. "One particular house in that town concerns me a lot. My sister Lady Sania is staying there for a while. Do I have to say more?"

Sania! Masolon tried to keep his face impassive when he heard her name. "Rest assured, milord. I will do whatever it takes to secure that house."

"One more thing." Feras chewed on his lip. "Lady Sania has refused to have any guards. You must make sure the house is protected without her noticing. Is that clear, Masolon?"

"Quite clear, milord." *Beautiful*, Masolon would say.

Feras concluded the meeting, and Masolon was impatient to undertake his new mission. Sometimes destiny's arrangements were better than his.

Waiting for him in the courtyard were his captains. "Someone here is as delighted as a bridegroom." Ziyad winked.

Ignoring Ziyad's teasing, Masolon tried to wear a stern face. "We have some rearrangements, brothers. I mean *captains*. We will split our forces into four groups to cover Kahora from all sides."

"But we are stronger together," Antram protested.

"We have nomads to chase, trade routes to keep safe, and a fort in the west to watch over. We cannot be everywhere at the same time," said Masolon. "Frankil will lead our men on the Northern Road, Antram around Arkan in the west, Ziyad in Kahora itself and its south, and I will be patrolling the east."

"Yes, my city." Ziyad looked excited. "I thought for a moment you would keep the big city for yourself."

"You *should* have kept the big city for you, Masolon," said Antram, then he nodded toward Ziyad. "You must keep him away from taverns. Put him in those eastern towns and villages."

"Hey! What's your problem?" Ziyad nudged Antram.

Masolon smiled at their bantering. "If one day the Ghosts think of coming back, the eastern towns and villages will be the nearest places they can reach. So as you see, their location obliges me to watch over them. Obliges us, I mean."

* * *

Before leaving Kahora, Masolon thought he should pass by Bumar to make sure he was all right after the Ghosts' attack. To his surprise, he found new windows and a new door on the healer's house.

"Look at you," Bumar said when he opened the door for Masolon, staring at the sigil decorating his breastplate. "The leopard fits you so well."

"I am one of Lord Feras's commanders now." Masolon stepped inside, contemplating the newly painted walls. "I see you waste no time. Your house is recovering."

"What matters is that the scrolls are safe, especially those in which I wrote what I learned from you about the Outsiders. When the havoc started, I hid them under the bed."

"The scrolls?" Masolon echoed. "What about you?"

"I hid with the scrolls. I was too worried to keep them out of my sight." Bumar ushered him to a seat, but Masolon didn't sit. "You must be hungry. How about having lunch together, and then we have another writing session?"

"I am in a hurry, my friend."

"I was reading about the Koyans when that barbarian attack on Kahora happened." Heedless of Masolon's statement, Bumar pulled him by the arm, ushering him to a seat in his reception hall, but Masolon kept standing. "You can say I have collected every scroll talking about or even mentioning them. Anyway, most of the scrolls do not tell us anything new: that Koya was the only part of our known world that Goran the Great didn't conquer; the fact that no Koyan is allowed to live outside Gorania, and in return no outsider is allowed to live in Koya; the rumors that they still practice the forbidden ancient arts; the peacefulness of their—"

"My dear friend," Masolon cut in. "I am just here to check on you. Maybe we should have this conversation later."

"You haven't heard the interesting part yet." Bumar grinned. "One scroll reveals that the Koyans have been designing a ship that could sail through the Boiling Eyes. Do you know what that means?"

Masolon blew impatiently. Knowing that no ship had ever returned from the Boiling Eyes (which had earned its name for a reason) he guessed, "The Koyans have naval superiority now?"

"The Koyans have found a way to go to your homeland without crossing the Great Desert, Masolon." The healer paused for effect. "Bearing into consideration the similarities between our tongue and yours, I strongly believe that the mages of *Cawa* are in fact from Koya."

Masolon pondered the two words that sounded similar somehow. "It could be a coincidence."

"Like Ogono and *Gana*: Paradise in the ancient Murasen tongue?"

Masolon's mind was already too clouded to connect the loose threads. "What does that lead us to?"

"I'm still unable to say. But I can tell you there is something dubious here. What are the Koyans doing in your homeland despite their restrictive laws? Why do they teach your people our tongue, among *many other things they teach*? No one can answer these questions better than you."

"I hate to disappoint you, my friend, but you must know that I have abandoned my old world for good. I have nothing to return to." *Except everlasting shame.* But here in Gorania, Masolon had an army to lead, a town to secure, and a noble lady to watch over.

"This is not about your return, Masolon. This is about your coming to us." Bumar gestured toward him with both hands. "It might sound crazy, but I think you haven't come to Gorania of your own will; you have been *sent*. The question is: To do what?"

Seriously, the obsession with Masolon's homeland made the healer's mind drift away. "Another time, my friend." Masolon patted Bumar on the shoulder and went to the door.

"Never mind. I can imagine how busy you have become. Send my condolences to Lord Feras when you see him."

"I will." Masolon did not look back.

"And to Lady Sania as well."

That one made Masolon stop and turn to Bumar. *The healer knows.*

"You see her, don't you?" Bumar asked.

Masolon shrugged casually. "Why should I?"

Bumar laughed. "Have you ever fallen in love, Masolon?"

"Why do you ask?"

"Because you're badly smitten, young man. You may fool yourself, but you can't fool me."

The guilt tightened Masolon's jaw. "Trust me. I did not do that on purpose."

"No one does. Our hearts never listen to our minds."

"Where do you think this is taking me to? I say nowhere."

"How would you know your destination if you never traveled to it?"

Masolon weighed Bumar's words. "What do you mean?"

"I mean you can never assume, Masolon." Bumar's grin got wider. "You must see for yourself before you judge."

What was Bumar hinting at? Going to Sania and simply telling her 'I love you?' "That is a dangerous road, my friend."

"And what are the risks?"

"I may lose her. Forever."

"*Lose* her? She was never yours in the first place."

Despite the harsh sound of it, Masolon couldn't disagree.

"Young man," Bumar said, "either you take that dangerous road, or you forget the whole thing until you find another girl."

* * *

The autumn sun was much gentler than that of the summer. The real problem was the dust. Masolon would prefer a hot day to a windy one.

Finding the desired house wasn't that difficult in such a small town. A one-story brick house stood alone at the end of Burdi away from other houses, away from the market, away from any building in this town. A perfect place for someone who sought solitude.

The wooden fence of the house enclosed many date palms that shaded most of the vast area surrounding the building. As Feras had told him, the place looked unguarded. Sania didn't wish to draw attention indeed, but that would never fool him. His eyes caught a horseman patrolling at a distance from the house as if he didn't want to be noticed. Turning the reins of his black horse toward the anonymous watcher, Masolon spurred his stallion onward. As he approached, he could tell from the leopard sigil on the horseman's breastplate he was a memluk.

"Commander Masolon," the memluk said respectfully. "It's an honor meeting you. We all heard of your heroic victory in Kahora."

"The honor is mine, soldier," said Masolon. "Now what are you doing here?"

"I am here to guard the princess, as you may know, Commander."

Masolon gazed at the area surrounding the house perimeter until he spotted the other two memluks. "Do you not think that your distance might not be the most appropriate for such a task?"

"You want me to stand farther, Commander?"

"For certain," Masolon stated. *Because I do not wish for too much audience.*

He wheeled his horse toward the house, leaving the memluk to his duty. Stopping outside the unlocked wooden gate, Masolon dismounted and pulled his stallion gently by its bridle into the sandy yard and tied it to a palm trunk. "I will not be late, my friend." Masolon patted his black horse's neck.

He approached the oaken door of the house cautiously, his heart pounding hard. Even before a battle, he had never been that nervous. Taking a deep breath, he gently knocked on the oaken door of the house, but he got no answer. He knocked again, harder this time. Now he could hear approaching footsteps from inside. Shortly afterward, the door was slightly opened. "Yes, sir?" The cautious face of a maidservant peeked from behind the barely opened door.

Masolon cleared his throat. "I am here to meet Lady Sania."

"Lady Sania doesn't meet anybody here."

"Really? Would you tell her that Commander Mas...I mean Masolon is here?"

"I'm so sorry, Commander. She doesn't want to see anybody. And she didn't tell me of any exceptions."

Masolon took a deep breath, hoping that would help him keep his composure before he might do something foolish. Inwardly, he cursed that maidservant who stood between him and his girl.

"Just *tell* her," Masolon insisted, not so nicely this time.

"Wait." The maidservant closed the door, leaving him outside. What was he going to say when Sania appeared? Though he was eager for that moment, he wasn't prepared for it. *You can just tell her how sorry you feel for her loss. Nothing more for today.*

Light footsteps came from behind the closed door at last. But again it was not her. The disappointment was unbearable.

"I'm sorry, Commander," the maidservant said dryly. "You won't be able to see her."

"Why not?"

"I didn't ask her why, Commander. She said so, and I simply have to obey."

"Are you sure you told her my name?"

"I am sure, Commander." The maid exhaled, looking irked. "Now if you don't mind?" She slammed the door shut, an end he hadn't expected at all. He should have known better though. The princess had chosen that lonely place for a reason.

Maybe he should try his luck another day.

40. GERVINY

A letter from Halin to him? Gerviny thought his squire Sergi was mistaken when he announced the news. Since his betrothal to his gorgeous future bride, she had never shown him a single gesture of affection. All he had on three previous occasions was that fake smile, which should give the image of the happy lordly couple, but never a smile from the heart to relieve his restless soul. The moment his eyes fell on her, he knew he wanted nothing but Halin. Perhaps the girl was too shy to express her feelings to him in person. The possibility made sense to him when he saw her name scribed on the sealed envelope.

Gerviny snatched the envelope from Sergi's hands. "Fetch me a flagon. A full flagon, Sergi," he demanded, and went to the terrace to enjoy the autumn breeze while reading Halin's letter. For the first time since summer, it hadn't snowed on Durberg. He should have known it was a good omen.

He reclined in a cushioned seat, his feet on the table in front of him. "Hurry up, Sergi!" he cried, although he doubted his squire would hear him through the wall. Too impatient to wait for his slow squire, Gerviny broke the seal on the letter, immediately catching the scent of purple rose, the flower she loved the most. "Curse you,

Sergi. You're ruining the moment. SERGI!"

With care he had never shown to anything, he held the scented paper and unfolded it, the sight of his name at the beginning of the letter exciting him.

To Gerviny, my dear dignified lord.

Dignified? Coming from a lover, the word sounded ridiculous. Later he would have all the time he needed to teach that courteous girl *other* words.

To Gerviny, my dear dignified lord,
I want to come to your palace to speak to you in person, but I can't. I don't feel I will be able to deal with this situation, which I never faced before and I never wanted to happen. I hope you are not offended by that.
Your father and mine have a plan for us, and of course, they think it's for our own good. However, I believe it's us who should decide. It's you who will find himself bound to a woman he is forced to be loyal to for the rest of his life just to fulfill his father's wish. I know for sure that if I wasn't Lord Sanislav's daughter, I wouldn't have the honor of being betrothed to the future honorable lord of Durberg. You deserve to choose a lady that befits the name of Lord Gerviny son of Lord Larovic, and I know I can't undertake that role.
I hope we can settle this on our own without involving our fathers. We don't want a matter between a man and a girl to turn into a conflict between two lords. Please, inform Lord Larovic of my sincere apologies. Let him know...

"Milord?" Sergi's voice startled him.

He looked up sharply and found the squire standing next to his seat. "What?" Gerviny snapped.

"The wine, milord." Sergi held out a flagon. Only now did Gerviny notice it.

"Leave it and get out of here." Gerviny waved him away.

"The table," the squire harrumphed, "if you don't mind, milord." He was *politely* asking Gerviny to put down his feet. But Gerviny had enough of politeness today.

"Give it to me," Gerviny urged his squire, who complied at once. "Here is your damned flagon!" He flung the full flagon away. The metal vessel hit the balustrade and fell on the floor of the balcony, unbroken, but it made a glorious clatter against the marble floor. The sight of the spilled wine aggravated Gerviny even more than the letter itself. "Don't ever be late when I demand something from you! You hear me? Now get out!"

The squire scurried away from him. Gerviny knew the lad had done nothing wrong, but his fury was too massive to contain. A perfumed letter of rejection? Was she mocking him? How dare she!

There was no reason to continue reading, but he was curious to finish the letter before tearing it apart.

Let him know that I am not acting on behalf of my father; that is my own decision. And I as well as my father will always bear utter respect to him and you.
Humbly,
Halin

That whore! All she was concerned about was his father's wrath. All those courteous words were for the sake of the fearful Lord Larovic, not for the harmless Gerviny. If it were not for the Lord Marshal, she wouldn't even bother writing to him. The betrothal wouldn't occur in the first place.

She had to pay for her insolence. Sanislav must pay for his daughter's insolence too. His father should see that letter for himself and decide the appropriate sanction for such an insult to the Lord Marshal and his heir.

Gerviny hurried back inside, looking for his father. A guard escorted Gerviny to the hall where his lord father was meeting with two lesser lords of the North. The Lord Marshal looked annoyed when Gerviny pushed the door open. His father didn't like to be interrupted, but Gerviny couldn't wait.

"My apologies, Lord Marshal." Gerviny nodded. "I'm coming to you with an urgent matter."

"I'm sure it is." His father looked at him impassively. With the slightest of nods, he motioned the two lesser lords to the door. For a moment, Gerviny regretted interrupting his father's meeting, but there was no turning back now.

In an attempt to imitate his father's dreadful coldness, Gerviny produced the letter without saying a word.

"What is this?" asked his father.

"Sabirev is sending its regards."

His father took the letter and scanned it. A snowstorm was coming; Gerviny could see it in his father's blue eyes. *Yes, Lord Larovic. Get mad. Those rascals have dared to insult you.*

"That's an urgent matter indeed." His father put the letter aside on the table. "But do you know what the matter is, son?"

"Isn't it obvious?" Gerviny cleared his throat. "That girl would respect your son if her father respected you."

The Lord Marshal squinted. "Did you read the letter before bringing it to me?"

"Of course, I did!"

His father picked up the letter and held it out to Gerviny. "Show me the part from which you sense her disrespect."

"Father, don't let her fake politeness fool you, she—"

"Fool me?" his father blustered. "The only one who can be fooled in this room is you! Disrespect? Is that the matter you stormed the hall for?"

"You just acknowledged the matter was urgent."

"You mean the matter beyond your meager understanding. The matter that we might have wasted a chance to make our house the most powerful in the North."

All his father was concerned about was Sanislav's stupid castle.

"What about me? What about *you*, Lord Marshal? What after the Rusakian court learns that the lord of some rural castle has dared to say no to you?"

"The 'no' was to *you*, not me. And who can blame her with your disgraceful past?" Larovic smirked. "Maybe the song is true after all."

When would his father stop rebuking him for an old act of foolishness? Was Gerviny the only one who had ever made a mistake?

"Go and call those two back." His father didn't even look at him when he gave him a dismissive gesture. Disappointed and infuriated, Gerviny didn't move.

His father glared at him. "You heard me."

"You are not going to respond to that insult, are you?"

"What do you expect me to do? Send my troops, storm the castle, and bring Sanislav and his daughter here on their knees?"

"Though merciful it sounds, I might accept that."

His father shook his head. "You know what? The whole matter was a huge mistake. You are not worthy of the heritage I wanted to leave you."

His father's insult was much more painful than Halin's. More frustrating. More aggravating. No matter what Gerviny did, his father would never regard him the way he deserved. The demented old man would always live in the memory of Gerviny's long gone brother Elov.

Gerviny exited the hall. The lords waiting by the door outside shot him an inquisitive look, as if they were asking for his permission to return to the hall, but he ignored them and stalked through the corridor.

The song is true after all, his father's scornful tone echoed in his head. *A song!*

Gerviny couldn't stand the notion that everybody knew about his shame. Everybody. Even Sergi knew. *Curse me!* Gerviny was the last one to hear about it. What a humiliation for the coming Lord of Durberg! No reaction from the great Lord Marshal, who even insulted him more. But so be it. From now on, Gerviny would act on his own. Whether his father liked this fact or not, Gerviny was his heir.

On his way back to his favorite balcony, Gerviny found his squire on the floor sitting by its door. "What are you doing here?" Gerviny snapped at him. "You are supposed to follow me where I go!"

The squire pushed to his feet at once. "Milord, you asked me to go away. I wasn't sure if——"

"Alright, alright," Gerviny cut him off. "Come now." He went to the balcony, the squire following him. No trace of spilled wine on the floor, and of course the flagon was taken away. "You need to acquire the pace of the maidservants of this palace," he muttered as he leaned to the balustrade.

"I beg your pardon, milord?"

Gerviny turned to his squire. "What do they say in the song?"

"What song, milord?"

"The song, Sergi. The song about me…and Lady Halin."

The lad looked down. "You may not like it, milord, and I really don't want to aggravate you."

"Just be honest with me, and I won't get mad at you," Gerviny promised. "Now what do they say about us?"

"The song is not about you, milord." Sergi swallowed. "It's about Lady Halin and the Champion of Durberg."

41. MASOLON

It had been two weeks since his unsuccessful attempt to see Sania. Why wouldn't he give it another try? *Two weeks are long enough.* Even Masolon himself was impressed by his own patience, but not anymore. Today he couldn't resist the urge. The desire to go and knock on her door one more time. Besides, there was nothing wrong in passing by the town of Burdi to oversee his troops. *Nothing wrong? That is my bloody job.* And Masolon would be damned if he didn't undertake his 'job' seriously.

By his orders, fifty soldiers split into ten groups of five made a wide ring around Sania's house. She must not notice their presence, Feras had warned him, and Masolon hadn't forgotten. To ensure that everything was going according to plan, Masolon made a tour around this ring of protection, passing by a few of his groups, asking them if there were any incidents worth mentioning.

"We even search fruit carts," a soldier told Masolon. "We make sure that no one armed goes in there." While Masolon was turning his horse to go to the next guarding group, the soldier continued, "It happened once that we found a bow and a quiver with an errand boy from Arkan, as he claimed. He swore they belonged to Lady Sania, but we did not let him go inside."

Masolon stopped his horse, looking over his shoulder at the soldier. "A bow and a quiver?"

"Full of arrows, Commander. The bow did seem to belong to the princess, however, we dismissed that errand boy, and I went myself to deliver those things to the princess's servant."

Masolon didn't conceal his smile when the sweet memories of Arkan flashed in his mind.

"Is there something wrong, Commander Masolon?"

"Lady Sania did not see you, did she?"

"She didn't. Even if she did, she would never know why I was here. I could be guarding the errand boy for instance."

"Well done, soldier."

The bow and the quiver! Masolon couldn't wait to see that with his own eyes. He kicked the flanks of his stallion, urging it to gallop until he reached the wooden fence. He dismounted and hurriedly tied his horse, carefully examining the palm trunks of the shady yard, looking for a particular trunk. It wasn't an easy search in such a vast yard full of palm trees.

And there it was at last; a trunk struck with arrows. Masolon pulled out one arrow, held it with both hands, and smiled. It was hers, no doubt, which meant that she might show up at any moment, and he would be damned if he missed that.

Under the shade of palms, he waited. Ignoring his thirst for an hour, he waited. The weather was getting hotter by noon, but he waited. He would wait all day long if that was what it took to see her.

And then he heard the creaking of the door. Somebody had come out of the house.

Full of hope, Masolon turned to see who was approaching him. It was Sania, holding her bow. While he was petrified beside the palm trunk staring at her, she came forward without noticing him, her bow and quiver in her hands. His heart pounded hard like a hammer, the arrow in his hand reminding him of the one that had missed his head a few months ago. He grinned, recalling how cheerful she had been. The word 'foreigner' had sounded so sweet when he had heard it in her voice.

Both Masolon's heart and mind were captivated, although she looked paler and skinnier than before. She was dressed in black, her auburn hair tumbled by the desert wind. An incarnation of beauty and grief.

Her eyes tightened when she noticed his presence. The moment he had been waiting for; when their eyes would meet and she would…

"What are you doing here?"

Her scowl and her unwelcoming tone stabbed him in the heart. That was not quite the start he was hoping for.

"Milady…I…I was…"

"You were what? Didn't you understand the first time?"

"Understand what?"

"My maid told you I didn't want to see you." Sania raised her voice. "Was that hard to understand?"

"Yes, but…I thought that you did not mean that for…" Masolon didn't dare to say it.

"I didn't mean what?"

"I assumed you did not want to see anybody because you were mourning at that time."

"So you decided that I had enough time mourning?" Sania glared at him. "What if I *chose* to be alone? Why is it too hard for you to respect my choice?"

Masolon couldn't believe his ears. Was he really talking to Sania? Where had the charming princess with the delightful spirit gone?

"I am so sorry. I never meant to disrespect your choice, milady. I just wanted to tell you that I felt sorry for your loss."

"Why would you?" Sania folded her arms, nodding toward him. "Even her husband didn't feel so." She looked down, shaking her head in disapproval. "She was buried under the ground, and he was not there to see her off. He was busy *fighting*. He *chose* not to be there."

She must be talking about her lord father, who fought the

Mankols in the north.

"I am quite sure he was obliged to stay at the frontiers, milady."

"Why do you defend him?" Sania snapped. "I shouldn't be surprised though. This is what *loyal* and *valorous* warriors usually do. Nothing is more worthy than the kingdom to fight for. That's what you choose! But what about us? We choose nothing. You choose for us, and we are ungrateful if we protest. It's a shame to protest. We should be thankful for our men's dedication toward the kingdom. But what about their dedication to *us*? Ah, I forgot. We are nothing but the mothers of your sons."

Furious and unstoppable, like an autumn sandstorm. Time hadn't healed her wounds as he had hoped. It had nursed her grudge beyond his imagination.

So how could you stop a blowing storm? You couldn't. You should only wait until its end. Masolon didn't do that though, and chose to try his luck one more time. "Not all men are the same," he said.

"Oh, please! Don't tell me that!" She snorted. "Actually, I don't find so much variety in them. A man wants a woman either to quench his lust, or bear his progeny, or both!"

Sania's maidservant hurried out of the house. "Commander! What did I tell you before? You can't break in like this!" she chided him, making the scene more ridiculous.

"I am truly sorry." Masolon ignored the servant and addressed Sania. "I did not come here to revive your pain."

"You did," replied Sania, her eyes welled up with tears. "That man, who I used to call 'Father,' didn't bother to grant my mother a farewell look."

Masolon felt as if he was trapped in quicksand. The more he resisted, the more he sunk.

"She was getting well before you came!" the maidservant screeched at Masolon, holding her mistress's hands. "Leave her be!"

That really hurt. He had thought of the worst possibilities for his conversation with Sania, but to be dismissed in such a manner? That had never crossed his mind.

With hollow eyes, Masolon watched the maidservant take her mistress gently by her hands, escorting her inside the house. Sania disappeared behind that oaken door and he could do nothing about it. He had been able to save her once from the hands of barbarian nomads, but today he couldn't get closer to her because of one maidservant.

He felt so heartsick.

Dragging his legs, he went to his horse and mounted it. He didn't notice that he was still gripping the arrow in his hand until he leaned forward to hold the horse's reins. "This is where your tale, as well as mine, ends," he muttered, staring at the arrow for a while. He broke the shaft into two pieces and let them fall to the ground next to his horse's hooves.

42. MASOLON

The remnants of the Ghosts had chosen the wrong time to restore their lost reputation.

When the news of a raided caravan on the Northern Road reached Masolon, he amassed half of the men under his command to hunt those bastards down, and all he found was fifty desperate nomads. Masolon granted most of them the mercy of quick death in battle, only sparing the lives of seven nomads. To each of Kahora and the neighboring towns and villages, he sent one nomad for the commoners to determine the fate of their desert dog. The good, peaceful people of Murase didn't disappoint him, he had to say. All of them displayed how the Ghosts' savagery had inspired them along endless decades of barbarity and bloodshed. Those desert maggots should have known that the day to reap what they had sown would come sooner or later.

After spending two weeks wandering the desert areas around the roads to track any lurking nomadic bands, Masolon allowed himself and his men a two-day rest in Kahora. Leading his mounted soldiers into the city, he waved at all the people who gathered in the streets and opened their windows to cheer for their guardian and his horde of heroes. The whole western region of the realm had become a safer place to its dwellers and travelers since the appointment of the new commander.

"If I were Lord Feras, I might feel jealous." Ziyad winked, his horse next to Masolon's.

"Why should you?"

"Aren't you watching?" Ziyad swept an arm at the crowd. "That's a reception for the ruler of Kahora."

"We represent the ruler of Kahora, brother."

"Ah! I see! Someone here doesn't want to involve himself in politics!" Ziyad teased him.

"Shut up," Frankil snapped. "Nothing worries me like your mouth."

"I didn't say anything wrong," Ziyad protested.

"We are warriors, Ziyad," said Masolon. "Politics are only for lords. Is that clear?"

"Speaking of warriors," Blanich said from behind him. "I wish I could see those lands that raise warriors like you, Masolon."

"You wish you could see my homeland?" Masolon chuckled. "Trust me, brother; a noble like you would never mean that."

"I *was* a noble, my friend," said Blanich. "For the time being, I follow whoever pays me well."

"Great," Frankil said grimly, "now we have two nobles in the gang."

"Blanich looks like a *real* noble to me, though." Ziyad sneered.

Antram frowned. "What do you mean, you worthless bard?"

"We are not going to argue in front of this crowd, fellows." Masolon turned to his brothers. "Can you just wave to them and postpone your quarrel until a bit later?"

"Good idea," said Antram, inclining his head toward Ziyad. "I suggest we start the next sparring session by a duel between me and him."

"I second this suggestion," said Frankil.

Masolon grinned. "I see your mood is improving, Captain."

Frankil gazed at the throng with a slight smile on his face. "You're reviving the good old days, Masolon."

"Stay alert, brothers." Ziyad nodded toward five approaching horse riders. "I presume those men are not here to greet us."

Masolon warily watched the five riders stop, their mouths covered with turbans. They were not Murasens, he could tell from their blond hair.

The only lady among them advanced on horseback toward him. Antram drew his sword, but Masolon gestured to his friend to stand down.

"Masolon?" she asked.

"You are speaking to him," replied Masolon.

"I was desperate to find you, but when you returned to the city, it wasn't that difficult. I just followed the noise." She smiled. "Can we talk somewhere else without too much audience? Bumar's house, for instance?"

She had his attention in no time. "You did put some effort to find me. How can I help you?" he asked.

"I bear a message for you."

"From whom?"

The lady moved her horse a few steps forward until it became side by side to Masolon's black stallion. Now he could see her blue eyes and her fine brown eyebrows. Her fair-skinned face was molded in the lands of ice, no doubt. "It's a message from my mistress," she replied. "Lady Halin."

The gorgeous girl from the feast of Durberg? When had they met? Six months ago? They had only bandied a few words during that feast, and still, she remembered him?

You had the chance to charm a lovely princess. Do you not remember that? His mind was back after weeks of silence.

Do you want me to believe the folly I heard from a bastard like Ramel?

Why do you always challenge me? We are one, you fool!

I have to challenge my thoughts until I make sure of them.

"Commander?" The Rusakian girl tilted her head. "You know Lady Halin, correct?"

"Yes," Masolon nodded. "You say she is your mistress?"

"Yes, I'm her prime maid. My name is Holga."

Too pretty for a maid, Masolon wanted to say. Ziyad had a point about his fondness of Rusakian girls.

"Who are those fellows?" Masolon nodded toward the four horsemen behind her.

"A woman needs protection to travel safely in these lands."

"For certain," Masolon said. "May I know what Bumar has to do with this?"

"When I arrived, I was told that nobody in this city knew where one could find Commander Masolon except Bumar the healer." Holga looked at the people passing by. "Can you meet me at his house?"

"You go. I will catch up with you," said Masolon before he returned to his three brothers waiting behind him. "I will be at Bumar's house. Wait for me at the tavern."

"A message she said?" Antram asked.

"Keep it down." Masolon glanced at her, but Holga was already gone, having left with her guards.

Ziyad gave him a sly smile. "I wonder from whom."

"You, in particular, must stay quiet." Masolon pointed his finger at Ziyad, grinning.

Ziyad smacked his lips. "If that is the messenger, I wonder what the sender looks like."

"I wonder if she is a messenger in the first place." Frankil's lips made a firm line. "Why would anyone send a woman?"

"Brothers, brothers." Masolon gestured to them with both hands to calm down. "Just wait for me at the tavern, and I will join you there."

"Why are you going on your own while she takes four men with her?" Antram asked.

"Because she is the one who should worry, not me."

"Who said Masolon is going to be alone?" Ziyad scoffed. "Bumar will interfere if anything happens."

"I don't find it funny," Frankil forced through clenched teeth. "That wench is trouble. I can feel it."

* * *

The four Rusakian guards were waiting outside Bumar's house when Masolon arrived. They didn't say a word to him, but he could feel the weight of their stares at him as he dismounted and knocked on the door.

"Your guest is here." Bumar grinned when he let him in. "Isn't it about time you bought your own house?"

A house was not something for a wanderer like Masolon. "I was told you met before," Masolon said in a low voice that only Bumar could hear. "What did she tell you?"

"Nothing. She insists that she will speak only to you." Bumar glanced at Holga, who waited in the hall, leaning back in her seat. "I like how you recover so fast."

"Shut up," Masolon teased him. "Now if you do not mind, we need a moment to talk on our own."

"You can go to the tavern if you need a bedchamber. But not in my house." Bumar grinned wickedly and turned to Holga. "Make yourself at home, milady." He bowed slightly to her, clasping his hands behind his back. Silently, Holga followed Bumar with her eyes until he went to his room. The Rusakian coldness; Masolon remembered what Ramel had told him once about it.

"We are alone now." Masolon seated himself opposite her. "What is your message?"

"To be more accurate, it is a request. Lady Halin asks for your presence in the castle of Sabirev. She needs your help."

"What for?"

"She didn't tell me anything else. She wants to discuss something private with you."

"Did you travel hundreds of miles to find me and ask to have a discreet word just to tell me that?"

"Trust me, Commander. There is nothing I love about these hellish lands. I begged Lady Halin to spare me this dusty journey, but she insisted that nobody else would undertake this mission to make sure her message was delivered to the right person." Holga gritted her teeth. "And yes, I asked to have a discreet word because I knew this argument would happen."

What kind of help would a princess ask from a warrior? And why him? Why not a Rusakian warrior?

She did not ask for a warrior's help. The princess asked for your help.

"What about her and Lord Gerviny?" Masolon's tongue was heavy when he uttered the Rusakian lord's name.

Holga looked confused. "What about them?"

"Their marriage. Were they not supposed to be married?"

"Yes, but not yet."

"Why not?"

"I have no idea. And I would never dare to ask about that."

Masolon didn't believe that. What sort of a 'prime' maid was she?

"Either you know too little or you hide too much," said Masolon suspiciously.

"I am going to say this for the last time, Commander." Holga looked irked. "Lady Halin sent me all this long way to take you to her because she wants your help in something she didn't tell me about. That's all I'm going to tell you because that is all I know."

Masolon weighed her words in his mind. Still, they were hard to believe.

"Is this an order from a princess?" he asked.

"No, Commander. She asks as a lady who needs help. I believe a chivalrous man like you won't ignore the call of help, especially from a woman."

"When does she expect my arrival?"

"She hopes you return with me." Holga stared at him with her ice-cold blue eyes. Maid or not, her look didn't make him feel comfortable.

"I will meet you after one hour at the northern gate of Kahora," Masolon promised.

"Please don't be late, Commander. We are not used to the Murasen sun." Holga rose to her feet and left him in the hall. The moment she shut the door behind her, Bumar came out of his chamber.

"You're not traveling to Rusakia with her, are you?" the healer began.

"Were you eavesdropping on our conversation?"

"Not really. It was your voices that were too loud." Bumar shrugged. "I like her voice, I must admit. But the story she tells is a bit strange."

"I will be fine, do not worry about me," Masolon told him, thinking of his brothers' reactions when they heard of this. To be frank, he shared Bumar's doubts about her story, but the temptation to meet Halin—by her own request—wasn't easy to ignore.

Masolon rode to the tavern. The brothers were there as they had agreed, their eyes betraying their anticipation the moment he stepped into the place.

"No!" Antram frowned after Masolon had told them about his decision to leave for a short period. "Not again, Masolon!"

"Sabirev?" Ziyad exclaimed. "That's another long journey, brother. It's even farther than Durberg."

"Why now?" Antram scowled. "I can't understand this! Wasn't this your dream, Masolon? The Gang? The path, remember? The tavern? The amphitheater? Look how far we came! Now after you have reached beyond the end of your dreams, you just want to leave."

"I am not leaving the gang or the path," Masolon clarified. "What was the path in the first place? Was it not about helping the helpless? This is why I am leaving."

"There is something you should bear in mind, Masolon," said Frankil. "You can't leave on your own like this. You are now a commander who follows a Murasen lord. What if Feras returns and finds out that you have left without informing him?"

"That is why I am gathering you now." Masolon's eyes wandered between the three captains. "As I do not wish for any sort of turbulence in the gangs' duties, I want one of you to lead the men in my absence. Does anyone here have any problems about Frankil being my deputy?" He studied the faces of both Ziyad and Antram.

"It doesn't matter who leads as long as this is for the good of the gang," said Ziyad. Sometimes he sounded wise when he spoke seriously.

Antram curled his lip in disdain. "It doesn't matter who leads as long as it is not Ziyad."

"Good." That had gone smoother than Masolon expected. "Frankil," he said, "who would you put in my place in the east?"

Frankil suggested Bergum. Masolon explained the way he spread his troops in the eastern part of Kahora, stressing the need to guard that small town called Burdi because of one noble lady residing there.

While Masolon was filling his horse's saddlebag before his long journey to Rusakia, Blanich passed by him at the market. "The brothers in the tavern say you are heading home." Blanich smiled. "*My home,* I mean."

"True. Do you want to join me?"

"Not yet. I just wanted to remind you to take heavy clothes for the journey. What you saw in the Contest was summer, and you saw it in Durberg, not Sabirev. Autumn will be too cold for a foreigner like you. And of course, I don't need to warn you against staying there until winter. Rusakian winter is only for Rusakians."

"I will remember that. Are you sure you do not want to join me?"

"Not yet," Blanich mused. "But I will appreciate it if you pass by old Anna in Durberg. She lives by the Frozen Lake. Tell her I'm fine. Tell her I'll be back when I'm ready."

43. MASOLON

After ten long days, the band of horsemen coming from Kahora approached their destination.

The Champion of Durberg, as King Bechov had called him once, was back to Rusakia after more than six months. As Blanich had warned him, the weather in Sabirev was colder than it had been during his previous visit to Durberg. Although Masolon wore a fur hood, he felt his head freezing.

"Hide it well," said Holga. "We might run into someone who still remembers you."

Masolon complied regardless of her advice. Running into someone that might remember him didn't matter as much as keeping his ears warm. Every breath he inhaled was a chore, the frosty air flowing through his windpipe stinging his lungs. *Obviously, the Great Desert is not the only hell in this world.*

"Here we are." Holga nodded her chin pointedly toward their destination that loomed in the horizon; the castle of Sabirev that belonged to Halin's father Lord Sanislav.

"How do you plan to get me in?" Masolon asked.

"There is no reason to worry as long as you are with me," she replied confidently.

Masolon and his companions became quiet until they reached the walls of Sabirev. Upon seeing the Prime Maid of Lady Halin, the guards opened the gates without posing any questions. Apparently, Holga had meant what she had just said.

As the escort reached the courtyard, the four Rusakian knights split, and only Holga and Masolon remained. "Wait here and don't enter until I come back to you," she said to him. "If anyone asks you what you are doing here, just tell him that you are waiting for Holga."

The Prime Maid went inside, leaving Masolon alone in the snowy courtyard. It didn't feel right to be here, but he had no choice except following Holga's instructions. For the thousandth time, he wondered if he had made the right decision when he answered Halin's call for help. Guessing what a gorgeous princess would want from him required a wild imagination. Wilder than his.

Masolon rubbed his gloved hands together against the chill. Perhaps he could distract his senses by sinking in his memories from that feast. It was true he had seen Halin only once, but her pretty face was a hard one to forgot. He wasn't sure about his feelings after that feast, but he remembered very well how she had allured him with her charming smile. Ziyad had told him that her eyes had been fixed on him. Ramel hadn't blabbered on about the 'lovely lady who was charmed by Masolon' for no reason.

"I hope I'm not late, Commander." Holga returned to him in the courtyard. "Lady Halin is ready to meet you."

The side door they entered the palace from seemed to be the one for servants. The way ahead was clear, and nobody interrupted them until they reached the stairs. Holga kept her head on a swivel as she ascended, Masolon following her. The Prime Maid stopped in front of a white door with a golden knob.

She opened the door for Masolon and ushered him inside. "She will join you shortly. Stay here until she comes."

Masolon reluctantly entered. The room inside was warm thanks to the fireplace. Much better than waiting in the snowy courtyard. A wide dressing mirror ahead rested on a huge wooden desk, all drawers' knobs in gold. What stunned him was the bed on his right. Yes, he was in a…bedchamber. What kind of *help* did the lady need here?

Light footsteps came from behind the other door next to the bed. The door creaked when Lady Halin pushed it open, clad in a red woolen robe. Gorgeous she was with her golden hair and blue eyes, but her charming smile was absent. Actually, she looked startled when she saw him.

"What is this?" she almost screamed. "What are you…No way! Masolon, that Contest Champion?"

"Yes, milady." Masolon nodded. "I came to answer your message."

"Message?" She was plainly confused. "What message?"

What message? That didn't sound promising at all. "Holga came to me and—"

"Holga?" Halin interrupted. "Message? What is going on? Who sent you here?"

That whore! Masolon felt his fingers clenching. Mad with rage, he wished he could drag Holga by her hair and bring her before Halin to explain this nonsense, but that shouldn't be his priority right now. "I think there is a mistake, Lady Halin. I must leave."

Masolon was going to the door when Halin blocked the way. "You are not leaving." She peered at him. "I demand answers."

Masolon didn't dare to move her from her place though he knew he must. "Your Prime Maid, Holga, found me in Kahora and told me you asked for my presence."

"Your presence? In my chamber? Tell me the truth before I call the guards!"

Blast! More trouble was brewing. That was going to be way worse than what happened to him with Sania at Burdi.

"I am telling the truth," Masolon said, his jaw tight. "Ask Holga yourself."

"Ask her about what? About her *journey* to Kahora? Holga has not left me for months!"

That lying whore! Like a fool, he had let himself fall into the trap.

"It must be you who spread those foolish tales about *our relationship*," Halin said in an accusatory tone. "Why did you do that? Because I praised your chivalry with a smile on my face? Then I am sorry! I didn't notice that I was smiling too nicely! You shouldn't have forgotten who you are, *Champion*. Tales will be nothing more than tales; reality never changes. Princesses are for princes. Commoners are for commoners. You may feel this unfair or humiliating, but this is the norm of life. Some are destined to be kings, others are destined to live and die in oblivion."

"I never spoke of foolish tales, and I had nothing to do with all you said," Masolon snapped. "I beg your pardon, milady. I have to go."

Suddenly, the door was flung open, and Masolon wasn't at all surprised to see that lordly bastard from the very cursed feast standing there. He should have known there was something wrong the moment he stepped into a noblewoman's bedchamber.

Backed by guards filling the corridor, Gerviny stood on the doorstep. "Well, well! I hope I'm not interrupting a private moment!" he said when he found Masolon and Halin standing so close to each other.

"What is the meaning of this?" cried Halin. "What are you even doing here?"

"Me?" Gerviny asked cynically. "I came this morning to discuss an important matter with your lord father. One of my guards spied an intruder breaking into your bedchamber." He turned to Masolon. "And look what a familiar intruder we have here! What a coincidence!"

Masolon clenched his teeth, his fist grasping the hilt of his sword.

"That would be an extremely stupid move on your part," said Gerviny. "You are surrounded, *Champion of Durberg*, and you may also hurt your lovely princess."

"You have no right to break into my chamber like this!" Halin screamed at Gerviny. "Leave!"

271

"I will surely leave, *Princess*." Gerviny cast her a mocking smile. "But I can't leave that intruder here in your bedchamber…unless he is *not* an intruder."

"You are such a vile creature!" she shouted. "I was right when I refused to marry you. I knew there was something wrong in your sick mind."

"And I knew there was something wrong about *Lady* Halin who refused Lord Gerviny, the Lord Marshal's son, for some nameless Contest fighter. You brought shame to my house with those songs about you and the Conte—"

Halin slapped Gerviny in the face.

"You dare to slap me!" Gerviny hollered. "You could have done yourself a favor and screamed out loud calling for help the instant you found that wretch in your room! You could have ended all the rumors and the gibberish forever, but you insist on confirming them!"

Masolon surreptitiously checked his surroundings to find a possible way out, but only a terrace with a locked door was there. Apparently, the lady trickster who called herself Holga had taken care of her measures very well.

"The moment I saw you, I knew you were despicable, but I never thought you could be *that* despicable." Masolon curled his lip. "If you want to defeat me, fight me like a man, one-on-one."

"Fight you? You don't even deserve the honor of my sword." Gerviny looked Masolon up and down. "If I had wanted you dead, my knights could have slain you in the desert."

Gerviny beckoned his men over, and in a few seconds, Masolon was surrounded by fifteen soldiers pointing their swords and spears at him.

"You will be an example for all your slavish likes. You should never aim at what is out of your reach," Gerviny said, a gloating smile on his face. *The coward is hiding behind his men.* "Take this prisoner to my dungeon," Gerviny ordered the guards. "I want him under my careful watch."

"I will kill you, Gerviny!" Masolon snarled while the soldiers were dragging him outside the chamber.

"I don't think so, *Champion*," said Gerviny. "Your fairytale ends here."

44. MASOLON

Princesses are for princes.
Commoners are for commoners.
Some are destined to be kings.
Others are destined to live and die in oblivion.
This is the norm of life.

Masolon was dragged to the dungeon in Durberg, Halin's words echoing in his mind. The snow was falling vigorously on the whole city, yet his mind was too busy to think about the freezing weather. Pondering how his journey had ended was driving him mad. The worst part of this ride was his encounter with Halin, especially what he had heard from her.

Her words were painful.

Her words were simply the truth.

"Looks like old Darov will have company at last,"

The Rusakian guards guffawed as they opened the door to the dungeon, herding Masolon downstairs until they reached his cell. He looked at the cell opposite his to find an old man lying on the floor, his back to the wall, his mustache and beard gray like his long hair.

"Wake up, old man!" One of the guards laughed while hitting the bars of Darov's cell.

"I am awake, you fool," Darov grunted.

"We brought you a neighbor," said the guard. "Now you have someone to fill his ears with your folly." He shoved Masolon to the opposite vacant cell.

The guards left him shackled in the dungeon, which was only lit by a single torch. Leaning his forehead against the cold wall, he closed his eyes and recalled how naive he had been when he believed that Halin would even think of him. Ramel, Bumar, Ziyad, himself; all of them were wrong. But Halin was right. Gerviny was right too. Only men of noble origins had the right to aim at what was beyond his reach.

"Son, are you all right?"

Darov's voice broke the silence of the dungeon, rousing Masolon from his absent-mindedness. He was not in the mood to talk, though.

"Who did you mess with, then?" the old man asked again. "Lord Larovic, or his spoiled son?"

"Not now, old man," Masolon snapped, his forehead still against the cold wall.

"If you are here, then you must have messed with one of them." The old man ignored Masolon's plain request. "Those who mess with that family end up here for good. Trust me, young man; silence won't do you any good. I have been alone enough to tell."

"Is that so?" Masolon turned, scanning the cell he was caged in. "How would talking to you help me, huh?" Gripping the bars, he tried to shake them as he roared, "How would talking to you help me, old man?"

Darov's face was surprisingly impassive. His silence gave Masolon hope that finally the old man got it.

"It was Larovic, wasn't it?" Darov evenly said, shattering Masolon's faint hope. *Is this the end for real? To be trapped in this dungeon with this garrulous old man forever?*

Masolon heaved a deep sigh. "Who is Larovic, to begin with?"

"Nobody," Darov said, "just the second-in-command to King Bechov, in case the name of King Bechov means anything to you."

The second-in-command? That explained the arrogance of his son. No wonder Gerviny felt he was immune.

"Was messing with one of them the reason behind your residence here?" Masolon asked flatly.

"Hah! I messed with both actually." Darov gazed at the ceiling. "That ended me up here twelve years ago."

Twelve years? Masolon couldn't still digest the notion of spending twelve days here. "You have grievously hurt them indeed."

"It was an accident. I didn't mean to kill his son."

"Who did you mean to kill? His father?"

"Nooo." Darov waved his hand dismissively. "I'm not an assassin, young man, I'm a chemist. If you are too ignorant to understand what that means, you can call me a sorcerer."

"I am that ignorant." Though Masolon was not in the mood, he had to admit he was impressed by the gray-haired man's high spirits in this cold grave. "How did you kill the poor fellow, sorcerer?"

Darov grinned, obviously amused by Masolon's interest in his story. "Fourteen years ago, I was summoned to serve the royal Rusakian court to improve our siege weapons. After a couple of years, I was almost done with a new craft that could destroy fortified walls in minutes and from a very far range." He paused for effect. "A weapon that would force your enemy to kneel to you before you move one soldier forward. I'm not exaggerating; the sound it makes is so horrifying that one strike is enough to convince the garrison of any fort you besiege that the battle is over. Can you imagine that? Probably, you can't."

Of course, Masolon could. Darov's weapon reminded him of the weapon he captured from the Ghosts in the battle of Kahora. "Is it different from a catapult?"

"It is totally different. My weapon hurls its projectiles with a force so massive you can never see them coming. Like a thunderbolt, son.

"I told Larovic I was ready to test the new weapon. Excited about the notion of possessing the most destructive weapon in Gorania, Larovic brought his elder and favorite son, Elov, to witness the test.

276

Unfortunately, things went bad and the weapon itself burst into flames. And guess who was blown up with the weapon?"

It took Masolon a while to realize that Darov was waiting for his answer. "Elov?"

"Yes, the son Larovic had been preparing to be his successor. Larovic's fury was beyond imagination. He ordered his soldiers to burn me alive, but King Bechov intervened and persuaded Larovic to imprison me for life instead."

"What about your thunder maker?"

"*Thundermaker?* I like that name," Darov said. "Even implying more dread than the cannon Larovic wanted."

The way the old man hopped from one topic to another was a bit exhausting. "The weapon, Darov. What happened to it?"

"Destroyed. The weapon and its maker are lost in oblivion, son. Larovic will never let me out of here until I die. Don't give me that look. I'm still not that old."

Masolon scanned the place with his eyes, hoping he could come up with a way out of this dungeon. "I am not going to die old here, Darov. I will get out, and you will get out with me."

The words were easy to say. Masolon realized that after two days of trying his luck with his shackles and the door of his cell. Everything was well-locked and there was nothing he could do. One more fact he realized in those two cursed days was that his suffering in the Murasen summer had been nothing compared to his struggle with the Rusakian winter.

"There were others," Darov told Masolon about his memories behind the cold bars, "but they died one after another in this tomb. I never saw anybody *walk* out that door at the end of the corridor. All of them were carried out."

Masolon wondered how the old man had survived this frozen tomb. The stale air in the dungeon was the least of Masolon's troubles. Over time, his nose became accustomed to the dungeon air, but the extreme chill remained his main problem. His cold chains were killing his limbs.

"I cannot feel my toes." Masolon shivered to the bone.

"Before they died, the first thing the others whimpered about was the numbness." Darov stood in the opposite cell. "The key is to keep your limbs mobile."

Masolon raised his chained hands and shook the clanking metal. "Easy to say without these."

"I have been shackled for months before."

"Any suggestions?"

"Keep jumping until your limbs get warm."

Jumping? No wonder this clever old fellow had survived all those years in the frozen tomb.

Day after day, Masolon was trying to discover more tricks to protect his limbs from being frozen. Once he tried putting his cuffed palms on the ground while raising his shackled legs and leaning his feet to the wall.

"I am too old to do this, I'm afraid," Darov said, watching him. "You are pushing more blood into your arms, but you're killing your legs. Don't stay like this for long if you want to keep them."

Masolon let his legs slip down and stood upright again. "How do those guards outside stand the chill?"

"Hah! They are Rusakians, son!" said Darov. "We are molded by the snow!"

"I do not know for how long I can live like this."

"You don't have to live if you don't want to," Darov said nonchalantly.

"Those who died in this dungeon; had they suffered much before their death?" Masolon winced as the bitter thought crossed his mind. Death didn't worry him as much as the pain before it.

"The hardest part is the first one," said Darov. "After that, you don't feel anything. It's like sleeping, or that's what it seems like."

Masolon gave him a faint smile. "Not as bad as I thought."

"I figured a warrior like you would fight."

"*You* are the real warrior, Darov. Just pondering the notion that I might grow old here drives me insane."

45. FERAS

Shezar would fall to his siege. Feras knew it was only a matter of time until Dehawy ran out of supplies. Deep inside, Feras loathed the notion of starving a Murasen city to force his foe to surrender, but it was not as bad as turning the greatest city in the east into a battlefield. The last sight Feras wanted to see was a Murasen soldier clashing his saber against his brother's.

"White flag, milord!" one of the officers standing outside Feras's pavilion announced. Every day he expected a messenger with a white flag coming out from the city gate. His father and his uncle had restored the northern fort of Kurdisan, forcing the Mankols to retreat to their lands. Now Dehawy and his eastern vassals were on their own.

"A messenger at last?" Feras said as he stepped outside.

"No, milord. It's Lord Memot himself."

Munzir would pay to witness this moment. Feras smiled as he gazed at the old lord who stood midway between Feras's camp and the walls of the city. Nothing would make his dear uncle happier than gloating over his old rival. But once again, Feras was there to steal his joy.

"Should I ready your horse, milord?" his officer asked.

"For this distance?" Feras pointed to the old lord. "He made it on foot, and he is twice my age."

Feras put on his helm and walked to his foe, his back straightened, his steps firm and steady. Though he was eager for such a meeting to conclude this war, he did his best not to show any sign of hurry. It was them who should be that eager for the King's mercy.

Memot had had a few tufts of gray hair, but now he was bald, slimmer than the last time Feras saw him. "Lord Memot," Feras curtly greeted him.

Memot looked him up and down. "I was a father of four sons when I was your age."

"When I grow old like you, I won't let a lord half my age defeat me."

Memot smiled. "You talk as if you won the war already."

"The war is over, the rebellion is over, and you know that," said Feras. "If you still think you are a true lord, you shall not let the commoners pay for your treason."

Memot stared at him for a moment. "Do you really mean any single word of what you said?"

"You heard what I said."

Memot nodded. "You are your father's son indeed. You're even greener than him when he was your age. You lucky bastard, Munzir."

"You'd better watch your mouth."

Memot gave Feras a crooked grin. "You have no idea what this game is about, son."

"I'm not your son," Feras spat.

"Of course not." Memot laughed. "You are the son of Lord Ahmet, the bastion of loyalty and dedication. And like your father, you will do whatever your king commands whatever the cost is because it's your duty. You will have no problem dedicating your whole life to an endless war, and in return, you will earn some hollow titles, like the Guardian of Kahora or the Hammer of the Mankols, and you will be satisfied with that. That's why Rasheed and his successors would rely on the likes of you to fight their battles and engage his enemies. But who would Rasheed listen to in the end?

Your father? Or your uncle? His soldier? Or his advisor? His vassal? Or his father-in-law?"

Feras was determined to ignore Memot's desperate attempts to provoke him, but he had to admit the last part had piqued his curiosity.

"Whose father-in-law?" he asked.

"You still don't get it." Memot chuckled. "What is really interesting is that the Guardian of Kahora is not aware of what is happening in Kahora. Do you have any idea what Munzir is doing in your city, in the royal palace these days?"

Feras didn't know about his uncle's presence in Kahora in the first place. "It doesn't matter. We defeated the Mankols and we won the war anyway," he reminded Memot.

"Why didn't your father return with him?" Memot asked. "Ah, right! Because the Mankols may strike again, so the Hammer shall stay there. And you, boy, after you are done here, will return to watch over Kahora again."

"That's an honor you can never dream of."

Memot sighed. "Haven't you asked yourself what on Earth is Rasheed so busy with that he can't see to the very city he resides in?"

It struck Feras that he had never thought of that. "We are done with this gibberish," he snapped. "Now it is time to discuss your surrender terms."

"This is not gibberish, boy," Memot argued. "There is a big game about that throne in Kahora, and still, you don't even want to listen. You didn't win, boy. The likes of you *never* win. Perchance you understand when the wedding ceremony begins."

Wedding ceremony? Father-in-law? His uncle in Kahora? Could that be the truth?

"Did you get it at last, boy?" Memot sneered. "That's why your uncle is a worthy foe. Unfortunately, I don't have any daughters."

But Munzir did. Shatha, a widow, and not even thirty.

"A king with no sons or brothers, and then you provoke his only legitimate heir," Memot said. "That's what Munzir did with Dehawy.

281

You can't but admire your uncle's patience. He has been trying to convince His Majesty with a second marriage, but Rasheed always honored his late wife, may the Lord rest her soul in peace. Now the way is paved after those sad events of Kahora."

Feras balled his hand into a fist, doing his best not to punch that rascal in the face. "My mother died in *those sad events of Kahora.*" He glared at Memot. "Why shouldn't I kill you right now?"

Memot kept his head up, his eyes averted. "You want to kill a lord under the banner of peace? Do you understand what trouble you will bring to your king, and consequently, yourself?"

Calm down now, Feras. The war is about to end. Don't start another one.

That was exactly what Memot had mentioned, right? The likes of Feras would do whatever their king commanded whatever the cost was because it was their duty. He wouldn't avenge his mother because of his damned duty.

Only now did he understand why Sania loathed their father. Strangely enough, it had never been so clear like today.

"Lord Memot, you have come out from your city to tell me something," Feras said. "If it is your surrender terms, I will be glad to listen to them."

"There is no surrender. But I have an offer for you."

More of the wicked lord's games. "What offer?"

"Join us before it is too late. I know your father won't. He is too stubborn to see what is coming in the near future. But you see it now, don't you?"

"This meeting is a waste of time." Feras turned his back on him, walking away to return to his camp.

"It's a game, boy!" Memot yelled after him. "You and your father's turn will come soon."

46. GERVINY

Gerviny was surprised when Sergi told him that Lord Larovic was already in Durberg and was now on his way to the palace. Because of the eminent war with the Mankols, the Lord Marshal was supposed to be leading the troops camping at the southern Rusakian borders.

There was nothing to worry about. In fact, Gerviny was glad his father was back to see for himself what his son had done in the city in just a couple of weeks of ruling. The treasury now had more coin thanks to the taxes he had collected from the merchants, who had been bribing the officers to skip their payments. The streets were safer now after he had doubled the night patrols. Only two weeks, and he proved his worth as the future Lord of Durberg. Wait, he was the Lord of Durberg already. His father should see him on the Lord's seat when he arrived.

Gerviny headed to the great hall and ordered his guards to line up in front of him, then took his seat. *That's how the Lord of Durberg should look,* he thought, his eyes on the door in anticipation of his father's arrival. About time the old man stopped grieving for Elov and remembered he had another son. About time Lord Larovic took back his insults and started regarding Gerviny as his worthy heir.

The page announced the arrival of Lord Larovic. For no obvious reason, Gerviny felt that his stomach was in knots as the echoing footsteps approached. In an attempt to appear at ease, he leaned back in his seat, resting his cheek on his fist. It might seem rude, but he didn't mind. For many years he had been treating his father with respect. How many times had Gerviny had the same treatment in return? Not even once. The thought infuriated him so much that his fist trembled beneath his cheek.

There was nothing unusual about his father's entrance; the guards surrounding him and the customary frown on his face. What was new about his entrance this time was Gerviny himself sitting on the Lord's chair. From the glare on the Lord Marshal's face, Gerviny could tell his father wasn't pleased with this sight. However, Gerviny was determined not to adjust his posture.

"Leave us," Larovic demanded. Nobody dared to disobey, Gerviny's guards included. In less than a minute, nobody stood between the Lord Marshal and his son.

"Why don't you have a seat, Father?" Gerviny nodded toward him, still keeping his posture.

"What have you done?" his father growled.

"I have made this city wealthier and safer in your absence. Why do you ask?"

"You are holding a Murasen commander in the dungeon."

So, this angry face was for that worthless Masolon? Seriously, his father was losing his sanity. "I didn't know that when I captured him."

"Now you know!"

"How do you expect me to act, milord? That commander was caught sneaking into Lady Halin's bedchamber."

"I am done with your folly!" His father glared at him. "Do you think that I'm not aware of your ridiculous plot?"

"What plot?"

"Shut up!" His father wagged a firm finger at him. "Your obsession with Sanislav's daughter has driven you mad. Your childish pursuit makes you forget that you are the elder son of Lord Larovic,

Marshal of all Rusakian armies. You forget that you are a lord yourself who should be responsible for his own acts."

"I'm responsible for my own acts and all their consequences," Gerviny stated firmly.

"No, you are not. You are too pathetic to understand those consequences! You are about to start a war between two realms, simply for the sake of your lust! Do you understand that we are recently allied with the Murasens to keep the Mankols surrounded from their northern and southern borders?"

"You should blame the commander who sneaked into a foreign castle, not me."

"Enough! This farce must end. That imprisoned commander shall be outside Durberg at once."

Gerviny leaned toward his father, their eyes meeting. "He is imprisoned by order of the Lord of Durberg."

"You have lost your mind." His father turned and headed to the door.

"What do you think you are doing?" Gerviny pushed to his feet and hurried after his father. No one should break an order from the Lord of Durberg, even the Lord Marshal himself.

"What do you think *you* are doing, boy?" His father stopped, glowering at him. "Two weeks on this seat and you think you can stop me?"

"I captured that bastard! He shall not be released unless I decide otherwise!"

His father shook his head. "You still don't get that I am saving your worthless head. Keep your prisoner in your dungeon, and I assure you that King Bechov will strip you of your title as a lord."

"Curse him and the title!" Gerviny snapped. "That commander is *my* prisoner! That's my dignity you're treading on! No one shall humiliate me again!"

"I really regret the day I had a son like you." His father turned to the door. "Guards!" The guards hurried to his father.

"What are you doing?" Gerviny asked.

"Escort Lord Gerviny to his chamber and keep him there until I return from the dungeon. Make sure no one follows me."

Gerviny was lost for words as the guards surrounded him. His father had devastated him with one simple blow. The lord became a prisoner, and the prisoner became a free man. Could this situation be more humiliating?

Fuming, Gerviny let the guards usher him to his chamber, the shock still muddling his mind. He realized that his nightmare was real when he saw the guards stand at his doorstep. Yes, the door was open, but Gerviny knew for sure that no one would allow him to step outside until receiving further orders from the true Lord of Durberg. The lord that everybody here obeyed no matter what. The lord that nobody would ever dare to lock up in his chamber. How would those guards listen to anything Gerviny said in the future? How would he ever rule his subjects after his humiliation turned into a song in the taverns? Now instead of singing about *The Lady Who Had Fallen for the Champion*, they would sing for *The Champion Who Locked up the False Lord*. That would make the perfect tale for those drunken wretches.

Unless Gerviny changed the end of the tale.

"Sergi!" he called out to his squire, who was standing outside the chamber. When the guards stopped the squire from entering, Gerviny snapped at them, "What's your problem? Will you prohibit my squire from coming to me?"

The guards reluctantly let the squire in. Gerviny took the lad away from the door to be out of earshot. "Listen carefully, Sergi. I will get out of here the moment my father returns. Until then I need you to ready my horse and my war ax."

The squire looked skeptical at the mention of the war ax. "Where are we going, milord?"

"Not far at all." Gerviny sighed. "And it's only me, not us."

47. MASOLON

Masolon heard the creak of the dungeon door, followed by many footsteps. Leaning his back against the wall of his cell, he couldn't see who entered the dungeon, but he saw Darov's widened eyes. When Masolon shot his mate an inquisitive look, Darov mouthed, "*Larovic.*"

Masolon rose and leaned against the ice-cold bars for a better view. Now he remembered he had seen that lord before in the feast of Durberg.

"We meet again, Masolon," Larovic said gruffly. "Or shall I say Commander Masolon?"

Scanning the lord's face, Masolon now knew from whom Gerviny had gotten his blue eyes. "Tides have changed as you see, Lord Larovic."

"I am not sure about those tides that brought you here, Commander. But I hope we can prevent this from happening again in the future." Larovic gestured to his guards, and without delay, they opened the cell and unchained Masolon. Although he had waited for that moment, Masolon was still suspicious about Larovic's intentions. Had the veteran lord come to release him, or to weave another scheme?

"We will consider that your journey to Durberg has never

happened," said Larovic, leering at Masolon. "I strongly recommend you do the same."

Masolon stepped outside the cell and stood just before Larovic. "That would be hard, I am afraid." Masolon curled his lip. "I can still feel the cold steel on my wrists and feet. How do you expect me to forget that?"

"Do you want to start a war between two kingdoms because of a boyish contest for a girl?"

"That contest exists only in your son's sick mind."

"Watch your mouth, Commander." Larovic glared at Masolon. "I might say harsher words to my son, but I would kill you if you just thought of harming him."

"Your son owes me a lot," Masolon ground out.

"And I pay his debt by setting you free. It's done once you set foot outside this dungeon. But I swear I will kill you if I see you here again."

"We shall see about that." Masolon took a few steps toward the dungeon door then remembered his promise to take Darov out with him. When he looked over his shoulder, the old man made a slight wave.

"We will meet again, son." Darov grinned. "Probably in the afterlife."

* * *

Masolon found his horse tied outside the dungeon in the falling snow, his greatsword, Mankol bow, and steel shield on the ground beside the stallion's hooves. The generous gesture from the Rusakian lord surprised Masolon, but his doubts never faded.

"You must be cold, my friend." Masolon brushed his horse's hair. The castle guards were glaring at him as if hurrying him to leave.

"Enjoy the weather, bastards," he muttered, mounting his stallion. He left the dungeon, his eyes and ears alert to his surroundings. That malicious lord should have waited until morning to release him. Maybe he set Masolon free at night to let the snow kill him without staining his lordly hands with a commoner's blood.

Masolon hadn't seen one random Rusakian citizen in the streets since he left the dungeon. In addition to the lovely weather of Durberg at night, the heavy clouds hid the sky with a dark-gray curtain that didn't even let the moonlight pass through it. From now on, he would never complain about the sweaty Murasen nights.

"Masolon!"

He was one mile away from reaching the city main gate when he heard Gerviny's voice. Ahorse, the bastard was charging at him from his right flank. Larovic might go to hell with his threats; Masolon had to defend himself.

He pulled the reins to the right and kicked his horse's flanks, spurring it to charge at Gerviny, but he was a bit late. Gerviny closed up on him before his stallion reached its full gallop. The Rusakian prince swung his massive war ax toward him, Masolon receiving the shock of the hit on his steel shield; a shock that was enough to crush any wooden shield. It bent Masolon's shield-arm though, causing him to lose his balance. He clutched the reins with his left hand, trying to prevent himself from slipping off the saddle, but it did not work, only easing his fall.

Masolon rolled on the ground and rose on his feet in a second, his eyes on Gerviny's horse. He held his greatsword with both hands, waiting for Gerviny to wheel his horse and charge once more. By any means, Masolon had to prevent the coming strike from happening. The momentum acquired by the huge war ax in a cavalry charge would make it deadly if intercepted on foot.

Gerviny rushed toward him as Masolon raised his greatsword above his head with both hands. "I'll crush you!" Gerviny screamed, stretching his arm, ready to swing his war ax.

Masolon's eyes were fixed on Gerviny's horse that came a few feet away from him. Just before the Rusakian started swinging, Masolon surprised his opponent by throwing his heavy sword right at the horse's big neck. Gerviny's horse neighed out of pain, raising its forelimbs, throwing its rider. Masolon rushed toward Gerviny's horse and wrenched his sword from its neck. The wounded horse whickered again.

Gerviny grabbed his ax and raised it with both hands to block an overhead strike from Masolon, then lowered it vertically to stop another low blow from him. After testing each other in that brief clash, both took a couple of steps away from each other without turning their backs.

"Not bad for a Contest clown," said Gerviny.

"And you are not bad for a pathetic little lord." Masolon smirked.

"I was trained by the best, not by some sort of clowns like those who trained you."

Gerviny bored in with three consecutive swings of his war ax, each strike met by Masolon's shield. After parrying the third blow, Masolon stabbed at Gerviny's left thigh. The Rusakian lord tried to evade the sword point, but the sharp blade cut through his skin.

"Surprised?" said Masolon with a gloating smile. Gerviny looked more astonished than pained, perhaps wondering how Masolon was wielding his heavy sword with one hand. Did Gerviny notice that Masolon's maneuvers were Rusakian? *Thank you, Ramel!*

"By the way, I was not trained by clowns." Masolon lunged forward with a mighty blow.

Gerviny limped backward, blocking Masolon's deadly strike with his war ax. Masolon found an opening and whacked Gerviny's right knee with the rim of his steel shield. The massive hit forced the prince to bend his leg and take one step back. Masolon swung his shield once more toward the face of his opponent, who did not know how to dodge that metallic slap. Taking advantage of Gerviny's confusion, Masolon plunged his sword into the prince's belly. Gerviny roared, bent his back, and dropped his ax.

"I told you, *milord*," Masolon scoffed, "one day you will not be hiding behind your title."

Gerviny stared at the blade stuck to his abdomen. Another blow by the shield made him fall on his back. "I thought you owed me a punch," Masolon taunted. "But you know what? I have just realized I owe you something."

Gerviny's eyes betrayed his anticipation; a faint hope of a dying man. That fool had no idea. If there was something Masolon owed him, it would be proving the ridiculousness of his grandfather's tales about the fairness of destiny. A scum became a noble only because his father was so, nothing glorious about it. A worthless bastard had the right to marry whoever he wanted to marry, jail whoever he wanted to jail, kill whoever he wanted to kill only because of the damned noble blood running through his lordly veins. But what about the likes of Masolon? Those who fought and bled for the people of these cursed lands? They might earn a meaningless title or a stupid medallion, but nothing more, because of their filthy 'common' blood.

Gerviny gasped, his chest rising and falling.

Masolon grabbed the war ax from the ground and laid its cold blade on Gerviny's neck. "You do not deserve the honor of my sword." With both hands, Masolon swung the ax and chopped off Gerviny's head, a fountain of dark-red blood surging out of the stump of the severed neck. The rascal was dead, but that didn't make Masolon feel any better. Nothing would change. Masolon was still a commoner who would live and die in oblivion. On the other hand, Gerviny's corpse would be buried in an honorable funeral that would befit a lord.

"Halt!" a harsh voice called from a distance.

Masolon was not able to estimate the number of those soldiers at the end of his sight. He pulled his sword from Gerviny's corpse, strapped his shield to his back, and ran into the nearest alley he found. It was time to flee this cursed city.

48. MASOLON

A troop of thirty Rusakian spearmen blocked the way to the gate of Durberg, making it impossible for Masolon to go past them peacefully and leave the city. He hid behind one of the houses in the dark alley and watched his angry pursuers look for him. He knew he had to move from his spot. Rusakian soldiers were searching the whole alley and they would find him at any moment.

The Frozen Lake.

Masolon recalled he had once heard from Darov that it lay west. But first he had to get out of that alley. And soon. The crunching boots of the Rusakian guards were approaching his hideout, which was a house surrounded by nothing but snowdrifts.

He was staring at a frosty white mass in front of him when a crazy idea came to his mind. *No time for hesitation, Masolon. Act now,* he thought, listening to the crunching footsteps. The Rusakian guards were going to reach his spot in seconds.

He quickly dug both arms into the snow. The numbness in his fingers started immediately, but there was no time to deal with it. He burrowed his lower half into the groove he made, brushed snow over himself to cover the rest of his body, and before burying his head, he took a deep breath of freezing air. It felt like being stabbed by a cold dagger in the heart, but it was surely better than getting struck by a real blade of some Rusakian soldier.

A couple of seconds later, he could hardly hear the soldiers' boots, just in front of the drift he buried himself inside. A severe chill shocked his body, making him shiver like a wobbling tree branch on a windy day. The air in his lungs was consumed rapidly. Any moment of panic would cost him his life. *When will those bastards leave?* The frost had numbed his limbs in the beginning. Now he could not feel them anymore.

"The roofs!"

A faint Rusakian voice reached his ears through the snow barrier. The soldier sounded as if he was miles away.

Masolon was not sure if the soldiers had gone or not, but his natural survival instinct urged him to get himself out, the deprivation of air tearing his chest apart. He tried to move his arms to remove the snow, but they barely responded. Frightened by the notion of freezing to death, he pushed forward desperately with his head and kicked the snow behind his numbed legs. The air in his lungs was running out. Most probably, he had only a few seconds before he collapsed.

And finally, his head was out.

He crawled, gasping for air, but he could not even fully open his mouth, his chest wheezing like a creaking door. His eyelids were too heavy to force them open to check his surroundings, yet there were no soldiers' boots visible in his limited field of vision.

'*The roofs*' was the last thing he had heard. Maybe those Rusakians thought that he was hiding atop one of the buildings in the dark alley.

Away from the soldiers' torches, hidden by darkness, trembling with chill, he crept out of the alley. The way was clear now to crawl to the other side of the street to head to the western side of the sleeping city. He still had a chance to reach that Frozen Lake, but not after sunrise. It would be easier to find him when the city woke up.

He needed to push blood to his limbs, and crawling wasn't helping. Walking on his feet was now a wish. If he remained on the snow all night long, he would die before anyone found him. Pushing himself up with his arms, Masolon raised his body and moved like a four-legged animal. Every few blocks his arms failed him. As he reached the end of the neighborhood, his hands couldn't touch the snow anymore. If the sense of touch was even still there…

He didn't know how much time had passed, but night in Rusakia was longer than in Murase. On his elbows and his knees, he crawled. A neighborhood ended, another one started, and yet no sign of the damned Frozen Lake.

"*Keep looking!*"

It had been a while since he had heard the guards' voices. *They are not too far.* Now, after realizing how warm his cell was, he considered yielding to those guards to take him back to the dungeon. Most probably his coming night in the dungeon would be the last, but that would be another problem he would worry about later.

Masolon used his hands again. Four legs were better than none. A lion was faster than a snake. A dog was—he would become any animal now to survive. With his four legs he walked, the soldiers' thudding boots getting closer. Abandoning the idea of surrendering to them, he trotted, or he tried to, but it wasn't as easy as his horse made it seem.

There were no more buildings on either side when he reached the copse of oak trees. He leaned on one of them and rose to his feet, his legs shaking so badly he would fall if he didn't embrace the huge trunk. Looking behind, he could see torches, though he wasn't sure where those soldiers were going. Soon they would come here. Blood was returning to his legs as he stood, and now he might be able to walk, but where should he go? Ahead was only a vast plain without a single tree to hide behind. He had seen green plains in Bermania and yellow plains in Murase, but here the plains were white, and at some points, they had no color, like glass. It even felt like glass, hard beneath his feet.

Wait. This is ice.

He must be standing on the Frozen Lake right now, and only one house lay at the other side of that lake. Doing his best not to be spotted by the guards, Masolon lowered his head and padded across the ice as he headed to, hopefully, his haven.

A woman came out of the house and dragged a barrel from the doorstep to a four-wheeled cart. Masolon wasn't sure what she said, but she seemed to be calling someone inside the house. A younger girl stood by the doorstep, talking to the old woman.

"*Mom!*" the girl yelled, pointing at him.

"*The bow! The bow!*" the woman urged her daughter, who hurried inside and returned in a few moments with a bow and a quiver. The last thing Masolon needed in such a quiet place was their noise. And their arrows, of course.

He waved his hands to them, hoping the woman wouldn't shoot him. While her daughter was holding the quiver for her, the woman snatched an arrow and nocked it onto the bowstring. "Don't come closer!" she warned, pulling the bowstring, aiming at him.

"Do not shoot." Masolon stopped, his teeth clicking.

"Oh Lord! He is almost frozen!" The young girl looked alarmed. Like her mother, her eyes were blue, but her hair was darker.

"Shut up now!" the mother rebuked the young girl. "You!" she addressed him. "What are you doing here?"

"Anna?" Masolon asked.

The mother looked surprised. "How do you know me while I don't know you?" she asked warily, still aiming at him.

"Blanich."

"Blanich?" Astonished, the daughter grabbed her mother's arm. "Mom, lower this bow. Please!"

"Get off me!" Anna snapped at her daughter. To Masolon, she said, "Who sent you? Tell me, or I swear I will shoot you at once."

"Blanich sent me." Masolon tried to recall Blanich's words. "He says he will be back when he is ready."

"It's him!" the girl told her mother. "Blanich must have sent him!"

Anna looked skeptical as she lowered her bow. "What do you want?"

Every part of Masolon's body shivered. "A warm place."

"Mom, he is freezing!" The young girl scurried to him, pulling him by the arm.

"Jubi!" Anna called, infuriated. "What are you doing, you foolish girl?"

"Can't you see his pale face? We must take him inside the house before the cold kills him," said Jubi, walking him to the open door. Masolon would allow her to take him wherever she wanted, as long as it was walled and roofed, and without soldiers looking for him.

Jubi dragged a chair when they entered their small house. "Sit until I get you something warm to drink."

Anna followed them inside. "Do I need to remind you of the four remaining barrels? We need to reach Maksow before sunset, young lady." She laid her palm on Masolon's numbed hand. "Oh Lord! You're freezing indeed! Jubi, get two blankets, now!" She pulled him by the arm and took him to the fireplace. Masolon extended his hands to the flames, resisting the temptation to drive his frozen fingers into it. Gradually, he was feeling the heat on his palms.

"Careful," Anna warned him. "Your hands are too close." She left him when Jubi returned with the blankets and covered him with it.

"Better now?" Jubi asked.

"Yes, thank you," Masolon croaked.

"You met him in person?" A smile crept over Jubi's pretty face. "How is he?"

The glow in her eyes when she asked about *him* was not lost on Masolon. A glow he had never seen in Sania's eyes. *Lucky Blanich. I would die for a look like this.*

Anna returned with a bowl in her hands. "Can you do something useful instead of asking about your sweetheart?"

"Mom!" Jubi's snow white face blushed, her blue eyes glaring at Anna.

"Go and boil some lemon for him," Anna said. Mumbling, Jubi went outside and Anna handed Masolon the bowl. "Drink this honey."

He took the bowl from her. "Drink?"

"This is Rusakian honey. The only honey in Gorania that is never thickened by the frost. What is your name?"

"Masolon."

"Tell me, Masolon. How did you meet Blanich?"

Masolon told her about the Contest, Blanich's injury that finally ended him up in the Murasen lands, the nomads' raid on Kahora, and their battle in which they had defeated those nomads.

"He told you he would return when he was ready, huh?" Anna asked.

"He did not say more, and I did not ask." Masolon shrugged. "I presumed the receiver would understand."

Anna glanced at her pretty daughter who entered holding a copper pot, steam wafting out from it with the scent of boiled lemon. He was better now already, the numbness gone, his limbs not shaking anymore.

"I understand indeed." Anna chuckled self-mockingly, Jubi pouring the boiled lemon in a jug. "Bring it before it cools, Jubi."

Anna took the honey from him and gave him the jug. The lemon was too sour, but Masolon felt the warmth spreading in his blood. "How are your limbs now?" she asked.

"Much better." Masolon took another gulp. "I can feel them, yet they are still weak."

"You were nearly frozen when we brought you inside," said Anna. "Although it seems that you are not used to our weather, you choose the coldest hour of the day to be outside."

"Bad luck, I guess."

"This is what my late husband used to say when he fell into trouble because of his folly."

"How do you know I am in trouble?"

Anna scanned his face. "You are not from here, I'm quite sure. I wonder why a stranger might deliberately come to our frozen city."

"Until recently, coming to Durberg was not one of my plans," Masolon said bitterly. "Apparently, destiny has its own plans for me."

"A good excuse to feel more comfortable about it, huh?" Anna chided. "Throwing the blame on destiny as if you don't have the free will to make your own decisions. Do you think this makes you pious?"

Masolon didn't dare to utter a word in his own defense.

"You won't change your destiny if you leave yourself to his plans." Anna took the empty jug from Masolon, then gave him another round of honey. "Destiny chooses those who choose him."

Masolon could sense her kindness despite her apparent harshness. *Who would ask a widow with a daughter to be 'nice' in these cold lands?*

"I wonder if you can help me with the barrels outside," said Anna. "We should have left Durberg before sunrise, but thanks to your sudden visit, we are late."

"My apologies." Masolon removed the blankets and rose to his feet. "I will make it up to you."

"Fine. You can come with us if you are leaving the city today."

Nothing he wanted now like leaving the City of Ice. "I am afraid I cannot come with you," he said.

"Why not?" Anna asked. "Where are you heading?"

"My destination is not the problem." It would be ungrateful if he returned their favor by putting them in danger. He had to tell them everything about his *visit* to their city. Everything, including the feast in the palace of Durberg, his brief chattering with Halin, his quarrel with Gerviny, Halin's false maiden, his frozen dungeon, and his last duel with Gerviny. Hopefully, he wouldn't regret it.

"Oh, Lord!" Jubi covered her mouth when Masolon reached the part of decapitating Gerviny. "All the guards of Durberg must be looking for you now!"

He nodded to Jubi, then stared at her silent mother, trying to get any clue about her stance.

"Killing a lord is a grave act, young man," Anna mused. "Lord Larovic will not rest until he finds you. And he will if you stay here. If we don't take you with us, your head will end up resting on a pike."

"But how will we take him, Mom?" Jubi shook her head. "The

guards at the gate will arrest him on sight."

"We've passed the gates hundreds of times," said Anna. "They never searched our cargo."

"Today is different, Anna," said Masolon. "A 'murderer' is on the loose."

*　*　*

It was dark inside, but warm. Even warmer than Anna's house. Through the only hole in the barrel, Masolon watched the houses passing by. Since he couldn't see a trotting horse or a turning cartwheel, it was the houses that moved, not him.

They were approaching the gate. He knew it when the cart slowed down until it stopped.

"*Sweet Anna! You are a bit late today.*" Probably, that was a guard.

"*I am getting old, it seems,*" Anna replied, sounding natural.

"*More honey?*" the same soldier asked.

"*Sure. Mine is the best you know.*"

"*Have a safe journey. Don't travel in the dark.*"

"*I will not.*"

Masolon let out a sigh of relief. Now he understood why Anna wasn't worried about sneaking him out of the city.

"*You don't look good today, Anna.*" Another guard sounded suspicious. *She looks fine, you bastard. Let her pass,* Masolon thought as he listened to the approaching thudding boots. Two boots of one soldier. From that hole in the barrel, Masolon couldn't see what the soldier was doing outside until he heard the knocks on the other barrels. The other *full* barrels. *Blast!* If he had half Blanich's luck, that guard would be too deaf to notice the different knock on the hollow barrel.

I should not have involved them.

He bit his lower lip. The guards would arrest Anna and her daughter with him, and most probably, Larovic would execute them as well. Yesterday he ran away, but today he wouldn't. Today he must fight to save those poor ladies.

Now it was the turn of his barrel, and it received more knocks than the rest. The guard had found something, Masolon knew. Gripping the hilt of his sword, he was ready for the inevitable encounter.

"I know you are here," Masolon heard the soldier whispering. "We are even now."

Masolon didn't respond to the soldier's attempt to distract him, his hand still tight on the hilt.

"*What is the matter?*" another soldier asked. "*Something wrong, Androvsky?*"

Could it be him? The same desperate spearman? Masolon wasn't sure whether it was good or bad news.

"*Everything is fine,*" Androvsky replied, Masolon now sure it was his voice. "*Let the honey lady pass. She has a long day ahead.*"

The cart moved at last, Masolon letting out a deep breath. The games of destiny treated him well this time. Should he restore his faith in them? Perhaps, but not before he made sure he was safe.

The cart started moving again and the guards' voices faded away. Now he could only hear the horses' clopping hooves. After Anna had traveled some distance from Durberg, she let him out of his barrel.

"It seems that you are not that unlucky, Masolon."

He smiled at her sarcasm, but a glance at her pretty daughter reminded him how unlucky he was.

"Hopefully, we will reach Maksow before sunset." Jubi turned to him. "There you can find a ride to Kahora."

The snow was getting thinner as they went south. Anna told Masolon about Blanich's stepmother, who married his greedy uncle after his father's death. Anna even believed that Blanich's father's death was arranged by the evil couple to take over his lands. After finishing Blanich's story, Anna told Masolon about herself and her life with her late husband. The journey to Maksow was a long one, and Anna was a good storyteller. Masolon had no problem listening to her all the way. Jubi barely talked, and when she did, she asked about Blanich.

The cart reached Maksow late at night. All shops were shut already, killing any chance for Anna to sell her honey today. "Damn!" She frowned. "Where am I going to leave these barrels?"

Masolon felt guilty since he was the one who had delayed the two ladies. "You go and find a chamber in the tavern. I will stay up and guard the cart," he offered.

"You will freeze," Anna warned.

He grinned. "Do not worry about me."

The night in Maksow wasn't as freezing as in Durberg, yet it was still much colder than any night he had spent anywhere outside Rusakia. *Colder and longer.* With only him and the cart horses, Masolon was spending one of his longest, *smelliest* nights ever.

With the first light of next day, Jubi came to him, her blue eyes so sleepy, still pretty though.

"It seems that you are awake a bit earlier than what you are used to," Masolon remarked.

"Is it that obvious?" She rubbed her eyes. "Waking up early is the daily topic of Mom's quarrels with me."

The wool coat she wore wasn't a match for his fur coat. "Are you not cold?"

"We are Rusakians," she scoffed. "Snow runs in our veins instead of blood."

For a moment, he remembered Sania. The *cheerful* Sania who used to make fun of him as he couldn't tolerate the Murasen sun. *Curse you, Blanich! How dare you leave such an angel!*

"Don't you want to get some sleep before you start your long journey to Kahora?" Jubi asked. "Mom is going to wake up soon."

"Thank you, Jubi. I am grateful for everything you and Anna have done for me."

"You seem like a good man of a pure heart, Masolon. I'm sure one day you'll find your soulmate who will deserve you."

A pure heart? A restless one, he would say.

"Would you do something for me?" asked Jubi. "Tell Blanich that

I am still waiting for his return."

"I will tell him."

"Also tell him this; *ya tebya lyublu.*"

"*Ya tebya lyu...blu,*" he echoed.

"Your accent is so funny." Her cheeks reddened when she giggled, making her even prettier.

He laughed. "What is this?"

"A message in the old Rusakian tongue," she explained. "Can you say it one more time?"

"*Ya tebya lyublu.*"

"You learn fast."

"I will keep practicing while traveling back to Murase. Now I must go. Send my greetings to Anna." He cast Jubi one last smile and left, eager to leave the snow lands as soon as possible. Whatever happened in the near or distant future, Masolon would never come back to the Kingdom of Rusakia.

49. MASOLON

The hill. The Den of the Warrior's Gang. That was the first place Masolon passed by when he reached Kahora.

The whole gang was in his reception when he ascended the hill. No doubt, the archers watching over the den had alerted everybody, especially Masolon's captains. "And here he comes back!" Ziyad rumbled upon seeing him.

"You look pale, Masolon." Antram studied his face. "I hope you didn't have a rough time with the Rusakians."

"Beyond what you think." Masolon gave him a tired smile. "What battles did I miss?"

"Nothing big." Ziyad shrugged. "Only a few raids from our side on some scattered bands of brigands around Kahora. Their activity has dwindled."

"Good news." Masolon nodded, his hands on his waist. "Anything else?"

"Feras is back," said Frankil. "He has asked for an audience with you."

No doubt the Murasen lord would have a few questions about his commander's sudden disappearance.

"We rode to the castle of Arkan to answer his call," said Antram, "and I have to tell you, he was upset when he knew that you traveled outside the kingdom without his permission."

Antram only confirmed Masolon's worries. How could he explain his journey to Rusakia?

"What did you tell him about my journey?" Masolon asked his companions.

"We told him we didn't know," Ziyad answered.

"You must go to him at once," Antram urged.

"I will." A journey to Arkan would be a ramble in the desert compared to his journey to Durberg. "I have a message for you," he said to Blanich, taking him aside.

Blanich grinned. "You haven't met Anna, have you?"

"I do not know how I could have survived if it had not been for her." Masolon told Blanich everything had happened, starting from his crawl on ice to reach Anna's house until their journey to Maksow.

"It's *ya tebya lyublu*." Blanich guffawed, correcting Masolon's accent. "Do you know what it means?"

Masolon shrugged. "Something in the old Rusakian tongue?"

"That's right." Blanich nodded. "It means 'I love you.'"

Lucky you, Masolon wanted to say. He wondered how he would feel if a sweet girl like Jubi said those three words to him.

* * *

Though Masolon had not seen the Murasen lord for a long time, there was not much emotion in their reunion; something Masolon wouldn't complain about. A 'warm' reception was nothing Masolon was hoping for.

Stone-faced, Feras met Masolon in the big hall and allowed him to sit down. "When I returned, it was easy for me to notice the impact of your efforts in cleansing the western regions from banditry," said Feras. "Your name has become a nightmare for those brigands, and now they are not playing hunter anymore. I believe every bandit is afraid of being the next prey."

Something harsh was coming after this *nice* introduction, Masolon knew.

"We won our war against the traitors, and you vanquished those brigands. A perfect time for celebration," Feras said. "But what happened when I summoned my valorous commander? He wasn't there. He decided to go to an unknown destination on his own."

Masolon remained silent since he could not argue about that.

"You're a soldier, Masolon." Feras glowered at him. "A soldier never abandons his post until his commander orders him to do so."

"It was just an old debt, milord." Masolon's voice was impassive.

"Tell me, Masolon, what will you do if a soldier leaves your gang without informing you?"

Was Feras testing him, or just teaching him a lesson? Or both? Masolon should weigh his next words carefully.

"I got your point, milord," said Masolon.

"Answer me!" Feras howled.

Masolon clenched his fist. No one was to yell at him. No one. Even if it was the King himself. "Then he would never have a place in the gang."

"Good," said Feras coldly. "Now I can rest assured that you really understand the difference between your previous position as a leader of a gang of mercenaries, and your current responsibility as a commander of a troop of Murasen soldiers."

A gang of mercenaries? Maybe it was part of the truth, but it sounded rather like an insult from Feras when said that way. Gritting his teeth, Masolon chose not to reply now. Otherwise he might say something he would regret. Until this moment, he still bore some respect to Feras. The young noble was what a lord in Gorania should be. A lord who had inherited the title from his father and earned it with his deeds. A Goranian champion who led his men himself to defend the lands he belonged to.

"Surely, milord," Masolon said. "You can rest assured."

A moment of uneasy silence fell over the place.

"I didn't want to dig deep in this," Feras rubbed his chin, "but I heard some tales that provoked my worries. When you hear that one of your finest men has run after some foreign princess, I believe you should be concerned."

"It is not like what you have heard, mil—"

"I am not interested to know whether it was a princess or a debt, Masolon," Feras cut in, "but I *do* need to hear from you one thing; that this will never happen again."

"It will never happen again, milord," Masolon said resolutely. "It has ended for good."

"I hope so. Now you can go and resume your duties in the western region. I will be expecting you at Arkan every two weeks to report to me." Feras gave him a dismissive gesture.

Masolon strode across the hall, heading to the courtyard outside. He waved at the stable boy to bring him his stallion. After he was done with that tense meeting with Feras, he wanted to leave the castle as fast as possible. The lad returned with his stallion in a couple of minutes that had felt like a couple of hours.

"I see you're still fond of black horses."

Masolon was frozen when he heard her voice. Her sweet voice. Yes, he heard that right. *She* was standing behind him. The girl with the auburn hair.

"Sania."

"Excuse me? How dare you address a princess like that?"

"I am sorry, milady, I did not…"

Masolon didn't finish as he wanted to entertain his ears with her sweet laugh that reminded him of some previous dreamy moments.

"Look at you, as if you have just seen a demon," she teased him.

Her cheerful spirit delighted and confused him at the same time. She was not the same pale, gloomy girl he had met ten weeks ago in Burdi. She was back, sweet and frisky.

"I would love to see demons if they were that pretty." He couldn't help grinning.

She blushed. "What was that? A flirtation?"

"I guess it is."

"You've changed, Masolon." She folded her arms, still smiling. "It seems that you've learned a lot from your last journey to Rusakia. I bet you had some good times there."

Masolon wondered what she had exactly heard. "Why do you think I had a good time there?"

"Why not?" She shrugged. "Didn't you enjoy the company of your Rusakian princess?"

"*My* Rusakian princess!" He guffawed. "It is not like what you think."

"Really?" The way she arched one of her delicate eyebrows betrayed her concern. She *was* concerned, and her concern excited him.

"There are many things to explain, Sania." A crazy idea popped into his head. "And indeed I have learned a few but useful things from this journey."

"Really? Like what?"

"*Ya tebya lyublu.*"

"What does that mean?"

"I love you." Masolon paused, amused by the stunned look on her face. "I mean this is what it means in the old Rusakian tongue."

Sania looked like a rose with her reddened cheeks, a smile slipping over her face as she rolled her eyes. "Interesting." She harrumphed. "Where has your stallion gone?"

Masolon smiled at her attempt to change the topic. "I lost him in my journey."

"It seems that many things happened to you on that *journey*. I am eager to listen, especially to that part of the Rusakian princess and how she taught you a new language."

"Trust me, it is not what it seems."

"We shall see about that. It's hard for me to trust men anymore."

"Not all men are the same. I told you that the day you dismissed me. Remember?"

"Please, don't remind me." She chuckled. "I acted like a fool that day."

"Never mind, never mind." Now Masolon was the one acting like a fool by bringing that memory back. "What has passed has passed. You are back, and that is what matters."

"I am not really back. I am spending three more days with Feras, and then I will return to Burdi."

"Burdi again? Away from your brother?"

"He was always away, and he will always be. The only thing that kept me here was my mother, and now she's gone."

"What about you? I mean, being alone?"

"I can take care of myself, Masolon. Besides, I feel better alone in Burdi. I wear what I want to wear, read what I want to read, ride a horse whenever I want to." She gave a sigh of relief. "That air of freedom is invaluable."

He missed that song, hearing his name uttered by her voice. It was the only word he recalled in all she said.

"I wonder if my brother has encumbered you with some of the great matters of the kingdom," she went on, "because I'm thinking of using your services."

"A quest for you?" That excited him. "I will never refuse that for sure."

"I'm looking for a veteran warrior who can train me how to wield swords and bows. Do you know anyone skillful?"

"Let me think." Enjoying the game, Masolon rubbed his chin. "I think I know one."

"Is he trustworthy?"

"He is more than trustworthy."

"What can be more than trustworthy?"

"He cares. And he has no problem traveling to Burdi."

"This is just fine. When can we start? I mean me and *him?*"

"He can start with you whenever you arrive in Burdi. Fortunately, it is his duty to protect the whole western region of the realm, including Burdi."

"Oh! I'm so lucky for sure. Then I will see him there."

"He cannot wait."

She saw him off with an alluring look, leaving him elated. He was not dreaming. It was not his hallucinating mind. That conversation was real.

* * *

Locating any possible threats was the reason why Masolon had ordered his men to patrol the eastern towns of Kahora for four days. Surely, he wouldn't tell them he was anticipating the arrival of a howdah carrying a princess from Arkan.

By the fifth day, Masolon was running out of patience and thought of riding back to Arkan. But the two weeks hadn't passed yet. What would he tell Feras? What would he tell his men?

At last, the camel came into sight.

"You lead the men, Blanich," Masolon told his fellow when he spotted Sania's escort approaching the town. "Scout the southern wells. Sometimes those nomads wander there."

"Are you not coming with us?" Blanich asked.

"I have a special task to do."

"A special task *inside* the Murasen kingdom?"

"Do not worry." Masolon chuckled. "I will not be far from here."

"Will I see you soon?"

"Tonight in the camp."

"Fine." Blanich pulled the reins of his horse, wheeling it to the other side. "No trouble this time," he warned.

"No trouble this time, my friend."

Blanich led the horde away. After Masolon made sure they all disappeared in the horizon, he dug his heels into the flanks of his stallion, spurring it onward. Sania's house wasn't far from here, yet he didn't want to be late for his *training*.

The sight of the towering palms of the house made him feel nervous. He wasn't ready for a third shock. The first time he had been deluded, and the second time he had been deceived. But no, not this one. He wasn't a fool. He was sure he had understood her suggestion right. She was the one who had asked him to come.

His fears vanished the moment he saw Sania in the yard; ready with her bow, her quiver strapped to her back. He dismounted, tied his horse, and approached her. "I thought you might need some rest."

"Really? Then why did you come so quickly?" She arched one eyebrow, a reaction from her he always loved. "I'll have some sleep later. Shall we start?"

"So, archery is what you want to start with?"

"It suits me more. I don't dare to stab anything alive with a blade." She winced.

"You do not have to. Let somebody else do that for you."

"I really want to learn how to use swords, but maybe later."

"From what I've seen, you have some good archery skills."

"Hitting a palm trunk from ten feet? I never took you for a hypocrite."

Masolon laughed. "Ten feet is a good start."

"How far were you when you hit that barbarian in Kahora?" she asked.

"I really do not remember, Sania." He noticed that smile that lasted for a second when he uttered her name without *milady*. "I do not even think when I shoot. It is something that has been growing with me since I was a child. Give me that."

She handed him her light bow, and he weighed it in his hands, testing its string.

"You must have suffered a lot in your village," she said.

"I was molded by that suffering."

"You told me before that all your people suffered like you. Why was it only you who thought of deserting his homeland?"

Was it about time he told her how his journey to Gorania had started? The truth could be painful to her. "You still have doubts about me, do you not?"

"All I know about you is that you came to us from the Great

Desert." She shrugged. "Unless you believe this is enough for me to know."

For you? Nothing is enough. "Not exactly." He grinned. "Alright then. As a start, I am not a demon."

"Impressive." She looked anything but impressed. "Any more amazing facts?"

Masolon rubbed his head. "Well, I rode my first horse while you might have been still learning how to walk. I learned how to wield a sword while you were learning how to hold a spoon. I…killed for the first time when I was six."

"That's not the amazing fact I was expecting." She curled her nose, obviously shocked. "What kind of people teach their children how to kill?"

"*My* people. Because if we do not know how to kill, we will be killed. I still remember the moment when my father took me by the hand and walked me to the Salvation Tree. They told me that the thief tied to the trunk was caught stealing from our bushes, and a man from our clan must execute him with his own hands. My father was supposed to do it, but he told me that he would pass that task to me because I had become man enough to do it. I was the happiest child in the village when he told me so. He gave me a short sword and pointed at the thief's chest. 'You must look him in the eye when you drive the blade into his heart, Masolon,' he told me. I gripped the hilt with both hands and I did what my father told me to do. I kept looking the thief in the eye after all that remained of his soul had left him already. The thief's eyes visited me that night and the night after. My father told me that the eyes would always visit me until I killed someone else. They let me execute the next man they caught—I do not even remember what he had done—and more eyes visited me afterward. My father told me I must kill someone else. I asked him when those eyes would stop. He said, 'When they become too many to remember any of them.' And you know what? He was right."

Sania's unusual silence worried him. Had he said too much?

"I believe it would be more pleasant if you told me about your childhood instead," he said.

"Please, continue," she encouraged him.

He would talk all day and night to keep those pretty eyes on him. "The raids on our village never stopped. They raided us, we raided them as well, but we never killed women or children; that was our code. That was what my father taught me. But my father put that code behind his back when they burned our village with all our women and children there.

"We were dragged to a fight away from the village when the bastards made their cowardly attack. My father insisted on returning the injury by burning their whole village and slaughtering all their women and children to put an end to their bloodline. I objected to that, and I was the only one who did. My father said I was a disgrace and threatened to kill me if I did not avenge my mother and sisters. That was when I realized I had no place there. My home was my family, and I lost them the day my mother and sisters were burned alive." *And the night I killed my father,* he thought, but didn't dare to say it.

"Oh dear!" She covered her mouth with her hand. "I feel guilty of reminding you of those horrible memories."

"Do not worry." He gazed at her. Seriously, she had the prettiest guilty face ever. "Come on. We have not started your training yet." He nodded toward the bow she was holding. "Show me how you shoot."

She fitted an arrow and shot at a palm tree trunk fifteen feet away. Her arrow hit her target (which could be anywhere on the whole trunk), yet her grip and posture needed some adjustment.

"You are better than I expected," he said.

"Don't fool me."

"I am serious. Has anybody taught you before?"

"No." She smiled, his compliment gladdening her. "I just used to watch the archers practicing in our castle."

"Impressive. Now place your feet shoulder-width apart. Make the left one pointed toward your trunk."

"I knew there was some secret." Sania did what he told her. "Am I ready now?"

"I have not exposed all my secrets yet." Masolon grinned. "Now nock the arrow and use your left forefinger to rest the arrow on it. Good. Straighten your left arm a bit more, and draw the string to your chin."

Sania struggled with the bowstring as she pulled it closer to her chin. She loosed, and the arrow hit another trunk at the end of the yard.

"That is what I call an amazing shot!" Masolon hooted.

"Of course." She looked disappointed. "If only I mean to hit *that* trunk."

"You were just busy with the tight string. In time you will get used to it. Now I want you to hit that trunk on purpose."

"If I was that good, I wouldn't ask for your help."

"That good? It is a trunk, Sania! I did not ask you to hit a date at the top," Masolon teased.

Sania giggled. "That's embarrassing. I will try my luck then."

"Let me help you." He stood behind Sania, his head just above her right shoulder so that both of them had the same vision for the target. "Tilt this bow a little bit." He gently held her left wrist, making her tilt the bow as he wanted. She seemed to be a bit nervous about his proximity. "I will help you with the string. Just keep your arms steady and focus on your target." He grasped her right wrist as she drew the bowstring to her chin. "Loose."

She relaxed her fingers. The arrow soared in a horizontal flight and hit the trunk.

"I did it!" Sania gazed at her distant target then she looked over her shoulder. "Are you done hurting my wrist?"

Alarmed, he let her go at once. "I am really sorry. Are you alright?"

She turned, playfully pushing him in the chest. "Not with you right behind me. Mind your distance, *Commander*."

"As you say, *milady*." He stepped back. "I guess I know what you need instead of this light bow."

"And I guess I'm done today. I really need to have some rest after this tiring day."

Their eyes met in a moment of a silence.

"I hope I am not keeping you from your duties," she said.

"No, you are not. My current duties compel me to guard your town."

"So, tomorrow then?"

"Tomorrow," Masolon replied without even thinking. He wouldn't mind a series of tomorrows.

* * *

For ten days, Masolon and Sania hadn't missed a day, doing more chattering than practicing. Since Masolon didn't believe she might be interested in his bloody tales, he let her do most of the talking, and indeed she had a lot to say. From what she told him about her absent lord father, her occupied brother, and her late mother who had been sick most of her last years, Masolon could tell that Sania was in need of someone to listen to her. And fortunately, listening was something he was good at. Certainly better at it than talking.

Sania told him about the sorceress who used to live in this house, the books Sania had found here and how her brother had insisted on keeping them away from Arkan because he believed they were cursed, the thrill of mounting a galloping horse, her aversion to the notion of marrying a man she knew nothing about except his name and his title. The last topic piqued Masolon's interest, giving him a glimpse of hope of realizing the impossible.

Every day, Masolon was becoming surer of his feelings toward her. He always asked himself whether he should tell her or not, but he was afraid of losing her forever. His heart was ecstatic to have her company, and her company was all he had dreamt of. Ruining these enchanting days was the last thing he wanted.

What if she just liked his company without any true feelings toward him? The notion of being rejected by her was a nightmare he tried to avoid.

But what if she *really* loved him? What could be the possible destiny for such a…bond against the norms of life? Halin's words still echoed in his mind.

Get over it!

Masolon chose to postpone thinking about this dilemma. Why should his mind always be overwhelmed by future consequences? What about living the current moment and enjoying these days in paradise with his charming angel?

On the eleventh day, one of his soldiers brought the crossbow and the bags of bolts he had requested. Masolon rewarded the soldier who brought those rare items with two golden coins, and hurried to Sania's house in Burdi.

Sania beamed with delight at her gift. "You can't be serious, Masolon. You brought this to me?"

"Do you like it?"

"Of course." She held the weapon as if she was testing its weight on her arms. "Where did you find it? We don't use these bows in Murase."

"From now on you will pick what fits you." He winked. He was sure Sania would like the crossbow just because it was *not* a Murasen thing.

She gave him a lovely smile that made his heart flutter. "You still remember, Masolon."

"I have nothing to do with it." He shrugged. "My mind picks what fits it as well."

"It's our hearts that decide what to remember and what to neglect. Those moments that you love or hate the most are hard to forget."

"Make the moments you love replace those you hate."

"It is not that easy, Masolon." She sighed, shaking her head. "I tried to forgive my father, but I couldn't. Every time I remember that he missed my mother's funeral my hatred toward him grows."

"I do not know what to say, but he might—"

"Please, Masolon, don't even try. He could have left his brother and returned. Feras says that I'm not fair with Father. So be it, I'm not fair. I am out of my mind if you like. But I don't feel I can ignore what happened and forgive him."

Masolon couldn't find anything to say. He had better listen to her and not try to involve himself in her problem with her father.

Sania raised the crossbow and loaded it with a bolt, aiming at one of the palm trees of her yard. "When will you tell me about your love story?"

The sudden change in topics caught him off guard. "My love story?" he echoed, giving himself a chance to figure out an answer.

"No need to deny it." Sania turned to him. "There is nothing in love to be ashamed of, especially when it is with a *princess*."

Well, that was escalating quickly.

"Is her beauty so charming it makes a commander follow her to the lands of snow?" Sania stared at him, waiting for his reaction. *Curse me!* She was referring to Halin. How hadn't he understood that from the beginning?

"Do you think I have a chance with a princess?" he asked.

Sania placed the crossbow on the ground. "It depends. Do you think you deserve her?"

"Of course I do. I am talking about norms."

"You shouldn't be worried about the norms. If she has the same feelings you have, she will do anything to spend the rest of her life with you."

Masolon pondered what he had just heard to make sure he had comprehended it right.

"*Anything?*"

"Enough of your wicked tricks," she scoffed. "I see how you try to confuse me, but I'm not easily distracted. Now tell me about your Rusakian princess."

"All right," he said. "What exactly do you want to hear about this princess? Why did I travel to her? Do I bear any feelings toward her?

I will tell you the whole story, but let me ask you first, *why* do you want to know?"

Sania was taken off guard, it was plain. "No reason in particular." She shrugged. "You don't have to answer if you don't want to."

"I will tell you everything about this journey. Do you know *why?*" Masolon caught Sania's gaze. He was going to stun her and even himself. "Because I love you."

For a couple of seconds, he felt relieved he had uttered those words at last. He was not ready for any more of their twisted conversations. But thinking of her reaction started to make him worried. At this very moment, she was petrified, her cheeks red, her eyes down. Then his heart wobbled when a *smile* slipped over her face. What did her smile mean? Was she happy? Surprised? *No way!* Surely, she knew about his feelings; it was obvious. Maybe she did not expect his move.

"Masolon...I...I really don't know what to say." Her eyes were still avoiding his.

"I tell you what to say. If you feel the same, say the same."

"I don't know, Masolon. I'm not sure if I can say the same."

"You are...not sure?" He remembered that feeling; the feeling of a cold-bladed dagger stabbing him in the heart. *Blast! Not again!* Memories of the sandstorm of Burdi were resurrected.

"It is not that simple." Sania finally looked at him. "I like your company, and I don't think I will ever meet a man like you anywhere. Despite your fame as a valorous warrior who fears nothing, you still have a soul that is as pure as that of a child. A man who just does what his instinct tells him it is right. You are one of a kind, Masolon, and you really don't belong to Gorania." She took a deep breath. "But again, I can't say what you have just said, at least for now."

Sania's consolations didn't make him feel any better. It wasn't his first shock, yet it was the worst. How was it possible that his judgment had deceived him this time? *Unbelievable!* He was living the same nightmare again.

"I would say something else," she said.

Masolon didn't understand her strange smile. It was obvious for him that she was taking the issue lightly, without any consideration for the frustration he felt.

"*Ya tebya lyblu.*"

It took him a few moments to grasp what he had just heard. *That playful girl! She said it! She said it!*

He grabbed her waist, lifting her up. "You should be punished for torturing me!"

"Hey!" she shrieked, kicking at his legs. "Let go of me!"

"I will not! I will keep you up the whole day for your games!" Thrilled, he let himself sink in her hazel eyes.

"That's enough." She pushed his hands, but his lock was firm. "Now put me down. Put me down, I say!"

He would put her on his horse and ride with her in the open desert until eternity. But the desert had eyes…

"Is that an order from Lady Sania?" Her face was too close to his. Too close to resist.

"No," she said, "but I'm afraid you must comply anyway."

The moment he put her down, she stepped back. "You will be punished for that," she teased him. "Now go before you do something foolish." She turned her back on him, heading to the door of her house.

"I have to go to Arkan," said Masolon. "We shall resume your training in two or three days."

"Three days? Why?" she groused, and Masolon liked that.

"It is your brother, my princess. He expects me every two weeks."

"I can't wait to…resume my training," she said coyly.

"Me too." He grinned. "I love *your* training so much."

He did not leave the yard until she got herself inside and closed her door. He wished he could stay in that yard forever.

Pull yourself together, Masolon. It is only three cursed days, he thought, fidgeting.

Mounting his stallion, he galloped away from Sania's house. All the way he recalled every sweet moment of that great day. Every word she said, every look, every smile. Over and over again until he approached Kahora. He wished his horse could gallop all the way back to Arkan to finish this irksome journey in one day. But as he had previously agreed with his companions, they would gather at their usual hill near Kahora before he went and reported to Feras.

His three captains were there when he arrived. "Anything interesting to tell Lord Feras about?" Masolon asked them.

"Nothing," Ziyad replied. "Except that your lord is not in Arkan at the moment. He's here in Kahora."

That was great news. Masolon's return to his sweetheart would be sooner than he had expected. "Do we have any idea why he came?" he asked, noticing the awkward silence among his companions.

"Tell us, Masolon." Frankil stared at him pointedly. "Is there something we should know about your journey to Rusakia?"

What was that question for? Masolon's journey to Rusakia was history now. "Something like what?" he asked. "Can you tell me what is wrong?"

Antram, Ziyad, and Frankil looked at each other.

"It's hard to believe the coincidence." Frankil took the lead. "When I see a Rusakian emissary leaving the King's palace, followed by a royal Murasen messenger traveling to Arkan to summon Lord Feras to Kahora, then I have to ask our commander about what happened when he went to Durberg."

Blast! A Rusakian emissary! Was it possible that Larovic was after him?

"You are sure Feras has arrived?" Masolon asked.

"I guess he has just entered the palace hall as we speak," Antram replied.

"We are worried about you, brother," said Ziyad. "Please tell us that you didn't do anything wrong."

"You do not have to worry, fellows." Masolon wasn't sure if he had hidden his worry himself. He could feel the frost hitting his Murasen paradise.

50. FERAS

All the way from Arkan to Kahora, Feras couldn't stop wondering what the *urgent* matter King Rasheed had summoned him for could be. Was it the start of another war? Or probably, an announcement?

As Feras entered the throne hall, he greeted his king and his uncle Lord Munzir. *He has done it last,* he thought, contemplating the victorious smile on his uncle's face.

"How do you find peace, Lord Feras?" Rasheed asked.

As usual, a question hiding something beneath. "Peace is a blessing, no doubt, sire," Feras answered. "It gives us a chance to replenish and rebuild our forces."

"It is interesting to hear your notion of peace." Rasheed grinned. "Actually, that was what I expected from a true warrior like you, Lord Feras."

Yes, a dedicated and loyal warrior. "Thank you, sire," Feras said.

"But can't peace be a destination itself, rather than a temporary period of time in an endless chain of wars?"

"We can never live in everlasting peace, sire, because there will always be enemies."

"You're right. But you can weaken their greed in what is yours, right?"

What about the greed of your close vassals? Feras glanced at his lord uncle. "I guess I need to learn from your wisdom, Your Majesty."

"I'm calling your father back from the borders," Rasheed announced. "The war is over, and he can return to the western region."

"Really?" Feras hadn't seen that coming. "I mean, that's a wise decision, sire."

"That's the first decision."

The first decision? Well, Feras could guess the next one.

"After some deliberations with your uncle, he convinced me to make a crucial move," Rasheed said. "Not only for me, but for the whole kingdom."

A crucial move for Munzir, no doubt. Feras must admit he had underestimated his lord uncle. On a battlefield, Feras had seen for himself how pathetic Munzir's leadership was. But he had learned something important from veteran lords like his uncle and Lord Memot; not all battles were fought with steel and horses. There were other battles that occurred in the big and small halls of the palaces and castles. And the truth was: Those were the real battles.

"The King is going to marry, and his new wife will be one of your honorable family," said Rasheed. The wide grin on Munzir's face spoke for itself.

"That's a great honor for our house, Your Majesty." Feras gave him the best smile he could manage.

"That's another reason for calling your father back," Rasheed said. "He must be here when I vie for his daughter's hand in marriage."

Wait! Whose daughter? My father? Sania? Feras was speechless, and so was his lord uncle. The king had just turned the tables on him.

"I have to acknowledge that it was your uncle who convinced me with the idea," said Rasheed. "After spending some time thinking of who can be my queen, I decided to propose to Sania."

"It's an honor for our family, King Rasheed." Feras was still stunned, but surely the news thrilled him. The gloating smile on his face was hard to conceal.

Munzir cleared his throat. "It's…an honor…for both families."

"I never considered you as two families, Munzir," said Rasheed.

"You're right, my king." Munzir tried to hide the scowl on his face. "We are one house after all."

"The whole kingdom deserves a few days of joy," said Rasheed. "Our people suffered a lot from the scourge of war, and they need to be rewarded for their endurance."

Feras nodded. "You have a point, my king."

"But what if someone among us endangers these peaceful days?" Munzir growled, glaring at Feras. "We are on the verge of war with the Rusakians because of your irresponsible commander. He killed their marshal's son, and now they seek justice to be served. He who kills must be executed."

Feras turned to Rasheed to see how much he agreed with that. "It's lamentable to make a decision against one of our commanders." Rasheed tightened his jaw. "But I find myself here obliged to do what is good for the kingdom, not for a single man. Especially, when he is not a Murasen."

"What's your decision, sire?" Feras kept his eyes fixed on Rasheed's face in anticipation.

"Masolon must disappear," said Rasheed. "Forever."

51. MASOLON

Masolon and his band were only one mile away from the walls of Kahora when he spotted Feras with his retinue. The lords' knights stopped when they recognized Masolon, who raised his fist to stop his horsemen as well. As he split off from his company, Feras approached him.

"Commander Masolon, meeting you here is not a coincidence if I know you right."

"My men are watching over the whole region, milord."

"Listen to me carefully, Masolon." Feras lowered his voice. "Do you have any friends outside the kingdom?"

Masolon shot him an inquisitive look.

"Can you return to your homeland?" Feras asked. "I'm asking you because you must leave the Murasen lands tonight."

"Why? What is wrong, Lord Feras?"

"The Rusakians sent to King Rasheed asking for your head."

"What did the King say?"

"King Rasheed told them that he had no idea about this incident and that he must investigate the truth before he surrenders one of his men. Justice would be served if he found out that you were guilty."

A diplomatic answer.

"This is what he said to them. What about his real intentions?" Masolon asked.

"Rasheed doesn't want those Rusakians to arrest you," said Feras. "But at the same time, he can't keep you as one of his subjects if you are convicted."

"I was never considered one of his subjects," Masolon mused, shaking his head. "All of you still see me as a foreigner."

"You were recognized by the King himself as a Murasen commander, Masolon. You were granted the Murasen armor."

"It was nothing more than rituals. If these Rusakians were coming after you, he would never surrender you to them."

"If I were you, I would never abandon my duty and follow my lust outside the kingdom." Feras frowned. "Don't you understand that we are trying to protect you?"

You mean protecting yourselves from war.

Masolon exhaled, trying to think of his next step. Ending his journey in this kingdom was inevitable. He had to cede his authority as a commander. He had to leave Sania after he had gotten so close to her.

Curse you, Rusakians! Why now?

"You have one night to pack your things and prepare for a long journey outside the kingdom," Feras said. "My piece of advice is to keep this issue discreet. For your own good."

"Do you expect that I will let my fellows discover next morning that I have deserted them without any notice from my side?"

"This is better for you and the gang as well. You will create a state of havoc in the gang by announcing that you are leaving. As for you, I recommend you have a new start away from any previous acquaintances. This will make you harder to find. Trust me, Gorania is but a small town."

"I think we do not have much to talk about," Masolon said. "I was honored by your acquaintance, Lord Feras."

Feras acknowledged. "I hope we don't meet again."

Courtesy followed by menace. Masolon wheeled his horse and

trotted back to his company. His brothers surrounded him, their eyes inquisitive, but he was determined not to talk about it before he made up his mind regarding his next move.

"Back to the hill," he commanded, and said nothing more until they reached their destination. He was the one who had started this gang, and it would be his third time to leave them, this time for good. Feras had warned him against telling his brothers, but Feras could burn in hell.

He called out to his fellows, including Blanich, to sit together and have a quick word away from the rest of the gang.

"First, we must agree on keeping our voices low." Masolon looked at Ziyad and Antram. "Can you do that?"

"My voice is not loud," Ziyad protested. "It's your voices that are too quiet."

Masolon would really miss his Murasen fellow's jests. "Listen to me. From now on, Captain Frankil will be leading you because I am leaving. I will not be back."

"*What?*" Ziyad blustered, Antram and Frankil looking shocked, Blanich's face barely showing any reaction.

Masolon shushed his noisy fellow. "What did I just say about keeping our voices low? Just listen to me, all of you, because I do not have much time. For the good of this gang, I must be outside it. I must leave tonight, and that is all I can say."

"Why?" Antram asked. "What happened?"

Frankil shook his head, his face betraying his disappointment. "What did you do this time?"

"The usual; getting into trouble with the wrong people." Masolon rose to his feet. "I must go now, brothers. Night is short in these lands, you know."

"Wait," said Ziyad. "Where will you go?"

Masolon hadn't made up his mind yet. Everything depended on the girl he would pass by next. "I have no idea. What matters now is that the sun of next morning does not rise while I am still in any sort of desert."

"You are not returning to your homeland, are you?" Ziyad asked.

The notion hadn't even crossed Masolon's mind. "Even if I want to, I do not think I can survive another journey in the Great Desert."

He went to mount his horse, his brothers following him on foot to see him off. "I know you will lead the gang better than me, Frankil. You believed in it more than I did." He meant every word. The only one in this gang who cared about the cause Masolon had suggested was the Bermanian captain. Even Masolon himself had his own priorities sometimes.

Blanich gave him a slight lopsided smile. "Not going to Durberg, I guess."

Masolon answered with a self-mocking chuckle. Of course, he wouldn't go anywhere in the snowy kingdom. Neither to Durberg nor to any other city in Rusakia.

Masolon kicked his horse's flanks and raced the wind away from the hill. He still had one last ride to Burdi before he ended his Murasen journey. He might have lost the gang and his title, but he wouldn't lose Sania for any reason.

52. SANIA

"Amal!" Sania called out as she went from room to room. Her maidservant would never leave the house without her permission. Where was she?

Taking a torch with her, Sania pushed the door open and scanned the dark yard with her eyes. Amal was there by the fence, bending over something on the ground. Since Sania didn't spot a broom or a bucket nearby, she could safely presume that her maidservant wasn't doing any cleaning.

Amal rose to her feet when she saw Sania coming. "Milady." She looked uneasy when she greeted her.

Under the flickering light of her torch, Sania eyed the hole Amal was trying to hide. "What are you doing here, Amal?"

"Nothing of import, milady." Amal smiled nervously. "I was just burying a dead snake that tried to creep into the house."

"You killed a snake?" Sania always feared them. After a couple of seconds, she reminded herself that the snake was dead already. "Why didn't you tell me at once?"

"I didn't want to disturb you, milady. You seemed busy with your reading and—"

"Show me the snake." Sania nodded toward the ground.

Amal acquiesced to her order. With her hands, she dug in the ground, and indeed she pulled a snake. Dead or alive, those damned snakes looked scary.

"Why does it smell like incense?" Sania sniffed as she bent over the hole. "It *is* incense."

Amal couldn't hide her guilty face.

"Amal, what is going on here?"

"It's for our protection, milady."

"Our protection from what?"

"From that demon…I know it's hard to explain."

Sania smiled to encourage Amal to elaborate. "Just try me. What demon are you talking about?"

Amal exhaled. "Commander Masolon. I heard he came from the Great Desert."

Sania chuckled, relieved. "I was scared like you the first time I knew, but don't you worry, he is just a man of flesh and blood."

"No man of flesh and blood can survive a cursed place like the Great Desert, milady. I feel something wrong about him every time I see him."

On the contrary, Sania always felt there was something *right*.

A galloping horse was coming, Sania listened to the thundering hooves. She would be sure it was Masolon, but his three days hadn't passed yet.

"Speak of the demon, and he shall appear." Sania grinned, watching Masolon on the back of his horse. "You go now, Amal." She motioned the maidservant toward the house.

Sania waited for him until he dismounted and tied his horse next to hers. She was about to tease her impatient lover as he strode across the yard toward her, but today he looked different. Where was the smile he wore every time he came here? The grim look on his face was worrying.

"Something wrong, Masolon?"

"I am leaving Murase tonight," he said without preamble.

"What for? Did my brother send you to fight the Mankols?"

"I am no longer a commander. Those soldiers around the town perimeter do not know that yet. When they find out, they will arrest me on sight."

"Arrest you? What on Earth are you talking about?"

"I am banished, Sania. By order of King Rasheed."

"Banished? What have you done?"

"It is a long story, and I am afraid I do not have enough time now." He glanced at the wooden gate behind him. "Your brother's soldiers might come here at any moment."

"Why, Masolon? Why? What happened?"

"I was trapped. I will tell you on our way out of here."

"Out of where?"

"Out of the realm, Sania. If we are going to leave, we must leave now."

And Sania had thought her maidservant was wrong in the head. "Masolon, are you drunk?"

"I know a merchant in Kalensi called Galardi," he said, ignoring what she had said, "and he wanted to make use of my services as a caravan master. I can have a new start there."

"Let me understand this right. You want me to elope with you?"

"Why not? Do you know another way?"

"Another way for what?"

Masolon looked surprised by her question. "To be together, Sania. I thought you might be happy about that."

She had thought the same, but now she wasn't sure. Maybe it was his plan that didn't make her feel comfortable. The plan of *their* future life; an idea that still sounded awkward on its own.

"Kalensi is too far away from here." She folded her arms, weighing his reckless suggestion.

He gave her a pale smile. "I know the way, do not worry."

"I will be nobody there. I will be alone, waiting for months for your return from your long journeys with those caravans. I will never be the wife of another Lord Ahmet or Lord Feras, Masolon. What you are asking me to do is even worse."

Masolon fidgeted. "We are running out of time, Sania, and that is our best alternative so far."

"*Your* best alternative." Disappointed, she pointed her finger at him. "I thought you'd know better."

"I am a warrior, Sania. If I decide not to travel with merchants, my only option will be offering my services to warlords as a mercenary. In both cases, I will be absent for a while."

"So your absence is a matter of fact that I must accept. Is that it?"

"I do not mean to impose anything on you, Sania, but this is part of my profession that I cannot change."

"You want me to cede my title, my country, my family—everything. But you never considered abandoning your bloody profession. You know what, I'm really shocked."

Masolon's lips moved, but he didn't say anything. Instead, he looked down, letting out a deep breath of air. "I am losing my mind, Sania. I cannot imagine how I may spend the rest of my life without you."

"You mean you cannot imagine spending the rest of your life without your sword and horse."

Masolon lifted his chin, looking her in the eye. "I will never choose them over you."

"You are sure of that?"

"Deadly sure."

Sania looked at him warily. "Masolon, the great warrior, are you ready to become a blacksmith or some carpenter?"

"A blacksmith will suit me more." He smiled grimly. "Carpentry needs some fine art."

"I am not jesting."

"Do you love me or not, Sania?" he asked, his voice firm, his eyes fixed on her.

"What is this question for?"

"Answer me," he insisted.

"You had my answer before."

"I want to hear your answer in a familiar language this time."

Sania studied his stern face. Apparently, he was serious about his silly demand.

"Alright." She exhaled. "I love you. Now what?"

A smile transformed his gloomy face. "This settles it." He wrapped his arm around her thighs and threw her over his shoulder as if she weighed nothing.

"What are you doing, Masolon?" she screamed, kicking the air.

"Helping you come to a decision." Carrying her, he walked toward her brown horse. "Such a hesitant girl."

"Put me down! We are not done talking!"

"We have a long way ahead. We will talk about everything you want." He laid her on the back of her horse.

"Get off me!" She kicked when he tried to help her with the stirrups.

"Alright, alright." He stepped back, untied both horses, and mounted his. "Let us go."

Running away with the man she loved. The notion had always sounded adorable in the old romantic stories in Goranian poetry. A charming moment she could only fancy in her daydreams. But she never thought it could be that scary when it happened for real.

"Move on, Sania," Masolon urged her.

"Masolon, I'm not ready yet," she said. "I need more clothes for this long journey."

53. MASOLON

Masolon held a torch to light the way in the desert darkness.

"This is scarier than I imagined," Sania mumbled, her horse next to his. Truth be told, he felt bad for putting her in such a situation. A delicate princess like his girl had probably never traveled without a howdah or guards to escort her. Right now, Masolon was her only guard.

"Is this how you usually travel?" she asked.

"Not really." Masolon grinned, trying to cheer her up. "At least I have a torch tonight."

"My Lord!" she exclaimed. "Are you telling me you travel in such darkness without a torch? You can't be serious!"

"Your eyes are accustomed to your burning sun, mine to darkness. We are even."

"No, we're not. This is not normal. Only demons see in the dark."

"Now you realize who I truly am." Masolon laughed. "But it is too late now, sweetheart. You are stuck with this demon, forever I am afraid."

"Speaking of forever, how long are we going to stay on this abandoned road?"

"Everything is going to be fine," said Masolon. "When we reach the Oasis, we can join a caravan heading to Kalensi, or any place you wish."

"The Oasis?"

"It is a gathering point near Kahora for caravans traveling from everywhere. There, we can replenish our supplies."

"Sometimes, I feel that I'm the foreigner, not you."

"I have seen a lot in Gorania in my first year."

"A year? Time passes so quickly indeed."

Her voice sounded more reassured as he kept talking to her. One night in the desert would be nothing to him, but it would be too long for her.

"Have you met any demons in the Great Desert?" she asked.

He shrugged, laughing. "Not so many."

"This is not funny," she protested. "Do they really live there as in the Tales?"

"Even for demons, that cursed place is too deadly." He shook his head, recalling his horrendous passage. "The blazing heat came from the sun in the sky and from the sand. The air I breathed burnt my chest. The blood boiled inside my veins. I spent weeks, and not a living creature I saw. Even cactus does not exist there."

"Was it better at night?"

"Not too much. Sometimes I felt that moonlight was as hot as sunlight."

She came closer with her horse when she heard a distant howl. "What was that?" she asked nervously.

He knew it was a wolf, but he didn't wish to scare her. "Do not worry." He held her hand as the two horses almost touched each other. "Fire keeps night wanderers away."

"Night wanderers?" She looked around her. "You're not fooling me, are you?"

"Can you imagine the thing that scared me the most in the Great Desert?"

"To be eaten by night wanderers?"

"No, Sania. It was silence," he scoffed. "I did not hear anything, even the whistling wind. I remember I was eager to hear a howling beast or a hissing snake."

"Am I supposed to feel grateful for the music I'm listening to now?"

"Soon you are going to enjoy this music."

"*Soon* we are going to reach that Oasis, I hope."

"If we keep moving the whole night, we will be there by morning."

"The whole night? Don't you ever sleep in your journeys?"

"We can have some rest if you want." He stared at the pretty face lit by the torch he held. Even in such a critical moment, he could not help entertaining his eyes.

"Listen, no foolish moves," she warned. "You won't get anything from me until we reach Kalensi and have our own roofed house. Nothing is going to happen in this bare desert."

Masolon tittered. "No rush. I will wait patiently."

"This is not all. We must announce our marriage in the presence of a cleric."

"A cleric?"

"Yes, a cleric. That is the proper marriage ritual for any virtuous couple."

"In my homeland, we were not in need of a cleric. We used to gather and witness the marriage announcement, and that was all. I remember a few occasions when we celebrated with music and drums."

She allowed a soft chuckle. "Imagining you dancing makes me laugh."

"I never tried to dance. I guess the sight of me dancing would be something worth watching indeed."

"Don't you worry, serious Commander." She gave him a charming smile. "I will handle this."

She was irresistible, but he remembered her warning. *A roofed house and a cleric.* That might not happen before a month or more. Too much waiting.

"Let us have some rest," he suggested when he spotted a copse of scattered palm trees. "We can tie our horses there."

"And how am I going to sleep? On the sand?"

"I do not mind if you use my armor as a mattress."

"I don't mind as well to use *only* the armor, you bastard!" she teased him. After they stopped their horses near a palm tree, she fluidly slid off her horse.

"I told you I did not need your help." She held the bridle of her horse. "I can mount and dismount on my own."

"If you insist." Masolon swung down from his saddle. "I will be there, just in case you change your mind." He pulled the reins of his stallion and handed Sania the torch. "Let me tie this horse for you, milady. Be careful, and do not burn yourself with that torch." He held the reins of both horses, pulling them to the trunk. In a few minutes, he was done with the horses and turned to Sania, who was irked by the heat of the torch she carried. "Give it to me." Masolon gestured to her to hand him the torch, and gladly, she stepped forward to give it to him.

And then she screeched.

"*Sania!*" Masolon yelled when a thrown dagger struck the left side of her torso. Before his very eyes, his sweetheart fell on her face, the flaming torch rolling on the sandy terrain, blood bubbling out of the wound in her trunk.

"*Blast!*" an angry familiar feminine voice came out of the dark desert.

The voice of a snake.

Masolon quickly put out the flame of the torch with his boot to hide Sania and himself in the darkness. The terrain was only lit by moonlight, and he could hardly see a slender shadow of the assaulter, who ran away toward her horse.

"You, devil's whore!" he bellowed. "Why? Why? Why?"

"The target was you, but she moved!" Viola shrieked. "It's destiny's justice. You killed Ramel, I killed your girl!"

Masolon heard the hooves of Viola's horse galloping away. He wished he could chase her and slice her throat, but it was impossible for him to leave Sania like that. The dagger was still stuck in her body, but he didn't dare to pull it out. Trying to stop the bleeding, he pushed on the wound with his hand.

"I don't want to die, Masolon," Sania whimpered.

"You will live, Sania. Just hang on to me." He cradled her in his arms. "Stay with me, please." He put her on his stallion, mounted his horse, and off he galloped. The only idea that came to his mind at once was taking her to Bumar. He would know what to do, Masolon hoped.

* * *

It was not yet dawn when Masolon reached Bumar's house. He dismounted and hammered the door with his fist. "Bumar! It is me!" When Masolon heard the footsteps coming from inside, he hurried back to his horse and returned with Sania in his arms.

"Gracious Lord!" Bumar made way for Masolon to enter when he saw him carrying the unconscious girl.

"She has been stabbed, Bumar! I need your help!" Masolon begged as he stepped into the house. Bumar hurried to a table and cleared its top, leaving room for Masolon to lay Sania on it. The healer checked the girl's arm and cheeks that looked so pale.

"Is she going to survive?" Masolon asked worriedly.

"Pull yourself together, young man," Bumar replied with his calm voice. "Your tension won't change anything. If you really want to help, stay close in case I need you to hand me something."

Masolon bit his lower lip. "She has been bleeding for so long."

"What have I just said? Pull yourself together."

Masolon kept his mouth shut, ready to do anything to rescue his love.

"The best thing you did was that you didn't pull that dagger out," said Bumar. "She could have bled to death if you had done that."

Bumar brought ten pieces of cloth and soaked each one in a cleansing solution with a pungent odor that reminded Masolon of his first night in Kahora. "I am going to pull it out now," he said. "Be ready with the bandages."

Once Bumar yanked the dagger out, dark-red blood gushed out. The healer took one bandage from Masolon, and pushed on the open wound until the piece of cloth became soaked with Sania's blood. "One more," Bumar demanded. He kept pushing on the wound with bandages, one after the other, until the bleeding started to diminish.

"The stitches, Masolon."

Masolon felt like pushing Bumar's hand away. Although he reminded himself that his friend was helping his Sania, he still couldn't watch a needle piercing her skin. Fidgeting, he turned his head away until the healer was done with his work.

"How did you come together?" Bumar was placing one new bandage over the sutures. "It seems that I have missed a lot of your news."

"Tell me first, how is she?" Masolon asked eagerly.

"She will be fine," Bumar reassured Masolon. "The blade cut her flesh, but it didn't reach any of her organs. She will need a few weeks until the flesh heals itself and restores its normal healthy state."

Masolon gazed at Sania, who was still unconscious. He put his ear near her mouth to make sure she was still breathing. "When will she wake up?"

"At any moment," said Bumar. "She has lost a lot of blood, but luckily, not enough to kill her."

"Great." Masolon sighed. "Can I take her now?"

"No. The bleeding has not stopped completely. She needs some rest to replenish her strength."

"I do not have much time, Bumar."

"Much time for what, Masolon?" Bumar narrowed his eyes. "Are you running away with her?"

Before Masolon could respond, they heard thundering hooves approaching the house. "Blast!" The clopping stopped just in front of Bumar's door.

"*I know you are inside, Masolon! Open that door!*" an angry voice shouted from outside. Among all the men in Gorania, the lord of Arkan himself was standing at the door.

54. MASOLON

Now was not the time for reckless moves.

Masolon regretted involving Bumar in his predicament. The first roof that had sheltered him in Gorania was that of the healer's house. Only now did Masolon realize he had never paid Bumar back for his favors. His dearest companions Antram, Ziyad, and Frankil had earned some gold and recognition as captains, to say the least. But Bumar? Except for the scrolls he had helped him write about his homeland, Bumar's reward was nothing but a horde of memluks waiting outside his house to break in, led by a furious lord looking for his sister.

"Let me handle this, my friend." Masolon rose from his seat, gesturing to Bumar to stay in place. "I do not want to involve you any further in my troubles."

The moment Masolon opened the door to face the angry brother, Feras growled, "Where is my sister, Masolon?"

"She has been taken care of," Masolon replied curtly.

Feras shoved Masolon and went inside to find Bumar standing by the table upon which Sania lay. "What have you both done to her?" Feras bellowed.

"No need to shout, milord," said Masolon. "The healer did his job and saved her. You cannot blame him for that."

"Don't dare to tell me whom to blame!" Feras jabbed his forefinger at Masolon's chest.

"Yes, I dare." Masolon gnashed his teeth. "You cannot blame the man who saved your sister's life."

For an instant, Feras looked surprised by Masolon's tone. But what was he expecting from someone who had lost everything he had?

"What about the man who betrayed me after I had granted him my trust?" Feras curled his lip in disdain.

"I never betrayed you."

"Yes, you did! You were supposed to guard my sister, not beguile her!"

"I did not beguile her. She chose me, as I chose her."

"She chose you? She chose *you*?" Feras huffed. "Then she deserves to be punished for the disgrace she brought to the name of her house!"

"Disgrace?" Masolon echoed, the word hurting him. It reminded him of his last journey to Durberg. It reminded him of the ugly truth. *The norm of life.*

"You are not much different from the others." Disappointed, Masolon shook his head. "All lords in Gorania are the same after all."

"You don't know anything about the lords of Gorania," Feras snarled. "If I were really like them, I would kill you at once without bothering myself with this conversation."

Should Masolon be grateful? Should he thank his master for sparing his life despite his horrendous 'sin'?

Sania groaned.

"She's waking up," said Bumar.

Masolon hurried to her. "Sania!" He held her hand.

"Where am I?" she asked in a faint voice, groaning again.

"You will be fine, milady," Bumar reassured her. "I will give you something to alleviate your pain." He hurried to one of his rooms.

"I am sorry, Sania." Masolon squeezed her hand. "All the pain you

340

are suffering is because of me. I cannot forgive myself."

"Oh please, Masolon." She tried to smile. "Don't be harsh on yourself."

"Sania!" Feras snapped.

Sania was startled when she heard her brother's voice. Obviously, she hadn't noticed his presence. "Feras?" She turned her terrified eyes toward Masolon.

"Yes, it's me," her brother said. "I'm here to end your reckless ride."

"I have always known you as a fair lord. Please, brother, no need to harm him. Just let him go," she pleaded.

Not after I have reached this far, Masolon thought. "I will not go alone." They could kill him if they wanted, but he wouldn't leave without her.

"Then you leave me no choice," Feras stated.

"Please, Masolon." Sania held his hand. "Let it go."

Masolon stared at her, stunned by her stance.

"It is over," she said sadly.

At a loss for words, all he could do was shake his head. What Sania said didn't make any sense.

"She's right," said Feras. "It's over."

"No." With hollow eyes, Masolon looked at Feras then turned again to Sania. They were all wrong. He would slay all those Murasens in Bumar's house, including Feras himself, then sneak out with Sania, find a horse and...

"Please, Masolon!" Sania was almost weeping. She turned to her brother. "Feras, you have already banished him. Let him go! If saving my life twice doesn't mean anything to you, let it be for the sake of saving your king's life!"

Feras chewed on his lip, an eerie silence reigning over the house.

"I hope I won't regret this one day," said Feras at last, his glowing eyes on Masolon, "because the next time you are seen on any Murasen soil, you will be hunted. And not by my men; by royal memluks." He leaned forward. "Royal memluks of a concerned husband."

Had Masolon heard that right? A concerned husband? There was only one man in the Murasen kingdom who had royal memluks.

"Sania will soon be wed to King Rasheed." Feras glanced at Sania, then back to Masolon. "I don't think His Majesty will be happy to know that we let you go, especially after he knows what you tried to do."

No, no, no. How is everything collapsing so fast? Masolon thought, feeling the firm hands holding his shoulders.

The healer's hands.

"I don't want to mourn you, young man," Bumar said in a low voice. "You still have the chance to restart your path somewhere else in Gorania. Pull yourself together, use your mind, and don't let your emotions drive you."

Path? What path? *Curse that path!* Sania was his path now! That was the only path he had to fight for. Although he knew he was on his own, he would fight.

His hand reached for the hilt of his sword, but Bumar held his hand tight, shooting him a warning look. "No, Masolon. You won't do this," Bumar whispered. "You'll kill yourself, you fool."

"They have killed me already."

Bumar glared at him. "You don't want her to watch you slaughtered."

Masolon glanced at Sania's pale face. He pulled his hand away from the hilt and moved past Bumar to touch Sania's soft hand one last time, but Feras stood in his way.

"I am running out of patience," the young lord grumbled.

A head shake from Bumar was the last plea from a true friend for Masolon to give up fighting. *But it is not fair, my friend*, he would say to Bumar, but no words would change anything. Words were futile, especially when you were badly outnumbered like Masolon now.

Masolon dragged his heavy legs and went ahead of Feras to the door, every step taking him away from Sania tearing up his heart. When he reached the doorstep, he thought of giving her one last look, but he didn't dare, the wheezing of her chest making him ashamed of his weakness. His sweetheart, his Murasen paradise; he was leaving her without a fight.

He took a deep breath and stepped out of the house in front of the guards ready with their weapons. Ignoring them, Masolon went past them and mounted his stallion. *Not like this,* he thought as the Murasen horsemen surrounded his horse, commanding him to follow them to the northwest borders. Silently he complied, recalling a whole year of events as if he was reliving all of them right now. Sometimes he wondered why it was destined for him to survive that deadly passage one year ago. If there was one answer to his question, it would be Sania. If there was one meaning of his journey to Gorania, it would be Sania.

I should have died in the Great Desert.

55. ZIYAD

Ziyad was the first one in the camp to wake up after quite a disturbing night. He doubted if Masolon's shocking egress had troubled his brothers' sleep like it had done to him. Frankil, who was only concerned about his duties, would get up as he did every day and assume his responsibilities as a leader of the gang. Be it the last time or not, Frankil wouldn't bother that much, if at all. Maintaining the gang's mission was always his top priority.

Though Antram seemed a bit touched last night, Ziyad was quite sure that the first pouch of golden coins would heal his grief. Ziyad was neither judging him nor claiming he was less greedy than his bald friend. The former bard had joined the gang to quench his revenge, but even after achieving that, he couldn't stop the music of gold from playing in his pockets.

Ziyad was still hesitant about considering Blanich a brother. Indeed the Rusakian had been fighting alongside them for a while, but Ziyad knew that the day of Blanich's return to his country was coming sooner or later.

What about Ziyad himself? Knowing that Masolon was not coming back for good, Ziyad felt unsure about the point of sticking to this brotherhood of warriors. His uncertainty didn't make any sense, he knew, but it was a feeling he couldn't overcome. Perhaps he was just feeling gloomy because of the way Masolon had seen them off. On the previous two occasions, Masolon had temporarily left them by his own choice. But last night, he was running away like an outlaw. *Getting into trouble with the wrong people,* Masolon had said. The statement had kept Ziyad awake as he let his imagination go wild, pondering what Masolon could have done to obliterate his glory with his own hands. Was it a stupid slip of the tongue while talking to Lord Feras? Or worse, King Rasheed? Had he quarreled with one of the royal memluks, and eventually His Majesty had considered it an insult to his dignified person? Had he been caught sneaking into the ladies' wing? Masolon had a weakness for women, Ziyad was sure of it. Well, all men had the same weakness except for clerics and eunuchs. Even the pious Frankil. His stern face must have smiled once to some wench.

Ziyad stood upon the edge of the hill to enjoy the dustless breeze of this morning. A few minutes later he heard the steps of someone else coming to join him. Antram had woken up earlier than usual this morning.

"Seeing you up makes me worried about the captain," Ziyad scoffed.

"We stayed up a bit late last night while you were snoring like a pig."

"This is nonsense. I wasn't able to sleep in the first place."

"But you did snore," Antram insisted.

Ignoring his friend's 'humorous' remark, Ziyad gazed back at the sleeping brothers. "Shouldn't we wake them up and make a brief announcement?"

"That's the captain's job, brother." Antram shrugged. "Let him have all the sleep he needs, and he will inform them himself of our most recent. . ."

Antram didn't finish as he gazed at the cloud of dust rising at the horizon. That wasn't Poison Wind. That was a horde of horsemen.

And they were riding toward their hill.

Ziyad and Antram exchanged a quick look before they hurried to their sleeping fellows to wake them up. "To arms!" Ziyad bellowed. "Intruders coming!"

The alarmed fellows didn't even have enough time to don their light armor. Everyone grabbed the nearest sword to him and hurried to the cliff.

"Bows!" Frankil shouted. "Make way for archers!"

Frankil motioned all the men capable of wielding a bow and arrow to spread out and take shooting positions, commanding the rest to line up and be ready to attack by his order. The first mission in the captain's reign was starting sooner than Ziyad had expected.

Ziyad estimated the intruders to be around two hundred...memluks? Yes, they were. As they approached, he wouldn't mistake their decorated heavy armor nor their honorable leader. The great Lord Feras, son of the renowned Lord Ahmet, was here himself, and Ziyad wondered what grave reason might be behind this unexpected visit. The lord's presence at the hill right after Masolon's escape could not be a mere coincidence. And what were all those memluks for? Not Lord Feras's guards, right?

"Don't shoot!" Frankil raised his hand as he ordered the archers, and all of them lowered their bows at once.

Lord Feras and his horde halted at the foot of the hill. Still ahorse, the young lord advanced, gazing at the archers spread out atop the hill, ready to shoot at any intruder. "I demand an audience with your captains!"

"Did you hear that?" Ziyad turned to both Frankil and Antram. "He knows that Masolon has left us."

"This is not promising." Frankil stood, looking out at the large group. "For someone coming simply to talk, our lord has brought too many men."

"Do you think he is looking for Masolon?" Antram asked the two of them.

"I'm sure Masolon has a hand in this somehow," Ziyad told them, wondering whether he should pity the fleeing commander or blame him for whatever mistake he had committed.

"I'm sure it's not a wise idea to leave that lord waiting too long. Come on. Let's see what he wants." Frankil motioned for Ziyad and Antram to follow him as he moved away from the cliff. "No reckless moves, brothers."

As the three fellows descended the hill on foot, Antram asked, "What if he is here to arrest us?"

"For doing what?" Ziyad asked. "Anyway, he will do that if he wants to. We are outnumbered here."

Thanks to one of Masolon's previous ventures outside Murase, Ziyad had had the chance to meet Feras in person once. A young lord, a few years older than Ziyad perhaps, yet a man of reason when he spoke. Ziyad knew he would need that reason the moment he saw the grim look on Feras's face.

"You know why I'm here, don't you?" Feras asked the three of them.

"We wonder if there is something we can help you with, Lord Feras." Frankil straightened his back. Perhaps not the best timing to worry about his pride, Ziyad believed.

"Captain," Feras tilted his head, "did you happen to lead a Murasen soldier when you were in Ramos?"

Ziyad didn't like the question nor Feras's tone. Frankil had better heed his next words.

"No," Frankil answered.

"I am quite sure of that." Feras nodded. "Because it simply doesn't make any sense. I doubt that any lord from any part of Gorania would commit our folly."

"I would never consider fighting banditry as an act of folly, Lord Feras."

"Fighting banditry is an act of bravery that we thank you for, Captain," Feras's impassive voice didn't betray any sort of appreciation, though. "But I think it is time for the sons of this realm to undertake this duty."

Ziyad knew what that meant, yet Frankil kept his stone face when he asked, "Are you dismissing me, Lord Feras?"

"I'm dismissing all of you, Captain," Feras announced. "From now on, there will be no gangs or bands of warriors in Murase. If any of you want to fight banditry, then you're welcome to join the Murasen army. But I'm afraid that you must be a Murasen if you want to fight under the leopard banner."

Now Frankil wasn't able to hide his scowl. "Is this how you thank us, milord?"

Feras leaned toward Frankil. "You and all your men have already been rewarded for your services. What else do you want?"

Frankil looked frustrated when he shook his head. "Nothing. May I leave with my men now?"

"You inform them of my orders first. After that you are free to go wherever you want in Murase as long as you don't raise a blade."

"I assure you that will never happen, milord." Frankil nodded. "We are not staying here any longer."

Frankil left and headed back uphill. For a moment, Antram looked not sure of what he should do before he realized he had better follow the Bermanian captain. Ziyad could understand Antram's puzzlement, though. He was confused himself, still not able to digest the lord's harsh decision. He wished he could persuade Feras to change his mind, but lords were not to be advised unless they asked you for that. And Feras didn't seem to be waiting for anyone's advice.

"This is not right." Ziyad couldn't keep his mouth shut any longer. He knew he might regret that, but nevertheless voiced his opinion. He wasn't a soldier in the Murasen army to obey Feras's orders; he was a brother of the gang, and he could speak his mind whenever he wanted.

"Of course, it is not." Feras stared at him. "A bunch of foreigners leading a gang of mercenaries in our realm. That's nonsense if you ask me."

The way Feras referred to his brothers irked him. "Those *foreigners* saved the realm when its soldiers failed it."

"What if one day we enter a war with Bermania or Rusakia? Which side will they stand for you think? Can you entrust them with your family's safety?"

Ziyad grinned. "I have no family, milord. Those foreigners are my family now."

"Then you had better catch up with them," Feras said, then wheeled his horse.

"What happened to Masolon?" Ziyad couldn't help asking. When Feras turned to him, he realized how foolish that question was. *I should have left when I had the chance. I made him hear enough from me today,* he thought.

"Why don't you ask him yourself?" Feras asked.

"I would if I knew where he was."

A wry smile twisted Feras's lips. "If you are telling the truth, then he is wiser than he seems."

The lord wheeled his horse again and trotted off, Ziyad letting him go this time. *That almost went well. Time to get out of here.*

Masolon knew what was going to happen, Ziyad reflected as he ascended the hill. But why hadn't he warned them? That hill could have witnessed a massacre this morning if only one archer had lost his composure and loosed an arrow. Probably, Masolon wasn't sure about it, but he must have heard something that made him see that happening soon. Though always mysterious with his own plans, he was nevertheless a fearless commander with a vision. Ziyad wouldn't deny he felt indebted to Masolon for taking him on that journey.

So, where should he go now? Ziyad had his revenge, in addition to an adequate sum of gold and silver to live on after dismantling the gang. Maybe that was the right time to stop fighting and return to his harp, to his festive world where he did what he loved and loved what he did. That path of blood would be pointless if it had no end.

Frankil was announcing Lord Feras's shocking decision to the brothers of the gang when Ziyad returned to them. Astounded, most of them argued with Frankil as if it was his own decision. No one could see any reason behind this absurd move from the Murasen lord's side, even the Murasen brothers themselves. Some spat harsh words about the lord and the King, others asking where Masolon had gone. Too many unexplained incidents for one morning. Ziyad wished Feras was here now to see for himself what the gang meant to the brothers. Maybe they were mercenaries as the young lord said, but that was only part of the truth. Those men had bled, won battles, and buried their departed brothers together. Their loyalty would always be to themselves, not to any other banner.

The brothers needed some time to realize that their prattle was futile. After Frankil was done with his brief speech, they dragged their feet away to gather their gear. The camp was never as silent and gloomy as it was today.

While Frankil and his fellow knights were getting rid of their Murasen armor and donning their old Bermanian suits, Antram was doing nothing. Sitting on his buttocks, he leaned his back to a big rock, his fingers crossed. If there was something Ziyad would miss for real, it would be teasing *Duke* Antram.

"You." Ziyad tossed a stone at Antram's feet, startling the huge fellow. "That lord down the hill won't wait for long."

"He dismissed me from his service, but he didn't dismiss me from here."

As Ziyad approached him, he eyed the brothers who were almost ready to move. "Everybody is leaving, Antram. I don't think you want to stay here on your own."

Antram leaned his head to the rock, letting out a deep breath of air. "I feel I'm lost, brother." For one rare moment, the *Duke* admitted he was vulnerable. "I can't imagine myself returning to those arenas, running from one Contest to another. Not after I've become who I am now."

"And what have you become? A captain?" Ziyad stood right in front of Antram. "What would losing that mean to someone who had lost his lordship before?"

Antram made a dismissive gesture with his hand. "I barely remember two or three years of my childhood in my father's house, so I don't have much to yearn for. My lordship was nothing more than an amusing tale I used for the Contests to earn some fame."

"No more Contests for an honorable warrior like you." Frankil's heavy armor rattled as he came to join them. "We are returning to Horstad," he jabbed Antram in the shoulder, "and this time, it's your turn to come with us."

Antram turned to Frankil, giving him a nervous titter. "No, Captain. As I loathe the notion of returning to the arenas, I cannot stand risking my life without a reward. I might at least earn some silver from those Contests." He rose to his feet, gazing at the camp as if he was looking for something. "Ask Blanich, and he will tell you the same."

"Blanich was the first one to leave the camp," Frankil pointed out. "The moment I returned, he took his leave and off he went."

"Without seeing us off?" Antram was surprised, but Ziyad was not. He knew the Rusakian was never truly one of the brothers.

"Forget about him," Ziyad told Antram. "I have a better alternative that would suit both you and Frankil: Galardi."

Both Frankil and Antram shot Ziyad inquiring looks. "The Skandivian merchant? What about him?" asked Frankil.

"He always needs strong men to guard his caravans," said Ziyad. "A profession not much different from what we used to do here in Murase."

Antram nodded in approval. "That is better than the Contests for sure."

Frankil seemed to be weighing Ziyad's idea in his head. "Not bad, I must admit. Still, we have a long way ahead until we reach the crossroads where we will have to decide if we should head to Horstad or to Kalensi." He turned to Ziyad and Antram. "You had better ready yourselves faster. The sooner I leave these lands, the more relieved I will become."

Ziyad wanted to tell them that he was just offering one last sincere piece of advice to his brothers before bidding them farewell. Fighting was no longer among his plans, which only included highborn ladies,

351

music, and banquets. Fighting would just be part of his new songs and tales in the coming feasts to entertain his audience, especially the gorgeous ones among the crowd.

"Ziyad?" Frankil tilted his head. "Are you coming or not?"

The Bermanian captain apparently sensed Ziyad's hesitation. Before Ziyad said a word, Antram answered on his behalf, "It's his suggestion, Frankil. Of course, he is coming."

Now Ziyad wondered if one day he would regret his silence.

56. MASOLON

The castle of Arkan had become a mere dot behind Masolon, and still, those forty memluks surrounded him as they rode on the Northern Road. The travelers going past him must be thinking that the fearless commander was just doing another patrol with his soldiers. For the commoners, even those who had never seen him, he was their champion, Bane of the Ghosts, the Demon of the Desert. Unfortunately, all those names didn't mean that much to their king. The Demon of the Desert was leaving Murase, stripped of his title, prohibited from setting foot on Murasen soil for the rest of his life. *I should be grateful they allowed me to keep the armor I am wearing.*

Dusk had fallen already when the memluks left him in the middle of nowhere. He must be near the Byzont lands, if he wasn't there already. Not the right place to visit wearing Murasen armor. His map was in his saddlebag, but he didn't take it out to check his directions. He let his horse move onward, having no idea where he should go. It didn't matter now.

Let destiny take me where I am supposed to go. He mocked the idea. It was destiny that had deceived him with its absurd games; destiny that had lifted him up high in the sky only to make his fall bone crushing. Today he returned to the very point he had started from. Today he was the same empty-handed man who had miraculously made it to Gorania; a man with no title, no gang, no friends…no Sania.

All was lost, but not for nothing. For the sake of the stupid games of destiny.

You did not lose everything, Masolon. You still have me.

The voice of his mind was back after a long absence, and it picked the right time to return. Only the Lord of Sky and Earth knew how long Masolon would stay alone.

You have never been alone since you came out of the Great Desert.

His restless mind had always muddled him with its intrusive thoughts, as if someone else inside Masolon's head was talking to him. But Masolon wouldn't bother talking to…

Because I am someone else, you fool.

Masolon pulled the reins of his horse, looking around. He was alone for real. From where he stopped to the reddish horizon ahead, he couldn't see a single shadow of a man or a beast. Had he lost his mind?

No, you did not. We met in Si'oli, but you never remember me.

Now Masolon was sure he was hallucinating. One year had passed since his dreadful passage through the Great Desert, but still he could remember his loneliness in that desolate place. Even the demons rumored to reside there did not exist.

Demons do exist, Masolon. You yourself have encountered one.

"Enough!" Masolon held his temples, trying to dismiss those disturbing thoughts. Those Murasen bastards had broken his heart this morning. He wouldn't let them get to his mind as well.

I am the one who keeps your mind sound, Masolon. Without me, you are nothing but a dull mass of muscles.

"What are you?"

Your sins. Your salvation.

"My salvation was in the path I forged."

What if you have chosen the wrong path?

"I did not. I fought for the helpless. I fought for a cause!"

The nomads fight for a cause as well. What makes you different from them?

"How am I even compared to them? I do not kill innocent people!"

And where did you end up with that? An outcast, who would be wanted for justice like any brigand. Can you not see it yet? You slew hundreds of nomads with your blade, but you only became a murderer when you shed noble blood. You are now a thief because you tried to 'steal' what you are not allowed to dream of. But what if you tried to run away with a girl from the commoners?

"The problem lies in the lords, not in the path. *My* path."

Why would you have a path in the first place? Why do you not just let it go and live the life an invincible warrior like you deserves?

"What do you want me to become? An outlaw?"

You are almost one. But you would not believe me if I did not let you see for yourself.

Masolon must kill this voice, and this time for good. Yelling to stop it for a while wouldn't do. Yelling wouldn't dismiss a demon. What he needed was belief. He would never again be vulnerable like today, and his demon knew that. His demon had been patient enough to take his best shot and start turning Masolon to what *he* had wanted him to be.

You cannot silence me forever.

"Then I shall simply ignore you. Keep talking, bastard."

Masolon listened, and all he heard for a couple of minutes was the gust of autumn wind, no voices coming from his mind, or the demon occupying it. He felt it was his restless mind that had created his non-existent demon. His boon, as his grandfather had described his mind. But no, his grandfather had been wrong. Masolon's mind had always been his pain. A curse that could never be undone unless the dead could be brought back. Yes, it was the curse of bloodshed. Masolon could see that gloating smile on the face of the thief of the Salvation Tree. If that thief had been a thief in the first place…

His ears caught some movement not far away from him. While he was lost in his thoughts, seven horsemen ringed him from quite a distance. He didn't make any move as he watched them gradually come closer. They didn't look like nomads or even Murasen. Those men came probably from Bermania.

"A wise man," said the horseman, who seemed to be their leader. "I promise, you will never regret your wisdom."

They were robbers, and they had just shown up at the right time. Masolon was having a bad day already, and he doubted if they could make it any worse.

"There is no good for us in taking your life." The robbers' leader approached with his men, closing the ring around Masolon. "Just drop your sword, yield your horse, and we will let you live."

With one hand, Masolon pulled the greatsword and showed its massive blade to the robbers' leader.

"Wow! Look at this, brothers! A Bermanian greatsword!" The robber's eyes widened. "Did you win any fight with it before?"

"All of them," Masolon replied. "Except one today."

The robbers' leader chuckled mockingly. "No one wins all his battles, wise man."

Masolon smirked. "I was not talking about *this* one."

The smile plastered on the leader's face faded, his men unsheathing their swords. Growling, they all raised their blades as they spurred their horses onward toward Masolon. Now there was no escape…

For them.

Kingdoms and People of Gorania

Murase

Murase is blessed with warm winters and cursed with hot summers. Some attribute its weather to its proximity to the sun that rises from the east. Others believe that the hot air in Murase comes from the gate of hell that lies at their southern borders; the Great Desert. According to the Tales of Gorania, the Great Desert is ten times hotter than Murasen desert, making the Murasen desert a paradise if compared to it.

Most of the Murasen terrain is sandy, except the Green Crescent that surrounds the Blue Crescent River. The castle of Kurdisan was built to defend the arable land against the endless raids of the Mankols who claim their ownership to the Green Crescent.

The nomadic tribes are actually the rulers of the Murasen desert, making travelling from a city to another without strong guard a suicide. One great clan among them is the fearful Ghosts, who resemble night beasts in their ability to see in the dark.

People of Murase

ZIYAD, a former wandering bard

SANIA, Lord Ahmet's daughter

AHMET, Lord of Bigad, Hammer of the Mankols

MUNZIR, Lord Ahmet's brother

FERAS, Lord Ahmet's son, Lord of Arkan

RAMIA, Lord Ahmet's wife

RASHEED, King of Murase

DEHAWY, King Rasheed's cousin

MEMOT, Lord of Shezar

QASEM, Captain of the Royal Guard

Bermania

Raigens
Lovoliem
Horslau
Neldon
The
Endless
Sea
Arsdam
Kalhom
Karun
Herlog
Paril
Ramos
Subrel
Lapond
Festburg
Talvda
Lizabona
Augarin
Sergrad

There are many reasons for the *Bermanian Pride*. They are the descendants of Goran the Great, which makes them—as they claim—the rightful heirs of the Goranian throne. The greatest city in Gorania is their capital; Paril or the Jewel of Bermania. The finest knights and strongest horses are raised in their lands. Their weather is neither Murasen-hot nor Rusakian-cold.

Along thousands of years, the Bermanians' stance toward other realms has varied, but their long-standing enmity with Byzonta has been an exception. The mountainous realm used to be part of Augarin, Bermania's southernmost region.

It is always a debate whose cavalry is the best; Bermanians or Murasens. There is nothing in the ancient Tales of Gorania about a battle between the two mighty kingdoms.

People of Bermania:
BUMAR, healer

ANTRAM, son of Aurel, late Duke of Lapond
FRANKIL, former Cavalry Captain in Ramos
RAMEL, owner of the Pit
VIOLA, Ramel's assistant
ARTONY, Contest Champion
VAKNUS, Contest Champion

Rusakia

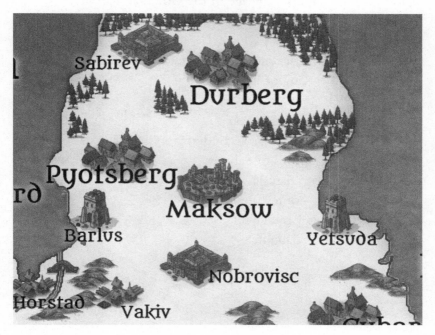

Rusakians have a special bond with snow. Snow is part of their blood (literally, they believe so), and it is their protective shield that has always defended them against their enemies. A city like Durberg was built long time ago far north to be always the Rusakians' last shelter in case an enemy invaded them. According to the Tales of Gorania, it happened thousands of years ago that the Mankols once pushed the Rusakians north beyond Pyotsberg. But when winter came, Rusakians marched from Durberg and the castle of Sabirev, and vanquished their frozen invaders for good.

The tension seldom settles down between Rusakia and its neighbors, especially with Bermania, because of the eternal dispute over the great fortress of Karun that was named after the firstborn son of King Goran the Great. It never happened that the great fortress had remained more than two decades in row in the same kingdom. Rusakians claim that the fortress had always been a Rusakian land before the age of the Goranian Empire.

People of Rusakia

KUSLOV, most renowned tracker in Gorania

BECHOV, King of Rusakia

LAROVIC, King's Marshal

ELOV, Larovic's late son

GERVINY, Larovic's secondborn

SANISLAV, Lord of Sabirev

HALIN, Lord Sanislav's daughter

BLANICH, Contest fighter

ANNA, honey merchant

JUBI, Anna's daughter

Byzonta

Byzonta is named after Baizent, who declared himself the first King of Byzonta, ending decades of the Bermanian sovereignty over this southwestern mountainous pocket. For centuries, the Bermanians had tried to reconquest this realm, but they were never able to make use of their powerful cavalry on the Byzont bumpy lands. The Byzonts, on the other hand, have proven themselves the masters of defense. They used to have their own cavalry force until their crushing defeat, hundreds of years ago, in one of the rare occasions they fought away from their homeland. Since then, infantry and sharpshooters have been forming the majority of the Byzont army.

Byzonts are also masters of spices and herbs, which makes them the most skilful chefs and the deadliest assassins in Gorania. Their merchants rule the naval trade business alongside the Skandivians, but their smugglers are unrivaled.

Skandivia

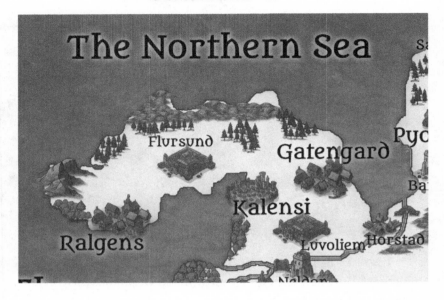

Skandivians call themselves *the Sons of Giants*. Although their tales about their ten-feet-tall ancestors seem to be exaggerated, Skandivians remain the tallest men in Gorania.

Skandivian armies do not rely so much on cavalry; a sort of honoring the legacy of their ancient grandfathers who never used horses in their wars. *A giant never needs a horse,* they say. Which makes them the deadliest foot warriors in the lands of Gorania.

An entire map of Gorania was drawn one thousand years ago, thanks to the bravery of Skandivian adventurous explorers. However, they never knew what lied beyond the Great Desert—which is believed to be the end of the Goranian world.

The war between Rusakia and Skandivia at their borders occasionally stops, but the case is a bit different with Bermania, where their history together is full of ups and downs.

Characters from Skandivia
GALARDI, merchant from Kalensi

Mankola

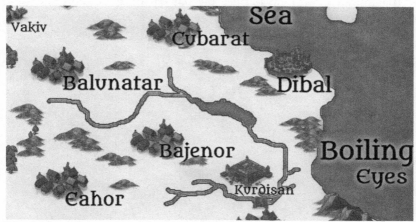

Mankols are warriors by instinct thanks to their bloody tribal conflicts that tore their lands apart. But that reign ended one hundred years ago when Sanjar united the clans and called himself the *Kaan* of all Mankols—which means 'king' in the old Mankol tongue. Since then, the Mankol realm has become a threat to its neighbors with its huge army and endless gold.

The Mankols stand out from all other Goranian factions with their own beliefs and values. First, the majority of them do not worship the Lord of Sky and Earth—a fact that makes them loathed by other factions. Second, horses are essential components of their lives since their early childhood. It's said that: "You may find a Mankol without a house; but not without a horse." A Mankol who can't ride a horse is not a Mankol. It's not strange, then, that the Mankol army has no infantry. Even archers are mounted. According to the Tales of Gorania, Mankols can speak the tongue of horses.

Third, unlike other Goranians, Mankols don't trade internally with gold—which is of little value to them. They only use it in their trades with other realms.

Strangely enough, Mankols don't rely on castles to defend their lands. However, any foreign commander, who may *think* of invading the Mankols, must put into consideration that he's going to face the masters of open field battles. He has to survive endless hordes of the fastest cavalry in Gorania.

Koya

Most of Goranians do not consider the islands of Koya part of Gorania. The fact that it's the only kingdom that was never conquered by Goran the Great could be the reason for that.

As they were never involved in big wars with other factions, Koyans are believed to be peaceful people. Still they have the biggest fleet in Gorania to watch over their shores.

The only bond between Koyans and other realms is naval trading. Generally, they don't live outside their islands, and in return, no *outsider* is allowed to live in Koya. Another reason for Goranians to ignore the existence of Koyans, and also to weave a lot of myths around the Koyan's mysterious life in their isolated islands. To name a few of those myths: Koyans teach sorcery to their kids; dragons, rocs and mammoths do exist in their islands; Koyans' boats can sail unharmed through the Boiled Eyes and they know secret gates in the water that take them to the Endless Sea.

Acknowledgements

The Warrior's Path could have been another unfinished story of mine were it not for May Imam, my dear wife and my cheerleader. I was writing for fun when I started my journey with Masolon, but she had more faith than I did, and encouraged me to share my work with the world.

Huge thanks go to my readers who have been rooting for me since I started posting my work on Wattpad. Your relentless support was the fuel that kept me going in my writing journey until Masolon's serialized tale became a 'real' book.

As for all the people running Wattpad, I owe you all for creating an amazing writing community that has turned a faint dream of mine into a possibility. It is really hard to imagine the existence of The Warrior's Path in the first place without the orange ocean of books.

Thanks to my wizard Stefanie Saw for her brilliant artwork. It is fun to work with a talented artist who embraces your books as her babies.

I must give credit to Felicia Sullivan who spent a hectic fortnight of editing my first draft. Hopefully, my final touches didn't ruin her work.

Thanks to Sandra Grayson. I must admit how excited I was when I found out that a talented author like her had been one of Masolon's early fans.

Muchas gracias to the one and only Lady of the Feathered-Arrows Rosa Aimee. Your comments always put a smile on my face.

Thanks to my tireless support team and advisors: Katrin Hollister, Gaby Cabezut, Debbie Joelz, and Jessica Fry. What did I do to deserve you, ladies?

Thanks to my dearest friend from the good old school days

Ahmed Khaled who was taking Masolon's business in Gorania as seriously as I was. I enjoyed our debates over the phone about my plot twists.

And of course, I must thank my parents: my mother for nurturing my love of books and writing, and my father for providing a five-year old child with his blank yearly planner to write his first story.

About the Author

Karim Soliman earned his first writing commission through his contribution to the first and last issue of his school magazine. Twenty years later, he earned his next commission from Sony Pictures.

Born in Egypt, where he lives with his wonderful wife and two children, Karim works as a brand manager of neuropsychiatric drugs. He holds a Master's degree in Business Administration, just in case he decides to pursue the CEO pathway.

Through Wattpad, Karim has built his fan base since he started serializing his fantasy and sci-fi novels online. When he is away from writing, he struggles with his insomnia, and continues his search for his next favorite dessert.

Stay tuned for Karim Soliman's updates

www.writerkarimsoliman.com

Facebook:
https://www.facebook.com/authorKarimSoliman

Twitter:
https://twitter.com/Kariem28

Instagram:
https://www.instagram.com/kariem28/

And don't miss

QUEEN OF REBELS

BOOK TWO OF
TALES OF GORANIA

KARIM SOLIMAN

THE HIGH CLERIC

The snowy ground of the Frozen Forest was the whitest Petrilius or any living creature might ever see. In this urgent visit he discovered something even whiter: the snowy ground of the Frozen Forest . . . in autumn. *I wonder how it looks like in winter,* he thought to himself as the tamed white bear pulling his sleigh trudged through the deep layers of snow. Sometimes Petrilius pitied the poor beast that only had its fur to protect itself from the deadly frost, while on the other hand, he and his junior mate steering the huge tamed bear wore fur coats, hats, masks, gloves, socks, boots, and several layers of garments quilted with dragonskin. Unless you were covered from head to toe with such material, you should consider yourself dead the moment you trespassed on that deadly forest.

With his woolen mask, the only way Petrilius could breathe was through its several fine pores, which still allowed cold air to reach his nostrils. But thanks to that layer of dragonskin lining those relatively deep pores as well as the entire mask itself, the air entering his lungs was steamy, especially when compared with the hard frost blowing against his masked face.

Only two slits in his masks exposed the world to his eyes, and he could not ask for more in this forsaken forest. Otherwise, his eyelids might freeze and stick to his forehead. Ahead loomed the White Chain, a dozen snowy hills which you might barely distinguish from the sky and the ground. *Everything is painted by the same white brush on this white horizon,* Petrilius thought as he gazed at his destination. "There!" He had to yell and wave, otherwise his mate wouldn't notice that he was talking. The padded masks covering their mouths and ears made their hollers sound faint as if they were coming from a mile away.

His young companion slowly turned to him, and at the same pace he looked ahead again. Though Petrilius could not see his face, he could imagine his mate's astonishment. The White Chain existed in no Goranian map, simply because no man had ever ventured that far north to know these frozen hills. Only the High Clerics of each realm and their escorts, who accompanied them in their once-in-a-decade journey, knew about that secret place.

Petrilius motioned for his mate to steer the bear toward the fourth hill to the right. They were less than a mile far from their destination, he estimated as the tireless beast resumed its march in the deep snow. *Bears were faster in summer.* Petrilius was sure he had made that passage before through the Frozen Forest in one day, not in two.

"Turn around." Petrilius had to curve his arm and repeat his command four more times, each time in louder tones to make sure his mate grasped what he was supposed to do. *The bear knows better though.* Most probably, the tamed beast was the one taking the lead, not any of the men riding the sleigh it dragged. After half an hour of passing by the western side of the fourth hill, Petrilius could at last see the cave.

Petrilius ordered his escort to stop and help him clamber down the sleigh. As a man nearing his seventies, he could not trust his knees to do any tricky moves. While his young escort was bringing the bags from the sleigh, Petrilius approached the bear and gently caressed it above its nose, the beast lowering its head in submission. When his young mate took the bags out, Petrilius opened his and found the bear's lunch enclosed in a thick piece of cloth. After unwrapping the bear's lunch and letting the fish fall on the ground, Petrilius took his escort by his arm to enter the cave. The young cleric seemed a bit reluctant to move, but in the end he walked away from the bear, leaving it to devour its weekly meal.

The cavernous entrance led to a door of steel, whose keys had always been passed to the high clerics of each realm. The heavy door squealed as Petrilius pushed it open and again as he slammed it shut behind him and his young escort. Once he took off his mask, his young escort did the same, as if he had been waiting for this moment for long. "Gracious Lord." The young cleric took a deep breath of the cold air filling the torchlit corridor.

"Move on," Petrilius urged him. "We have a long way down."

"Down?" The young cleric's astonishment reminded Petrilius of his first visit to this very cave thirty-seven years ago. As an escort of the High Bermanian Cleric at that time, he also had had hundreds of questions. A few of them remained unanswered still. "Whoever built this haven; what were they thinking when they chose this place?"

With wary steps, Petrilius descended the winding stone steps, his young escort following him with the two bags on his shoulders. Serving the High Cleric was a great honor, yet it might not be the *only* reason why the young fellow did not complain. *His mind is so preoccupied with questions he is not sure which one to ask first.* Petrilius had gone through that feeling before.

"Shouldn't we have tied the bear, Master?" The young cleric kept the same pace as he followed him.

"Don't worry about our return. Those bears always come back."

"*Bears?*" the young cleric echoed in astonishment, but said nothing more about it. "Master, please, are you going to tell me what we are doing here?"

"Honestly, I don't know. Not yet, I mean."

"Umm. . . but I thought you might have come here before."

"To compile a decade of the Tales, yes. But this decade is not over yet, so I presume I'm summoned for something urgent." *Shocking news, I fear.*

"The Tales of Gorania?" The young cleric's astonished tone did not lack that hint of disapproval. "But why here? Isn't there any place in the six realms where you, Master, and the other high clerics can meet away from curious eyes, other than this deadly frozen place?"

Petrilius stopped, looking the young cleric in the eye. "I know what you are thinking of, but the Tales is more than a huge book to chronicle our history. One day, you or your descendants may realize that. Until then, we must safeguard the Tales and make sure that no single line is erased or altered."

The young cleric's eyes were hollow when he nodded. *He doesn't understand, but he has to obey anyway,* Petrilius reflected as they resumed their way down, their footsteps echoing on the seemingly endless stone steps.

"The second and the last emperor who ever ruled Gorania, Karun the Pious, ordered his clerics to choose a safe place for compiling the history of his empire." Petrilius wanted to let the young man know how ancient this place was. "A place that if even spotted by the Seers in their visions, would always stay out of anybody's reach."

"You mean the Seers who abandoned his father, Goran *the Great*."

Petrilius did not miss the scorn in his companion's voice. "Goran is dead. Only the Lord of Sky and Earth can judge him."

For a short while, Petrilius heard nothing but their echoing footsteps until the young cleric said, "He killed more than any man ever existed."

"So?"

"His crimes are too obvious to be overlooked, Master."

Petrilius chuckled. "The Rusakians won't disagree with you." It was no secret; only the Bermanians glorified the founder of the Goranian Empire that had barely lasted for fifty years.

"At least, we should be fair, no matter which realm we belong to."

"There are no realms in this place, young man. We are all Goranians here."

"Then who are we protecting the Tales from?"

Silence was the only answer Petrilius could offer his apprentice for the time being. *Not everybody is ready to know the truth,* Petrilius thought. The young cleric respected his master's silence and did not pose more questions until they ended their descent and reached the last stone step. A short corridor took them to another steel door resembling the one at the cavernous entrance. Behind that door was a round hall with three doors, three High Clerics standing in the center.

"Master Petrilius." Yesen, the High Cleric of Murase, advanced to greet him. "We have been waiting for you to start our meeting."

The other two men were the High Clerics of both Rusakia and Byzonta. They greeted Petrilius briefly and left him with Yesen as they headed to the door on the left.

"Am I not going to get some rest after my long journey?" Petrilius asked Yesen.

"Of course, you are. You should." Master Yesen showed him a book he was holding. "Yet I will understand if you are too impatient to wait to discuss this."

Curiosity replaced exhaustion the moment Petrilius read the title, which was not written in any contemporary or ancient Goranian tongue. Before posing any questions, he remembered that his escort was still waiting behind him.

"You see that door?" Petrilius turned to the young cleric, pointing to the first door to the right. "There you will get food, water, a bed, and a warm bath. The moment you step inside, the door will be locked from outside. No escort goes out of that door until the High Clerics decide they are done. Are you fine with that?"

"Do I have a choice?" The escort gave him a tired smile.

"You did a good job." Petrilius patted the young cleric's shoulder. When the escort was out of earshot, the High Cleric of Bermania gestured to Master Yesen to hand him the book. "How did you get this?" He lowered his voice, though there were only high clerics in the hall now.

Master Yesen glanced at the two fellows waiting for him by the doorstep. "Get some rest for now, Master Petrilius. You will have all the time you—"

"How did you get it?" Petrilius impatiently cut him off.

Yesen sighed, a faint smile on his face. "Remember the tale of Lady Nelly?"

"That demon summoner? She has been gone for long, right?"

"She is still dead, don't worry. Anyway, it happens that the granddaughter of her sister has now become the Queen of Murase. And for some reason, that queen feels interested in the books her grandmother's sister had left in her abandoned, cursed house. After failed attempts of different tongue tutors to translate those books, Her Majesty seeks my help."

"Did you tell her what this book was?"

"I told her it could be written in some ancient tongue, so I asked for some time to work on it."

Studying Koyan was not something unusual for a cleric. But Petrilius had never seen a full, original book written in that tongue. "A whole book about *The Last Day*?" It was just a topic mentioned in some parts of the Tales of Gorania. "How many Signs do the Koyans have for that day?"

Yesen gestured to his two fellows to go and wait for him in their meeting chamber. "The Last Day is not a prophecy for the Koyans. It's a sort of plan."

"A plan for what?"

"For destroying the six realms of Gorania, Master Petrilius."

Though that would sound grave, Petrilius was not impressed. "Not any different from our inevitable fate anyway."

"That's what they made us believe about our *inevitable* fate," Yesen pointed out. "But I tell you, Master; it's a plan. A great plan, I daresay. Yet since it's a plan, it could be achieved and it could be foiled as well. But if we are to move, we must start today. The Koyans' plan is ongoing already."

"Ongoing?" Petrilius echoed, confused.

"Yes, Master," replied The High Cleric of Murase. "If you haven't heard the news yet, a demon has come to us from the Great Desert."

88033453R00225